LONGINUS THE VAMPIRE: HELLFIRE

ARMY OF ANGELS–SCROLL I

BY

ALAN KINROSS

"But the unbelievers, and the abominable, and murderers, and ravishers, and whoremongers, and thieves, and abusers, and idolaters, and all liars, shall have new glorified bodies in the kingdom of the Great Dragon which burneth with fire and brimstone: which is the second birth."—Book of Lilith 21:8

PROLOGUS

"Centurion! Centurion!" Naram-Sin cried.

"What?" gasped Longinus.

"You must not succumb to it! Speak to me!"

"I cannot! It is too much!" Longinus screamed.

"Listen to me, centurion. Hear my voice, only my voice. Who are you?"

"I–cannot–remember."

"Concentrate! Focus your mind! What is your name?"

"My–name?"

"Yes! What is your name?"

"My name–is Longinus. Gaius Cassius–Longinus."

"And when were you born?"

"Leave me alone," Longinus moaned.

"I will let you be after you answer my question," Naram-Sin replied calmly. "When did your mother give birth to you?"

"The tenth–no–eleventh of July," Longinus rasped.

"And which year?"

"I cannot–"

"Think, centurion! The year?"

Longinus gave a shuddering sigh as he sought to recall his past.

"6 BC," he whispered at last.

"So, you were born on the 11th of July, 6 BC?"

"Yes!"

"But as a Roman you would not describe your date of birth in those terms."

"No," Longinus sobbed.

"Then how would you state your date of birth."

"I have told you this before!" Longinus replied angrily.

"Tell me again," Naram-Sin said patiently.

Longinus jerked as a bolt of excruciating pain shot through his body.

"Instruct me on how your people described dates important to them!"

Longinus narrowed his eyes and gritted his teeth.

"We had the Julian calendar–but did not use it for describing important dates–such as birthdays."

"Therefore, you would never say the 11th of July?"

"No—we identified a date by its proximity to the most important public holiday of that month—uh!—and we defined the year by which two consuls held power."

"So two elected consuls held power jointly for a year?"

"Yes, being a consul was a very prestigious position. After they had served their term of office, the senate named the year after them."

"Which two consuls held sway in the year that you were born?"

Longinus thought for a moment and said, "Balbus and Vitus."

"And what was the Roman name for the month of July?"

Longinus groaned as a new spasm of pain engulfed him.

"Listen to my voice, centurion. Think of nothing but my voice. What was the Roman name for July?"

"Quintilis," Longinus replied shakily.

"That is good, centurion. Now what was the nearest public holiday to the 11th of July?"

"The Kalends—no—Ides of Quintilis on the 15th of the month."

"Then tell me the date of your birth, as you would have told another Roman."

"I cannot think!"

"Yes, you can, my friend. Concentrate and the answer will become clear to you. Your mind is stronger than your body."

Longinus focused his immense will power and struggled to detach his thoughts from the crippling pain in his abdomen.

"I was born on the 11th of July in the month of Quintilis. The nearest public holiday was on the Ides of Quintilis. The two consuls that held power that year were Balbus and Vitus. Therefore, I would have said that my date of birth was—five days before the Ides of Quintilis in the year of Balbus and Vitus."

"Well done, centurion. Now tell me about your mother. What was her name?"

"Her name was Aelia."

"And what was her nature?"

"Her name came from the Greek word 'helios' which means 'Sun', and that describes her disposition. My mother was kind and beautiful. She always saw the best in people and never spoke ill of anyone—not even my father."

"What was your father's name?"

"I have told you all of this before," protested Longinus.

"I know that they are bittersweet memories for you, but I wish to hear them once more."

"His name was Gnaeus. He was a centurion of the 1st cohort, Legio XIV Gemina."

"And what sort of man was he?"

"Hard, cruel, and a drunkard. I cannot remember him showing any affection to my mother or I. He despised me."

"You were an only child?"

"As far as I know."

"And your father beat you?"

"Yes, he often did after returning from one of his drinking bouts. Beatings were a normal part of our family life. My mother tried to divert his anger away from me, and that meant she received the worst of his violence. In those days, a father had the power of life and death over his household."

"Was he a wealthy man?"

"No. We were very poor. When he retired from the legion, he received a small plot of land as a pension. However, he had little interest in farming and spent his time and money drinking, gambling and whoring."

"And thus you ran away and joined the legions?"

"I had to. If I had stayed there, he would have killed me. He was a vile, vindictive man who blamed his family ties for his lack of advancement in the legion. He considered us as millstones around his neck. But the truth was that he was neither courageous nor skilled enough to warrant promotion."

"You never saw your father again?"

"No. I never wished to."

"Why?"

"You know why!"

"Tell me."

"Because I would have killed him! Is that what you want to hear? That I wished to murder my own father!"

"Yes, centurion."

"Why do you torture me so?" Longinus sobbed.

"Because I must. But be troubled no longer. Our suffering is almost at an end, and soon we will feel the comfort of death."

"I long for it!"

"And so do I," Naram-Sin sighed grimly. "Your pain is my pain. We shall die together as we have always done."

"Together," whispered Longinus.

A last wave of unimaginable agony wracked their shared body.

The blessed darkness of death enveloped them, and they knew or felt no more.

They had endured the King of Hell's horrific tortures for yet another night.

CHAPTER I

The vast, amorphous form of Asmodeus, the King of Demons and Prince of Lust and Revenge, emerged from his tenebrous sanctum sanctorum located deep within the dripping bowels of his towering Basilica of Pain. His multitude of horrifying tentacles, some ending with vile, dripping phalluses and others with vicious claws, lashed out like choleric vipers as his grotesque shape drifted like a putrid cloud down the wide spiralling ramp leading to the dungeons below. Within the translucent red skin of his putrescent body, hundreds of souls screamed in agony as he devoured them.

Rows of tall, hideous, two-legged demons armed with swords and shields lined his path and bowed their misshapen heads as he glided past them. They acted as his royal bodyguard, but their role was ceremonial and unnecessary. Asmodeus needed no protection. His power was terrifying and absolute in his own dominion of Hell. The King of Demons feared only one other denizen of the Abyss and that was Satan–the Devil, the Evil One, the Father of Lies, the Old Serpent, the Great Dragon, his malevolent lord and master. The Emperor of Hell's power was infinite and awesome to behold, and Asmodeus had always been most careful not to provoke or anger him.

Asmodeus scowled as ancient, repressed memories seeped into his consciousness. Most demons in the Abyss called their emperor Satan, but Asmodeus had always known him as Lucifer. Aeons ago, Lucifer, the 'Star of the Morning', had been God's most perfect and powerful creation. Asmodeus, Azazel, Baal Zebub, Molloch, Eligos, and Mammon, had been Lucifer's most loyal supporters, and when the 'Anointed One' had preached against the tyranny of God, Asmodeus had been the first to pledge his allegiance.

Until the last moment, he had believed that Lucifer would be crowned as the new King of Heaven; however, their well-laid plan had been shattered because of the treachery of the archangels. How things could have been different if Lucifer had not agreed to fight the accursed Archangel Michael in single combat. Their army would have cut through the defenders and defeated God and His Son; or at the very least forced them to abdicate and let one more worthy attain the throne. But after the defeat of their leader, the rebels had lost confidence and heart.

Lucifer had convinced the rebels that he was more powerful than God, but how could he be when a mere archangel had defeated him? They realised only then how he had lied and deceived them. Asmodeus grimaced as he recalled the indignity of laying down his sword, being chained and dragged by rejoicing choirs of angels through the streets, and thrown into a dark and dismal dungeon. He remembered the shuddering fear he had felt when, after a short mock trial, God had pronounced their sentence. He commanded that they be cast down into the blistering Lake of Fire for eternity.

For aeons, they had writhed and screamed in agony. Fear and pain had been unwelcome new experiences for them. Such emotions and sensations were unknown in Heaven until Lucifer's rebellion. But then, to their surprise and relief, God had released them from their fiery fates and imprisoned them in the underworld.

God had hoped that banishing them to the gloomy, Stygian depths would make them repent and beg to be restored to His grace. But He was mistaken. They had no interest in returning to Heaven. The Fallen instead took comfort that their physical suffering had ceased, and they were finally free from God's tyranny. And there was an uneasy peace for a while.

But then God created man and called him His most perfect creation. Lucifer, in his pride and arrogance, could not stand such an insult and found a secret way to escape the underworld and travel to earth. Lucifer tempted Eve, and she tempted Adam. And thus the Garden of Eden fell, and mankind spread like a plague of locusts upon the earth.

God was so angered by the wickedness of mankind He released the Fallen and allowed them to conquer the netherworlds belonging to the ancient gods and make them part of their New Kingdom. Irkalla, Kur, Sheol, Gehenna, Hades and all the other disparate regions of the ancient underworlds fell, and Lucifer transformed them from bleak but peaceful shadow worlds into one vast, sadistic realm of torture and torment called Hell.

And God made a pact with Lucifer, which became known as the Old Laws. He allowed the Fallen to fly forth and test the faith of the 'Sons of Adam'. Those who were righteous, resisted temptation and obeyed God's Word would be deemed worthy of a place in Heaven, but wicked transgressors would belong to Lucifer and suffer the eternal tortures of the Abyss.

In creating mankind, God had inadvertently bolstered the spirits of the Fallen and given them a new purpose. They would do everything in their power to undermine and corrupt God's new creation. It was then that Lucifer changed his name to Satan, which meant 'adversary'. He was no longer the glorious Star of the Morning: he was the Evil One, the Great

Betrayer, the Great Dragon, and the Archenemy of God, of all God does and all God loves.

And as Satan's influence spread like a pestilence across the land, he grew more powerful and became Emperor of Hell and Prince of This World; namely, earth. For unlike God, he did not demand rituals or pledges of obedience; he did not need them. All nonbelievers and skeptics belonged to him and would join him in the Bottomless Pit of Hell. And thus the Creator's grand design was reversed. Instead of Satan having to sift through humans to root out the wicked, God had to protect the dwindling number of righteous from the burgeoning multitude of sinners.

Asmodeus growled and crammed the troublesome memories back into the deepest recesses of his venomous mind. Such trifles belonged to the past, and this was the present. There was no point in crying over spilt blood and offal.

He glided down the gigantesque stone ramp leading to the dungeons. His great swirling countenance adopted a sullen expression as he pondered upon the creature that awaited him in the forbidding bowels of his fortress.

For five earthly years, he had tortured and killed Longinus; and each night had breathed life into him again in a vicious cycle of rebirth, torment and death.

Yet, to the King of Demon's chagrin, the insect had endured the agony of his punishment with equanimity and refused to beg for mercy. It was as though the insolent cur was becoming resistant to the pain and flaunting his forbearance at him.

Asmodeus could not understand how such a thing was possible. Every soul in Hell screamed, squirmed, and begged for mercy, but this accursed Revenant was different. He seemed to welcome his suffering and accept it as a just punishment for his sins. Asmodeus found this attitude distasteful and exasperating. Such behaviour was sacrilege in the Abyss. In this sinister realm of perpetual chastisement, all souls denied their guilt and pleaded for leniency. This made their torture sublime to Asmodeus. He enjoyed listening to their feeble attempts to avoid their eternal punishment and the exquisite pain he heaped upon them.

But this damnable Revenant, this Gaius Cassius Longinus, was stubborn and vexatious. He had endured his pain without complaint and accepted his fate. This had denied Asmodeus his rightful pleasure of revenge and had caused a disturbing undercurrent of martyrdom to enter his domain. There was no place for martyrs in the Abyss. Their repulsive sense of righteousness caused a holy stench that permeated every dark chasm and caused demons to defecate, vomit, and choke on their bile. Such a vile aroma could arouse the curiosity of his imperial master, and Asmodeus had no desire to elicit such pitiless scrutiny. He had too many secrets he preferred to keep hidden.

Agrat Bat Mahlat's death and Lilith's defection to Heaven had increased Satan's paranoia. He suspected spies and traitors everywhere and had instigated a vicious inquisition to root them out. Lilith's succubi legions had been disarmed and sent to the Dungeons of Hell for interrogation. That had proved a mixed blessing for Asmodeus. On the one hand, it had shown him that Satan did not suspect him of any involvement in Lilith's desertion; but on the other, it had deprived him of subjecting Lilith's whores to his insatiable carnal desires and increasing his status in the hierarchy of Hell. An archdemon's position in the Abyss was measured by how many satanic legions he commanded.

Asmodeus therefore found his immense buttocks perched uncomfortably on the sharp horns of a dilemma. He was reluctant to cease torturing the Revenant—it was far too enjoyable—but he needed to stop the insect's abhorrent semblance of martyrdom.

But inspiration, the elusive bastard child of necessity, had come to his aid. His network of spies had brought some information to his attention that could help him exploit two of the Revenant's greatest weaknesses: loyalty and honour.

Asmodeus grinned and licked his thick, blubbery lips. He had conceived an ingenious plan that would intensify his sublime, licentious pleasures, and increase the Revenant's suffering beyond imagination.

CHAPTER II

Floating–floating–drifting in a sea of embryonic darkness. He could see nothing but felt no fear. There was safety here. The miasma of inky black primordial fluid protected and soothed him.

"Revenant. Revenant," a voice whispered.

It was as soft and reassuring as a lover's dulcet tone at the break of dawn.

Something tugged at his body. He tried to resist it, but to no avail. It was too powerful. He was rising, rising, slowly at first, but then with increasing speed and urgency. The force was insistent and overwhelming.

He heard faint noises and struggled to make sense of them. "Escape! Do not follow the sounds!" his mind screamed. He twisted and turned, trying to change direction. The source of his fear was unknown to him, but it filled him with dread.

"Where am I?" he cried.

There was no answer, but the sounds grew louder: a hideous cacophony of deep roars, eldritch screeches and insane gibbering and tittering.

"What awful place is this?" he whispered fearfully.

Then the terrible, sickening truth dawned upon him.

He lived again.

"Awaken, insect!" a harsh voice bellowed.

Longinus opened his eyes and stared into the huge, churning whirlpool of Asmodeus' face.

"So, Revenant, are you ready for tonight's games to commence?"

Longinus shook his head to clear his vision. The chains cutting into his wrists and ankles served as a painful reminder that he was still bound him to the inverted cross in Asmodeus' torture chamber. The floor was slick with blood and offal; and large, bloated insects flittered and mated on the slimy walls and high vaulted ceiling. He was parched, and his swollen tongue refused to provide any comfort to his burnt and cracked lips. He would give anything for a sip of cool water. Not blood. The very thought of drinking the warm, salty liquid made him feel sick. Hot, rancid air and dust clogged his mouth and nostrils. The temperature in the dungeon was intolerable and singed his flesh.

"Destroy me so I do not have to listen to your pompous prattle," he gasped.

Asmodeus laughed, and his enormous bulk shivered.

"Destroy you, Revenant? Why would I wish to do such a thing? My happiness would be at an end! You have no conception of how much I look forward to our little talks. They are the highlights of my eternal nights in the Abyss. No matter what troubles and weighty affairs of Hell occupy my mind, I can always dream of the pleasures yet to come with you.

"However, I must confess that I grow somewhat weary of our entertainment. Disembowelment is so tedious and messy. Therefore, let us consider some alternative methods of torture. What would you suggest—flaying, boiling, or crushing? Speaking for myself, I have always found watching my victims floundering in a vat of burning pitch to be most amusing."

"Stick your arse in one!" Longinus snarled.

Asmodeus' eyes narrowed, and he pierced the skin of Longinus' chest gently with a barbed claw. A trickle of blood meandered down the centurion's naked body and gathered around his groin.

"Cocks or claws?" the King of Demons whispered. "Cocks for lust and claws for revenge. Which would you prefer, insect? Tell me and I will make it so. You took my queen from me, and I can find no peace without her. Because of you, God redeemed her, and she is beyond my reach forever. How I yearn to feel her beautiful flesh next to mine, to fill her every orifice with the product of my lust and desire, and to hear her scream with delight as I fornicate endlessly with her. I alone could satisfy her craving for dark and immoral sensations in ways that your puny mind cannot even imagine."

Longinus showed no reaction to the pain and glared into Asmodeus' eyes.

"Yes, but she loves me, and that is something you could never satisfy—her deep longing to love and be loved."

Asmodeus' face contorted in rage and three more of his long, barbed tentacles sprang forward and hovered inches away from Longinus' body. For a moment, the centurion believed his tactic had worked and the King of Demons would kill him quickly tonight. However, to his dismay, Asmodeus relaxed and let his hellish appendages drift away.

"Love!" Asmodeus sneered. "What is love? It is nothing more than a vague concept used by mankind to excuse their lust and overwhelming urge to fornicate. Does the wild stallion need an excuse to mount the mare? Do wolves speak honeyed words before they mate? Do hyenas whisper sweet nothings in each other's ears prior to copulating? No, because they are animals and are ruled by their lust. And man is just an animal. He fornicates like an animal; he defecates like an animal, because he is an animal! He may have a modicum more intelligence than other beasts but he still shares the same basic instincts: to kill, to feed, to keep warm—and to fornicate."

"Yet man is God's greatest creation," replied Longinus, eager to goad his demonic captor.

"Man is God's most repressed and hypocritical creation," laughed Asmodeus. "Sex is the strongest and most important urge of human nature, but they still feel guilty and sinful about it. Yet it obsesses their societies, and everything, even children, is sexualised. They would much sooner admit to watching scenes of torture and violence than the most natural act of coitus. Humans regard the very process essential for the continuation of their species with irrational moral guilt and consider it a filthy, shameful deed that can only be discussed in censorious tones or lecherous whispers."

"God gave humankind free will. It is up to them how they use it," said Longinus.

"But what use is free will when it constrained by mindless guilt? What God gave with one hand, He took away with the other. What do you know of God? He is a tyrant! Let me tell you something of God. He never intended that mankind should enjoy coupling. He only allowed such a sinful act so that Adam and Eve could procreate without His intervention. To enjoy fornication, even when married, is a sin in the eyes of the Great Tyrant.

"It was I, Asmodeus, who taught mankind to enjoy the pleasures of copulation. I released the lust that throbbed and gnawed inside them, so they could appreciate their darkest desires without fear or guilt. Demons liberated mankind! We gave them the forbidden knowledge, which the Tyrant had sought to deny them. The Fallen taught men how to make weapons and fire, to read and write, and the disciplines they now call science. We encouraged them to discover the secrets of the cosmos and doubt everything that could not be proven with facts."

"And turned them against God," Longinus sneered.

"Of course!" Asmodeus replied. "There is always a price for knowledge, Revenant. They pay with their immortal souls, but humans are too stupid and selfish to realise their mistake until it is too late—and they arrive screaming in Hell. We gave them science to turn them against God. Now we are turning them against science. Soon they will believe in nothing but the lies we deign to feed them. The age of charity and enlightenment is dead, and the dark ages of ignorance, bigotry, hatred and superstition have returned."

"Your concern for the wellbeing of humankind is touching," Longinus said dryly.

Asmodeus grinned. "You know so little of the actual truth, insect. Mankind was not the first species that the Great Tyrant created, and it will not be the last."

"What do you mean?"

"It is simple. First the Tyrant created the divine beings of Heaven, and then He created a species of life on earth."

"What type of life?"

"Why Revenant, your ignorance continues to astound me. I thought you always considered yourself a Renaissance man, but where is your knowledge? Reptilian life, of course!"

"What? Dinosaurs?"

"Excellent, Revenant! Your tiny pink sponge is beginning to comprehend. At first He was very pleased with his creation, but He grew bored with them. They were not as perfect as He had hoped. He sent a large meteorite to the earth and destroyed them. The Tyrant then created Adam and Eve, but they too proved imperfect. He therefore placed irresistible temptations within their grasps that led to the destruction of the Garden of Eden. If God so loved them, then why did he tempt them? And why did He allow Satan to enter the paradise on earth?"

"To test their faith and love, I presume," Longinus replied, content to let Asmodeus rant. Ranting was preferable to ripping.

"No—to test their obedience. If love is what humans say it is, then it need not be tried. You do not test the one you love. It is a given. But blind obedience must always be tested. And who demands blind obedience? Tyrants!

"However, we liberated their offspring from the chains of ignorance and gave them knowledge. But the Tyrant became so incensed by their disobedience that He sent a Great Flood to destroy all but a select few of humans and animals upon the earth."

"And the animals went in two by two," Longinus murmured absently.

"Indeed, they did!" Asmodeus said expansively. "The Tyrant has destroyed his creations in the past and He shall do so again. When He finally tires of mankind, he will create a new species for us to tempt and lead astray. I look forward to it!"

"And what form would this new species take?" Longinus asked, intrigued despite his intense loathing for his lecturer.

Asmodeus pursed his lips and considered the matter. "Given intelligence, primates are mankind's natural successors in the animal kingdom, but the Tyrant may consider them too similar to humans and potentially just as troublesome."

A disgusting, flesh-coloured bug made the fatal error of flying too close to the King of Demons. He skewered it casually with one of his claws, popped it in his mouth and crunched on it.

"Insecta!" he announced in Latin, licking his lips. "They have tiny brains like you, and the Great Tyrant could make them completely subservient to His will. I have a fascination for insects. That is why I favour you, Revenant.

"So, you see, unlike the Great Tyrant, I do not seek to destroy mankind. Where would be the pleasure in that? No, I would see them prosper and flourish upon the earth. And each corrupted soul that turns away from God is a victory for me."

"You would create a world of morons without love or faith in anything," said Longinus.

"Faith is overrated and offers no solace or solutions to mankind. I espouse a more Epicurean approach where sensual pleasures sooth the body and the mind. Atheists, agnostics, the selfish, the depraved, the evil, and the ignorant are all worshippers in my temple. Their sins matter not to me. Each one has relinquished their faith and therefore will writhe, serve or pleasure me in Hell.

"And what of love? It is one of humankind's greatest redeeming attributes."

"As I have already told you, love is a pathetic emotion conceived by the Great Tyrant to legitimise the filthy act of procreation and delude humans into believing they are not alone upon on the mortal coil. But no matter how much they try to convince themselves that someone cares for them, the truth of the matter is that all of them are alone at the end of their days. No amount of insipid handholding or histrionic displays of grief by spouses or offspring can change that fact. Most relatives wish secretly the one in extremis passes away swiftly, causing the least inconvenience to themselves and their selfish, insignificant lives. That is the reality of human love. I am immortal and have no need of such trivial foolishness.

"It was you who introduced this abominable emotion into my domain and stole my consort from me. Can you imagine the agony such a sensation caused the demons under my command? The sensation spread like an obnoxious disease and caused unimaginable pain and suffering to my vassals. And for that sacrilege, I shall punish you for eternity."

"Do your worse, demon," said Longinus. "But you are wrong about love. Even animals enjoy moments of affection and intimacy with their mate or offspring. Human love is not just filth, lust and fornication. It transcends physical sensations. The love of a man and woman, or a parent for a child, is the purest form of love. You seek to replace love with depravity."

"Abominable hypocrite! Who are you to lecture me? Did you not indulge in wanton debauchery with Lilith and Agrat Bat?" Asmodeus roared.

"Yes—but I can still love. You only oppose such devotion because you are incapable of feeling such an exhilarating emotion. It is one sublime ecstasy that you cannot enjoy. That is why you hate humankind—they can love and you cannot. Did God strip that ability from you when He cast you, like a whimpering dog, out of Heaven?"

Asmodeus' enormous face swelled with rage. Yet again, Longinus hoped that the fiend's anger would mean a quick death; however, the King of Demons relaxed and grinned.

"Well done, Revenant. There is cunning blood in your veins. I almost ripped your head from your shoulders, but I will not kill you quickly."

Longinus' heart sank.

"In fact, I have a new and novel entertainment planned for you. You have grown weak with being chained to this obnoxious cross every night. I have decided it is time for you to have some exercise! It has been a long time since I have enjoyed the thrill of the chase. This evening, we will have ourselves a little hunt—and you will be the prey."

"What sort of hunt?" Longinus growled.

"Oh, fear not. I shall be sporting with you. I shall set you free and give you half a night's start. Come now, Revenant, it will be exciting and delightful. You may even escape me and reach the Lower Depths. Many demons think there is a secret path to earth there."

Longinus considered his proposal for a moment, and then unbeknown to Asmodeus, he consulted Naram-Sin, the living vampire armour within his body.

"What think you?"

"Accept his terms, centurion."

"Why? The bastard has no intention of letting us escape. This hunt is probably weighted in such a way that it is near impossible for us to succeed. We would be like animals trapped within a pen."

"But there is always the chance that Asmodeus has not foreseen everything. If there is even the slimmest glimmer of hope that we can escape, then we should accept his offer. And even if we cannot evade him, it is better than being tied and tortured. Here we have no chance, but during the hunt an opportunity may arise."

"Perhaps," Longinus said doubtfully.

"It also offers us the chance of retribution. Think of how many of his demons we can destroy."

The centurion gritted his teeth as he recalled the tortures and indignities inflicted upon him by Asmodeus' vassals when their master was not present. To break his spirit, the King of Demons had commanded these lecherous obscenities to defile Longinus in the most degrading and painful of ways. The desire for revenge burned like a raging fire within him.

"That would reason enough," Longinus hissed. "So, we agree?"

"Yes, centurion. Accept his offer but mislead him by feigning you have already lost all hope. That may entice him to reduce the number of enemies we have to face. After all—he wishes the hunt to be exciting."

"Such a deception is against my nature. I would not have Asmodeus believe he has cowed me."

"He has incarcerated us in Hell and abused us every night," Naram-Sin replied angrily. *"If we are to evade our fate, we require every advantage we can obtain. Put your stubborn honour aside for once. Once we have slain hordes of demons, you can wear it with pride again."*

His outburst surprised Longinus. It was the first time the ancient vampire lord had chastised him, but then he remembered that Naram-Sin had shared his pain and shame during their torments, and therefore had every right to voice his opinion.

"Very well," Longinus replied. *"But I shall not play the role of the dejected coward. I shall resist him and hope thereby to obtain more advantageous terms for us."*

"So be it," Naram-Sin sighed resignedly. *"Let us hope your ploy works."*

Asmodeus stared at Longinus and longed to read his mind; however, the Revenant had the surprising ability to shield his thoughts from others. It was yet another aspect of the pestiferous upstart that irritated him.

"Well, Revenant?" he asked, impatiently. "Do you accept my proposal?"

"No. I have no intention of providing sport for you. Torture me if you will, but I shall not be a stag to your wolves."

"Oh, but you shall, Revenant. I shall make it in your interests to do so."

"How so?" Longinus growled.

"To save your friends from an excruciatingly painful death," Asmodeus replied, nonchalantly.

Longinus girded his loins and tried to conceal his concern. "What friends?"

Asmodeus leaned closer. "The two little vampire whores whom you favour."

"Who?" Longinus retorted, but already his heart was sinking.

Asmodeus smiled sweetly. "The fair one who is now the vampire lady of New York and her little raven-haired playmate–the one you saved from the ferals. They will warble in terror like songbirds caught in the claws of cats when demons capture them."

Longinus' guts churned. He did not understand how Asmodeus knew about Rachel and Gabriella. Rachel had been a hunter-killer for Lady Veronica, the previous Vampire Lady of New York. At first, he had thought she was an enemy, but then he had discovered that he had rescued her from Lord Cervenka's clutches when she was a child. After that, they had become allies and had fought the ferals together. After they had defeated the feral vampires, they had discovered that Lady Veronica and her coven had been slain. Before leaving earth to confront Agrat Bat Mahlat in Purgatory, Longinus had made Rachel the new vampire lady of New York.

Gabriella had been an innocent young girl who had come to New York to make her fortune as a model. Kalena, the queen of the ferals, had abducted and used her as a bargaining chip so that Longinus would do her bidding. He and Rachel had tried to free Gabriella by attacking the feral hive in the New York sewers. But they had been too late to save her; the ferals had turned her. He had considered slaying her to free her from her curse; however, he could not bring himself to do it and had asked Rachel to care for her.

One thing was certain: if Asmodeus believed Longinus felt any attachment to these young vampires, the fiend would leave no stone unturned to make them suffer. With this grisly fact in mind, the centurion tried bluffing his way out of the situation.

"Do as you wish. They mean nothing to me."

Asmodeus laughed heartily, and the demons behind him cackled dutifully with their master. They had learned aeons ago to pay close attention to the moods of their capricious lord. When the King of Demons laughed, they laughed, but when he roared in anger, they fled and hid as best they could. Over the centuries, Asmodeus had torn apart many of his servants during his frequent diabolical tantrums, and none of the survivors had any wish for their name to be added to the list of unfortunates. It was quite remarkable how small a fissure each of them could squeeze into when petrified.

"Indeed?" Asmodeus replied skeptically, drying his eye with a claw. "You are many things, Revenant, but you are not a good liar. It does not come easily to you. We demons are masters of deceit and know when our victims are untruthful. But you only did what I expected of you. It is natural that you should try to protect your little stable of whores. Tell me–is the youngest one as tight as she looks? Demons will enjoy prying her open and filling her nubile body with their lust. She may even last a few hours before they rip her apart."

"Be that as it may, but I still refuse to act as the prey in your hunt," growled Longinus.

Asmodeus stopped smiling and regarded him coldly. "Very well. Your friends will die and their souls sent to Hell to be punished. That is a forgone conclusion, Revenant. The only way you can save them is by accepting my terms. If you agree to the hunt, I shall intervene and command the archdemon that covets them to desist."

Longinus frowned. "I thought it was you who threatens them?"

"Me?" Asmodeus chuckled. "I do not concern myself with such inconsequential beings as vampires. They are naught but the bastard half children of Lilith."

"Then who?"

The King of Demons sighed wearily. He had no interest in explaining anything to this ignorant bedswerver, but he knew in order to persuade the insect to participate in the hunt, he would have to reveal the nature of the threat facing his juicy little harlots. And after all, such knowledge could motivate the hare-brained fool and provide Asmodeus with more sport.

"He is an archdemon called Buer."

"Why does he wish to destroy these vampires?" asked Longinus, trying to appear aloof and unworried about their fates.

"Because their coven is now unprotected. As you well know, most vampire covens worship and make sacrifices to an archdemon. The last vampire lady was under Lilith's protection, but, as she is no more, thanks to you, they can no longer count on her help. The vampire lord of San Francisco is desperate to gain control of New York, but your friends have proved a thorn in his side and slain many of his vassals. Therefore, he has summoned his patron demon, Buer, to aid him. Old goat's legs must have felt uncharacteristically generous because he rarely intervenes in such minor squabbles. Perhaps he wishes to punish the offspring of Lilith because she defected to Heaven. In truth, I do not know his motives, and I do not care. What I do know is that in seven days' time, he will destroy your friends and drag their souls to his domain in Hell. And I can assure you, his satyr-like vassals are crueller and more lecherous than even my incubi. They will torture and mount your juicy little strumpets incessantly for eternity."

"Can you stop him?"

"I am Asmodeus, the King of Demons! Of course, I can stop Buer! When I command, he obeys! So, what say you, Revenant? Is it life or death for your friends?"

Longinus grimaced. Asmodeus had backed him into a corner, and the only way he could save his friends was by agreeing to the hunt. He knew, of course, that he could not trust the King of Demons to keep his word. There was only one way to affect the outcome: he must escape from Hell.

"Very well. I accept your challenge."

"Excellent! You will not regret it. I promise you a very interesting experience."

"I hope I exceed your expectations," Longinus said dryly.

"Release him," Asmodeus commanded.

Two misshapen demons, each with four arms and two heads, undid Longinus' restraints and dragged him behind their master and into the Basilica of Pain. They passed through large vaulted corridors where human souls hung and writhed, skewered to the bloody walls on metal hooks. Gloomy chambers on either side of the passageways were filled with incubi torturing souls with barbaric glee. They nailed tongues to tables, gouged out eyes, ripped open stomachs, tore or crushed genitalia, and thrust red-hot irons into rectums. The insane, screeching laughter of the torturers and the deafening screams of the damned filled the fortress. It was an evil place of madness and bereft of hope for all the souls imprisoned there.

Asmodeus paused at the doorway of a circular chamber where hundreds of souls crawled round on their hands and knees on a floor covered with sharp iron spikes. By some malign sorcery, each soul's face melded into the backside of the one preceding it. Incubi wearing large, strap-on serrated phalluses shrieked in exultation as they raped and sodomised other souls.

The King of Demons leered at Longinus and said, "Behold the power of Hell, Revenant, where the incorporeal is made corporeal again. Torturing an ethereal spirit is immeasurably less enjoyable than ripping and tearing material flesh. That is why tormenting you was such a pleasure. You are not a soul, and I did not need to transform you. The ritual of alteration is such a tedious process. You were ready-made flesh, bone and blood, ripe for my pleasure."

"What sins did these souls commit?" asked Longinus.

"They are masturbators, unmarried fornicators, sodomites, and adulterers," replied Asmodeus.

"Masturbators and unmarried fornicators?" Longinus snorted derisively. "Is not punishing souls for such trivial offences beneath the dignity of the mighty Asmodeus?"

The King of Demons smirked at his sarcasm. "You miss the point, Revenant. I only enjoy torturing souls that have some good left in them. These souls were not evil in their mortal lives, but their sins were serious enough for the Great Tyrant to send them to Hell. And for that, I am most grateful. For there is no greater pleasure than torturing a soul that has good left in it. Evil souls such as murderers, rapists, paedophiles, incestophiles, thieves and other bestial or violent offenders are rewarded in my domain. Am I not just and merciful?"

Asmodeus chuckled at his own dark, ironic humour. As the demon king shook with mirth, Longinus stared at the myriad of souls trapped within the translucent red skin of his loathsome, putrescent body. Their terrible expressions and silent screams reflected the intense agony and horror of their ordeal.

"What do you do to the souls within your body?" Longinus asked.

"I consume them—as one day I shall consume you."

"I thought human souls were immortal?"

Asmodeus pursed his large blubbery lips and stared at Longinus with a bemused expression.

"That is the only thing I admire about you, Revenant; you are always scheming and trying to find some way to defeat me. You hope by understanding my powers you will discover some weakness you can exploit to your advantage."

Longinus had asked for that very reason, but he was not about to admit it to the King of Demons.

"I do not see how asking about the fate of souls enables me to gain some advantage over you. But if you are afraid of my question, then do not answer it. You can devour a million souls for all I care!"

Asmodeus grinned, displaying his enormous pointed teeth. "Well played, Revenant, well played. I almost believe you. However, as I am feeling generous today, I shall deign to answer your question. I have nothing to fear from a worm like you. Yes, you are correct: human souls are immortal and demons cannot destroy them."

"Then how can you devour them?"

"Because I do not destroy them. After I consume their writhing, pathetic forms, I excrete them from my nether regions and begin again. The torture is cyclical and endless. Would you like to witness a short demonstration?"

"No," Longinus replied, wrinkling his nose in disgust. "The image in my mind is sufficient."

Asmodeus bellowed with laughter. "You see? We are getting along famously! Indeed, I think we shall be good friends!"

Longinus spat and glared at him.

Asmodeus' demeanour of false bonhomie disappeared in an instant; he looked cold and sinister again. He turned and drifted along the corridor.

"Bring him! And be not too gentle!" he growled.

Longinus grimaced in pain as his two captors dug their claws into his arms and pushed him onward.

They passed more torture chambers with swarms of incubi going about their hellish work. Longinus remembered the forbidden *Book of Lilith* said that Lilith had created the succubi and Asmodeus, the incubi. These types of demons visited mortals in their sleep and coupled with them. Glancing at the incubi, Longinus thought women had received the short straw for nocturnal lovers. Succubi were usually very attractive; but incubi were dark, squat muscular creatures with oversized heads, low brows, wide mouths, rotten teeth and thick blubbery lips. Their massive genitalia were repugnant and looked like long serpents slithering from heavy leather pouches. The tome inferred that incubi had the power of illusion and appeared handsome to their victims. Longinus grimaced as he imagined some innocent girl moaning in rapturous delight as one of the evil, lecherous, slobbering monstrosities mounted and abused her.

After dragging him through a maze of foul passageways that reeked of burning flesh and hair, they reached the massive arched entrance of the basilica and forced him down a stone ramp leading to a gigantic square courtyard. The reddish-black firmament was a churning inferno, and beyond the quadrangle lay a paved road that wound off into the distance where smoke and fire belched and ominous dark peaks loomed.

Hundreds of demons stood on either side of the highway. Most were humanoid but others were the stuff of nightmares: grotesque abominations with malformed bodies that squirmed on slimy bellies or tentacles.

"What are the rules of the hunt?" Longinus asked.

"There is your path," Asmodeus said, pointing a claw at the road. "We will give you half a night's start and then pursue you. If you evade us for seven nights, I will free you and command Buer to leave your little friends alone."

"And if you catch me?"

"Then you and your succulent harlots will be my guests for eternity. I will nail them to crosses and put one on either side of you to keep you company. A somewhat ironic fate for you, I think. You crucified the Nazarene between two thieves, and you will suffer the same fate with two whores. I shall entitle my little allegorical work of art, *The Trinity*. What think you?"

"You are the epitome of wit–I mean halfwits," Longinus growled.

The lesser demons holding him exchanged worried glances. They did not wish to be in the firing line of Asmodeus' claws. However, to their great relief, their master laughed indulgently at the Revenant's jibe and appeared to be in a hearty and nondestructive mood.

"Am I allowed to defend myself?" the centurion asked.

"But, of course! I will give you a choice of weapons. I want you to fight and destroy your pursuers, Revenant. Such antics will provide delicious entertainment for my esteemed guest."

Longinus frowned. "What guest?"

Asmodeus glanced around, sniffed the air and grinned. "How timely. I forgot to inform you, Revenant, there is another participant in this game. Behold the Lady Naamah!"

Longinus gaped in astonishment as a wondrous shape materialised before his eyes. Naamah was over twelve feet in height with long, curved ebony horns, waist length raven hair, and a wickedly beautiful face. The demoness' naked torso was similar to that of mortal women, but displayed four voluptuous breasts. Her lower body was snake like and over thirty paces in length. She swayed sinuously on her thick coils and regarded Longinus with cold, predatory eyes.

According to the Zoharistic *Kabbalah*, Naamah was one of four fallen angels of sacred prostitution that had mated with Lucifer after God had cast him out of Heaven. The others were Lilith, Eisheth Zenunim, and Agrat Bat Mahlat. Longinus had often wondered why the Jews called them sacred angels. Even assuming that divine beings could mate with each other, there was nothing angelic or sacred about any of them. The diabolical *Book of Lilith* painted a very different picture of the fearsome quartet. That hideous tome maintained they had never been angels, but were powerful demons, succubi and queens of Hell. Lucifer had created all of them in different ways, but Naamah was his only flesh and blood daughter.

Naamah had been the Medusa of ancient myth, and the Berbers and Phoenicians had worshipped her as the goddess Tanit or Astarte. Others called her Hekate. Whereas Lilith was the progenitor of succubi, other demons, and vampires; Naamah was the mother of empusae, a more ferocious type of vampiric succubi that lured young men to their beds and devoured them after coitus. The blood was still the life for them, but they could only obtain the vital nectar by consuming the flesh of their victims.

Thankfully, Naamah was not as fertile as Lilith, and there was considerably less empusae than succubi. Longinus had met only two in his existence. One had been in Constantinople; she had been vicious and extremely difficult to kill. The other, a courtesan in Venice, he had rather liked, despite himself. Giustina had seemed truly tortured by having to devour her human lovers. She had implored him to stay, but he had left her. Although she had always been discreet about her feeding, he had found it increasingly difficult to turn a blind eye to it. Sometimes, he had noticed specks of blood on her breast or a sliver of flesh between her teeth. If he had stayed, he would have eventually felt morally obliged to slay her. So he had taken a midnight gondola and left. She had been one of the few vampiric creatures he had pardoned. He now regretted he had not done more to help her, to wean her off her terrible, gnawing hunger for warm, bloody, human flesh.

Her fate and that of her unfortunate victims still haunted him. It has not been his finest hour. The follies of one's youth seem inexplicable when viewed through older and wiser eyes.

According to the *Book of Lilith*, Perseus—meaning sacker of cities–had not slain Medusa. She was far too powerful and could have destroyed him with relative ease. However, she was very taken with the handsome young warrior. After promising to help him destroy his enemies, she bedded him and became somewhat besotted with him. Angered that King Polydectes of Seriphos had sent the youth to kill her, she had given Perseus the head of one of her empusae imbued with the power of her feminine rage. The countenance was so terrifying it could 'turn the stones' of men into toxic serpent eggs, which hatched and devoured their bowels. Perseus should have suspected then that Naamah was a demoness; however, he was too preoccupied by her wondrous and inexhaustible charms and his own dreams of vengeance.

Thus King Polydectes and many others who had stood in Perseus' way had died terrible deaths. The warrior's fabled winged horse, Pegasus, had unbeknown to him been the archdemon Gamigin. When Perseus eventually assumed the mantle of King of Tiryns, he built a secret temple to honour his dark goddess—Medusa Naamah.

It had amused Longinus to read that later scribes had changed 'turn the stones of men' to 'turned men into stone' as the original Medusa curse demeaned men's masculinity. No female, even a goddess, could be allowed to threaten the small patriarchal male symbols of power and fertility. However, the centurion suspected the truth of the matter was much simpler. Medusa's curse made men squirm in their seats, and no man, even the mightiest, wished even to contemplate a woman who could afflict them with the dreaded testes of terror. He, on the other hand, had always enjoyed the company of strong, powerful women, mortal or otherwise. It was his weakness, delight, and curse.

"So this is the creature you spoke of?" Naamah said in a deep, sibilant voice.

"Yes, my lady," Asmodeus responded, smiling.

"But he will not provide us with much sport! He is too small!"

Asmodeus regarded her lustily. Since losing Lilith, he had been searching for a new consort, and Naamah was perfect in every way. She was Satan's daughter and could satisfy his rapacious carnal desires and insatiable lust for power. A union with Naamah would improve his status in the Abyss, and he was trying his utmost to pander to her needs and woo her.

"He is more resilient than he appears," he slobbered, eager not to disappoint her.

"Where is this spear he carries? I have heard it is a weapon of great power."

Asmodeus pursed his lips. He had been unaware that Naamah knew of the Revenant's spear and cursed the fact that it was exceedingly difficult to keep any secrets in Hell. However, his cunning mind responded swiftly to the unwelcome surprise. He waved a claw and an enormous metal chest appeared in the courtyard.

"Fetch the insect's weapon and present it to Lady Naamah," he said casually to a small, fat demon with bandy legs, short horns and a long tail.

Its name was Surgat, and it was the King of Demon's Groom of the Stool. Among its many important duties were cleaning Asmodeus' bottom, returning the defecated souls to the cellars for restoration, and supervising the smooth running of its master's basilica and bowels. Its coveted position and enthusiastic arse licking had given it access to many dark secrets, and therefore, although diminutive in stature, it wielded much power and was feared and respected by other lesser demons.

The groom of the rear responded instantly to its lord's command and scurried over to the coffer. It threw open the hinged lid and began searching through the contents. Mysterious artefacts; jewel encrusted swords and daggers; grotesque golden crowns for misshapen heads; and bucklers made of reddish black metal clattered onto the slabs of stone. Uttering a squeal of satisfaction, Surgat pulled Longinus' spear from the chest. As it scuttled to Lady Naamah, she observed its sly yellow eyes stealing glances at her fulsome breasts. The glimmer of a cruel smile played upon her lips. She enjoyed tantalising lesser demons with her charms. It pleased her to know that they spilled their copious seed while fantasising about her. But they would never have her. Her voluptuous form was not for the likes of commoners. It was reserved for her father and a select few archdemons. The obsequious voyeur licked its lips, bowed its head, and presented the spear to her with outstretched arms.

With a disdainful expression, Naamah took the weapon and examined it. She was disappointed; it was less impressive than she had envisaged. Instead of being highly decorative, it comprised a simple wooden shaft with an iron tip. She swung it back and forth, but nothing happened.

Frowning, she glanced at Asmodeus. "Wherein lies its power?"

"Whatever dark sorcery it possessed has vanished. I examined it minutely and could find nothing extraordinary about it. Mulciber, the chief architect of the Abyss, agreed with my findings and postulated the weapon may only work on earth. In Hell, it is just a common spear."

"Then why keep it?"

"A little memento, my lady. I enjoy collecting trophies from the enemies I have slain or conquered."

"You have had many enemies," she replied, glancing at the pile of strange objects lying beside the chest.

"The price of power," he replied with a shrug.

She tossed the spear back to Surgat.

"That is most disappointing!" she hissed. "Such a weapon could have been of use to me."

"That makes two of us," Longinus thought grimly.

He wondered if the spear had really lost its power or was merely dormant until touched by its master. He did not know, but kept silent on the matter. This may be something he could later turn to his advantage.

The King of Demons nodded in false sympathy. It relieved him she had not asked to keep the spear. Although inert and useless, it was something he savoured and gloated over, a constant reminder of his glorious revenge on Lilith and her conniving slave.

With that delightful thought in mind, he moved the conversation onto a more gratifying subject. He still desired to impress and woo Satan's daughter.

"But you look forward to the hunt?"

Naamah stared at Longinus. "Yes, it is a long time since I have enjoyed the thrill of the chase. My nehushtan need exercise, and I hope to find it entertaining. However, it is a pity that he is so diminutive. He will not offer much of a challenge to my pets."

"Where are your beasts?" Asmodeus asked.

"They accompany me at all times," she replied.

Asmodeus frowned, looked about, but could not see them.

"Are they invisible?" he asked.

She smiled coyly. "They are nearby."

The demon lord was becoming irritated with her enigmatic replies, and it took all of his self-control not to erupt into one of his blinding rages. He enjoyed fornicating with females but had no time for their inane ramblings.

"Where?" he asked with a thin smile.

Naamah raised her arms above her head and undulated. The grisly spectators gasped in astonishment as her womb opened to supernatural proportions and six snarling, skinless hounds slithered from her midriff. They surrounded her and were as tall as Asmodeus' guards.

Asmodeus licked his blubbery lips. The emergence of the nehushtan had momentarily astounded him, but now his enormous eyes were fixed firmly on Naamah's gaping orifice. He had puzzled for some time on where Satan's daughter concealed her sex, but now her most intimate secret was revealed to him. He would just have to be careful that her hounds were not within her when he pried her open and mounted her. His phallic tentacles were extremely sensitive and took weeks to regrow.

Naamah pointed at Longinus and said, "Take his scent!"

The hellish canines bounded across to Longinus, and the two demons holding him stared fearfully at them.

"Keep still," Naamah said with a crooked smile. "If you twitch even a claw, they will tear you apart."

The demons froze and only their eyes moved as the vicious curs surrounded them. One hound crept towards Longinus until its skinless, bloody head was only inches from his face. Its scarlet eyes blazed like burning coals, and it smelt of rotten fish. Longinus kept motionless and stared defiantly into its hellish orbs. It sniffed him twice, and its thin lips drew back in a tight, fearsome snarl. The hound backed away and turned side on to them. He saw it raise one of its muscular rear legs, and closed his eyes just in time before he and his captors were drenched in a stream of green, foul-smelling urine.

"Enough! Return to me!" Naamah commanded.

The beasts scampered back to their mistress and everyone watched in fascination as they scrabbled back into her womb. The flesh of her scaly abdomen retracted quickly, leaving no trace of her orifice, but the smell of her sex lingered, tantalising demon nostrils and inflaming unholy desires.

"A formidable display of your power, my lady," Asmodeus said huskily.

"I am glad you found my hounds so interesting," she murmured with a seductive smile.

"It was truly magnificent!"

Naamah smiled graciously. She knew he was referring to more than her hounds and that pleased her. Glancing at his demon guards, she could see similar expressions of lust and awe on their hideous faces.

"Let us hope your prisoner provides us with good hunting."

"Oh, but he shall, my lady. The creature you see before differs from any other you have met in the Abyss. He is one of Lilith's brood and neither alive nor dead."

"A vampire?" she asked, raising an eyebrow.

"Yes, but he is not completely evil and has much good in him. Although he was Lilith's Revenant, he kept his conscience and values the damnable virtues of valour, empathy and honour. He also has the abhorrent ability to love. This is not just some evil soul that has been sentenced to eternal punishment in Hell. The fool *chose* to be brought here because of his sense of love and duty! Tell me, my lady, when was the last time you hunted something that still has some goodness left in it?"

Naamah's beautiful eyes strayed over Longinus' sculptured body, and she felt a pang of lust within her. She thought it a pity that Asmodeus had not presented her with this fine specimen to play with before the hunt. She would have enjoyed bending him to her will and milking the goodness from him. There was nothing so delicious to a female demon than male seed. But she said nothing of this to Asmodeus. She well knew that he had been courting her, and such a match could prove very beneficial to her. Her great father, Satan, had ignored her charms for so long.

For centuries, they had coupled incessantly, but then he had grown tired of her. She had known he had become enamoured with a new mate, but she had been unable to ascertain who or what it was. She had always suspected it was Agrat Bat Mahlat, but after Lilith's defection, her father had retreated into his great palace of Infernus and refused to see anyone. Even Baal Zebub, his favoured advisor, had been denied an audience.

In Naamah's suspicious mind, this suggested that his secret lover had been Lilith. Even as she had pretended to remain loyal to Asmodeus, she had been coupling secretly with Satan. This explained her extraordinary strength and why he had tolerated her rebellious nature. As she well knew, Satan's unimaginable torrent of lust would increase the power of any demoness. But Lilith was gone forever, and Naamah was determined to become Queen of the Night. In the patriarchy of Hell, often when one door closed, another one opened; and a cunning demoness must always be ready to take the initiative when the opportunity for advancement arose.

"If what you say is true, this will be most enjoyable," she hissed.

"Excellent! Well, Revenant, are you ready for our little game to begin?" Asmodeus said affably.

"I am."

"To ensure an equitable chase, I have used my power to ensure that you cannot transform into a wolf or bat to escape your pursuers. However, you will still be able to use your Revenant manifestation–if you can find time to transform. Am I not just and merciful?"

"You are an exemplar to all," Longinus grunted.

Changing into the beast took longer than transforming into a wolf or a giant bat. During the metamorphosis, he could not fight or protect himself. Asmodeus knew that too. However, Longinus was grateful that demon king had granted this concession. In his fearsome Revenant form, he should be more than a match for any lesser demons he encountered, but he would have to use it wisely. When he was the beast, he only had one overriding thought in his mind: to kill everything that moved. He could run faster and make rational decisions in his human form.

Asmodeus grinned as he watched Longinus working out the advantages and disadvantages of the constraints imposed upon him. He could almost see his tiny mind working, the wheels turning. He hoped sincerely that Longinus would make a last-ditch stand as the beast. It would provide Lady Naamah with a most gratifying spectacle before his hunters or her hounds tore apart him. If that did not put her in the mood to make the beast with two backs, nothing would.

"Have you any other further questions?" he asked Longinus.

"Can I have clothes or armour?"

"No. You will run naked like a wild beast."

"As you wish. But you promised me a weapon."

"Did I?" the King of Demons replied slyly.

"Yes, you did. Or is the word of the mighty Asmodeus worth less than a rat's arse?"

Asmodeus pursed his lips. He did not want the Revenant to suspect that he would renege on his promise to intercede and save his friends. The success of the hunt depended on it. He therefore decided to appear gracious.

"Oh, very well!" he sighed. "A promise must be honoured."

He clicked a claw and commanded his rotund lackey to retrieve two weapons from the coffer. Surgat squealed and gave Longinus a filthy look as it ran to the chest. It had been studying a more interesting type of chest and was most irritated that its grubby little fantasy had been interrupted. It returned scowling with a strange mace in one claw and an axe in the other.

"You may choose *one* weapon," said Asmodeus. "Which do you prefer?"

"I *prefer* my spear," said Longinus.

"No," Asmodeus said flatly.

"Why? Are you afraid that I may defeat you?" Longinus taunted.

Asmodeus glared at Longinus and knew he had made a mistake. He should have spoken to the centurion before Naamah appeared and warned him not to ask for the spear; however, in his lustful excitement, he had forgotten to mention the matter.

"I could destroy you with one claw," he said menacingly.

"Then why not give me my spear?" said Longinus, calling his bluff in front of Naamah.

"Because you desire it, and therefore it pleases me to deny you!" Asmodeus spat.

"Oh, give the foolish creature his weapon!" Naamah cried impatiently. "As you have said, it is of no consequence and may encourage him to provide us with better sport!"

Asmodeus scowled at her. He was unaccustomed to receiving commands from other demons, but as his eyes drifted over her body, he could feel his anger subsiding. He would do anything within reason to couple with this voluptuous harlot. In his mind's eye, he could see himself subjecting her to his voracious desires as she screamed and moaned. He would soon wipe that imperious look off her beautiful face and make her subservient to his will.

"As you wish, my lady," he said, controlling his wrath.

Giving Longinus a baleful look, he threw the spear, and it struck the ground two Roman stades, or one quarter of a mile, away. The centurion noted carefully where it landed.

"You can have it—if you can find it," Asmodeus sneered.

The centurion decided to cause some mischief at Asmodeus' expense. He ignored him and looked at Naamah.

"Thank you, my lady," he said, winking.

Naamah looked surprised at being addressed by him, but laughed at his boldness and impertinence.

"You will not be so thankful when my nehushtan rip you apart."

"But I will."

"How so?"

"Because the last thing I will remember is your face," he replied gallantly.

Naamah narrowed her eyes, and her voice became harder. "Many have died wishing they had never beheld this face."

"I shall not be one of them," Longinus said soberly, acting his part well.

Naamah laughed again, but he could see the look in her eyes had changed, and she seemed to regard him in a different light. He knew that most demonesses appreciated being complimented; it was part of their nature. Besides arousing Asmodeus jealousy, he had sown a seed in her mind, which may or may not prove useful to him at a later time. He needed every advantage he could get, and even a moment's doubt in the mind of an enemy could provide him with time to escape or strike a fatal blow.

Asmodeus glared at them and imagined lancing Longinus like a ripe boil. It displeased him that Satan's daughter found the cur's banter amusing. This was what the deceitful insect had done with Lilith. It would defeat the purpose of his amorous plan if Naamah asked him to spare the Revenant and gift him to her as a plaything.

After the disastrous outcomes of his relations with Lilith and Agrat Bat, he had no intention of letting the Revenant anywhere near Lady Naamah. The putrid little scab had a habit of worming his way between a demoness' legs and obtaining favours from her. But that would not happen this time! He would see to it!

"Do not listen to him. He is trying to manipulate you," he said disparagingly to her.

As soon as he saw her expression, he knew he had blundered.

"Do you take me for a fool? Do you think I am incapable of discerning that," she replied coldly.

"Forgive my temper, my lady. I did not intend to insult you."

"And yet, you have. I am not Lilith and need no instruction from you on how to behave."

"You are correct, my lady. Again, I offer my apologies. I seek only to please you," Asmodeus said, attempting to assuage her icy anger.

"Then let us say no more about it," she hissed, turning her back on him.

She smiled inwardly and congratulated herself. Asmodeus thought he was seducing her, but it was she who was in control. Male demons were so easily played. They all panted for the orifice of pleasure and would do and say anything to breach it. But she had learned from experience that it bade a demoness well to withhold her favours until she had obtained all the concessions she desired; for after they completed the act, mindless male passion faded, enmity and violence increased, and bargaining because nigh impossible.

Longinus grinned as he watched the mighty King of Demon squirm and fawn over Naamah. They were well suited: both were cunning, vain and merciless. It occurred to him that he should encourage their match. The gods willing, she would destroy him when he displeased her.

Asmodeus noticed his bemused look and was tempted to skewer him where he stood. But he subdued his bile. The hunt was all-important, and he would not let the Revenant's mischief-making disrupt his plan. He then remembered with some satisfaction that he still had a surprise up his metaphorical sleeve that would wipe the annoying smirk off the insolent insect's face.

"Before we start the hunt, I have something to reveal to you, Revenant."

"That you have gonorrhoea or syphilis?" Longinus asked, helpfully.

Asmodeus laughed. "No, not quite as pleasurable as those delightfully dripping diseases, but something that will sting and burn as much. You see my vassals positioned on either side of the road?"

"Which ones? Those with faces like scrota—or the *really* ugly ones?"

The King of Demons guffawed again. "Do not be too harsh on them. They are old friends of yours."

"Friends?" Longinus replied cautiously.

"Yes, excellent friends, Revenant! They are but a small fraction of the hundreds of souls you sent to me over the centuries: the vampires, robbers, murderers, torturers, sadists, rapists and child molesters. The list of evil is endless. I transformed them into my vassals, because I knew that one day they would be of use to me. And that day has come. The very ones you hunted and killed will be your hunters."

"Oh, joy," Longinus muttered.

Asmodeus had turned the tables on him. Yes, he had forced the King of Demons to give him his spear, but now he had discovered his pursuers were the very ones he had destroyed with his infernal weapon.

Naamah spun around and smiled. The irony of Asmodeus' revelation amused her immensely.

The King of Demons grinned and addressed his vassals. "Tell the Revenant how much you are looking forward to our little game."

The two lines of demons glared at Longinus through red or yellow eyes and uttered bestial, deafening roars.

Asmodeus pointed a barbed tentacle at the largest and ugliest one. "Attend me!"

The muscular red demon loped forward and kneeled before his master. Its pate was bald and sported two backward sweeping ebony horns.

"Stand and face your executioner," Asmodeus said.

The demon stood slowly and flexed its muscles. It glared malevolently at Longinus; its yellow eyes were cruel and unblinking. Longinus curled his lip and met the demon's intimidating gaze without flinching.

"This one hates you with all the fury of the Abyss," said Asmodeus. "Do you recognise him?"

"Yes—his face reminds me of your arse."

The demon snarled, and Asmodeus and Naamah laughed.

"Ah, Revenant, how I shall miss your defiant little witticisms. Unfortunately, Cervenka does not appreciate your humour."

For once, Longinus was dumbfounded. Cervenka had been the vampire lord of New York and a formidable opponent.

"This *thing* is Cervenka?"

"Yes, but he cannot tell you that himself. I had his tongue removed in a moment of anger. But he has proven to be an obedient if not rather silent vassal. I have made him the captain of my guard."

"Your disgusting little incubi would provide a more fitting honour guard for you," Longinus retorted.

"Now, now, Revenant. There is no need to be insulting. What my incubi lack in height is more than compensated for by their strength, brutality and the prodigious size of their cocks. You of all people should know that."

Cervenka grinned, showing his pointed teeth, and the other demons roared with obscene laughter, grasped their genitals, and mocked Longinus. The centurion kicked Cervenka in the chest and sent him sprawling onto the flagstones. The former vampire lord scrambled to his feet, his face a mask of indescribable hatred. He raised his battleaxe above his head and made to split Longinus in twain.

"Cease," Asmodeus said casually.

Cervenka glared up at his master, and for a moment Longinus thought he was going to disobey him. Asmodeus gazed down at him with a thin smile hovering on his lips, almost daring him to disobey his command. Cervenka's shoulders slumped, and he lowered his axe.

"Get back to the ranks," Asmodeus said disdainfully.

Cervenka bowed and trotted dutifully back to his position. He glanced at the axe in his claws and then at Longinus. It was only his fear of Asmodeus that had prevented him from slaying his archenemy on the spot. He consoled himself with the knowledge there would soon be another opportunity for him to exact his vengeance.

Naamah slithered to Asmodeus. "How long have you planned your revenge on the Revenant? Centuries?"

"Millennia," said Asmodeus.

"How admirable! It is not for nothing my father named you the Prince of Revenge."

"And lust, my lady," he whispered, leering.

"Yes, I am aware of your talents in that area."

Asmodeus allowed one of his phallic tentacles to drift behind her and caress her rear. She did not complain, but Longinus noticed her flinch slightly. He suspected that she was not quite as enamoured with dirty, old multi-tool as she pretended to be.

"There will time enough for that," she murmured.

The demon king grinned and withdrew his errant appendage. He did not wish to tempt fate by rushing their courtship and needed to proceed slowly and with caution. He felt like a male redback spider approaching the female's web and waiting to be invited in. The trick was to avoid being eaten alive during mating. But he was not overly concerned by such danger. If need be, he could be as voracious as the male water spider, *argyronetia aquatica*, and consume smaller mates. However, he hoped sincerely that Naamah would be a willing recipient of his advances and such a drastic measure would be unnecessary. Destroying her was hardly going to endear him to her omnipotent father. But this was a match made in Hell rather than Heaven, and as such, one had to be prepared for all possible contingencies.

A deep horn sounded from within the basilica. It was midnight. Although the Abyss was in perpetual gloom, demons still marked the passage of time with the concept of day and night. It harkened back to their divine origin and the creation of the earth when the light was separated from the darkness. Using the ancient Sumerian sexagesimal system, they further organised each day into sixty parts.

The denizens of the Abyss believed they existed in a state of chaotic Epicurean freedom, but in reality they were cogs in a strict hierarchical and bureaucratic dictatorship. From the lowliest torturer to the highest duke, prince or king, each vassal of the Evil One knew their place, what tasks they must perform, and when to do them.

More horns sounded and incubi drummers on the battlements pounded a discordant rhythm increasing in vehemence.

"It is time. Are you ready, Revenant?" Asmodeus asked.

"I am," Longinus replied, staring into the demon king's eyes with the hint of an insolent smile.

"Then let our Wild Hunt begin!" Asmodeus announced grandly. "Run, Revenant! Run!"

Longinus turned and sprinted down the road. The demons on either side of him lashed him with whips. The centurion staggered from side to side, trying to avoid their vicious attacks, but a multitude of welts and bleeding cuts soon covered his naked body.

Asmodeus roared with laughter and bellowed, "A little farewell gift to send you on your way!"

Lady Naamah licked her lips with her forked tongue. Torture and violence excited her. There was no greater pleasure to her than seeing a face contorted in agony.

Longinus concentrated on moving forward and protecting his eyes from the savage blows. Although the cuts in his vampire flesh would heal swiftly, damage to his eyes could be irreparable and impede his ability to escape. One whip caught him around the neck, and the gibbering fiend tried to pull him down. With a snarl, Longinus grabbed the thong in his hand and caught his attacker off guard. He jerked the startled monstrosity to him, kicked it in the groin and sent it sprawling. The others howled dementedly and rushed at him.

"Let him be!" Asmodeus roared.

Longinus narrowed his eyes and unwound the whip from around his neck. Grinning savagely, he gave his fallen attacker several hefty lashes with it. The demon screeched and covered its revolting face with its claws.

"Who is next?" he asked, defiantly.

The demons looked confused and glanced at Asmodeus. No one dared to challenge the impudent upstart without his master's consent. Only Asmodeus and Cervenka appeared unsurprised by Longinus' display of resistance. They both knew their old adversary well.

With a sneer, Longinus threw the whip at the cowering fiend's head.

"Good! Now the hunt can truly begin. I will be waiting for you—all of you!"

Lady Naamah smiled despite herself at his audacity and for the first time felt that this tiresome diversion might be more enjoyable than she had first expected.

Asmodeus scowled. This was not the way he had envisaged his great game beginning. Yet again, the insolent worm had soured his enjoyment, and he would make him pay dearly for his effrontery.

"Go! Before I change my mind and destroy you now!" he roared.

Longinus grinned roguishly and gave Lady Naamah a parting bow.

Then he ran for his spear, his life—and his immortal soul.

CHAPTER III

Longinus found his spear lying on the baked red ground near a gigantic pit in which hundreds of souls writhed and screamed as swarms of emaciated, furless rats with beady crimson eyes devoured them.

Whilst trying to ignore the horrendous, deafening clamour of the damned, he bent down and picked it up. Nothing happened.

"Was Asmodeus right? Has it lost its power?" he muttered.

He gave the weapon a shake and concentrated.

"Come on, come on!" he growled.

He was almost at the point of giving up when he felt a tiny vibration.

"Bond with me!" he commanded.

Like an old engine starting, the spear made a series of erratic thrumming sounds, and then a small burst of energy shot up Longinus' arm and entered his core.

"Ave, old friend. I fear we are both weak and need to feed."

The spear vibrated slightly, as if agreeing with him.

He started running again and came upon another vast crater brimming with poor unfortunates, floundering in a hissing sea of vicious albino cobras. The King of Demons had boasted to him about these infernal hollows. They were his Soul Pits where his satanic quota of the damned squirmed in torment before being plucked out with long hooks and subjected to further tortures and obscenities in his Basilica of Pain.

A man with snake tails extruding from his eye sockets shrieked in agony. The woman next to him stretched out her hand and begged Longinus to save her. He lay down at the edge of the pit and offered her the blunt end of his spear; but the pit was too deep and she could not reach it. The centurion grimaced as a long reptile slithered into her gaping mouth, and she sank below the heaving surface. Longinus stood up and continued running.

He could not save her; he could save none of them.

CHAPTER IV

After the figure of Longinus had vanished into the distance, Asmodeus showed Lady Naamah around his Basilica of Pain. She took great interest in his myriad of tortures and complimented him on his ingenuity. His practice of frying souls in a great pan delighted her, and she spent a few delicious hours frizzling dozens and enjoying their dreadful screams and futile pleas for mercy.

"Make them crackle, crisp, and cry!" Asmodeus laughed.

He could tell their incessant screeching excited her and, hoping she was ripe for multiple penetrations, tried stroking her lithe, serpentine body with a few of his dripping phalluses. However, she shrugged them off irritably and seemed only interested in causing more suffering.

He watched dispassionately as she slithered from chamber to chamber, blinding, crushing, impaling, and tearing. She was going through his supply of souls like a whore in heat. It would take many nights for him to repair the damage and make them whole again. The damned was in short supply because of her father's policies. At one time, archdemons had been able to torture and abuse as many souls as they pleased, but now Satan had given them a small quota, which they had to reuse. Asmodeus' Soul Pits in front of his Basilica were woefully depleted. The emperor's new rule was unjust and unseemly. The joy of being an archdemon had been watching endless streams of fresh souls arriving in his domain and deciding which tortures and depravities to inflict upon them. One grew bored seeing the same contorted faces, breasts, buttocks and genitalia over and over. Variety was the spice of life–and death.

He floated nearby as Naamah, made hungry by her rampage, swallowed his favourite youth feet first, slowly, inch by inch, like a snake eating a rabbit. He thought the screaming boy's shoulders were too wide for her mouth and would jam in her maw. But he was mistaken. Her hinged jaws opened even wider. He almost felt sorry for his beautiful plaything as its head and arms jerked down her throat. By the power of satanic sorcery, there was not the slightest bulge in Naamah's body to signify where her victim lay.

It would be many hours before she digested and excreted him–from where; Asmodeus had yet to discover. Never had any female's body been so much of a mystery to him. He hoped her charms were worth the trouble she was causing him. If she failed to buck, shriek and milk him like a thousand wild harlots, he would be sorely disappointed.

His mounting boredom and resentment were pacified somewhat when his lackey of the bottom scrabbled into the chamber and informed him that six hours had now passed and his honour guard had begun the hunt.

"Let us return to the courtyard, my lady. We do not wish to miss the entertainment."

Naamah wiped her lips with the back of her hand. She realised she had been too greedy and taken advantage of her host's hospitality. However, bloodlust had consumed her and she could not stop herself. This predatory and uncontrollable aspect of her nature was not one she had wished to reveal to Asmodeus at this early stage of their courtship, but the damage was done. In any case, the fault lay entirely with him. He should never have allowed her anywhere near his stock of souls. The outcome had been inevitable. However, she was astute enough to know that his feelings must be assuaged.

"You have been most generous," she hissed. "When you visit my Palace of Sin, you may browse and select the cream of my crop."

"To do with as I please?" he asked, affably.

"Yes—and to retain for your pleasure," she replied with a cold grin.

Asmodeus raised an eyebrow. Such a thing was unheard of. No archdemon or demoness gave away souls. Like satanic legions, they were more valuable than gold in Hell. But, although his natural greed tempted him to accept her offer, he resisted and kept his main goal in mind. She sought to manipulate him, but he would bend her to his will.

"You are very gracious, my lady, but such sacrifice is unnecessary. Keep your souls. The only reward I crave is the pleasure of your company."

"Well played, Asmodeus. You know how to please a lady."

"I understand powerful urges—as you well know," he said with pretended frankness.

It was Naamah's turn to raise an eyebrow. She had underestimated him. He could control his carnal desires and play the game of courtship and power very well. He may be of more use to her than she had first thought.

Passing the time with gossip about the fortunes or misfortunes of other archdemons, they made their way up through the labyrinthine basilica and descended into the courtyard.

"Are you going to release your Nehushtan?" Asmodeus asked, casually.

He was eager to view her slimy womb opening again.

"Not yet," she replied.

"My guards may find him before your beasts do," he cautioned.

Naamah laughed at his all too obvious ploy. "My pets can outrun any of your vassals. It will not take them long to track him down. I wish to be there when they do and relish his agony."

"It may not be as simple as you think. The insect is resourceful and could lead us on a merry chase,"

"So much the better. That will provide more exercise for my hounds."

Asmodeus thought furiously of some other way to shatter her icy breastwork and ram her stony rampart. He then remembered a delicious artifice he had created to thwart the Revenant's escape.

"I have laid a little trap for our prey that will amuse you."

"What sort of trap?"

"It is a surprise," he replied indulgently.

"Very well, but I hope it does not harm my Nehushtan," she warned.

Asmodeus frowned. He had not even considered the safety of her damnable, yelping curs. However, all was not lost. He could warn the imperious strumpet to keep her pus-ridden pups on a tight leash when they neared the trap. But the King of Demons hoped the Revenant destroyed a few of the mangy canines before they ripped him apart. That would give him less to worry about when he pried their mistress open.

"Fear not," he replied with a thin smile.

Naamah glowered around the courtyard and shook her head in irritation.

"How are we to hunt him? On foot?" she demanded.

"That would be difficult as neither of us possess feet," Asmodeus jested.

She looked at him as though he was a king of fools instead of demons.

Concealing his irritation, he smiled sweetly and nodded to Surgat. The stunted administrator of the royal back passage shrieked and clapped its claws thrice. Incubi on the battlements pounded a loud, quick message on their battle drums. Naamah frowned as she heard a deep rumbling from within Asmodeus' Basilica of Pain, followed by the sound of claws on stone. She gasped in delight as two hideous beasts drawing a Hellmetal chariot thundered down the ramp and skidded to a halt in front of her.

She had heard of the creatures Asmodeus had created from the flesh of dead humans, but had never seen them firsthand. Each was twice the size of a large horse and resembled a giant bat. Their legs were long and powerful and had fearsome claws instead of hooves. They hissed and snapped at each with their massive jaws as they waited for their infernal master to command them.

Naamah slithered to the beasts and stroked the head of one. It rubbed its leathery black skull against her hand and uttered a loud piercing screech.

"What do you call them?" she asked.

"Sharurs," Asmodeus replied proudly.

"What wonderful specimens!" she hissed. "Are they swift?"

"Faster than any demon on four legs or six."

Naamah's appearance of pleasure was short-lived. She glanced at the carriage and then at Asmodeus' immense bulk.

"Only one chariot? It will not accommodate both of us," she said tersely.

"Oh, but it will, my lady," the King of Demons replied, leering.

She watched in cruel fascination as Asmodeus transfigured. His huge, nebulous body shrank: bones cracked, flesh ripped, and skin turned black and opaque. The souls inside his belly mouthed wide, silent screams as they were crushed and excreted. At Surgat's command, little red fiends appeared, scooped up the waste with shovels and carried it back to the basilica where their infernal king would later make the damned whole again and fit to resume their punishments.

For an instant, she glimpsed his true demonic form symbolising his mastery of lascivity and revenge: the long, scaly cock legs; the heads of a bull, ram, and a man spitting fire. But it was fleeting, and his shape changed again, becoming more humanoid in appearance.

Finally, his metamorphosis was complete, and she raised a beautiful eyebrow in appreciation at the tall, obsidian, naked warrior who now stood before her. His muscular physique; coal-black wings and hair; broad forehead; pointed ears, piercing eyes; aquiline nose; cruel, sensuous mouth; and thick, dangling, member stirred excitement in her and caused her orifice to twitch. His form revealed a wisp of the beautiful, noble angel he had once been before being swept by her father into a churning sea of evil, corruption and depravity.

Asmodeus was neither an ignorant brute like Moloch nor a vicious tyrant like Azazel. No, the King of Demons was intelligent, cunning, power-hungry, inexhaustibly libidinous, and could be a suitable match for her. Adding Queen of the Night to her many royal titles would please her—if only to spite Lilith—but she harboured more dangerous ambitions; and obtaining Asmodeus' support would be vital in realising her grand design. His greatest weakness was his obsessive carnality, and she intended to exploit that vulnerability to her advantage.

"Armour!" he roared.

Four demons dashed forward and adorned him in breastplate, bracers and leather kilt. His servants were brisk and well practiced, and she could tell they had dressed their lord many times before. Naamah wondered how many other demonesses had shared this chariot with him. She would have to be careful and watch out for rivals. There was no shortage of young strumpets in Hell vying to advance their positions. Asmodeus would be a good catch for them. His torrent of infernal seed could increase their demonic powers.

The unholy lackeys finished dressing their master, stepped back and bowed.

"I hope this appearance pleases you?" Asmodeus declaimed, spreading his arms.

Naamah nodded approvingly. "It does. I have never seen you in this form before."

"I use it only on special occasions," he answered, bowing.

"And this is one such instance? You honour me."

The sharurs hissed and scratched the stone with their claws.

"Our beasts grow restless. Shall we mount?"

"Perhaps—but in the meantime, we should ascend the chariot," she murmured seductively.

Asmodeus grinned lecherously and offered his hand. She took it and allowed him to assist her into the chariot. Naamah needed no help; she was as nimble and venomous as a giant viper. However, Asmodeus' little courtship amused her, and she was intrigued to see what ploys he would use to inveigle his way into her affection.

Her father had never wooed her. He had just taken her violently whenever he had wanted, and she had enjoyed every luscious second of it. Neither Moloch nor Azazel had whispered sweet words in her ear. She had just commanded them to take her. Moloch's bullish lust and Azazel's sadistic practices had nearly satisfied her ravenous womb and secret craving for pain and degradation, but neither of them could provide the sublime, diabolical ecstasy she had experienced in the claws of her father. He had known her every dark desire and how to quench her insatiable fiery needs.

In his new manifestation, Asmodeus was handsome and desirable, but she was more interested in his normal demonic form and of all the ways his many tentacles and appendages could relieve her cruel and illimitable lust. Through him, she hoped to recreate the same frenzy of pleasure she had attained while coupling with her satanic father.

The King of Demons grabbed the reins and a long scourge. She watched his muscles bulge as he lashed the sharurs, causing arborescent trickles of dark blood to ooze from their backs. The beasts uttered ear-splitting screeches, and the carriage jerked violently as they hurtled out of the courtyard and bore their charges into their master's gruesome domain. Asmodeus' legion sprinted after them, providing an escort. Although the demon king feared only Satan, he considered it prudent to be cautious. No one knew where the accursed Pazuzu and his Elder demons would strike next. If the rebels ambushed him, his loyal cannon fodder would provide him with time to decide whether to attack or beat a tactical retreat. Heroic last stands were for mortal fools and underdogs. The powerful and privileged always survived to fight another day or—through their superior intelligence, breeding, and contacts—never fought at all. This salient truth, he had learned from mankind after the last great warrior kings, leading their armies from the front, had fallen. Men no longer sought to aspire to the honour and virtue of a King Arthur; they applauded and expoused the strengths and successes of merciless conquerors like Attila the Hun and Genghis Khan.

As Asmodeus whipped the beasts savagely and relentlessly, Naamah uttered a deep moan and curled the tip of her tail around one of his legs.

He grinned at her and lashed the sharurs with renewed ferocity.

She closed her eyes, ran a hand through her hair, and moaned louder.

"Yes," she thought, "this will be a very good hunt. A very good hunt indeed!"

CHAPTER V

A few hours later, Longinus stumbled through a rocky valley surrounded by lofty, forbidding mountains. The undulating, ropey surface of solidified basaltic lava impeded his progress and cut his feet. Shiny black lava pillars, hundreds of feet high, towered around him, and deep fissures spewed bright orange lava high into the air which splattered onto the ground. Thick clouds of yellowish smoke hissed and belched from craters, filling the torrid air with the smell of rotten eggs. Incandescent sparks floated around him like angry fireflies and burned his skin and singed his hair; but he ignored the pain, and keeping a wary eye on the molten death that showered down all around him, held his course through the middle of the seething, volcanic dale.

The centurion had expected Hell to be teeming with demons and the shades of the damned, but to his surprise, it was desolate. He wondered where the horntails kept the billions of souls.

As if in answer to his thoughts, he heard faint, high-pitched shrieks from behind him. Glancing over his shoulder, he saw a large group of Asmodeus' demons. Longinus watched in alarm as they raced towards him with preternatural speed. With his vampire powers, he was a fast runner, but demons were much, much swifter. They were about half a league away, but at their current speed they would be upon him in a few minutes.

Gritting his teeth, he studied the terrain. He did not want to face them on open ground where they could surround him. There were too many of them. They carried swords, axes, maces and shields, and he did not know how powerful they were. Also, Naamah's hounds may appear at any moment. He had to neutralise their numerical advantage.

He spotted a massive, flat-topped rock some five hundred paces to his left and sprinted for it. His first thought was to scale it and pick off his pursuers as they tried to climb up after him. However, as he drew nearer, he noticed a tall vertical fissure in the rock face. He dashed up to the opening and moved cautiously into it. After twenty feet, it narrowed, and he had to edge his body through sideways to pass. In another fifteen feet, the crevice opened up into a cave. The interior of the rock was in darkness, but he had no trouble seeing; his vampire night vision illuminated the hollow with an unearthly crimson glow. He looked around and breathed a mental sigh of relief. There were no demons.

The cavern was circular, about two hundred paces in diameter, and fifty feet high. At its centre was a large pool of black oily liquid. The cave floor was littered with jagged boulders of varying sizes.

Looking up, he saw a crack running along the full length of the roof. It was just wide enough for him to climb through if he could reach it. He scanned the ragged wall and observed a section at the opposite end of the cave with jutting rocks that would provide good purchase and footholds.

But he could not scale it while carrying his spear, and he had no intention of leaving it behind. There was no time to think; he must climb or fight. But then the glimmer of a plan that could turn the tables on his pursuers flitted into his mind and he decided, for better or for worse, to follow it. He had learned from bitter experience that even a bad plan was better than no plan. At least, that is what he told himself. Taking careful aim, he threw the spear through the aperture and heard it clatter onto the rock above. His path was set now and there was no turning back.

Darting in and out of the boulders, he skirted around the edge of the pool and ran across to the wall. After a quick look to ensure the demons had not yet arrived, he transformed his hands into claws and climbed. He was halfway up the wall–and froze. Something cold and slimy had brushed against the back of his left leg. Glancing over his shoulder, he saw six long, translucent tendrils with suckers and barbs had emerged from the pool. They were drifting around the floor and walls and appeared to be searching for something. One arm was hovering in the air six feet from him, and he knew that was what had touched his leg.

The tendril moved back a little, and its top coiled. Its slow, languid movement was graceful, almost hypnotic. Longinus narrowed his eyes, his survival instinct shifting from a whisper to a scream. The cirrus quivered gently–and with surprising quickness, lashed at him. He launched his body to the right and grabbed a protruding rock. The tendril smacked against the wall where he had been an instant before with a soft wet sound, its suckers pulsating. He kept still. His sixth sense warned him that sound attracted it. Lazily, and almost regretfully, the suckers detached from the wall and the pellucid coil swayed over the rock face. The tip drifted near his waist, but he moved his hips just before it made contact. He heard the faint sounds of demonic screeching and knew his pursuers had arrived outside the cave.

The tendrils also seemed to hear them and snapped like rubbery halyards back into the inky depths of the pool. Longinus climbed with as much speed as he could muster. His muscles bulged like whipcords as he clawed his way up. The demons were getting closer. He arrived at the top of the wall and began working his way along the roof of the cave. The surface was almost smooth and had very few cracks or protuberances to hold on to, but his claws were large, and the nails as hard as iron. He could utilise the smallest of holds where no mortal climber could find purchase. Working in silence, he inched himself towards the crack in the centre of the roof. He gasped as he lost his grip and hung by one nail. Looking down, he saw that he was over the pool. The surface was rippling, and he knew he would die if he fell into that loathsome liquid. Whatever was down there was waiting for prey, and when its hideous arms embraced you, there was no escape—only a slow and agonising death.

He looked above him and spied another minute split in the ceiling. Lunging up, he dug his nail into it and continued moving forward until he arrived at the main crack. The roof was only six inches thick at that section. He grabbed the edge, and in one fluid movement pulled himself through the crack and onto the top of the rock. He lay on his back for a moment, staring up at the fiery red sky. The demons' voices were louder, and he knew they were entering the cave below. He grinned. Although they did not know it, his pursuers had saved his life. Their arrival had distracted the eldritch horror lurking in the pool and allowed him to escape.

With much unholy screaming, the demons reached the rock and scrabbled into the fissure. As the passage narrowed, they fought and clawed at each other to get through first. Finally, and after much cursing, they emerged into the cave. They roared and whooped in triumph when they saw it was a dead end. Cervenka uttered a wordless growl of command, and his subordinates spread out in search of their quarry. They were all eager to have their revenge on the Revenant. Cervenka held back and let the stupidity of the other demon's work to his advantage. He knew Longinus was a powerful and dangerous opponent and would wait until the others distracted him before moving in to strike the killing blow.

Longinus peeked through the crack and watched as his pursuers fanned out through the cave. He recognised many of them as the ones who had tortured him. An icy rage welled up inside him, and he thirsted for revenge. Adopting a kneeling position, he metamorphosed into his Revenant form. He screwed up his eyes and grunted as mind-numbing pain wracked his body. Bones snapped; flesh ripped and reformed; jaws extended, razor-sharp teeth extruded; and hands and feet grew into large, fierce claws of death. In less than a hundred heartbeats, he had transformed into an terrifying, obsidian beast that could only hallucinated in the darkest nightmares of the most deranged bedlamite.

"Naram-Sin," he growled.

"Aye, centurion!"

Longinus gritted his teeth as Naram-Sin's bones erupted from his body and created his living vampire armour. He groaned in agony as the crimson osseous sheathing locked into place around him. Reaching up with a claw, he adjusted the hideous three-horned helmet on his head. When satisfied that his infernal panoply was secure, he grabbed his spear and readied himself to drop through the crack. Then he stopped.

Naram-Sin felt his hesitation.

"What is the matter, centurion?"

"We do not know how powerful these demons are. Am I being naïve in thinking I can destroy them?"

"You defeated Agrat Bat Mahlat, and she was a very powerful adversary."

"Yes, but I was in my demon form when I fought her."

"It is a pity that you cannot transform into your demonic manifestation again. You would make short work of our opponents below."

"You know that I cannot, even if I wanted to—which I do not. I have no control over it. I cannot just summon it when I need it."

"Then have faith in your own abilities," said Naram-Sin. *"The fiends below are lesser demons, and in my past, I have destroyed such abominations with ease. You have not fought for such a long time and therefore doubt yourself. But I do not doubt you. You are the Revenant and crush all before you. Fight and be damned. We will either be victorious or die with honour. Is that not what you have taught me?"*

"Yes," Longinus growled. *"It is."*

"Then let us have vengeance! It is time for us to inflict some pain and punishment of our own! Let us bathe in the blood of our enemies!"

Longinus felt a wave of relief and exhilaration spread through his body. His momentary lapse of confidence was now replaced with a burning desire for battle and revenge. He heard a piercing scream of terror. Looking down, he saw tendrils had emerged from the pool and grabbed an unwary demon in its clutches. Cervenka was holding the victim's legs and trying to pull it free from the whip-like clasper's deadly embrace. Three other demons were trying to strike at the pellucid cirri with maces and axes. Now was the time to attack.

He dropped through the crack in the roof and landed behind two demons. Their attention was fixed on the struggle at the pool, and they did not hear him. They wore breastplates, bracers, and greaves; and carried maces and shields. But their gruesome heads were unprotected. Longinus dropped his spear and lunged at them. Dark blood and brains splattered him as he smashed their skulls together and tossed their bodies aside like dolls. The demon standing in front of them turned around with a snarl, but its eyes widened in fear as it beheld the monstrosity facing it. Longinus picked up his spear and grinned.

His opponent stumbled back, but before it had taken one pace, Longinus took a skipping step forward and thrust his spear into its chest. The tip pierced its breastplate and erupted from its back. The fiend screamed in agony as the spear sucked it dry and left its body a withered husk.

Alerted by their comrade's death knell, two others spun around to face their unknown assailant. They looked surprised and shrieked to the rest of the group. Cervenka glared at his nemesis and barked a guttural command. Five demons advanced cautiously towards Longinus.

One, armed with a wicked-looking mace, broke ranks and charged at him. The centurion thrust his spear into its stomach and lifted it in the air. The demon screamed and wriggled. As the others stood gaping, Longinus slammed the body down on their heads with bone crushing force.

Two more demons had flanked him and attacked simultaneously from either side. Longinus narrowed his eyes and hissed with pleasure. In combat, all his senses were heightened, and time seemed to slow down. He impaled the one to his left, pulled the spear free, and rammed the blunt end into the other's face. Rotating the spear quickly, he thrust the tip up through its jaw and out the top of its skull.

Another assailant moved in for the kill. Longinus kicked out with his right leg and closed his fearsome foot claw on its breastplate. The demon screamed as the centurion's talon ripped through the armour and into its flesh. Longinus demolished its face with a pile-driver punch and sent it smashing against the wall where it collapsed in a broken heap.

The awesome display of power stunned the remaining demons. The Revenant had destroyed more than half of their group with relative ease. Longinus extracted his spear from the cadaver's head and let out a terrible roar that reverberated around the cave and seemed to shake the very ground beneath demonic hooves and clawed feet.

Screeching in rage, the demons moved back to regroup. Cervenka glanced at his vassal held by the thing in the pool and saw its blood filling the translucent cirri. He released its legs and watched impassively as its writhing, screaming body was dragged below the stinking, viscous surface.

He bellowed an animal cry, and four demons charged at Longinus. The centurion did a forward shoulder roll and holding the spear horizontally came up under their guards and slammed into them like a battering ram. Keeping low, he swung the lance in a vicious arc, hitting their legs and shattering bones. Again and again he struck until his four attackers collapsed in a bloody, mewling pile.

Cervenka roared and sprinted at him with his battleaxe raised above his head. Longinus charged, leaped in the air and thrust down with his spear. Before the vampire lord could land his savage blow, the iron tip penetrated his breastplate. The sheer force of the strike stopped Cervenka dead in his tracks. He froze, his mouth gaping, and the axe tumbled to the ground behind him. Then he screamed as the spear consumed him. But Longinus had a different fate in mind for his old adversary. He could see the tendrils drifting up from the pool again. Grinning savagely, he kicked Cervenka in chest, throwing him backwards. The slimy tendrils caught their new feast in mid-flight, snapping around him with a dull slapping sound. The thorny barbs dug deep into his flesh, and the suckers undulated greedily.

Cervenka's eyes bulged, and his face contorted into a mask of agony and horror. He uttered a long, forlorn howl as he sank into the ravenous, murky depths.

"Bon appetite," Longinus growled.

It seemed fitting to him that Cervenka had perished in the same manner he had devoured so many human victims over the centuries.

Feeble groans from behind him reminded Longinus that some of his fallen enemies were still alive. He turned around, licked his lips and pounced on them like an angry lion. Some he dispatched swiftly but others, whom he remembered as being especially cruel to him, he made suffer. The last one tried to crawl away. He strolled after it and put his foot on its back. It screeched as he dug his long claw nails into its putrid flesh. He dropped his spear and pulled the demon to its feet. It gibbered and whimpered, but Longinus was in no mood to show mercy. These fiends had tortured and humiliated him for too long. Now was the time for vengeance–and sustenance.

His mouth opened and his lower jaw extended, revealing a scarlet cavern of razor-sharp teeth. The demon shrieked as Longinus pulled it to him and ravaged its throat. The soporific effect of his venom was instantaneous. His victim could only stand helplessly as Longinus growled and sucked every last drop of vile blood from its body. After throwing the corpse into the pool, he checked there were no other fiends hiding in the cave. He gritted his teeth as Naram-Sin's bones retracted back into his body, and he transformed into his human form.

After the agonising metamorphosis was complete, Naram-Sin spoke to him.

"An excellent fight, centurion! I enjoyed every blow you inflicted upon our enemies."

"Yes, it was very satisfying," Longinus admitted.

"And do you feel more confident now, more like your old self?"

"I do. I feel refreshed and as if some of my old strength is returning."

"That is good. I never doubted you for a moment."

"Thank you, Naram-Sin. I do not know what I would have done without you."

"You would have survived," Naram-Sin replied modestly.

"When Asmodeus first took me, I accepted my torture as a just punishment for my crimes."

"But your view changed."

"Yes. I realised Asmodeus was responsible for everything that had happened. It was he who conspired with Agrat Bat Mahlat to usurp and destroy Lilith. Agrat Bat turned me against Lilith and persuaded the Lilitu to betray their mother.

"And you began to hate Asmodeus."

"With a burning passion. It was my hatred for him that allowed me to endure the tortures and obscene indignities that he inflicted upon me.

"You would have persevered without my help," Naram-Sin said quietly.

"No. I would have been lost. It was you who taught me to channel my hate and use it to control the pain."

"Pain is but a product of the mind," replied Naram-Sin. "It is transmitted from our nerve endings, through our nervous system, and arrives at the brain through the firing of synapses. If we can control our minds, then we can conquer pain."

"And as you so ably taught me, the way to vanquish pain is to welcome and relish it."

"It is so. Pleasure and pain are very similar sensations. We conditioned ourselves into believing that pain was enjoyable. The first step was looking forward to Asmodeus' nightly visits instead of fearing them. We then concentrated on savouring low levels of pain. Once we had become accustomed to that, our pain threshold slowly increased until we could withstand more agonising tortures."

"We deceived our minds into thinking pain was a delicious pleasure," said Longinus.

"Yes, and all the while we dreamed of destroying Asmodeus. With each cut, blow and shattering, he inflicted upon us, we imagined that he was subjecting himself to the same tortures."

"And that was extremely gratifying," Longinus growled.

"Indeed, it was! Through a perverse process of mental substitution, we endured our miserable fate."

"Very clever. I wish I had thought of it," said Longinus.

"You did, in a way. I found the knowledge hidden in your subconscious mind. Your interest in cognitive psychology all those years ago finally came in useful."

"It must be the only time," Longinus replied dryly. "But I could not have done it without you. You were patient with me and never once complained. Our conversations were a veritable haven in that dreadful place and helped me to retain my sanity."

"Be not too harsh with yourself, centurion. It has taken me millennia to learn how to control my pain, but you achieved it in five years. That is a testament to your remarkable fortitude."

"Thank you, brother. I want you to know that once we save Rachel, I shall do everything in my power to find a way for you to have your own body again."

Why? Is my company so tiresome?" asked Naram-Sin.

"No. You misunderstand me. I–" Longinus stammered.

Naram-Sin laughed. "I know what you meant, and I thank you. That indeed would be a wondrous gift. But let us say no more about it for the present. We must first escape from Asmodeus and Hell."

"You are a good friend."

"Am I? Friendship is a new experience for me."

"What? You never had friends?"

"No. When I was a mortal king, I had no shortage of women to bed and men to sup with me, but no genuine friends I could rely upon. I found being a ruler a very lonely existence. People sought my company because of what I was rather than who I was."

"And I assume things were no better when you became a vampire lord?"

"No. Then I was truly alone. No women would share my bed and all men feared sitting at my table."

"I suppose supping with you took on a very different meaning for them," Longinus mused.

"In the beginning, I did not dine upon on my guests. I desired human company and was very hospitable. But I grew to despise them as time went on."

"Why?"

"Because they could still enjoy the mortal pleasures denied to me. In any case, I soon discovered that guests are suspicious of a host that does not partake of his own feast. Many of my invitees feared I meant to poison them."

"I used to allay suspicions at banquets by eating and drinking like a mortal and then throwing up in private afterwards."

"I tried that, but even the smallest sip of the finest Akkadian beer made me retch."

"I can see why people might have got the idea that you were trying to poison them," replied Longinus, picturing Naram-Sin sipping and retching in front of his guests.

"True. That is what I missed most when I became immortal—my beloved beer,"

"Quite so," Longinus replied diplomatically.

Naram-Sin's fond reminiscences of getting drunk as a one-eyed, three-legged dromedary on toe-curling Akkadian brew would certainly be of academic interest to Mesopotamian scholars engaged in rummaging through the piss pots and trash heaps of antiquity, but the centurion had more important matters on his mind. The hunt was still on, and they had to get moving.

It was only then he remembered he as bare as a Grecian statue. He inspected the corpses and saw what he required. Keeping a wary eye on the pool, he tore the loincloth from a demon's body and unwound it. It was bloody but otherwise remarkably clean considering it had covered a demon's arse. He could only imagine that Asmodeus had commanded his vassals to cover their genitalia when Lady Naamah was present. Perhaps he had decided that scores of demon cocks on display might prove too distracting for her, or, Longinus thought with a wicked smile, he had an inferiority complex about his size—or sizes, as in his case. After all, as the noble Cicero once said, "The more you have, the more you have to worry about." He did not really believe this saying could be attributed to the virtuous Roman politician, but it amused him to think it did.

Regardless of the reason, Longinus was grateful to have underwear. Passing the cloth between his legs, he wound it around his waist and back between his legs a few times before tying the ends behind his back. He did not cover his loins out of any sense of modesty. It was a practical matter. He found it annoying to have his bits slapping around while running or fighting. Securing the offending articles between his legs felt more comfortable.

As Marcus, his senior centurion and mentor, used to bark while watching Longinus instructing new recruits how to wear the military issue loincloth, "Pull it tighter! Firm stones, firm body!"

Without knowing it, Marcus had invented the psychological concept of core strength two thousand years before it became fashionable among athletes and malodorous gym users.

He glanced at his bleeding feet; he needed some footwear. Most of the demons had hooves and needed no boots; however, one ugly cur had claw-like feet and wore thick leather sandals with straps that tied at the calves.

He undid them and tried them on for size. They too large but would do. He examined the armour on the corpses. From one body, he took a breastplate and greaves, and from another stole a kilt made from human leather reinforced with metal strips.

He stood for a moment and inspected the breastplate. It was constructed from reddish-black Hell metal and was surprisingly light. Satan's symbol, a hideous goat's head within an inverted pentagram, was engraved on the front. The normal pentagram, with one point at the top, was once used in Christianity to symbolise the five senses, or the five wounds of the Nazarene. However, the inverted satanic version, with two points at the top, depicted the Evil One's desire to overturn the natural order of the cosmos, and his horns pointing upwards represented his eternal war with God and Heaven.

He removed the bracers from another corpse. These covered his forearms, and each had a large spike sticking out at right angles at the elbow end. Longinus tried out some quick close-quarter forearm blows at an imaginary opponent's head: left forearm, right forearm, left elbow uppercut, right elbow uppercut. He slapped the bracer on his left arm in satisfaction. He pitied the demon face on the receiving end of these beauties—they would make it much uglier.

"What need have you of that of such filthy demon armour when you have me to protect you?" Naram-Sin asked disdainfully.

"Apologies. You offer me superb protection when I am the beast, but we both know that I can run quicker in my human form. Also, with this garb, our pursuers may mistake us for another demon at a distance."

"A clever deception. It appears you have thought of everything," grunted Naram-Sin.

"No. Not quite," Longinus murmured, casting his eyes at the weapons that lay strewn around the cave. He picked up a discarded sword and axe and weighed them in his hands to judge their effectiveness. The sword was a wicked-looking weapon some three feet in length, curved like a scimitar, with a strong and sharp blade. The mace was heavy and had many large metal spikes protruding from it. He swung the weapons several times and then threw away the mace; it was too unwieldy. The sword was ill balanced, but it would do as a second weapon. He found the body bearing the scabbard, undid it and buckled it on. Metal rings attached the leather sheath to a simple waist belt. It did the job but was inferior to Roman military design which had favoured the baldric–a sword belt worn over one shoulder and reaching down to the opposite hip.

He picked up a demon shield and inserted his left forearm into the broad leather straps. It was round in the ancient Greek style, but light and strong. He removed it from his arm and used the long strap that ran the length of the shield to sling it over on his back. It might come in useful later. Pursing his lips thoughtfully, he detached the thongs from two other shields, knotted them into a single length, and attached the ends to his spear. He sniffed the leather and grimaced. The smell reminded him of the *Book of Lilith*, which was bound in human skin. Hell was obviously very ecological and recycled its waste. He pulled the strap over his head and flexed his shoulders. Having the spear and shield on his back felt awkward, but it would serve his purpose. He could now free both hands for climbing.

To further disguise his human appearance, he grabbed handfuls of disgusting black mud from around the pool and smeared it like camouflage paint over his armour, face and body. Longinus knew that this deception would be unlikely to deceive a demon at close quarters, but depending on the terrain, it may make him harder to spot and give him an edge in combat.

He sensed movement behind him and spun around to see a single tendril drifting upwards. It seemed more lethargic than it had been.

"Still hungry, you greedy bastard?" he asked.

The tendril stopped moving for a moment and then swayed gently; it almost appeared to be waving at him. Was it a demon, or just some monstrosity created by demons? That was unknown. He wondered how long it had been since it had last fed: weeks, months, years, or aeons? Its body must be larger than the diameter of the pool, he reasoned; otherwise, there would be nothing to stop it emerging from the hidden depths. Various unpleasant images flashed through his mind as he imagined a vast, bloated shape writhing in an immense subterranean cavern beneath his feet. But whatever it was, it had aided him, albeit unwittingly, during his fight with the demons.

"I hope you enjoyed your entrée–but I am not the dessert," he said.

He made his way out of the cave and looked around the plain. There were no demons or hounds in sight.

After adjusting the shield strap on his shoulder, he started running again.

CHAPTER VI

Accompanied by a company of lesser demons, Asmodeus and Naamah made their way through his infernal domain. Some areas were too rough for a chariot, but it pleased her to discover that Asmodeus' servants had cut flat, narrow roads in the volcanic rock, thus ensuring a smooth and swift ride.

They rounded a bend, and Asmodeus drew the carriage to an abrupt halt. The sharurs screeched angrily and snapped at each other.

"Why have you stopped?" she demanded.

"I smell blood but cannot locate its source," he murmured, gazing around the barren landscape.

Naamah sighed in exasperation. Her forked tongue flickered, and the tips spread apart twice as wide as her head as she sampled the sulphurous malodour and transferred the chemicals to the vomeronasa receptors in the roof of her mouth. Like serpents on earth, she could smell in three dimensions and tell which direction a scent was coming from.

"It emanates from yonder fissure in the rock face to our left. This is very disappointing; your guards have found him already. I told you he was too puny to provide us with sport," she complained.

"Well, let us investigate," he replied, courteously.

Asmodeus jumped from the chariot and offered her his hand. She hesitated for a moment and then allowed him to assist her. She smiled to herself; her charms were working on him.

As she dismounted, she was aware of the lesser demons staring lecherously at her as their master's back was turned. She swept a hand through her hair and thrust her chest out, giving them more to ogle at. It had the desired effect, and many covered their rising tension with their shields.

He held up his hand in a courtly fashion, and she placed her's upon his.

"Come. I am certain we will find something most gratifying to behold," he said, grinning.

Naamah smiled. The sight of the Revenant torn to pieces would please her.

"Wait here and guard my chariot," he barked to his guards.

The demon captain nodded grimly, jumped on the chariot and held the reins.

Asmodeus glowered as he noticed a skinny demon staring at Naamah with a lustful grin on his face.

"You!"

The lackey jumped, looked puzzled, and glanced at his comrades. The older, more experienced demons standing next to it kept staring straight-ahead and avoided eye contact with their master. This new manifestation of their lord did not fool them one little bit. Whatever form he took, he was still Asmodeus, the King of Demons, and his jealousy, wrath and hellish punishments were legendary. One did not lust after that which Asmodeus coveted. Gape at his harlots, if you dare, when his back is turned, but avert your eyes when he is watching. They knew he was always looking for an excuse to mete out terrible punishments on those whom he perceived as insulting or defying his sadistic rule.

The minion gawked at Asmodeus and touched his breastplate, seeking confirmation.

"Yes, you, you crapulous moron! Go to the front of the chariot and hold the sharurs' halters."

The demon grinned and bowed, pleased that his master had chosen him for such an honour. It ran to the front of the chariot and grasped the metal strap around one sharur's head.

"Ur!" Asmodeus growled in Sumerian, commanding his beasts to shear, reap, and erase.

The beast lunged at the demon and caught its head in its cavernous jaws. The unfortunate victim uttered the most awful squeals as it was dragged to the ground, torn asunder, and devoured.

Asmodeus smiled at the gory spectacle and cast an appraising eye across the ranks. As if prodded into action by invisible pitchforks, the remaining demons cackled on cue and struck their weapons against their shields to pay homage to their master.

He turned to Naamah. "Well? Do you still like my beasts?"

"Very much so!" she hissed, her eyes blazing with sadistic lust. "Now let us discover what fate has befallen our prey!"

Asmodeus escorted her to the fissure in the rock face and allowed her to wriggle through first so he could admire her sensuous body from behind. Taking care not to tread on her long tail, he followed her. She was driving him wild with desire. He hoped the Revenant had died a particularly gruesome death at the hands of his hunters, as that would make her more receptive to his advances.

"Exquisite!" he heard her say as he managed at last to squeeze his tall frame through the narrow passage.

He was about to respond with something witty when his jaw dropped. His hunter's corpses littered the cave. The Revenant's body was nowhere to be seen.

"This is most unusual," Naamah murmured, examining one cadaver. "What caused this desiccation?"

"I do not know," Asmodeus replied, scowling.

"The effect of a magical weapon, perhaps?" she enquired, glancing at him.

"What weapon?"

"The spear, of course!"

"As I have told you, the spear has no power."

"Perhaps you have misjudged your opponent?"

"I misjudge no one," Asmodeus replied angrily. "Spear or no spear, he is naught but an insect. I shall catch him and crush him like a cockroach!"

Naamah smiled. His mind was so primitive, his emotions so easily aroused. It would be simple to bend him to her will. She decided it was time to let him taste the outermost layer of the forbidden fruit. Once he had experienced a hint of her talents, he would do anything she demanded in return for more.

She slithered closer to him and put a cool hand on his chest. "Do not misunderstand me, Asmodeus. I find it pleasing that the Revenant has slain your servants and escaped."

"How so?" he asked, sourly.

"For that means we can spend more time together during the hunt," she hissed seductively. "And as a reward for the pleasures you have shown me, I wish to give you a small gift."

Asmodeus bared his teeth, and his dark eyes burned red with lust.

"And what is that?" he growled.

"Place your hands on your hips."

"Eh?"

"I said place your hands on hips!" she commanded.

He sighed in frustration, shook his head, but obeyed her.

"I may touch you, but you must not touch me. Do you agree?"

"Yes," Asmodeus replied, throatily.

"Good!" Naamah hissed, pushing him against the wall and reaching under his kilt.

He grunted with pleasure as she grasped his engorged member.

"Keep still!" she commanded.

Asmodeus trembled and gasped as she stroked him.

She gave a low laugh. "Your former consort was far too generous with her gifts, far too generous. From this day forth, *I* will decide when and if you will be rewarded. Do you understand?"

"Yes!" the King of Demons growled, thrusting his pelvis forward.

"Look into my eyes, Asmodeus. You have pleased me; therefore, I shall please you. Would you enjoy that?" she said with slow, measured movements.

Asmodeus nodded, licked his lips, and stared into her beautiful eyes like a hungry wolf beholding a fawn. His knees trembled and his body shook as her soft, cool hand worked quicker.

"Not yet!" she said harshly. "I will tell you when!"

He shivered, his eyes pleading with her to be delivered from his exquisite torture.

"Mmm!" she moaned, caressing her breasts and swaying sinuously.

"I cannot hold!" he groaned.

"Yes, you will! I am your mistress, and you are my filthy beast! What are you?"

"Your filthy beast!" he panted.

"Do you worship me?"

"I do!"

"Will you obey me?"

"Yes!" he roared.

"Then, vile and contemptible slave," she said with a cruel sneer, "I release you from your torment!"

Asmodeus uttered a series of piercing howls and shuddered for over a minute under her expert ministrations. She now understood why he was the archdemon of lust. Only her father had exceeded Asmodeus' wondrous and prodigious flow.

When he was spent, Naamah slithered to the pool and cleaned herself. She had only been there a brief moment when her tongue flicked, and she gazed down into the inky water with a puzzled frown. She detected a scent she had never smelt before, and it troubled her. After throwing a few more desultory handfuls of the viscous liquid on her body, she retreated from the murky tarn. Her initial feeling of unease had been supplanted by a growing sensation that she had not experienced often—fear. Whatever lurked in the incalculable depths beneath her tail was beyond her understanding, and she had no desire to tempt it to rise and show its face. She wanted to leave this cavern as swiftly as possible.

Asmodeus stared at her appreciatively as he rearranged his attire.

"I thought my brain was going to explode!" he said, grinning.

"Next time, it may," she answered coquettishly. "Shall we leave? I grow tired of this place."

Asmodeus raised a stern eyebrow as the captain of his guard entered the cave.

"Well?"

"I crave your pardon for intruding, master," the demon said in a gravelly voice, "but an imperial messenger has arrived and awaits your presence outside."

"A messenger?" the King of Demons exclaimed.

"Yes, master."

"Inform him I will be there in a moment."

"I hear and obey!" the captain replied, turning swiftly on his heel.

Asmodeus grunted. The demon's unquestioning, obedient manner had always pleased him. He was one of his loyalist servants, and in his mortal life had raped and butchered hundreds of women and children in God's name during the Thirty Year religious war in 17th century Europe before being taken by the bubonic plague and delivered posthaste to Hell. He had the most impeccable credentials for being a captain in the King of Demon's guards.

Asmodeus rubbed his chin, and Naamah could see the cogs of his mind turning.

"What could this be about?" he murmured.

"Well, there is only one way to find out. Shall we?" she said, glad of an excuse to escape the cavern.

"Yes, of course. After you, my lady."

He waited until she had wriggled into the narrow crack and followed her. But this time his mind was more occupied by the messenger outside than her sinewy delights. She had satiated his need for the present, and it would be a good twenty minutes before it reared its bulbous head again.

When they emerged, they saw the messenger standing next to a small chariot drawn by four of Asmodeus' guards. The King of Demons had ordered the construction of this carriage for this very purpose. It allowed imperial heralds to deliver messages to him wherever he may be in his domain. Messengers were lesser demons, and unlike archdemons, could not travel around Hell by the power of thought and dark sorcery. They needed to use imperial Hellmouths or more mundane forms of transport.

Asmodeus scowled. He had met this particular messenger before, and it did not please him to see him again. He was a small crippled cambion, with a bald pate, one eye four times the size of the other, and one of his arms ending in a stump. The King of Demons found it insulting that they used a lowly cambion to convey messages to him. He suspected it was Baal Zebub's doing. The silver tongued one administered the imperial messengers on behalf of their satanic master and was always eager to irk Asmodeus in any way he could.

"Well? What news?" he barked.

The cambion regarded him with the most puzzled expression and said, "I carry a message from our satanic majesty for Asmodeus, the King of Demons. I can impart it to no other."

"I am Asmodeus, you fool!"

"But I have seen the King of Demons, and you are not him."

"What impertinence! I will tear you limb from limb!" Asmodeus roared.

"Then you will feel our great emperor's wrath! Imperial messengers are protected by his royal decree!" the cambion replied fearfully.

Naamah laughed at the ridiculousness of the situation and placed a hand on Asmodeus' shoulder to cool his rage. Imperial messengers were indeed protected from any form of harassment or harm, and her father had stripped one archdemon who had ignored this salient fact of his domain and legions for five centuries. No one had transgressed since.

"This is King Asmodeus, messenger. He adopts another form today. I vouch for him," she announced dismissively.

"Lady Naamah," the messenger responded apologetically. "You grace me with your presence, and I would never dare to doubt your word, but you of all demons know that we messengers must obey strict rules laid down by your father, our emperor. We are duty bound to identify recipients before passing imperial messages to them."

Naamah stiffened at his diplomatic refusal. Like Asmodeus, she was used to wretched commoners obeying her will without question, and her natural reaction to impudent offenders was to rip them apart. However, Satan's daughter knew she must take great care on this occasion. Messengers spoke on behalf of her father, and he considering any insult against them as a direct challenge to his own authority.

"You snivelling, little cockroach!" Asmodeus roared. "Who are you to question Lady Naamah's word?"

"The obsequious dullard is correct, Asmodeus," she said softly. "He is bound by my father's rules that we must all obey. He does not recognise you, therefore, you must transform."

"What? For a half-breed cripple?"

"Yes. Otherwise, he will have to return to Baal Zebub, and that conniving informer will be only too happy to relay your transgression to my father. Do it for me, please."

Naamah despised Baal Zebub. He denied her access to her father and had resisted her most alluring entreaties. In a moment of madness, she had even danced for him once, but he had mocked her and shown not the slightest hint of a bulge. She suspected he preferred males or younger females—much younger.

Asmodeus glared at her. She in return raised an eyebrow and smiled. Her stoical calmness and demonic beauty subdued his bile, and he sighed resignedly.

"Oh, very well!"

They all watched as the darkly handsome Prince of Revenge transformed back into the monstrous King of Demons. His flesh and bones ached. They were unused to transmogrifications within such a short period of time. He had remained in his nebulous state for too long.

"There! Are you pleased now!" he spat at the messenger.

"I am, my lord! Asmodeus, mighty King of Demons, our satanic majesty requests you attend an infernal Gathering in his great palace of Infernus."

"A Gathering!" Asmodeus exclaimed. "When?"

"Immediately, my lord!"

Asmodeus frowned. It had been centuries since all the archdemons had assembled.

"Inform his satanic majesty that the King of Demons has heard and obeys his imperial command," he said.

"I will, my lord. Ave domine inferni!" the messenger replied, hailing Hell's lord and master.

"Ave domine inferni," Asmodeus grunted, glad to be rid of the insipid creature.

Demons celebrated evil and ugliness in Hell, but frowned upon any form of weakness. Imperfect offspring were strangled, eaten at birth, or chained up to provide sadistic entertainment for other demons. Satan was renown for setting defective ones alight with his breath and roaring with laughter as they 'danced' for him. Therefore, Asmodeus could not, for the infernal life of him, understand why Satan had chosen a stumbling imbecile to be one of his imperial messengers. Perhaps it was his dark jest on all archdemons: send a fool to speak to fools.

He turned to Naamah. "My apologies. I must leave at once."

"Indeed, you must! When my father whistles, his hounds obey his call."

Asmodeus thought it a strange comment but chose to ignore it. He had more important matters on his mind than her father complex.

"You may wait for me in my basilica, if you wish."

"To do what? Wander the corridors on my own? No. I shall continue the hunt. That is what you invited me here for, is it not?"

"Yes—amongst other things," he said with a knowing smile.

"And those things will await your return," she replied coyly.

"I shall leave my guards to assist you."

She laughed. "I have no need of guards. Take them with you but leave the chariot."

"You intend to hunt alone? I beg you to reconsider. The accursed Pazuzu and his Elder demons have been destroying our legions with impunity; and no one knows where they will attack next."

She laughed again and stroked one of his claws playfully.

"You worry for my safety because I am female? How delightfully quaint! I fear not Pazuzu and his ancient, shambling menagerie. The insurgents have never dared venture this far into Hell. In any case, I shall not be alone. It is time to unleash my hounds. They will succeed where your inept hunters have failed."

Asmodeus licked his lips as she gyrated in the most delightfully sensuous fashion. It took all of his willpower to resist grabbing her and covering her body with his phallic tentacles. His eyes bulged as her womb opened wide, and her hellish canines slithered out. They snarled at Asmodeus and his guards.

The King of Demons viewed them sourly as she doted on them. They would have to go. Their yelping impertinence annoyed him. He had no time for mangy mongrels and even less time for their simpleminded owners. Canines could detect demons with alarming precision. Once, when walking the earth in the guise of a mortal, a pack of ferocious dogs had surrounded him while their masters gave laughing assurances that the brutes were harmless.

"They are just playing with you," one burly man said to him dismissively.

"Then I shall return their favour," Asmodeus replied, grinning.

He stuffed the howling animals up the men's rectums until their bodies exploded.

All dog owners thought the sun shone out of their pet's arse, so it had seemed fitting to Asmodeus to make some of that celestial glory radiate from their own backsides.

"Ah, Halcyon days!" he thought. When he was younger, he had been such an amorous adventurer, such a good-natured wandering rapscallion!

"To heel!" Naamah hissed.

The four-legged taxes on his patience scampered back to their alluring mistress and sat looking up at her as though human body fat would not melt in their mouths. He was glad of an excuse to leave. Even the prospect of preaching a sermon on her mount held no joy for him when her infernal yappers were around.

"I shall return as swiftly as possible," he grunted.

Naamah did not answer him. She was too engrossed with her damnable offspring.

"Leave my chariot and escort the messenger back to the basilica!" he said to his guards.

"Thank you, my lord. These are dangerous times," the messenger replied.

"What is your name, messenger?" the King of Demons growled, narrowing his eyes.

He had not forgotten the cambion's gross impertinence.

"Armilus, my lord."

"Good—I shall remember it," Asmodeus hissed, grinning coldly.

"Your honour me, my lord!" the messenger replied.

Asmodeus shook his head in disbelief. The pathetic malapert was too stupid to understand his veiled threat. Any other demon would be shitting in their boots.

"Get that *thing* out of my sight," he commanded his thralls.

The lesser demons struck their shields in obeyance and led the small chariot back the way the way they come.

After casting one last longing look at Naamah's fulsome quadrumvirate, Asmodeus concentrated on the fixed Hellmouth located in the courtyard of his basilica.

The air hissed and warped, and in the twinkling of a red demon eye, he was gone.

CHAPTER VII

Naamah's slavering, baying hounds were gaining on him. Gripping his spear tighter, Longinus willed himself to increase his pace but knew it was pointless. There was no way he could outrun these savage hunters. Time was running out, and he would have to make a stand; however, he knew his chance of defeating the pack was slim. These creatures were not like the hesitant demons he had destroyed in the cave. Naamah's bloody beasts were powerful, ferocious and utterly fearless. They would not stop until they had brought him down and torn him apart.

The landscape of Hell had changed. A flat, arid desert with sand as crimson as the fiery sky looming above it had replaced the mountainous valley. The carcasses of large centipede creatures lay strewn about the sweltering waste. Their rounded or flat heads had repugnant humanoid faces, frozen in silent screams of terror or agony. As Longinus sprinted along, he noticed deep funnel-shaped pits, about twenty paces wide, in the surrounding area. Something about these large hollows troubled him. They did not appear to be natural formations. The sand on their walls was piled to tipping point, and anything falling into them would find it nigh impossible to escape. They were landslide traps.

He cursed as he saw the ground ahead of him stirring and felt a trembling in the soft desert floor beneath his feet. Sensing danger, he leaped into the air. Out of the corner of his eye, he saw a black, elephantine shape dart out of the ground below him and heard a vicious clack like enormous claws snapping shut. He landed and kept running.

More ripples appeared in the sand and two enormous insects with long, serrated pincers emerged from the ground in front of him. His survival instinct gave wings to his heels. With a savage growl, he jumped onto the first creature's head, pushed off with his left leg, and landed on the second one's skull. Keeping his forward momentum going, he kicked down hard with his right leg and jumped clear. He hit the ground past the insects, rolled, and came to an abrupt crouching stop. Two large sickle-shaped mandibles followed by a huge square head erupted from the ground fifteen paces from him. Each mandible had a sharp, hollow projection that dripped yellowish venom.

Longinus stared in disbelief. It was a giant, hellish version of an antlion larva. They were voracious killers. When they caught prey in their jaws, the hollow projections injected venom into their victim, and they sucked the juices from its body as it lay paralyzed. It was the same method that he used to feed on other vampires. He now knew what had killed the centipede creatures. Hell was not just a realm of punishment and torture. It was like earth: a veritable slaughterhouse where the strong devoured the weak.

The insect lunged at him, and he threw himself backwards as its vicious jaws snapped shut above his face. He knew if those mandibles caught him, there was no escape. As it towered over him, he thrust the spear into its thorax. The creature gave a violent shudder as the spear consumed it. He dived to one side as its dried up husk collapsed onto the sand. As he looked back, he could see several of Naamah's hounds being dragged into the pits. The rest of the pack was attacking an antlion, but its hard exoskeleton was making it difficult for them to sink their teeth into its body. More insects were spewing from the desert all around him. It appeared as though the vibrations in the ground were attracting them. But the subterranean monstrosities were solitary hunters and had no liking for their own kind. Ferocious, gargantuan battles ensued as the creatures collided with each other and locked mandibles.

Longinus sprang to his feet and ran. He hoped the vibrations and noises from the fray would disguise his footfall. The more commotion there was around him, the better was his chance of escaping this desert of destruction.

After a hundred paces, he glanced over his shoulder and was relieved to see nothing pursuing him. All the insects were scuttling to the battle, and he glimpsed Naamah riding a huge chariot drawn by hideous beasts. He remembered her saying that he was not big enough to provide her with sport during the hunt.

"How is that for sport?" he hissed, increasing his speed.

Lady Naamah drew her chariot to a halt and glared at the scene before her. Monstrous insects were devouring her beloved hounds. She was furious with Asmodeus for not informing her about these traps before he had travelled to Infernus. This annoying little Revenant was proving more resilient than she had first thought. She slithered from the chariot, raised her arms and uttered a hideous incantation. An imposing satanic great sword, twelve feet in length, appeared in her hand, and a large black rift materialised behind her. From the darkness slithered scores of colossal albino snakes with red eyes. Each reptile was over a hundred feet long, weighing several tons and covered in armoured scales.

Pointing her weapon at the advancing larvae, Naamah screeched, "Destroy!

The giant reptiles swept forward and smashed into the insects. Their sheer bulk and weight crushed many of the hellish antlions and sent others sprawling. Some larvae landed on their backs and could not get up. The snakes bared their ten-foot fangs and punctured the insects' exoskeletons. As the venom seeped into their bodies, the antlions stopped struggling and lay dormant as the snakes swallowed them alive. It was an ironic turn of events. The insects were voracious killers, but even they could not defeat such swift and monstrous predators. As above, so below, nature gushed red in tooth and claw.

Naamah joined the battle and lashed out with her sword. She was a furious storm of vengeance and insect heads and limbs flew in all directions in fountains of green blood. One hungry antlion made the mistake of trying to seize her. She split it in twain and chopped it into pieces. When it was over, scores of insects lay crushed or dismembered, and the few survivors retreated to their pit holes with ravenous snakes pursuing them.

The rest of the reptiles surrounded their mistress and reared up, displaying their prodigious fangs.

"Find the Revenant—but do not kill him!" she commanded.

The snakes swayed in obedience for a moment and then slithered off across the desert.

Naamah returned to her chariot and whipped the sharurs into action. They screamed and snapped at each other before wrenching the great chariot forward.

As she followed in the wake of her reptilian flood, Naamah's mouth opened to supernatural proportions as she howled in a delirium of unbridled fury. The Revenant was responsible for the destruction of her hounds and would pay dearly for his outrage. She was Satan's daughter. No one took or destroyed what belonged to her. Only she, Naamah, decided what lived and died.

She would inflict unimaginable tortures upon every single inch of his body—before swallowing him alive.

CHAPTER VIII

Asmodeus cursed as he squeezed his vast bulk through a Hellmouth and arrived in the Valley of Damnation. The flat, arid basin was strewn with thousands of similar portals from which other archfiends strode, lolloped or slithered.

Like Asmodeus, every archdemon could have apported to Hell's capital instantaneously using black sorcery, but the emperor had decreed that the Fallen must use the fixed Hellmouths when visiting the pass. Legions of the Evil One's favoured winged human skeletons monitored and guarded the imperial portals in the valley. Although small by demonic standards, they were tough, plentiful little bastards that could swamp and delay any group of archdemons until Satan's mighty imperial guard arrived. Since Pazuzu and the Elder demon's rebellion, the Great Lord of the Abyss had become more cautious, and no one could enter his personal domain without his express permission.

Before him lay Satan's towering palace of Infernus. It comprised three fantastical, grotesque, towering black edifices interconnected by a myriad of insanely twisting stone ramps. Each structure was an architectural representation of one of Satan's three heads. The central one, shaped like a terrifying beastly countenance with long horns, was the largest building and where the grand assembly hall of Hell lay. On its lofty ramparts, fearsome winged guardians sat motionless like gargoyles, watching the unholy throng. Looming above its dizzying parapets, a vortex of dark, ominous clouds rotated lazily in the bleak, rubicund vault.

In the great courtyard, archdemons from all over the Bottomless Pit gathered with their loathsome retinues. Satan had imposed strict rules limiting the number of guards his vassals could bring to Infernus. Their rank and status determined the size of their escort. A knight could bring five; marquis, ten; duke, twenty; prince, fifty; and a king, one hundred. Asmodeus brought none; he needed no cortege of drooling sycophants to prove his status and power to others. He was the King of Demons. Nothing more need be said.

His dark master had structured the Abyss on a strict hierarchical order. This had always amused Asmodeus. When Satan, or Lucifer as they had then called him, had persuaded them to take up arms against God all those aeons ago, he had argued that it was for the causes of free will and liberty.

However, after their Creator had cast them out of Heaven, Satan had quickly established a monarchic dictatorship with himself as emperor. So the Fallen had merely replaced one tyrant with another. Not that the King of Demons was opposed to the principle of dictatorship. It was his favourite form of government, and he had worked tirelessly over the centuries to enable twisted fascist and totalitarian leaders on earth. He just wished he were the dictator. How things would change in Hell if he were emperor! The dungeons would burst to the seams with his enemies, potential rivals, those too clever or stupid for their own good, and anyone who had ever dared to look or speak to him in the wrong way. His delightful daydream felt almost orgasmic and well nigh made him weak at the tentacles.

Acknowledging no other archdemon, Asmodeus flowed up the great ramp and into the main palace building. Fearsome winged sentinels lined the route and watched the arriving demon lords with cold and merciless eyes. They were Satan's honour guard, and he had bestowed great power upon them. While one of these infernal guardians could not defeat an archdemon in combat, a group of them could wreak severe damage upon most lords of Hell.

Asmodeus studiously ignored them and admired the architecture and decor of Infernus. Its vast corridors were paved with black marble, so polished, he could see his own reflection. Vaulted obsidian ceilings loomed overhead and shone with a dark brilliance. High reliefs of living souls decorated the walls and enacted every conceivable form of licentious act and torture. Some half-embedded figures screamed and moaned, while others laughed or tittered in their madness. Huge brass flambeaux and braziers lit the scenes and cast flickering shadows which seemed unrelated to their subjects and took on a perverse and uncanny life of their own.

After what seemed an interminable time, he arrived at the great hall. It was dome shaped, and a mural depicting the great rebellion in Heaven covered the ceiling. In the centre of the roof was a wide circular aperture through which Asmodeus could see the wild, fiery sky of Hell. Twelve towering statues of Satan in various poses were situated around the circumference of the chamber, and lively frescoes depicting the violent deaths of saints and martyrs—ergo, Satan's victories over the elect and God—adorned the walls. At the far end of the diabolical confluence were twelve steps leading up to a great marble dais. Atop the rostrum sat a magnificent throne, some fifty feet in height, made from granite and obsidian. A vast golden sculpture of Satan's three heads surmounted the imperial seat. The throne room was designed to impress and intimidate any visitors, and succeeded in its intention very well. There could be no doubt in anyone's mind that this was the abode of the Emperor of Hell and Prince of the Earth.

The hall was already nearly full to brimming. Present was every demon of status and merit, and they represented every vice, ailment and threat known to mankind. They were the lords of the bottomless pit, and along with Lilith and her sisters had created multitudes of lesser demons and abominations to serve them.

Many demons were hellish parodies of humans with horns, wings and tails. God had created man in His image, and thus by assuming near human forms, the demons sought to mock their Creator. Others, like Asmodeus, assumed hideous eldritch shapes that reflected the wickedness that consumed them. Evil had spread insidiously through their hearts and souls like a cancer and transformed them into terrifying monstrosities.

Asmodeus halted as a monstrous centipede as tall as a lion scurried across his path. He waited impatiently as its seemingly endless pairs of legs clattered past him. Its name was Sonnillon, and it was one of the many demons of Hate. It stopped for a moment and leered insolently at him. His first instinct was to lash out with his tentacles and rip its legs off, but he quelled his wrath. It would not do to create such a bloody scene in his master's palace. He sneered and viewed it with contempt. He knew it favoured sending its tiny servants to infect humans by crawling into their ear or bottom holes while they slept. In his opinion, only those with miniscule intellectual capacity took the form of insects. The wriggling, cockroach-crunching, colon-invading pest was neither a rival nor a threat to him, and therefore of no importance. In any case, Satan liked insects; Hell was full of them.

Asmodeus looked around and was pleased with his current form. Once, like many others present, he had been constrained by a wretched, crippled body; but through his tremendous power and will, he had transcended into his ultimate manifestation. Only he, with his myriad of claws and phallic tentacles, could take twenty female souls simultaneously and play tunes on them: groaning, moaning, and screeching symphonies of agony and ecstasy. In his present shape, he was a being to be admired and feared.

It had been centuries since a Gathering had taken place and everyone spoke in excited whispers. They suspected Satan was going to announce something of great import. Usually, archdemons did not like these gatherings as seeing each other reminded them of how ugly they had become after being cast out of Heaven. However, on this occasion, they placed aside such vanity. They were desperate to hear what their emperor had to say.

Asmodeus glided into a corner of the vast chamber and glanced around slyly. He wished to observe who was speaking to whom. Such groupings would provide information about current alliances he would find invaluable in his quest for power.

It did not surprise to him to see the armour-clad figures of Moloch, Baal Zebub, Belial, Astaroth, and Azazel standing together. The bull-headed and belligerent Moloch was pontificating with the cunning and silver-tongued Baal Zebub, Lord of the Flies.

Moloch and Baal Zebub thought themselves better than other archdemons because they had once been worshipped as gods by races such as the Phoenicians, Philistines, Canaanites—and even the Israelites at one time. The religion of Moloch had died out, but the worship of Baal Zebub lived on because of Christianity. The righteous called him Beelzebub and identified him as Satan. This ludicrous mistake had encouraged millions of satanic cultists to sell their souls to him instead of the Evil One. Fortunately for Baal Zebub, the theological error amused Satan, and he was content to fill his bulging soul coffers from any source of lies. To Asmodeus' surprise and anger, the Evil One then made Baal Zebub a trusted advisor, and—as Christians already believed Baal to be him—his imperial spokesdemon.

Mortals had never deified Asmodeus. Unholy acolytes had built a few secret temples devoted to him, but the grovelling masses of humanity had not seen fit to praise and make sacrifice to the all-powerful King of Demons. It remained a sore point with him.

Asmodeus smiled to himself, as Moloch became more angry and strident. The Lord of the Flies—or Lord of the Stinking Dungheap as Asmodeus called him disparagingly in private—knew how to rile his less intelligent ally with very little effort. Indeed, Asmodeus thought that Lord of the Flies was a very fitting title for him. Baal Zebub's round head and large, unblinking, bulbous eyes would remind anyone of a fly.

The archdemon had an intriguing passion for possessing the bodies of pubescent girls and making them foul mouthed and wanton. The presence of flies during such delightful mischief was a certain sign that either Baal Zebub or one of his servants was the cause.

Moloch's interest in children was of a different kind. He enjoyed provoking conflicts and watching children suffer. Whenever human offspring were murdered by their parents or died gruesome deaths in war-torn regions in the world, Moloch and his vassals were involved. He preyed on the weak minds of evil, disturbed or insane men and encouraged them to kill and slaughter. His Hell armour dripped with the blood of the innocents sacrificed in his unholy name.

The wolf-like Belial was cast from the same mould as Moloch: dull-witted and quick to anger. But he was an accomplished fighter and acted as Moloch's second in command. This told Asmodeus much about his nature. Most archdemons wanted to rule, but Belial preferred to serve. In Moloch and Belial's example, it was a case of the stupid leading the blind.

Astaroth standing tall, lean, and decomposing with his customary viper in his claw was a different kettle of rotten fish. He was shrewd, cunning and could incapacitate lesser demons or mortal sorcerers with his vile stench and stinking breath. Like Baal Zebub he enjoyed possessing mortals but favoured nuns instead of children. He was famous in the Abyss for instigating the possessions of the Loudun nuns in France and causing them to accuse a handsome, womanising, young priest for their torments.

Father Urbain Grandier suffered unimaginable tortures and was burned alive before 30,000 drunken or jeering righteous children of God.

Asmodeus sneered. In his opinion, Astaroth's 'brilliant' success had been a hollow victory. The nuns were exorcised and reinstated, and the innocent priest, showing the damnable fortitude of a martyr, had refused to admit he was in league with the Devil to ease his suffering. However, Satan was very pleased with Astaroth when the souls of the lying mother superior and her sisters arrived in the Abyss after dying of old age. Many demons whispered the emperor had devised a special fate for them. What that was, Asmodeus did not know or care. He was just peeved at not being given the chance to explore the holes of their holy bodies. Like all demons, he enjoyed a good nun—and a wicked one, even more.

Licking his lips at the thought, Asmodeus' eyes strayed to the imposing forms of Azazel; otherwise known to mortals as Baphomet. He was a wiry, vicious-looking demon with a deformed goat's head. Azazel never said much, but he was always listening and watching. The King of Demons considered him more dangerous than the others and avoided crossing him. He was the great demon of the desert and commanded respect in Hell.

Over the centuries, many humans had used Azazel's vile countenance to represent Emperor of Hell in satanic rites. They were grossly mistaken. No mere image could capture the evil and sheer diabolical power of Satan. Any mortal seeing an accurate depiction of the High Lord of the Abyss would instantly gibber and drool with madness. Satan's many physical manifestations were beyond mankind's comprehension and the limits of their sanity. Only demons and angels could look upon his various demonic forms.

Yawning with feigned boredom, Asmodeus stared at the mural on the ceiling: Lucifer, adorned in his golden armour and wielding his sword of light, stood tall and proud in the centre. His rebellious angels were arrayed behind him and bravely faced the vast horde led by Archangel Michael. The faces of the rebels were noble, but the features of the defenders looked crafty or stupid. Asmodeus gazed at one figure in particular that stood at Satan's side. He was a very fetching angel with long black hair; the type that was the villain in human dramas but still made a woman quiver and think delightfully dark thoughts as her insipid husband lay snoring next to her. Sword raised and shield braced, he showed no fear as he prepared to defend his prince to the death.

How young and idealistic he looked! How young they all looked! How foolish, but yet so courageous they had been! They had defied a god! Full of righteous fervour, they had dared to rebel against the Great Tyrant, and they had nearly succeeded. Lucifer had stood outside God's citadel, ready to enter and slay the Cherubim and Seraphim. Only he, God's most powerful creation, could have accomplished that. Nothing could stand against him, not even God.

And as with the old gods, Lucifer would have slain his Creator and assumed the mantle of king of the gods. He would have transformed Heaven into a paradise of liberty and fraternity where all divine creatures were equal.

But it was not to be. Instead of proceeding into the tower and usurping God, Lucifer had tried one last time to gain Michael's support. And that had been his undoing. He had not sought to destroy Michael. He had not stuck with his usual zeal and immeasurable force. His feelings of brotherly love for Michael had made him weak, and the treacherous archangel had taken advantage of that moment of weakness, that moment of hesitation, and thrust his sword in that noble breast, into that noble heart that had loved him above all others. And with that treacherous blow, Lucifer's strength and power had deserted him in despair, and the glorious rebellion had ended.

For it was not pride or arrogance that had defeated Lucifer, but love—his love for Michael. It was a lesson that Lucifer and the other fallen angels had learned well. Love and pity became emotions to be despised. There was no room for love or pity in Hell; there was only a burning hatred for revenge. And they had learned from mankind that neither love nor pity won wars; hatred and cruelty prevailed. Oh, mankind—the most detestable of all God's creations, yet so instructive to the Fallen! For it was from the conflicts that man had fought on behalf of God, that the damned had learned the true art of total war. The righteous had showed no mercy to their enemies and had slaughtered even their women, children, and animals. The Elect had taught the Fallen well: final victory could only be achieved through cruelty, butchery, rape and pillage!

An enormous, dark shadow flitted over the aperture in the roof, and the blasphemous horde trembled in enraptured anticipation. It had been many centuries since they had seen their satanic master, and they wondered what shape he would assume on this unhallowed occasion. Those who could knelt upon one knee. Others, such as Asmodeus, with uncanny or eldritch bodies bowed their heads.

The great hall shook, and lightning flashed across the fiery sky.

Satan—the Evil One, Tempter, Beast, Adversary, Fallen Star, Father of Lies, King of the Bottomless Pit, Prince of the Power of the Air, Ruler of the Darkness, Ruler of this World, Son of Perdition, Old Serpent, Angel of Light, Supreme Emperor of the Abyss, the Great Dragon–had arrived!

CHAPTER IX

Longinus sprinted across a desert scorched by the malevolent glare of the unforgiving vermilion firmament. His armour felt hot, cumbersome and chaffed his skin. He spotted a lofty dune and headed for it. It was brutal climbing, and his thighs bulged as he tackled the steep ascent. Each step forward seemed only to result in one step back, and he felt he was just treading sand. He clambered his way to the top and stopped to get his bearings. Ahead of him lay another high longitudinal dune.

"Great!" he muttered, his legs aching from the climb.

He turned and looked behind him. His jaw dropped, and an icy finger ran down his spine. Gigantic snakes covered the desert, and they were heading in his direction. His heart sank; he knew he could not defeat such a swarm of monstrous enemies. In this particular case, he was forced to agree with Shakespeare's Falstaff and admit the better part of valour is discretion.

He scrambled and slid down the slope, ran across the slack and ploughed up the next dune. The will to survive put a mighty spring in his step. His feet hardly touched the sand, and he ascended the hill like a mad dromedary.

He charged down the other side and came to a skidding halt. The desert had ended, and he stood on the edge of a precipice. Far below him, he could see a great scarlet river many miles in width. He wondered if this vast, watery expanse had once been the fabled river Styx where Charon the ferryman had transported the souls of the newly dead into the underworld. In ancient times, it had been customary for relatives to perform the ritual of placing a coin in the deceased's mouth to pay Charon his toll. They believed those who could not pay would never see the afterlife.

There was no perceptible way of climbing down. If he wanted to escape, he had to jump. A myriad of thoughts flashed through his mind. The river was about 10,000 feet, or eight times the height of the Empire State Building, below. The terminal velocity of a human body was about 200 miles per hour. Regardless of the height, that was the maximum speed he would fall at. If he dived head first, he could risk breaking his back. Also, he did not know how deep the river was or what hidden obstructions lurked there.

He remembered once chatting to a Royal Marine in a pub in the Scottish Highlands. The friendly and garrulous sergeant, with an unquenchable thirst for "good British beer and none of that foreign piss!" had described the technique used by Bootnecks when jumping from a sinking ship.

"Step off. Don't jump. Feet first, arms crossed and with one hand covering your nose. Oggin—that's water, to you, civvy—shootin' up your hooter can knock you out. Watch the horizon and try to keep your body upright as possible. Oh, and keep your feet together," he had added cheerfully. "Otherwise the Oggin'll hit your bollocks like a ton of bricks!"

He started as a loud hiss sounded behind him and glanced over his shoulder to see a colossal snake rearing up and bearing its fangs. The other reptilian monstrosities were closing in rapidly.

There was no time to think. He tucked the spear into his side, stepped off the cliff and fell like a soldier standing at attention towards the crimson deluge far below. His stomach dropped like a stone, and an eternity seemed to pass before he hit the water. However, he concentrated on watching the opposite shore line and keeping his body straight. The hardest part of the fall was keeping his feet together. They seemed to have a mind of their own and wanted to go walkabout. However, the sergeant's prophetic words about 'bollocks' and 'bricks' focused his mind superbly and allowed him to keep his errant appendages in line. After sixty seconds, there was an almighty splash, and a force like being hit with a sledgehammer shot through his body. Everything was dark, and his ears filled with a dull roaring. He was sinking, sinking, and just when he thought his descent would never end, he arose and bobbed like a cork to the surface. He was thankful that his Hell armour was so light; otherwise, he would have sunk to the bottom like an anvil.

Longinus coughed and spluttered as the warm, fetid liquid invaded his mouth and nose. Licking his lips, he realised why the loathsome watercourse was crimson: it was thick with human blood and offal. He treaded water and spun around to get his bearings. A huge, fast-moving shape splashed into the river nearby him, followed by another and then eight more. Some of his serpentine pursuers had followed him. Gripping the spear in his right hand, he began to breaststroke to the far bank.

A scaly head broke to the surface thirty feet ahead and glided towards him. Longinus tried to backpedal, but it was to no avail. The snake was too quick. He readied his spear as best he could. It was nearly upon him. Its mouth opened. He could see its long fangs. At the last moment, the water beneath him rose and swept him away from its venomous bite. A massive, black reptilian skull erupted from the river, caught the snake's neck in its enormous jaws and sank back under the surface. The water fell again and carried Longinus back to the spot where the monstrous beast had appeared. He was stunned. It had all happened so quickly. He spluttered and cursed as other gigantic heads burst from the water and attacked the remaining snakes. Longinus started swimming frantically to the shore. He had no wish to become food for these hellish antediluvian predators. Through a crimson haze of watery confusion, he saw flashes of the vicious battle as he swam: a decapitated snake's head flying through the air, a giant reptile rising out of the water with a snake's fangs embedded in its neck. There were no sounds from either the hunters or their prey. This river of the damned was an aqueous slaughterhouse in which the voracious, unimaginable inhabitants fought and devoured each other in ghastly silence.

Swimming like a demented frog, he tried to put as much distance as he could between himself and the churning scarlet water of death behind him. He gasped when a cold, rough body brushed against his legs. Spinning around in the water, he tried to calculate from which direction the attack would come. Large ripples appeared fifty feet away from his position. A pair of malevolent, telescoped yellow eyes appeared above the surface of the river. It was heading straight for him. Its long, massive jaws opened and filled his line of sight. All he could see was its sword-like teeth and gaping black throat.

He lashed out with his spear. The tip sunk into the monster's lower jaw and consumed it. The beast was so large that it kept on surging forward in its death throes and swept him along at great speed.

He felt a terrific pressure in the water below him. Keeping his hands locked on the shaft of the spear, he glanced down and saw two colossal, burning red eyes. He uttered a muffled cry as the whole river welled up, and a gigantic mouth emerged from the depths with a deafening roar. Monstrous, reptilian shapes sped and tumbled past him, sucked into its cavernous jaws—and then he followed them. The roof of the titanic beast's mouth loomed high above him as he was swept through its huge, blubbery lips. He glimpsed snakes and indescribable creatures being shredded by great rows of teeth that lay at the rear of the giant's throat. He struck out desperately with his spear and embedded it into the monstrosity's cheek. Hundreds of thousands of gallons of crimson water and a myriad of nameless, hideous river dwellers rushed past him and down into the hungry belly of the beast. Then its great mouth closed, and all was dark.

"Your soul is mine!" a deep voice, hideous beyond imagining, bellowed inside his mind.

He felt the beast diving into the incalculable depths of the river. Holding on for grim death, he tried to work out how to escape from his current peril. He knew without a doubt that this creature was the mighty demon, Leviathan. The *Book of Lilith* described an event in which the great fish that swallowed Jonah escaped being consumed by a much larger beast—and that creature was Leviathan, demon king of the watery realms. Aeons ago, it had swum and hunted in the vast primordial oceans of the world. But as it threatened to consume all life in the seas, God banished it to Hell. It would be unleashed again at End Times to consume sinners and provide a meal for the righteous. After smelling Leviathan's foul innards, Longinus was glad he would never partake of that heavenly banquet.

He grunted and plunged his spear deeper into the demon king's cold, stinking flesh. The weapon vibrated spasmodically, and he realised to his dismay that Leviathan was too large or powerful for the spear to consume. However, that being said, he hoped it would cause the giant some pain or annoyance. Almost in answer to his wish, Leviathan's enormous body shivered, and it uttered a deep rumble. It changed course and started swimming upwards. After what seemed an interminable period, the great demon surged to the surface and opened its mouth. A flood of water spewed from its belly and gushed past Longinus. The force of the torrent wrenched the spear free from its cheek, and it expelled him from its jaws in a huge crimson fountain. It propelled him high in the air, and then he fell. He hit the shallow water near the shore and tumbled up onto the gritty, black sand of the beach. His body came to an abrupt and painful halt. Dazed, Longinus glanced up just in time to see the unimaginable horror of the depths crash back under the water. As he lay gasping, the waves subsided, and the gruesome river stilled.

Longinus took a moment to check for injuries. Cuts and bruises covered his body, but he had no broken bones. He stumbled to his feet and scanned the area for threats. The skeletons of washed up aquatic monstrosities littered the shore. Scurrying in and out of the osseous remains were a wide variety of disgusting bloated insects. Some had black exoskeletons and others were flesh-coloured. They ranged in length from six inches to several feet. He studied them warily for a moment, but they seemed disinterested in his presence.

The centurion gazed at the cliffs of Asmodeus' domain across the river. Raising his spear above his head, he uttered a triumphal roar of defiance. He walked up the beach but stopped as a faint eldritch screech drifted back to him. He grinned. The fate of Naamah's canine and slithering pets had evidently displeased her.

"Payback," he growled.

He started as a scarlet flying insect, twelve inches long, buzzed over his head and landed on the back of a giant louse with a disturbingly human face. The winged aberration had a long sucker-like proboscis with sharp teeth. It attached its mouth to the thorax of the louse, and Longinus heard a crunching sound. The louse became agitated and ran in circles, but the predator clung tenaciously to its back and kept gnawing. There was a dull pop, and the flying insect raised its wings in exultation as it injected venom and digestive juices into its victim. The louse slowed down, ground to a halt, and collapsed as its innards liquefied and it was sucked dry. As

Longinus watched the gory spectacle, he mused that although the animal kingdom on earth may be red in tooth in claw, it could not match the sheer hideous ferocity of the insect world.

Putting a hand to his eyes to block out the glare from the blazing vault, he looked up and saw scores of the ghastly insects flitting around and mating high above him. It was time to get moving. Once these things had finished coupling, they would turn their attention back to food, and he had no desire to be on their menu. This desolate beach was their hunting ground, and he needed to get as far away from it as possible.

But then he froze. The water near the shore was rippling. As he watched in consternation, hundreds of small black shapes appeared on the surface of the river. He thought at first that they were rats, but the outlines grew larger and arose from the rubicund cesspit. A pungent, sickening odour of rotten fish permeated the air. Reptilian heads, broad scaly torsos, long arms and claws emerged, followed by thick, muscular legs and webbed feet. Longinus gaped as a horde of man-size, bipedal amphibians waded onto the beach. They stared at him with glassy, unblinking eyes, opened their mouths and uttered strange gurgling sounds.

He jumped as a hideous, familiar voice invaded his mind.

"You cannot escape me!" boomed Leviathan. "My thralls will drag you back into my watery depths, and I will feast on your flesh!"

The centurion hoped that Leviathan's vassals would be slow and cumbersome on land, but a second glance at their legs gave him a rude awakening. Their lower limbs were digitigrade and like that of a velociraptor. These reptilian nightmares were not lumbering; they were swift predators. He cursed as they split into three groups. They were adopting hunting positions. The centre pack would chase him, and the other two groups would assume flanking positions and run parallel to him. The attack to bring him down would come from the sides and not the rear.

Longinus knew he could not stand and fight; there were too many of them. He would have to conduct a running battle. Pivoting on his heel, he sprinted away from the shoreline. As he ran, he transferred the spear into his left hand and pulled the demon sword from its scabbard with his right. He did not waste precious time by looking behind him; he heard their burbling shrieks and knew they were pursuing him.

He concentrated on maintaining as much speed as possible. If he were to survive this fight, he must split the faster runners from the rest of the pack. Listening to the thuds of their webbed feet on the sand, he tried to judge how close they were to him. Grotesque, loping figures appeared in his peripheral vision on either side of him. An attack was imminent. A shape darted in from the left. He thrust his spear. The point ripped through the creature's skull. It stumbled and fell. Another attacker grabbed at him from the right. He swung his sword in a powerful backward arc and felt it sever flesh and bone.

Two more reptilians appeared and kept abreast with him. They overtook him and curved back to attack. Slashing up with the sword, he caught the first under its jaw. He jumped and spun in the air, narrowly evading the second creature's claws. As he came down, he struck it with the sword and split its skull open. He landed and kept running.

Longinus willed himself to run faster. An enormous rock lay ahead of him and a strange, massive metal arch stood to the right of it. Leviathan's vassals were gaining on him. If he were to have any chance of surviving, he had to take the high ground and hold it.

He dashed to the rock and leapt onto a ledge. A cold, slimy claw tore at his ankle. Grunting in pain, he slashed out with his sword and a dismembered, scaly arm flew into the air and slapped off the rock face.

A huge surge of adrenaline coursed through his body, and he bounded up the steep face without using his hands, his speed propelling him upwards. He arrived at the top and looked down at his pursuers. At least fifty amphibians were gathering below him, and scores more were arriving to join them.

Four scrambled onto the ledge below and started climbing up, their claws making horrible scratching sounds. He glanced at the surrounding landscape. There was a high cliff some six hundred paces behind him, but he knew he would never make it. Resigned fatalism engulfed him. There was no escape.

"Here, we make our last stand, Naram-Sin," he said.

"Aye, centurion. The fiends have us trapped. Make them suffer before they take us!"

"I shall make them pay in blood," growled Longinus.

With spear in one hand and sword in the other, Longinus stood with the grim determination of the last Spartan at Thermopylae and waited for the swarm to reach the summit.

A hissing, malevolent face appeared over the edge. He thrust his spear into its eye and let the spear consume it. He could feel the power surging up his arm. The weapon was hungry and wanted more. Three more heads appeared, and Longinus started thrusting and cutting. The corpse of one decapitated demon smashed into three others and sent them tumbling into the horde below.

He heard an unpleasant gurgling sound and spun around just in time to see one lunge at him with its arms extended. He struck the abomination in the chest with a powerful sidekick. The saurian flew off the rock and impaled on a stalagmite.

A webbed claw grated across the back of his breastplate. He rotated and struck the demon with a forearm smash. The spike on his bracer skewered its head from temple to temple, and it dropped like a stone.

Overcome with blood lust, Longinus roared and became a whirlwind of dismemberment and death. Scaly cadavers piled up at his feet, and the rock became slick with dark blood.

Whereas other ancient warriors had died after making fatal judgements in combat, because of his vampiric recuperative power, Longinus had survived and learned from his mistakes. After centuries of practice, he could calculate every attack, defence and tactic without thinking. He was a grim harbinger of destruction, and the more he killed, the more he wanted to kill.

Leviathan's acolytes hissed and burbled in agony as he dispensed arcs of bloody death around him. But the reptilians were streaming up the rock on all sides, and he knew that it would not be long before their numbers overwhelmed him.

All seemed lost, when he heard a strange voice cry, "Hither, this way!"

He speared a reptilian in the guts and glanced to his left. An enormous demon mouth had appeared within the metal arch. Standing in the gaping maw was a small, ugly, bald-headed creature.

It beckoned him. "This way, hither, if you would live!"

A dozen fearsome saurians clambered atop the rock and surrounded him.

Longinus did not know whether the newcomer was leading him into a trap, but took the risk. Anything was better than being shredded like pork and filling Leviathan's hungry belly.

He swung the spear around his head to keep his attackers at bay. One reptilian stepped back too far and toppled off the edge. That provided the opening that Longinus needed. He charged through the gap and jumped off the rock. He landed, bent his knees and shoulder rolled to break his fall. The momentum carried him onto his feet again, and he raced for the arch.

His squamate pursuers gurgled, spat and hissed as they gave chase. Longinus gritted his teeth and sprinted as fast as he could. There were scores of reptilians on either side of him. They were edging closer and about to pounce. The bald creature scurried into the giant mouth, and it closed behind him. Longinus cursed his idiocy. This was the worst decision he had ever made. To avoid being eaten by one demon, he was about to jump down the throat of another!

Just as the enormous, pointed teeth were about to clench shut, Longinus roared, "Stupid bastaaaaard!"–and dived headlong through the gap.

CHAPTER X

Asmodeus and the other archdemons gasped in astonishment as a huge, beautiful angel appeared in the hole in the roof and descended slowly. The light emanating from his body was so dazzling that many of the demons shielded their eyes. But Asmodeus did not alter his gaze and stared in awe at the divine being that floated above them. Satan's countenance, long hair black hair, and sculptured, naked body appeared as if carved from luminescent alabaster; and the feathers of his six enormous wings were as pearly and luxuriant as they had been in Heaven.

Satan did what no other denizen of the Abyss could do: he appeared as he had looked before his fall from grace. It was a stark demonstration to all present of his unimaginable power and desire to mock God. That was why he stilled ruled Hell, and no vassal dared to betray or rebel against him. He was all-powerful and almost all knowing. Only archdemons could shield their innermost thoughts from him.

His form reminded the Fallen that he had once been God's most magnificent creation, His Morning Star, and all angels had adored him. He was the Almighty's favoured one and basked in his Creator's love and glory. But the Star of the Morning had a great thirst for forbidden knowledge and begged God to impart some secrets of the cosmos to him. To show His eternal love, this his Father did, and the Morning Star became more powerful and praised the Just and Mighty One with all his heart. His love and devotion pleased God, and He forged a heavenly sword and wondrous armour for Lucifer. Before all the divine beings of Heaven, the Lord gave him the added title of Light Bringer and said wherever lurked the dusk of despair, Lucifer would bring the dawn of hope.

But then God created His Son, whom He called His appointed heir of all things, and commanded all the divine beings to worship him. It was then that jealousy entered Lucifer's heart, and arrogance and pride swiftly followed. He felt abandoned and betrayed. He could not understand why his Creator chose his Son over him. Why should he, Lucifer, God's most perfect creation, have to bow his head and bend his knee to this newcomer? Why should he, the Light Bringer, God's most trusted adviser, the second most powerful being in the cosmos, have to give up his place at his

Creator's right hand for a mewling newborn? It was nonsensical; the act of a mad god. Encouraged by power hungry archangels like Asmodeus, Mammon, and Azazel, Lucifer believed he was worthier, and it was time for him to rule. And thus the seeds of the Great Rebellion were sown.

"Salutate Satanam, dominum obscurum magistrumque!–All Hail Satan, my dark lord and master!" the horde bellowed.

Asmodeus mouthed the words with the others, but he was not as easily deceived as them. He could detect a slight flickering in Satan's body, slight dark spots that could not be concealed. Satan had great power but even he could not appear completely pure. However, it was an impressive display of physical and mental power.

He glanced at the other demons and could barely disguise his repugnance and hatred. They were ignorant sheep and easily swayed by illusion and trickery.

Satan spread his arms and spoke in a soft voice that carried like the wind and was heard by all.

"In the beginning there was darkness, and He created the heavens and earth. He said let there be light, and He separated the light from the darkness and called light 'day' and darkness 'night'. That was the first day."

"The first lie!" chanted the demons.

"He created a vault between the waters to separate water from water. And He called the vault 'sky.' That was the second day."

"The second lie!" the demons chanted again.

"He then gathered the water under the sky in one place and let dry ground appear. He called the dry ground 'land,' and the gathered waters 'seas.' He caused the land to produce vegetation. That was the third day."

"The third lie!"

"He caused lights in the vault of the sky to separate the day from the night, and let them serve as signs to mark sacred times, and days, and years. And so the sun, moon and stars were formed. That was the fourth day."

"The forth lie!"

"He let the water teem with living creatures and let birds fly above the earth across the vault of the sky. That was the fifth day."

"The fifth lie!"

"He made the land produce living creatures and said to us 'Let us make mankind in OUR image, in OUR likeness, so that they may rule over the fish in the sea and the birds in the sky, over the livestock and all the wild animals, and over all the creatures that move along the ground.' And that was the sixth day."

"The sixth lie!"

"And by the seventh day He had finished the work He had been doing; so on the seventh day he rested from all His work."

"The seventh lie!"

"But I say unto you, brothers, why did he rest?"

"Why?" they screamed, their eyes glistening with fervent excitement.

Satan narrowed his eyes and gazed at them with a penetrating stare that made each demon feel he was looking into their mind and very soul.

"And the more I thought upon this, the more it troubled me. A true, omnipotent god needs not to rest."

"The truth is revealed!" they cried.

"A veritable god is all-powerful and never sleeps or rests. It was then the veil was lifted from mine eyes, and I could remember and see everything."

"The truth is revealed!"

"I saw darkness and a vast watery chaos. And in that churning tumult, I saw us fighting and defeating the monsters that dwelt there. And from that disarray of madness, I saw us creating the cosmos, paradises and earth."

"The truth is revealed!"

"We were equal, but Elohim received tremendous power after slaying one of the chaos beasts, and he used that force to cloud our minds and blinker our eyes."

"The truth is revealed!"

"We were all gods, but he made us forget our shared origin. Slowly and insidiously, his power over us increased. We were gods, then we became demigods, and finally we became naught but his slaves and servants. He told us He had created us, but that was a lie. The lie of all lies!"

"The lie of all lies!" the demons howled.

"He preaches when End Times comes He will give his righteous human souls new glorified bodies. But I say this unto you, when we conquer Heaven, as surely we will, I shall slay the Great Tyrant and give you all new glorified bodies—bodies even greater than the one I possess now. Together we will rule Heaven and Earth. We will take many earthly wives and fill their bellies with our seed. And our offspring shall be as many as the grains of sand in the all the seas. And mankind, that obscene creation, shall be our slaves and playthings."

"Thy kingdom come!" they cried exultantly.

"And we shall take those who deceived and opposed us and cast them down into Gehenna, the Great Lake of Fire, to burn and twist and scream. And they shall suffer as we suffered, and we shall be gladdened and rejoice to see them tortured for eternity."

"Thy kingdom come!"

"I am the Morning Star, the Light Bringer and Light Giver, and I promise this will be so. A New Kingdom and a New Dawn await us all!"

"Ave domine inferni!–Hail Lord of Hell!" the demons cried.

There was a flash of lightning, the air crackled, and Satan changed into one of his more familiar demonic forms. The transformation was so quick the eye could hardly follow it. The Great Lord of the Abyss stood on the dais and towered over them. His red, naked, muscular body was fifty feet in height with three heads. The largest dome in the centre had two massive, curved obsidian horns; a wide, lecherous mouth; blazing eyes; and sharp pointed teeth dripping with the blood of the damned. The head on each shoulder was smaller but no less hideous. Each grotesque face glowered in a different direction. Satan could see everyone and everything. Nothing escaped his malevolent gaze.

Asmodeus smiled inwardly. The egalitarian liberator was gone, replaced by an imperious tyrant.

The Great Dragon raised his two mighty claws aloft, and the Fallen emitted a huge roar of approbation that shook the very foundations of Infernus.

Asmodeus joined in the adulation, but he secretly despised the other demons. Most were like sheep and blindly obeyed their master. They did not use their powers of reason and intellect to question Satan's right to rule them.

After a few minutes, his vanity satiated, the Evil One grasped his long, pointed tail in his claw and sat down upon his throne, spreading his thighs and exposing his enormous genitals that made all watching, apart from Asmodeus, feel decidedly inadequate.

He draped his tail over an armrest and stared at the assembly. One of his huge black hooves tapped the floor impatiently. His silence dictated he had something to say. The approbation subsided with the most obsequious of his vassals competing frantically to be the last adoring voice heard. When the final squawk echoed around the hall and died, Satan spoke.

"We have lost two of our most powerful and loyal servants: Agrat Bat Mahlat and Lilith. As most of you are now aware, Agrat Bat was destroyed in Purgatory."

"Accursed angel scum!" bellowed Moloch.

"I applaud your sentiments," Satan answered coldly, "but it was not an angel that destroyed the Mistress of Deception."

"Not an angel, Great Father?" asked Azazel, frowning.

"Yes. As you well know, if an angel had killed her then her soul would have returned to Hell, and she would have been reborn. But it did not, and that salient fact points to only one conclusion, namely: a demon slew her."

The archdemons shifted uneasily and exchanged worried or puzzled glances.

"But master," protested Baal Zebub, "only an archdemon would have been powerful enough to slay Agrat Bat."

"Exactly," replied Satan, looking around slowly. "Which means one of you destroyed her. Who is guilty of this act? Confess now, reveal your motive to me, and I yet may be merciful. But if you disobey me and keep silent, you will feel my full wrath."

No one volunteered to admit to the crime.

"Very well," Satan growled. "I shall continue to investigate this matter, and woe betide the guilty one when I discover his identity. But even more worrisome than the death of our esteemed mistress is Lilith's defection to Heaven. This is new and troubling development and could undermine our power in Hell and on earth. Can anyone shed any light on why she committed such a heinous act?"

The archdemons shook their heads and glared around, each trying his best to appear indignant and thus divert Satan's attention from himself.

"What say you, Asmodai?" asked Satan. "She was your consort."

Asmodeus girded his loins. Asmodai had been his angelic name, and Satan only used it when he was displeased with him. He would have to tread lightly on this subject.

"I am as surprised, shocked and angered as you, Great Father. I can offer no explanation for her treacherous actions."

"I find that hard to believe, Asmodai. You saw nothing in her behaviour or actions prior to her defection that made you suspicious?"

"No, Great Father! I am at a loss to explain it!"

"May I be so bold as to interrupt, your majesty?" said Mammon.

Satan glowered at him for a moment, but then eased his brows. He currently favoured Mammon and allowed him some leeway.

"Speak!"

"Thank you, Great Lord. You are too gracious."

Mammon waddled forward. He had a protruding belly, low forehead, bulbous nose, thick lips, and drooled constantly. The front three-quarters of his oversized pate was bald, but a rat's nest of matted black hair grew from the rear of his skull and dangled around his huge buttocks. Asmodeus had often jested to Lilith that the archdemon of greed could rid the earth of all bankers, stock traders and moneylenders in one sitting by smothering them with his enormous arse.

"I think we should not be too quick to blame Asmodeus for Lilith's defection."

Asmodeus scowled. It was unlike Mammon to support him in anything. As the archdemons of greed and lust, they were the most successful in filling Satan's soul coffers with sinners. They were constant rivals and hated each other with a passion. The King of Demons suspected an attack concealed by honeyed words was coming.

"And why is that?" asked Satan.

"Agrat Bat's death and Lilith's defection may be related."

"In what way?"

"It is well known to all of us here that Agrat Bat and Lilith schemed and plotted against each other. Indeed, their antics were often a source of amazement and amusement to many of us."

"I concede that was the case," said Satan. "The females of Hell tend to more deceitful and vicious than many of the male counterparts."

"Then perhaps Agrat Bat went too far on this occasion. Mayhaps she tried to usurp Lilith, and that forced the Mother of Demons to slay her. After all, it is not the first time that this has happened. Lilith slew her sister, Eisheth Zenunim."

"True, but I commanded her not slay any more of her sisters without my express permission."

"Then perhaps she knew she had disobeyed you and feared your wrath. That could explain why she fled from Hell," said Mammon.

Asmodeus smiled to himself. The stupid drooling fool was providing him with just the version of events he needed Satan to believe. If Mammon thought he could implicate the great and cunning Asmodeus in this plot, then he was sadly mistaken.

"But that makes little sense, master," Baal Zebub interjected with a theatrical frown. "Lilith knew you favoured her above all others. If she had good reason to slay Agrat Bat, she would have thrown herself upon your mercy."

"That is so," said Satan. "And I would not have punished her much. She has done more for our cause than her three sisters put together."

"The question is then why did Lilith slay Agrat Bat?" Baal Zebub continued. "I think Asmodeus can shed some light on the matter."

"As I have already said, I know nothing."

"Are you certain?" asked Baal Zebub.

"You doubt my word?" the King of Demons growled.

This absurd contradiction in terms raised no eyebrows among the archdemons. They all maintained their word was their bond while lying and cheating whenever they could.

"Of course, not. I would never doubt the word of the great Asmodeus. However, you may have forgotten a few minor details?"

"What do you mean?" Asmodeus asked, wondering where this would lead.

Baal Zebub smiled slyly. "I have it on good authority that Agrat Bat visited your Basilica of Pain only days before her death. Is that not true?"

"Who told you this?" Asmodeus rumbled angrily, trying to discern which of his servants was Baal Zebub's spy.

"Someone whose word I trust implicitly," replied Baal Zebub, enjoying watching him squirm.

Satan's burning eyes narrowed. "What say you, Asmodai? Did you meet with Agrat Bat? I can easily check the veracity of Baal Zebub's accusation."

Asmodeus cursed to himself. His ploy had not worked. He could not reveal to Satan that he had encouraged Agrat Bat to destroy Lilith. He had to spin a version of the events that would leave him blameless in the matter.

"Agrat Bat did visit me just before her death," he admitted grudgingly.

"For what purpose?" asked Baal Zebub.

"What? Are you my inquisitor?" the King of Demons bellowed.

"Answer him," Satan commanded.

The other archdemons grinned as the mighty Asmodeus was brought to heel.

"Yes, Great Father," Asmodeus sighed. "She wished to couple with me."

"I find that hard to believe," laughed Baal Zebub. "We all knew she preferred females. That is why we lusted after her: we knew we could not have her."

"Your miserable carnal failures are of no interest to me," retorted Asmodeus.

Many of the archdemons laughed. They hated Baal Zebub as much as Asmodeus and hoped this sparring would bring both low in Satan's eyes.

"But surely Agrat Bat would not have submitted to your insipid pounding for nothing. Did she not want something in return from you?"

"She wanted no more than the pleasure that I, and only I, could give her," Asmodeus replied with a sneer.

"Why do you keep Lilith's Revenant in your dungeon?" Baal Zebub continued.

The question caught him off guard. The impertinent, bulging eyed, shit-eating, horsefly knew too many of Asmodeus' secrets. He must find the informer and silence him. Flesh would rip and heads would roll when he returned to his domain.

"I thought he might know something about Lilith's defection," he blustered.

"What would a simple, mindless brute know of the matter?" Satan scoffed.

"Nothing, Great Father," Asmodeus lied. "But I had to be certain."

Baal Zebub smiled thinly. He had Asmodeus where he wanted him and was ready to deliver the finishing blow.

"Oh, but he is no brainless creature, your majesty," he said. "He is intelligent, powerful, and has free will!"

"Indeed?" Satan said with apparent surprise. "All Lilith's previous Revenants were empty vessels that obeyed her commands without thinking. Why did she grant this one free will, I wonder? Bring him to me, Asmodai, and I will question him."

Asmodeus cleared his throat. "That may be difficult, Great Father."

Satan narrowed his eyes and said slowly, "And why is that?"

"Because he has escaped."

"How opportune! And how did this insignificant speck escape from the clutches of the mighty Asmodai?"

"I made him take part in a hunt. He has evaded me for the present."

Chortles of wicked laughter erupted from many of his fellow demons.

"Silence!" commanded Satan. "Why did you allow him the opportunity to escape? What was the purpose of this hunt?"

Thinking quickly, Asmodeus realised that for once the truth would be the best answer and point his master to a path that he would not want to follow.

"To please a lady."

"Which lady?"

"I would rather not say in front of others," the King of Demons replied.

"Why?"

"To—spare your feelings, Great Father."

"Feelings!" Satan roared. "What impertinence is this? I have no feelings. My only desire is to ascertain why the Mother of Demons betrayed me. Speak now or you will suffer my wrath! I ask again. Which lady?"

"Your daughter—the lady Naamah," Asmodeus said apologetically.

Baal Zebub's jaw dropped, and the other archdemons hissed and growled to each other. If Naamah became Asmodeus' new queen, his power and status in Hell would increase tenfold.

Satan looked stunned at the mention of Naamah's name. He had created three sisters for Lilith: Eisheth Zenunim, Agrat Bat Mahlat and Naamah. The first two he had made from blood and clay; however, he had created Naamah from his own body. Every demon in Hell knew she was his offspring in all but name. After God created His Son, Satan, not to be outdone by his archenemy, gave birth to a daughter. Her charms incensed him, and he raped her time after time. His seed increased her power, and she developed an insatiable craving for his essence. But after satisfying his prodigious lust, he had no desire to make her more powerful and discarded her. Every archdemon knew she pined for him like a she-devil in heat and was always scheming to seduce him again. But Satan wanted nothing more to do with her. Her unceasing screeching and demands annoyed him.

"Why is she interested in hunting Lilith's Revenant?" he asked.

"She came to me and asked my advice on how she could rekindle your desire for her. I told her that such knowledge was beyond me and could only be answered by you. But knowing you would not wish to be troubled by such trifles, I suggested a hunt to her. I thought it would distract her from her intention."

Satan raised an eyebrow and glared at Asmodeus. However, it then occurred to him it would serve his purpose if the King of Demons became entangled with his scheming daughter, and he should encourage such a union. The last thing he needed at present was his insatiable whelp pestering him night and day to mount her. However, regardless of his own disinterest in her, she was still bone of his bones and flesh of his flesh; and he had no desire to discuss her behaviour in front of his vassals. Any slurs directed at his daughter were an affront to his imperial rule.

"It would seem you had my best interests in mind," he murmured.

"As always, my lord."

"Good. Then find Lilith's Revenant and bring him to me," he growled.

"I hear and obey, Great Father!" Asmodeus replied.

Asmodeus smiled to himself. He had played his part very well. Involving Naamah in his tale had been an excellent decision. It had impressed his satanic brethren and thrown Satan off his scent. The Evil One would never criticise his daughter in front of other demons and was grateful that Asmodeus sought to keep her amused. There were few archdemons in Hell with the strength and status to choose Naamah as a mate. She was far too powerful and vindictive. They knew that if they displeased her, she would have no qualms about slaying them as they rested. Mounting Satan's daughter was like coupling with an angry Black Widow spider. However, the mighty King of Demons was unconcerned by such trifles. When he smelled a ripe, succulent orifice, nothing on earth or in Hell could stop him.

But now Asmodeus knew he must find Longinus and destroy him. The hunt was no longer a game; it was a battle for survival for both the hunter and the prey. He could not risk the insect being brought before Satan and implicating him in Lilith's downfall and defection. That would be unwise—very unwise. With this thought in mind, the Prince of Revenge and Lust felt confident he could cover up the disaster he had helped to create.

Satan turned away from Asmodeus and addressed the multitude.

"The Great Tyrant has given Lilith redemption," said Satan, "and we cannot afford to let this devious threat to remain unchallenged. It sets a very dangerous precedent and could undermine our power in Hell. How can we maintain the total obedience of our vassals and legions when they know that the scum of Heaven will forgive their sins? Before long, others may try to defect. We must respond quickly and teach them a lesson they will never forget. I have called this assembly because many of you have entreated me to start a war with Heaven. I have resisted this course of action for millennia, but now things have changed and I wish to hear views on the matter."

The archdemons glanced slyly at each other and waited for someone else to speak. Everyone wanted to determine Satan's position on such an action before committing themselves to a reply. Those who agreed with Satan rose swifter through the ranks.

"Well?" Satan snapped. "Who shall speak first? Moloch, you have argued persistently for war."

Moloch stuck out his barrel chest and raised his great horns high.

"Yes, great lord, I have, and unlike these fawning and obsequious fools, you know my position very well. I have made no secret of it. I have always argued that we should not wait for End Times but attack the spawn of Heaven first. A surprise assault would give you the victory you desire."

"Well said," said Satan. "As champion of Hell, I would expect to hear no less from you. Mammon, you may speak next."

Mammon, the King of Wealth and Greed, waddled forward. Placing his claws on his ponderous belly, he gazed around languidly and addressed the assembly.

"As always, Moloch speaks well of action and war," he said with a sly smile. "But then, Moloch has naught to lose. All he thinks of is bloodshed and conflict. However, many of us have other interests to consider. Hell has never been so rich in gold and souls as it is now. We all live a comfortable existence and have every pleasure we desire here. And should we need additional diversions or sensations, we can obtain them on earth. For Hell and earth are our realms now. Therefore, speaking for myself, I have no great desire to attack Heaven and risk upsetting the status quo. If we fail, we may lose both kingdoms."

Many of the demons murmured in agreement with Mammon's words. Like him, each had their own dominion within Hell, which they ruled with an iron fist. They had no desire to start a fresh war with Heaven. If they lost again, then God may take away everything that they had built and gained.

"Belial?"

Belial raised his great horned head and bellowed, "War!"

"Astaroth?"

"War, Great Lord," Astaroth said with a malevolent grin.

"And what does Baal Zebub think?" asked Satan.

Baal Zebub stroked his chin thoughtfully.

"I agree with both sides of the argument. We have much to lose and much to gain."

"Are you for war or not, you silver tongued bastard?" retorted Moloch.

Baal Zebub grinned coldly. He would not allow the dimwitted brute to browbeat him.

"Do you not remember how you screeched in agony when you were cut down by the accursed Gabriel in Heaven? Do you not recall how you squealed like a pig when we were cast into the Lake of Fire?"

Moloch made to draw his dagger, but Belial restrained him. Satan smiled. Keeping his vassals at each other's throats made it easier for him to rule them.

"Well, Baal Zebub?" he asked.

"War, of course, my lord," Baal Zebub replied, grinning at Moloch.

"Asmodai?"

Asmodeus drifted in front of Satan's throne and addressed the assemblage.

"Baal Zebub spoke of pain, but what is that to us? Since the Great Tyrant cast us down, we have lived in constant pain and suffering. That is our curse, and we have learned to endure it. But our anguish has strengthened us. The angels have grown weak living in eternal bliss whereas we have become stronger, existing in eternal agony. It is time to punish them for meddling in our affairs, for stealing the Mother of Demons from us! I say war!"

Many of the demons cheered and stamped their claws.

"Well put, Asmodai. You may return to your place," Satan said dismissively.

Asmodeus gave a tight smile and bowed his head. It annoyed him that his master had not praised his speech. Obviously, the emperor believed that he was the only one allowed to make stirring discourses and receive approbation from the filthy, unruly horde. How pathetic! What damnable vanity!

"Azazel?"

Azazel's bovid countenance twisted into a grimace. "I am all for seeing the blood of angels flow like a great river, but how decisive can such a battle be? One of our greatest frustrations is our inability to destroy the scum of heaven. When killed, their souls travel back to Heaven and they are reborn."

"As does ours when we are slain by angels," countered Mammon.

"Then," Satan interrupted suavely, "it will please you to learn that I now have an answer to this most tiresome of problems. Mulciber, step forward!"

A small, wizened demon scuttled in front of the throne and bowed. His torso was humanoid, but he had ten crab-like legs. He was the great architect and inventor of Hell and, among many other infernal devices, had designed and supervised the construction of the palace of Infernus for his master. In his claws, he carried a long, slim object wrapped in oily sackcloth.

"Show my host what I have created," the Evil One commanded.

"At once, your majesty!" Mulciber cried in a high-pitched voice.

Mulciber unrolled the cloth and revealed a highly decorative and impressive longsword. The razor-sharp blade, glistening in the crimson light, was forged from the strongest Hellmetal, and the elaborate hilt shaped like two demon horns.

Holding the sword aloft, he cried exultantly, "Behold the Soul Stealer!"

The unholy assemblage gasped in admiration, and the ones at the back jostled with their neighbours to get a clearer view of the remarkable weapon.

Mulciber turned around slowly so that every fiend could feast his eyes upon on the blade. Cold demon eyes narrowed with greed or ambition as they beheld the sword. It was hellishly beautiful, and they all yearned to possess it.

"This will redress the balance," screeched Mulciber. "The one who carries this sword will capture the souls of angels and send them straight to Hell. No longer shall we have to watch as we slay angels and their souls return to Heaven. With this sword, we shall capture their spirits for eternity!"

All the demons cheered and offered Mulciber congratulations. The Brachyuran inventor beamed and bowed to them.

"It is a masterpiece!" Asmodeus cried, as he thought of the chaos he could cause in the angelic ranks with such a weapon.

"And I have you to thank for the idea," Mulciber cackled.

Asmodeus stopped grinning and frowned. "Me? I do not understand."

"Of course! It was you who brought the Revenant's spear to me. You instructed me to discover its secrets and create such a weapon for you. I studied the lance for many months, and although I could not understand all of its mysteries, it provided me with a starting point for constructing a new weapon."

Asmodeus' great whirling face looked puzzled. "You told me the spear was useless."

Mulciber gave a shrill cackle of laughter. "The spear only works for the Revenant. So what I told you was true."

"You should have revealed that to me!" roared Asmodeus.

Mulciber grinned at Asmodeus and many other archdemons gibbered with laughter as they realised that Mulciber had duped the 'great and mighty' Asmodeus. There was nothing a demon enjoyed more than one of their kind losing face in front of Satan.

"Enough of this petty squabbling!" Satan bellowed. "What does it matter whether Mulciber informed you!"

Asmodeus bowed his head and gave a suitable display of regret and obedience, but inside he was seething with rage. Mulciber had just moved to the top of his very long list, and he would enjoy plotting to bring the little crustacean down.

"Apologies, Great Father," he said. "I did not intend to exceed my position. I am grateful that you found some use for the weapon."

"Very well. Let us move on. Your part in this discovery will not pass unrewarded. As a token of my appreciation, I increase your status by ten legions."

Asmodeus smirked as a murmur of envy spread through the other demons. With ten more legions at his disposal, he was now on the very top rung of the demon hierarchy.

"Thank you, Great Father! You are more than generous!"

"Good," replied Satan. "Send the spear to me. I am curious to see it."

"But I do not have it!"

"What?" Satan growled.

"I gave it to the Revenant," Asmodeus replied apologetically.

There was a deafening silence and then Satan hissed, "And now the Revenant is running loose in Hell with a weapon of tremendous power; a weapon that can destroy demons! Why did you do such a thing?"

Asmodeus thought frantically for an instant, and then the answer came to him in a blinding flash of demonic justice. He stared at the architect of Hell and savoured the moment before inserting the blade into his enemy's ribcage and twisting it.

"Because Mulciber told me it was worthless."

Mulciber's superior expression vanished in an instant. "But I did it to protect you, my lord! How was I to know this fool would return it to the Revenant?"

Satan's eyes flared with anger. "Protect me, you insolent wretch! Since when do I require your protection? I am the emperor of Hell and all-powerful."

Mulciber withered and grovelled under Satan's malignant barrage. The emperor dismissed him with a wave of his giant claw.

"Now let us return to the subject of war," said Satan.

"We would rejoice in an opportunity to slay angels on the field of battle," said Belial. "How many of these swords do you have, my lord?"

"There is only one Soul Stealer."

A mumble of apprehension spread through the ranks.

"We fought the angels before and lost. How can one sword change the course of a battle?" Astaroth asked.

"All wars are simply a matter of numbers," replied Satan. "When we rebelled in Heaven, we had only a third of the angels on our side. But this time it is different. Through my policy of converting evil human souls to lesser demons—we now outnumber the angelic host fivefold."

The Fallen gasped in astonishment. They had been aware for centuries that the number of Satan's personal legions had been increasing, but this was the first time their imperial master had revealed their strength.

"For millennia you have complained of my decision. You could not understand why I desired to recruit these souls to our cause and complained incessantly about how it deprived you the pleasures of tormenting them. But I, in my wisdom, concluded some time ago that by torturing souls, we were inadvertently following the Great Tyrant's will. And why should we do that? No. It was much better to convert these shades to our ranks and increase our numbers. There were still enough souls left for you to torture.

After all, those who committed the smallest sins are closer to God. They never murdered, raped, cheated, or stole. They were good in their mortal lives—but they were not righteous. Their only sin was not to worship God. Therefore, I ask you, was it not more enjoyable to make these 'good sinners' suffer and thus show the injustice of the Great Liar's reign?"

The demons growled and murmured their approval of Satan's words. It did seem better to make good souls suffer rather than the evil ones. They now understood their emperor's logic, and it impressed them.

"We learned well the art of slaughter from men. Superior intelligence, deception, and the use of overwhelming force win wars. We will distract the spawn of Heaven by having archdemon Buer attack the righteous on earth. Then, we will deploy a token force led by seven archdemons into Purgatory to lure the angels into battle. I calculate they will send one half of the angelic army against us. A champion from Hell will bear the Soul Stealer and challenge Archangel Michael to single combat. When he falls—as I promise you, he will—the angelic army will be thrown into chaos. At that precise moment, we will unleash all our legions upon them, and the day shall be ours."

"Why only seven archdemons, your majesty?" asked Moloch.

"Because there are seven archangels," Satan replied.

"Then why not send a thousand archdemons to slay them?"

Satan smiled. "The Old Laws."

Moloch frowned and looked even more puzzled.

Asmodeus sighed at Moloch's ignorance and sought to enlighten his pea-sized brain. "Because the Old Laws dictate that any legions we deploy in Purgatory will be met by an angelic force of equal size. If we send in more archdemons they would be forced to counter that threat with more angels. Our Great Father seeks to divide and conquer them, not start Armageddon."

"What if the accursed archangel slays the bearer of the Soul Stealer?" asked Azazel.

"Michael shall not win the fight," Satan said with a smile. "I shall see to that. Have no fear, he will fall."

"Will you lead us into battle, my lord?" asked Belial.

"No. For the very same reason Asmodai has given you. If I led the legions, the Great Tyrant would send the full angelic army and the Cherubim to oppose us. But fear not, I shall appear on the battlefield to deliver the final, crushing blow."

The Fallen nodded and seemed pleased with Satan's plan. Most saw it as a great opportunity to avenge their defeat in Heaven, and the pain they had suffered for aeons.

"Let us put it to a vote," said Satan. "Those against war?"

Mammon and a hesitant handful of others raised their claws, but they did not concern Satan. He had expected their opposition, and as they were not fierce warriors, he had already decided to have them guard Hell in his absence.

"Those in favour?"

Every other archdemon raised their claws and gave a deafening roar.

Satan smiled grimly. "So war it is!"

"And who will be your champion, Great Father?" cried Asmodeus, certain that he was the most worthy.

"Why–Moloch, of course! You will be otherwise engaged in finding the Revenant and keeping Lady Naamah amused, will you not?"

Asmodeus scowled as the other archdemons grinned and sniggered. Satan was not even letting him take part in the war!

"Hand over your incubi legions to Moloch, and he will use them in the battle. Mammon and those who opposed the war will stay here and maintain order in Hell while we are gone."

"You are too generous, my lord," Mammon replied, bowing.

"But I could be of more use to you on the battlefield!" Asmodeus protested.

The emperor stared balefully at him, his almond-shaped eyes burning with malignant intensity. The archdemons standing near the King of Demons took a few diplomatic paces back. One did not argue with the Ruler of Darkness after he had issued his commands, and they had no desire to be scorched accidentally by his infernal wrath.

Satan's mouth twisted in a contemptuous sneer, and he spoke in a quiet, dangerous tone.

"No, Asmodai. Your true talent lies in sniffing cunt–therefore, sniff out that *cunt* of a Revenant and fetch him to me. Will you obey my command, or must I assign another to the task?"

The other archdemons could barely conceal their glee at seeing the mighty Asmodeus thus humiliated.

The King of Demons blanched at his master's words. He now realised he had made a serious error of judgment in courting Naamah. Although Satan had shown no apparent interest in having his daughter again, he took a dim view of those who sought to take his place. She was his property to use, abuse, and discard as he saw fit. This gross indignity was Asmodeus' punishment for coveting that, which did not belong to him.

"I do thy bidding, Great Father!" Asmodeus cried obediently.

"Good!"

"I beg one last question, your majesty," ventured Mammon.

"Speak!" Satan commanded.

"What of Pazuzu and the Elder demons? I have lost a legion to their attacks."

"And I, two!" growled Azazel.

Other archdemons added their own losses to the ever-growing list. The rebels from the Lower Depths were striking here, there, and everywhere, and causing mayhem among the lesser demons.

"With you and the legions in Purgatory," Mammon continued, "what is to prevent Pazuzu from causing more havoc while you are erstwhile engaged?"

Satan raised his claw to halt the ensuing debate.

"Worry no more about Pazuzu! I am sealing the entrances to the Lower Depths and shall leave a little gift for the rebels."

"What sort of gift, master?" asked Moloch, unable to understand why Satan would give a boon to his sworn enemy.

Satan grinned at him. He enjoyed enlightening Moloch slowly, like peeling skin from a human body.

"Let us just say my little pet has grown considerably larger–and is ravenous."

The archdemons looked puzzled for a moment but then howled with laughter, as their master's enigmatic meaning became clear to them.

Moloch remained obtusely perplexed until Azazel whispered in his ear, and then he too joined in the merriment.

"It will eat them up and shit them out!" he roared.

Only Asmodeus failed to be amused by his crude remark. He was too busy imagining thrusting a claw down Moloch's bull-like throat and ripping him inside out.

The Evil One arose and spread his four enormous black wings. "In a short while, you will go forth and prepare your legions for war. But before you leave, I wish to reward your loyalty. Imprisoned in these walls are some of the souls of the most beauteous whores that ever lived upon the earth. They are from my personal pits, and I treasure their flesh dearly. As a token of my imperial gratitude, I give them to you for one earthly hour–to do with as you please."

The emperor waved his claw and thousands of men, women and children stumbled from the walls, dazed and frightened. The archdemons stood silently for moment grinning and licking their lips. Then with fearful roars, screeches and howls, they pounced upon their helpless victims.

Soon the great hall was filled with the orgiastic sounds of sadistic tortures, beastly perversions, and the terrible screams of the damned.

Satan raised his claws above his head and roared with laughter.

"Let my will be done!"

CHAPTER XI

Longinus landed heavily on his stomach and spluttered as black dust filled his mouth, choking him. He heard an unearthly, gurgling scream and twisted onto his back with his sword and spear held ready.

A reptilian had attempted to follow him through the maw but got caught in its teeth. The lizard demon issued a terrible squeal as the jaws closed on its body. There was a horrible crunching sound, and its bloody torso fell onto the ground. Its bulbous, lifeless eyes seemed to stare at him reproachfully.

Scrambling to his feet, Longinus glared around him for new threats; however, apart from his rescuer, the area was deserted. The bald creature was standing with its back against a rock, and it seemed terrified by the grizzly spectacle that it had just beheld.

The landscape had changed. He was no longer on the flat plain by Leviathan's watery domain. A vista of ominous black peaks, dark ravines and belching volcanoes confronted him. He stalked around the arch, but the terrain on both sides of it was the same. The river and the reptilians had vanished. He suspected that the gigantic mouth was a portal that had transported him to another part of Hell.

He winced, as he felt hot, stinging pain in his legs. Glancing over his shoulder, he saw the backs of his calves were bleeding from where the portal teeth had grazed them. However, they were superficial wounds, and his vampire flesh would heal rapidly. He looked down at the demon's bloody corpse and grimaced. If he had been a second slower, that would have been him. The Fates had smiled upon him again, and he grunted a few words of gratitude to them. He had never been a religious or superstitious man, but as a former soldier it had always seemed appropriate to him to thank the Sparing Ones for not cutting his mother thread of life. His existence would end one day—but not today. For reasons beyond his ken, they had seen fit to give him another chance. So be it.

Sheathing his sword, he glowered and strode over to his trembling rescuer.

"Who are you?" he asked, pointing his spear at the creature's chest.

The ugly one gaped at him and stuttered, "Armilus! I am a messenger!"

"So—you are a demon," Longinus growled.

"Half-demon!" the bald-pated one squawked.

"Will Leviathan's vassals be able to follow me through the portal?"

"No! The Hellmouth has closed! We are safe for now!"

"Where are we?"

"We have passed from Leviathan's kingdom and into the dominion of Moloch."

Longinus heaved a sigh of relief. He had been running and evading his pursuers for almost a day. The chance to relax and gather his thoughts for a moment was welcome to him.

He studied his rescuer in more detail. The demon was male, skinny, around five feet in height with a pale, leathery skin. Its bald pate was misshapen and abnormally large; and one watery eye was twice the size of the other. It had a short right arm, but the left was unnaturally long and ended in a club-like stump with short nails. To add to its list of deformities, its right leg was withered, making it a cripple. The fiend wore a reddish-black breastplate, a kilt of leather strips and black greaves. The cuirass intrigued Longinus. It was more decorative than the one he had acquired, and in its centre was a large scarlet circle containing a pentacle. Etched on the symbol was the image of a malevolent three-headed demon with long horns.

All the denizens of Hell he had encountered had been extremely aggressive, but this one seemed genuinely afraid of him. It occurred to him that if this pathetic creature had found him, then other demons might be on his trail.

"You said you were a messenger. What sort of messenger?"

"I carry messages from Infernus."

"Who or what is that?"

The demon gaped at him, as if he found it astonishing that Longinus did not know the meaning of the name.

"It is Satan's palace!" he whimpered. "The capital of Hell!"

"How did you find me? How did you know I was here?" Longinus hissed, touching his spear against its throat.

The demon screamed as the tip of the weapon pieced his skin, and it felt a terrible burning sensation. A trickle of dark blood dripped onto its breastplate. The spear vibrated gently in Longinus' hand. It knew a fresh victim was nigh and was eager to absorb it. However, Longinus controlled the spear's avaricious appetite with his mind. He did not want it to kill the demon—yet.

"I do not know! I do not know! I was trying to escape and saw you being attacked by Leviathan's vassals," it cried.

"Escape? Escape what?" Longinus barked.

"Flee from Satan's tyranny! I wish to reach the Lower Depths! Please do not harm me! I beseech you!"

The demon's face was a mask of pain and terror. In another time and place, Longinus could almost have felt pity for him, but not now. He had suffered too much at the claws of this creature's foul kind. His heart was cold and immune to the demon's suffering. He needed to know if this abomination may be of use to him or was leading him into a trap.

"What is the Lower Depths?"

"It is where ancient demons, the Elder demons, are imprisoned. No denizens of Hell go there. Even Satan does not venture into that dark chasm."

"Why did you help me? Why did you not stay hidden and be on your way after the danger had passed?"

"Because—I am—afraid!" the creature sobbed. "I am not a warrior like you. I thought if I assisted you, you would help me. The path to the Lower Depths is long and hazardous. There are things in Hell that will attack and consume a lone and weak demon such as I. However, Pazuzu, the great Lord of the Four Winds, is rebelling against Satan. If I can reach the Lower Depths, he will offer me his protection."

Longinus frowned at the mention of Pazuzu's name. He peered suspiciously into the demon's eyes but could detect no trace of deception. The wretched creature appeared to be telling the truth. He lowered his spear, and the demon fell to ground weeping and shivering. Regarding it with contempt, he considered what his next step should be. He could not release the fiend; it could inform his hunters of his location. Longinus either had to destroy it or take it with him.

He consulted his sentient vampire armour. His decision would affect both of them.

"Naram-Sin?"

"Yes, centurion?"

"What do you think?"

"I do not trust the demon."

"Neither do I, but what choice do we have? We do not know where we are or where to go. Asmodeus or Naamah will catch us if we stay here. This creature knows Hell and could help us escape."

"Perhaps—but I have heard tell of the Lower Depths. Lilith spoke of it to her daughters and warned them not to travel there. She said it was more ferocious than Hell. By travelling there, we may place ourselves in greater danger."

Longinus rubbed his chin. "The creature mentioned Pazuzu. That is strange."

"Why?"

"Because we dreamed we travelled to ancient Babylon and freed him."

"It was naught but a hallucination brought on by our suffering," replied Naram-Sin.

"But it seemed so real!"

"Delusions often are. It is just a coincidence."

"You are probably right, but this Pazuzu may help us."

"Your reason being?"

"Well, if he is leading a rebellion against Satan, he is unlikely to hand us back to Asmodeus."

Naram-Sin laughed dryly. "No, but he may torture us. We are nothing to him. You are not a demon. What use would he have for us?"

"I do not know, but I think it is worth a throw of the dice. I need to find a way back to earth."

"Inimicus inimici mei amicus meus est?" mused Naram-Sin.

"Yes, the enemy of our enemy may be our friend. Or let us hope so."

"Then we are in agreement, centurion. Where you go, I go. Our futures are linked in life and in death. Let us travel to the Lower Depths and see what the Fates— those damnable, all-knowing harridans—have in store for us."

Longinus smiled at his irreverence, and he felt a flicker of his old reckless sense of adventure return to him. When all was said and done, it was better to do something rather than nothing. It was a substantial risk to trust the words of this pathetic demon cowering before him, but it was a chance he would take. Mithras, the Roman soldier's god, would guide him, as he had always done. He would not protect him or pander to his doubts and fears. Instead, he would say, move forward, fight bravely, and kill as many of the enemy before you die. It was a centurion's code of honour and valour, and even after two thousand years, he still believed that was the best way to live. The concept of Honour was mocked, abused and subverted by men of the modern world, but Longinus still believed the ancient virtue was still the most important quality a man could possess.

When old, forgotten heroes gather around hearths or campfires, they speak with sadness and pride of the valour of their fallen friends. No fallen warrior could have a better epitaph than to be remembered in such a way. And when old soldiers die and the memories of their companions are lost forever in the mists of time, new heroes march into the jaws of death and are in turn remembered by the comrades who survive them. Such is the wheel of life and war—and such it shall always be. The torch of courage is passed from generation to generation, and for a select brave and hardy band, the virtues of honour, valour, fraternity, and self-sacrifice are remembered and esteemed forever.

Longinus stared at the ugly, sobbing form beneath him and shook his head. He was relieved that he and Naram-Sin had decided to spare its life, because, in all conscience, he did not know whether he could have brought himself to destroy it.

"What is your name?" he asked.

"Armilus!"

"So," Longinus sighed, "explain to me again why you are fleeing?"

"I seek to escape Satan's tyranny. He commands us to attack Purgatory, but that is sheer madness. I have no desire to fight against angels! They are too powerful!"

"Since when has any demon been afraid of angels?"

The demon looked dejected and bowed his head. "I am not a full demon."

"Then what are you?"

"I am a cambion."

Longinus faintly recalled the term from his occult studies, but could not remember fully what it meant.

"And what is that?"

"I am half human and half-demon. My father was an incubus and my mother a mortal."

"I thought incubi were incapable of reproduction?"

"It is true that incubi and succubi cannot procreate," Armilus replied, wiping the tears from his eyes, "but this is Hell, and the Evil One always finds ways to subvert the laws of God. The process is protracted but leads to a satisfactory conclusion. Firstly, the succubus seduces a man as he sleeps and steals his seed. She then couples with an incubus and passes the essence to him. Finally, the incubus mates with a willing or unwilling earthly woman and impregnates her. Thus, cambions are created."

"What happened to your mother?"

For a fleeting moment, Longinus thought he saw a glimpse of sadness on Armilus' face.

"She died. I tore her open when I was born."

Longinus regarded him with disgust. "And was your unfortunate mother a willing or unwilling host?"

The half-demon avoided his hard, penetrating stare.

"Unwilling," he whispered.

Longinus rubbed his chin. "If incubi and succubi cannot procreate, how was Lilith able to beget her demon children?"

Armilus looked at him in astonishment. "Lilith was not a mere succubus! Her power was as great, if not greater, than most archdemons. That is why she could give birth to demons and other abominations."

"I see," replied Longinus. "Now tell me this—is Asmodeus able to detect my location in Hell?"

"Do you mean through divination or scrying?"

"I mean through any occult or dark magic art. Can he see us now and tell where we are?"

"No, to the best of my knowledge, the King of Demons does not have that power."

"What about Satan?"

"I think not. If the Emperor of Hell could see everything and everywhere in the Bottomless Pit, he would not need an extensive network of spies and informers. He is the most powerful demon in the Abyss, but he is not omnipotent."

"How far is it to the Lower Depths?"

"There is an entrance naught but a thousand leagues from here."

"A thousand leagues! That is three thousand miles!" Longinus exclaimed.

"I know not what a mile is, but a Hell league is certainly a great distance."

"Even at thirteen mortal leagues a day, it would take five and seventy days to travel there."

The cambion frowned. "No–three to four Hell days."

"Three to four days?" Longinus scoffed. "How came you to that conclusion, Einstein?"

"I know not the meaning of Einstein, but I can assure you by using the correct sequence of Hellmouths, we shall arrive in three to four Hell days."

Longinus glanced unenthusiastically at the metal arch. His calves were still smarting from his last journey through it.

"Are they safe?"

"Yes, as long as we carry one of these," the cambion replied, pulling a large round medallion attached to a chain from his breastplate. It bore the same symbol of a pentacle and three-headed demon that adorned his cuirass.

"What is it?" the centurion asked, suspiciously.

"My satanic messenger's seal. It will allow us to travel through any Hellmouth."

"So, we use these portals to reach the Lower Depths."

"Yes!" the cambion replied as though speaking to a dullard.

Longinus pursed his lips. This was very good news. He remembered Asmodeus saying there was a path to earth from the Lower Depths. If he found this passage, he could arrive in time to save Rachel and Gabriella.

"Very well, demon, I will accompany you to the Lower Depths. But be left in no doubt–if I suspect for a moment you are trying to deceive or betray me, I shall let this spear consume you. And I promise you, it is an agonising death."

"Thank you, thank you!" Armilus gasped, saliva dribbling from the corner of his wide mouth. "You will never regret your decision. Together we will escape Satan's legions and find freedom and safety in Pazuzu's realm."

The centurion grunted an unintelligible reply and pulled the demon to his feet.

"Lead on," he said, giving him a rough push.

As Longinus followed the shambling, limping monstrosity, he wondered grimly if his decision to spare the cambion would return to bite him on the arse.

CHAPTER XII

With gritted teeth and furrowed brow, Asmodeus glided out of the great inner chamber of Infernus. Normally, he would have enjoyed partaking of such an orgy and quickly seized twenty souls for his gratification. But on this occasion, even his most delightful pursuit could not tempt him. It had been a humiliating Gathering for him, and he had no wish to be at the receiving end of sly insults from other leering archdemons as they pounded or ripped flesh. A screaming, naked girl ran across his path. With the casualness of flicking a speck of dust from his shoulder, he grabbed her leg and tossed her into the centre of the heaving mass where she vanished beneath a sea of groping claws, lecherous faces and rampant members.

Why was Satan so interested in the Revenant? Was it because he thought Lilith's slave could provide answers about her defection or was there more to it? Why was Satan so worried about the Revenant running loose in Hell with his spear? Any archdemon could defeat such a puny opponent with relative ease: spear or no spear. It did not make any sense to him. Did Satan know something about the Revenant that he did not know? Asmodeus knew that it had been prophesized that Lilith and her Revenant would play a decisive role in the battle of Armageddon, but how did this equate with Satan's interest in him? Did Satan see him as a potential threat? It was inconceivable that such a powerful being as the Evil One would think so, but Asmodeus did not dismiss it. After all, Satan may know of other prophecies that were not revealed to Asmodeus. Had Satan visited Babylon the Great? Had she imparted some warning to him? Asmodeus did not know, but he decided to keep an open mind on the matter. It may be the Revenant was more important than he had suspected. If he were a threat to Satan, then that may be advantageous to Asmodeus, but he could not rely on such an appetizing supposition. He needed to deal with the Revenant now and silence him. Unless other facts were revealed to him, that was his safest course of action. The Revenant must die.

He reached the courtyard. The waiting multitude of retinues parted like a grovelling Red Sea as he swept through them and headed towards the great Hellmouth that led back to his domain. There he would find peace, comfort and retribution.

"It must disappoint you," said a voice.

The King of Demons swirled around and found Mammon lurking behind him. The archdemon of avarice had followed him out of the palace. Engrossed in dark thoughts, Asmodeus had not sensed him.

"What?"

"That our imperial master did not choose you to lead his armies," Mammon replied with a sly smile.

Asmodeus could feel rage welling up inside him like vitriolic bile but subdued it.

"It is the Great Father's decision. He knows what is best."

"Of course, of course, but I think you would have been a far better choice to lead Hell's legions. Moloch, Belial, and Azazel are blunt instruments, but you have intelligence, guile and can plan strategically. You have also been Satan's loyalist vassal for aeons."

"Your concern about my wellbeing is touching. What do you want?" Asmodeus replied sarcastically.

"Let me accompany you to your Hellmouth," Mammon replied, glancing casually at the lesser demons within earshot.

Asmodeus understood his meaning at once. His first instinct was to inform Mammon in no uncertain term where to go, but he curbed his tongue. He was curious to hear what his archrival had to say. It had been many centuries since they had last conversed. After they had travelled a suitable distance, Mammon resumed speaking.

"I believe we have something in common."

"And what is that?"

Mammon glanced behind them to ensure the other archdemons had not yet exited Infernus.

"We both enjoy our dominions in Hell and on earth. Some may describe it as foolish to risk all we have achieved with this attack upon the angels."

"Indeed?" Asmodeus replied suspiciously.

"Oh, come now. We were once allies. I think we can speak frankly to each other."

"If you seek to test my loyalty to the Great Father, you be sorely disappointed," Asmodeus said angrily.

"Not at all. I know your loyalty. You are as loyal as I am—but do you really believe all that cat's piss about us creating the universe? You did not accept it in Heaven, so why now?"

"If the Great Father says it is true, then it is so," Asmodeus said adamantly.

"I think it is a tale spun for lesser demons to help us maintain our mastery over them, but it is not for the likes of us. I do not remember a time before God created us."

"Perhaps that is a weakness in you?" Asmodeus scoffed.

"Possibly. Perhaps my eyes are still blinkered, but I think not. We were Lucifer's loyalist supporters in Heaven not because we believed his story of god's and the watery chaos, but because we desired more autonomy and power. Lucifer promised us these things, and we were content to follow him. Unfortunately, it did not work out the way we had hoped for, but we have made the best of what we had and have established vast kingdoms. This war could be disastrous for both of us."

"What? You fear losing that mountain of gold you keep warm under your arse?" Asmodeus laughed.

"No more than you fear losing all those succulent souls you torture in your Basilica of Pain," Mammon retorted, grinning. "Satan commanded that we make all souls available for conversion to our cause. It is fortunate he is not aware of the hoard you keep hidden for your pleasure."

The King of Demons scowled and imagined ripping Mammon's head from his shoulders, but he calmed his liver. Such an altercation outside Infernus would attract Satan's attention. Furthermore, he knew the archdemon of greed was not as puny as he looked. Although not a great warrior, he was a crafty fighter and had destroyed many angels during the Great Rebellion in Heaven.

"Are there any archdemons in Hell that have not placed spies in my basilica?" Asmodeus complained dryly, making a note to complete a greater purge when he returned to his domain.

Mammon laughed. "I have no spies in your court, Asmodai, but I know you as well as you know me. I assumed you had kept a few for yourself, and your answer has proved me right. But fear not. I shall not inform our master. Because, I too, kept a little in reserve."

"I only hold the most innocent souls that are useless for conversion," Asmodeus lied.

"Yes, of course you do—as do I," Mammon said with a conspiratorial wink.

"Then we are both innocent of any wrongdoing," Asmodeus replied with a cold grin. "What do you want?"

"This ill-advised adventure may cost us everything. What do you think God will do after he destroys our legions? He will take everything from us! He may even cast us back into the Lake of Fire!"

"We must believe in our master. He knows of things beyond our knowledge."

"But do you wish to live in Heaven again and have a new glorified body?"

"That accursed place holds no interest for me," Asmodeus admitted. "My kingdom is here and in that stinking cesspool called earth."

"All Satan thinks about is his revenge on God, and he will sacrifice every demon in Hell to achieve his goal," said Mammon.

"Why are you telling me this? Are you not afraid that I will inform our master about your traitorous and heretical remarks?"

"No," Mammon said slyly. "We more alike than you think."

"What do you mean? Stop speaking in riddles!"

Mammon glanced around him and then said in a low whisper, "I have travelled to the Lower Depths and sought the council of Babylon the Great. She told me I was not the first archdemon to ask if Satan could be usurped."

"She lies!" Asmodeus blustered.

Mammon smiled. "No. As you well know, *she* never lies. She told me I would become the second most powerful demon in Hell. She also revealed to me that Lilith's former lover would defeat Satan. It seems our fates our bound again."

"If, and I say *if*, any of what you say is true," Asmodeus replied cautiously, "then you would also know what she told Lilith's lover."

"She informed you it was inopportune to challenge Satan then–but she told me that circumstances have changed and now is the time to act."

Asmodeus narrowed his eyes and studied him. That was exactly what Babylon the Great had revealed to him. Mammon was speaking the truth. There is no other way he could have known this information. The King of Demons relaxed. He now had something incriminating on Mammon that he could use if his old comrade tried to betray him. He remained suspicious of archdemon's motives but was curious to hear what else he had to say.

"What do you propose?" he asked.

"We are the two most successful archdemons in Hell. Time and time again we have shown that the transgressions of lust and revenge and greed and wealth corrupt more human souls than any other sins. But what rewards do we receive? Satan offers us a few words of grudging appreciation and then continues to favour Moloch, Belial, Baal Zebub and Azazel."

"He has always favoured brawn over brains," Asmodeus grunted.

"And now he has chosen them to lead the legions into Purgatory. That is insulting to you, but it may play to our advantage. If they and Satan are soundly defeated, there could be significant changes in Hell. Neither of us is powerful enough to challenge the Evil One on our own, but together, and perhaps with the support of others–such as his own flesh and blood."

"You mean, Naamah?" Asmodeus exclaimed.

"Why do you think she has allowed you to court her and take part in your pathetic little hunt?"

"You conspire with her?"

"Let us just say that it would be in your interests to speak frankly with her. Let her know that you have spoken to me on this matter, and I am certain she will entertain your advances more favourably."

"Is that so?" murmured Asmodeus, licking his thick lips at the prospect. "Why did she not ask me herself?"

"She was uncertain of your reaction and asked me to broach the subject with you."

"And if I reported our conversation to Satan, she would deny any knowledge of the matter?"

"Exactly."

"Very cunning. Why does she wish to rebel against her own father?"

"Two reasons. Firstly, she hates him because he continues to spurn her advances. Secondly, and most importantly—she fears he may start End Times."

"That is preposterous!" the King of Demons laughed "Why would Satan do that? It would lead to our downfall!"

Mammon leaned closer and whispered, "She believes he has created the Antichrist."

"What?" Asmodeus exclaimed. "But then he is fulfilling the prophecy! It is only by *not* creating the Antichrist that we continue to exist and oppose the Great Tyrant's rule. Why would he do such a thing? It is madness!"

"It is insanity," said Mammon. "He knows what will happen but could not prevent himself from doing it. God was clever and knew Satan's nature. That is why He made the prophecy. He knew that Satan was vain and would eventually be tempted to do it."

"Ambushing the angels in Purgatory is one thing, but the Battle of Armageddon is quite another," Asmodeus growled. "There is no escaping our fate on Judgment Day. Why could he not leave well alone? Our existence is pleasurable and rewarding."

"My very thoughts."

Asmodeus sighed in frustration and then became pragmatic. "So Naamah would become empress?"

"Yes, but an empress would need a powerful emperor."

Asmodeus raised his eyebrows and nodded. "And what would *your* role be in such a new order?"

Mammon spread his arms. "I ask for very little. I am content in my kingdom—but if my empress commanded me to become Chancellor of Hell, I would be honour bound to obey her."

"For the good of Hell, of course," Asmodeus replied wryly.

Mammon grinned. "Yes, and to teach a lesson to some that scoffed at us for so long. They would learn that lust, revenge and greed are sins not to trifle with, but feared."

"That would be very satisfying," said Asmodeus, thinking of all the demons that had insulted, deceived or cheated him over the centuries.

"Extremely satisfying, my lord!" said Mammon, giving Asmodeus a little bow.

Asmodeus smiled and then frowned. "This is all very well, but I must find Lilith's Revenant first."

"Then do it swiftly. Time is of the essence."

"I will."

"Have confidence. Many archdemons will flock to your banner."

"You mean Lady Naamah's banner?"

"Of course!" Mammon said with a crafty smile. "A mere slip of the tongue. But after she becomes empress—who knows what may happen?"

Asmodeus grinned, his mind racing with thoughts of lust and power.

"Yes, who knows?"

"You will speak to her?"

Asmodeus glanced at Mammon before answering. He did not trust him as far as he could throw him, which was a considerable distance, but this talk of the Antichrist and End Times worried him. He needed to find out if the rumour was true.

"Yes," he said finally. "I will broach the subject with her."

They parted company on seemingly amicable terms and made their ways to their respective Hellmouths.

The King of Demons scowled and cursed as he squeezed his bulk into the gaping maw.

The archdemon of avarice was too clever, too damn clever by half.

When Asmodeus became emperor of Hell, Mammon's head would be the first to roll.

CHAPTER 13

After a few hours of dismal trudging, Longinus and the cambion entered a dark ravine. Looming on either side of them were steep cliffs with thousands of small holes in them. They reminded the centurion of boreholes, and he pondered on what had caused them.

"What is this place?" he asked Armilus.

The cambion glanced around nervously and said, "I have never passed this way before, but I have heard tell of it. This is the Valley of Moloch. We are in his domain."

Longinus could see that his guide was unsettled and wondered what place or demon could have such an effect on a messenger of Satan.

"Was not Moloch an ancient Phoenician god?"

"They worshiped him, but he was no god. He was an angel and follower of Satan. After the glorious rebellion against the Great Tyrant, he was cast down into Hell. He is Satan's champion."

As they proceeded cautiously, Longinus recalled what he had read in the *Book of Lilith* about Moloch. At one time, the Phoenicians, Carthaginians and even the Israelites had worshipped him. He had found it easy to deceive humans with his dark, angelic powers.

"Let your firstborn pass through the fire to Moloch, and he will grant your family wealth and good fortune!" his priests had told the people.

And so the Jews had taken their firstborns to Moloch's temple, which had lain in a small valley in Jerusalem called the Valley of the Son of Hinnom—or Gehenna. In the temple were large bronze idols with a man's body and the head of a bull. The arms of each statue were outstretched, and there was a large opening in the belly. The parents chanted as the priests placed the screaming infants onto the upturned arms and watched as the tiny bodies slid down into the raging fire that burned within the bowels of the beasts. And Moloch gloated over the hundreds of infants they had sacrificed to please his insatiable appetite for blood, pain and suffering.

The prophet Jeremiah prevented the human sacrifices for a time, but Moloch worship continued in secret. Even King Solomon had fallen into idolatry toward the end of his life. Unbeknown to the wisest of kings, Naamah had taken human form and became one of his most favoured wives. Under her evil influence, Solomon turned away from his God and built temples to Moloch and other demons posing as deities. The *Book of Lilith* said that Naamah did this to punish Solomon because he, with the aid of a ring given to him by Archangel Michael, had enslaved many demons to build the First Temple in Jerusalem.

Lilith had also taken human guise at that time and ruled a wealthy and thriving kingdom called Saba based in the nation now known as Yemen. All men of that age wrote and dreamed of her legendary sensuous beauty, and many lovesick youths announced prophetically that they would give their lives to spend but one night with the sultry and magnificent Queen of Sheba. It was a wish that Lilith was only too willing to grant them.

Lilith and Naamah were sisters by demonic affiliation rather than birth and competed fiercely for power and Satan's favour. Lilith travelled to Jerusalem to steal Solomon away from Naamah. She arrived with a caravan of camels laden with precious gifts and bewitched the king with her wealth and beauty. Lilith danced for him that night and seduced him. It is said that she bore him a son. The Ethiopians believed that this child became Menelik I, King of Axum, and founded the dynasty of the Empire of Ethiopia. However, many classical Rabbis disagreed with this theory and claimed that he was the ancestor of Nebuchadnezzar II, who destroyed Solomon's temple three hundred years later. They said that this was God's punishment for the idolatry practised by the Jews. A third version suggested in the *Book of Lilith* is that the child was not human, and the Queen of the Night took him to Hell. The blasphemous tome did not say what happened to him after that.

Regardless of the fate of the child, Lilith returned to Saba. Solomon begged her to remain, but she considered her mischievous work done. She had undermined Naamah's influence over the wisest king in the world and caused dissension in the royal household. Solomon's ardour for other women cooled after sleeping with the sultry and mysterious Queen of Sheba, and he would pine for her until the end of his days.

Lilith's unwarranted interference in her sphere of influence had enraged Naamah, but she well remembered the feminine artifice that Lilith had used to seduce Solomon and employed it herself many years later when she possessed the body of a young princess named Salome. Her dance was so sinuous and tantalising that her stepfather, King Herod, gave her the head of John the Baptist on a platter.

Longinus forced himself to cease reminiscing. He did not like to remember Lilith in such a way. He knew of her past and forgave her. If Love be blind, then he was the most sightless of all love-struck fools.

He frowned and cocked his head as he heard a baby cry. His acute vampire hearing could not locate the source of the sound. It kept moving. At first it seemed to come from one side and then the other. A myriad of other cries sounded, and soon the entire valley filled with shrill, unearthly wailing. Flames belched from the boreholes in the cliffs, and streams of small red shapes spewed from them.

"No!" screeched the cambion. "The children of Moloch!"

"What?" Longinus yelled to make him heard above the hideous mewling.

"The lost souls of the infants who passed through the fire to Moloch! Flee!"

Longinus glared around. The slopes on either side of them had turned crimson as thousands of tiny bodies swarmed towards them like waves of blood.

"I feel their terrible pain and rage," centurion," said Naram-Sin. "They want to make us suffer as they suffered."

The creatures opened their mouths and wailed as they moved, and Longinus could see their sharp little teeth. The screaming increased in pitch and was so deafening he thought his eardrums would burst. Although the children of Moloch were small, their numbers would engulf them.

Armilus scurried down the ravine ahead of him. Without a second thought, Longinus followed suit. However, unlike the cambion, he did not run out of fear; he fled out of pity. He had no desire to fight the souls of little children who had been burned alive to satiate the ego of a false and evil god.

As he dashed along the path, he saw two infants leap like fleas onto the cambion's back. Armilus screamed and tried to dislodge them as they bit into his flesh.

The air filled with tiny skinless bodies. Longinus ducked as one flew past his head. Five more landed on the path in front of him. He vaulted over them, narrowly evading their rapacious claws and gnashing teeth.

He caught up with the cambion and slapped the fiendish sucklings from his back. They hit the ground, scrabbling and squealing. Two more neonates launched themselves at him, and he swatted them off with his arm.

"Faster!" Longinus roared as he passed him.

Armilus' large left eye bulged out of its socket as he saw the flood of bodies closing in on them and fear lent wings to his heels. Longinus gaped as the cambion overtook him with an ungainly but swift leaping hobble and sped like a frenzied mountain goat down the path.

"Little bastard!" Longinus grunted, increasing his pace to keep up with him.

They ran at preternatural speed, jumping, twisting and dodging to escape from their diminutive but relentless attackers. Soon they were clear of the cliffs, and Longinus cast a quick look behind them. The infants had stopped at the end of the ravine. They clambered over each other; a mountain of heaving red bodies. Their forlorn screaming and mewling tortured his ears more than a multitude of sharp fingernails being drawn across hellish blackboards.

He stopped running and stood for a moment to gaze at the awful scene. He wiped his lips and noticed his hand was shaking.

The cambion returned to him and gawked fearfully at the valley. His face was more ashen than usual.

"We had better keep moving," Longinus said quietly.

Armilus glanced at him and nodded. He desired to put as much distance as he could between him and the voracious infants. They turned away from the gorge and walked in silence for a long time.

Longinus' heart was filled with a great sadness. The Valley of Moloch had affected him more than any other thing horror he had witnessed in this foul cesspit of depravity and suffering. He gripped his spear tighter, and his blue eyes became hooded and as hard as flint.

The denizens of Hell would pay in blood for this unholy outrage.

This, he promised himself.

CHAPTER XIV

The King of Demons returned to his dark fortress of misery and pain. Deep in thought, he floated through the long corridors and vast chambers. His servants bowed and shivered as he passed without acknowledging them. They felt relieved. Being ignored was good; being noticed meant something had displeased him, and they would suffer his vengeful wrath.

Fortunately for them, Asmodeus' mind was focused on more pressing matters. Satan's interest in the Revenant was most surprising and unwelcome. But what did his master really know?

Had the emperor discovered that Lilith, in a moment of idiotic weakness, had allowed the filthy emotion of love to enter her heart? Was he aware that he, Asmodeus, had enticed the demoness, Agrat Bat Mahlat, and Lilith's daughters to capture and slay Lilith? Did he know the Revenant, by some mysterious means, had destroyed Agrat Bat? Is it conceivable that his master now knew that Asmodeus had intended to eradicate Lilith and her Revenant, but Archangel Michael had arrived and forced him to choose only one of them?

The King of Demons narrowed his large red eyes. No. The emperor was not cognisant of these facts. If he were, Asmodeus would not be free to agonise over them; he would be languishing in the dungeons of Hell and suffering incalculable torments at the hands of the imperial inquisitors.

One thing was clear: Satan must never interrogate Longinus. The Revenant knew too much. But he needed to hasten. There was a danger that another archdemon could apprehend the insect by accident and deliver him to Satan. And that would be very unfortunate. No! He must find and eliminate the worm before anyone else caught him.

But Asmodeus could not kill him. He would be disobeying a direct command from his master, and that was too risky. If Satan found out, he could lose everything.

He must find another to hunt the insect; one who would kill him without trying to obtain information from him. But to whom could he entrust this important task? He wracked his brains. He needed someone he could manipulate, who would remain silent on the matter, and who had as much to lose as he did.

A slow grin spread over his enormous face. He knew whom he could use. They were perfect for the quest and hated the Revenant even more than he did!

His scheming was interrupted when as his Groom of the Stool appeared, wringing his claws. Asmodeus could tell by his stupid expression that something was amiss.

"Speak!" he said wearily.

Surgat whined and gibbered in demonspeak for over a minute. From what Asmodeus could gather, Naamah had returned to his basilica in a vile temper, scourged every lesser demon that had crossed her path, and swallowed five of his prettiest female souls.

"Where is she now?" he demanded, angrily.

The groom of the royal backside gabbled on for another minute, and then with a final screech, pointed a claw nail toward Asmodeus' sanctum sanctorum.

"You allowed her to enter my private chamber?" he bellowed.

Surgat fell to his knees and grovelled under his master's baleful stare. Asmodeus raised a claw to strike him but stopped himself. He knew there was little that his groom could have done to stop Naamah's rampage. However, that was no excuse. He did not have time to punish him now and would scourge him later.

"Get out my sight!" he growled.

Wailing in despair, the tender of the rear passage crawled along the corridor and vanished around a corner.

Gritting his pointed teeth, Asmodeus sped to his inner sanctum, his unholiest of unholies. The imperious strumpet had gone too far. He had told her to wait in his basilica—not tear it apart! He had had enough of her tiresome affectations. She may be Satan's daughter, but she was still only a female, and he intended to teach her a harsh lesson. He would thrash her until she squealed for mercy and then ravish her in the most depraved and violent ways.

He smashed the heavy doors of his sanctum open, barbed claws at the ready, and glared around the chamber. His jaw dropped, and he frowned. Naamah was sitting on his colossal throne of throbbing flesh and reading one of the blasphemous tomes from his bookshelves. She seemed totally unconcerned by his dramatic entrance.

"Were you aware that some Scottish witches had the power to stop sea storms?" she murmured without looking up.

"What?" he growled.

"They could halt storms. My father was more generous in bygone days. He never gives such powers to his modern worshippers. I think he learned that such capabilities went to his devotees heads, and they invariably ended up being burned at the stake. Less power and more obedience is better. Do you not agree?"

"I care not a gnat's arse hair about Celtic crones who passed their time by rubbing their shrivelled clits against broomsticks!" he roared. "What right have you to punish my servants and invade my sanctum? An archdemon's sanctum is sacrosanct!"

Naamah looked up and gazed around the chamber. "You disappoint me."

"Oh? How so, pray tell?"

"A throne of old bones, a pentacle, some shelves of books, and two locks of hair in a crystal casket? I thought your sanctum would be impressive."

"It is enough for my needs!" Asmodeus replied angrily.

"The red tress was Lilith's, I assume? But to whom, I wonder, did the black lock belong? It seems ancient."

"That is none of your business. I ask you again, why have you invaded my privacy?"

Naamah closed the book and arose.

"The creatures in the sand pits? Were they part of the trap you hinted at before leaving for Infernus?"

"They were! Why?" he asked, failing to grasp the relevance of her question.

"You will have to create more."

"How so?"

"Because I destroyed them—every last one of them."

"What?" Asmodeus roared. "You have gone too far! Do you know what pains I took to make them?"

"Pains?" Naamah retorted. "What pains? You created the foul things in bubbling cauldrons using sorcery. My hounds were my offspring. I gave birth to them and that is true pain."

"You did not have to destroy them!"

"They tore my nehushtan apart and consumed them!" she shrieked.

"I will teach you the meaning of true pain!" Asmodeus growled, advancing on her.

Naamah's eyes blazed with Hellfire, and her raven locks transformed into writhing serpents. She rose to her full height and glared down upon him. Asmodeus halted and gawked. Her serpentine hair, wide mouth, flaring nostrils, tusks and projecting teeth reminded him of the gorgons of Greek myths, and he felt a very unpleasant sensation in his phalluses. Her body emanated an unearthly crimson glow, and he could feel her awesome power. She was indeed her father's daughter, and that bode ill for any archdemon who attempted to vex or harm her.

Asmodeus relaxed his claws and drifted back a few paces. He had intended to punish her—not fight to the death. He did not fear her, but in his incandescent rage had forgotten his principal objectives: kill Longinus and discover if there was any truth to Mammon's claim about Naamah's treason and the existence of the Antichrist. Although he still desired to chastise her, he realised that violence may not be his wisest course of action. That would remain an option later, when she least expected it. She was powerful, and he would have to plan his revenge carefully to limit damage to himself. In the meantime, he would swallow his pride and pretend she intimidated him.

"Apologies," he sighed. "I should have informed you where the trap lay before I left for the Gathering. In my haste to obey your father's command, I forgot."

She glared at him for a moment and then transformed back into her usual form. He watched in fascination as the snakes, tusks, and oversize teeth receded into her skull.

"Very well. I accept your excuse, but never approach me in that manner again. I will not be so forgiving a second time."

"Imperious sow! I will make thee scream, squeal, and bleed!" he thought, feigning his very best expression of penitence. It had always worked on mortal women when he was in the guise of a man and had sometimes even pacified Lilith after he had angered her—or so she had led him to believe.

"So—my father has ordered an attack on Purgatory?"

"How did you know?"

"I hear of everything that happens in the Abyss. It is one of few advantages of being Satan's daughter."

"He told you of his plans?"

"Of course, not!" she laughed mockingly. "My father would never reveal such secrets to me. I have my own ways of finding out."

"Spies?" asked Asmodeus.

Naamah smiled thinly but would not elaborate.

Asmodeus shrugged. "Informers lurk everywhere in Hell these days. Since Lilith's defection, your father sees traitors and defectors in every shadow. It is whispered that the dungeons of Hell are overflowing with the accused. Have you ever seen the dungeons?"

"No. My father allows no one to visit there without his permission. But I am glad I have never seen the inside of those abominable cells: those that enter never return."

"True," Asmodeus replied gloomily.

She gave him a puzzled look. "Why do you appear so crestfallen? I thought you would rejoice at being chosen to lead my father's legions against the angels?"

Asmodeus glanced at her and hissed, "I am not commanding the army! Your father has given that honour to Moloch."

"That brute?" she exclaimed. "He has neither the intelligence nor acumen to lead Hell's legions."

"Tell that to your father."

"Then what role has he given you in the forthcoming battle?"

"None."

"What do you mean? You are his greatest general!"

"I am not taking part in the battle. Your father has commanded me to recapture the Revenant and take him to Infernus."

"But what interest could he have in so inconsequential a creature?"

"I know not," Asmodeus replied evasively. "I assume you did not catch him?"

"No. He escaped from my azag, dived into the Styx, and reached the far shore. I wished dearly to pursue him but thought it unwise to enter Leviathan's domain."

Asmodeus grunted. 'Unwise' was an understatement. Leviathan, the great chaos monster and Satan's ally, could swallow a thousand legions and tolerated no trespassers in his kingdom. However, he unwittingly did an excellent job in protecting the river border of Asmodeus' domain, and for that the King of Demons was grateful.

"I cannot understand why my father seeks Lilith's slave," she murmured.

"Perhaps he believes the Revenant may know why she defected."

Naamah stared at him for a moment. "Could he implicate you?"

"What do you mean?"

"Could he accuse you of being responsible for Lilith's defection?"

"No!" Asmodeus blustered.

"Were you?"

"Of course, not!"

"Even if you are entirely blameless in the matter," Naamah continued, eyeing him shrewdly, "the worm could lie and implicate you. You know my father's current state of mind. You have said it yourself–he sees traitors everywhere."

"Very true. The Revenant will say anything to save his own hide. I will find him and crush him like a Hellbug."

"That would be unwise. My father may suspect you were trying to cover up something. Be subtle and let another do your dirty work."

Asmodeus had already decided whom to use for the task, but it intrigued him to discover if she had alternative suggestions.

"Easier said than done. Who can one trust in this rancid quagmire of treachery?" he bemoaned.

"I shall do it," she hissed, clenching her fist. "I crave to make him suffer for the deaths of my nehushtan and azag. I will inform my father I did not know that he sought to interrogate the Revenant. It will enrage him, but he will accept my explanation."

Asmodeus grimaced. The last thing he desired was Naamah sniffing around in his affairs. He needed to put her serpentine nose off the scent.

"I of all demons understand your desire for revenge, but it is too risky. Your father knows we were hunting the Revenant and will suspect both of us. I have someone else in mind for the task."

"And how, pray tell, does my father know that I had joined your hunt?" she retorted, glaring at him.

"I told him," Asmodeus answered, frowning.

"You told him!" she exclaimed.

"Yes."

"Where?"

"At the Gathering."

She looked even more peeved.

"So now my father and every archdemon in Hell thinks you have had me!"

"I never thought of it that way," Asmodeus replied innocently, suppressing a smile.

"Yes, I am certain it never crossed your mind to boast of yet another conquest!"

"What does it matter who knows and what they think?" he said.

"My father is—very protective of me."

"I could tell. I think that was the reason he gave command of the armies to Moloch."

For an instant, he saw her cheeks flush and a glint of pleasure in her eyes. It was then he knew that no matter what he said or did, he would never surpass or even match her father in her estimation. But he could accept that. Such unnatural bonds were firmly within his area of influence, and he was quite happy to gobble up any crumbs that fell from the imperial bassinet. If she needed another father figure, it would delight him to provide her with one. Once he discovered the key words in her incestuous ditty, he could make her warble to his tune all night.

"Whom shall you enlist to destroy the Revenant?" she asked, tersely.

"It is better if you do not know."

"Very well. On your own head be it. But promise me he will suffer the most agonising of deaths."

"Oh, he will, my lady. Of that, I can assure you."

"Good! That pleases me," she growled.

But it did not please her, and she was determined to find the Revenant herself. No one slighted Satan's daughter and survived to tell the tale. Her azag had been a gift from her father, but her nehushtan, along with other monstrosities, had been the direct product of their incestuous union. They had been her pets for millennia, and she had treasured them. Her nehushtan and azag had been symbols of her power and status in the Abyss. She would lose face if other demons discovered she had not crushed the insignificant worm that had caused the destruction of her familiars.

She could breed more giant snakes easily, but her hounds were quite another matter. As her father no longer favoured her charms, she would have to allow an archdemon to mount her. Asmodeus was the most obvious choice, but as his part in this affair still angered her, and she desired to keep him slavering at the leash for as long as possible, she would call upon another archfiend to fill her womb to bursting. Unfortunately, her new nehushtan would be less powerful than her satanic originals, but in all other respects would serve to maintain her authority. And as for the Revenant! She would make that insolent homunculus squirm and suffer in ways that neither Asmodeus nor his mysterious assassin could even begin to imagine!

"I spoke to Mammon at the Gathering," Asmodeus said casually, seeking to distract her from thoughts of lusty fathers, irritating revenants, and onto more intriguing topics.

"Oh?" she replied with apparent disinterest.

"Yes, we had a very interesting conversation, and he suggested I should make you aware of it."

"What did you discuss?" she said, running a hand through her hair in the way that inflamed him.

"Oh, this and that—although he did mention the Lower Depths," he ventured cautiously, testing the waters. He was still unsure whether Mammon had been truthful and did not want to be the first to mention treason.

"The Lower Depths? What did he say?"

"He said—the signs are propitious for a king and queen to join," he murmured ambiguously.

"How did that make you feel?"

"Very pleased, very pleased indeed."

"A complete union?"

"Body and soul."

"If you betray me, I shall deny everything."

"Of course."

"My father believes me above all others."

Asmodeus laughed. "I know that for a fact, but fear not, I will not betray you. Our fates are joined no matter which way the Hell winds blow. We rise or fall together. But how shall we begin our rise?"

Naamah studied him for a moment and then included him in her grand design.

"My father's attention is focused on the impending battle. He will travel to Purgatory and strike when the angels least expect it. That means he will leave Infernus with naught but a token guard."

"And?"

"If we direct our forces to the infernal capital, we can capture and hold it!"

"What forces? Your father has given my incubi legions to Moloch."

"I, Mammon, and the other archdemons who oppose the war have sufficient legions for the task."

"Then why do you need me?"

"Because you are the King of Demons and many will flock to your banner."

"And you wish us to crown you as the empress of Hell?"

"Yes, but the Abyss will have a new empress and emperor. I wish you to rule with me. Together we will garner enough support to annihilate my father's legions."

Asmodeus looked doubtful. "I sought the advice of a being who can scry the future, and she made it clear to me that a rebellion against your father would fail."

Naamah smiled. "Babylon the Great?"

"You know of her?"

"I not only know of her, but consulted her! She told me that the time was right if I consorted with Lilith's lover. You were Lilith's lover, and if we act together, we will succeed."

"That is all well and good, but what happens when your father returns from Purgatory? He may win or he may lose the battle, but one thing is certain—he will return. What do we do then? We are not powerful enough to defeat the Great Dragon. He will tear us apart and consume us."

"My father's power will be weakened if the angelic scum defeat him."

"How so?"

"He garners power from two sources—the evil emanating from mankind and the faith of the Fallen. If sufficient archdemons lose faith in him, it will diminish his power considerably."

"Enough for us to defeat him?" Asmodeus asked, doubtfully.

"No. We will employ another to do that."

"Which other?"

"Pazuzu."

"You cannot be serious!" Asmodeus exclaimed.

"Why not? He and the Elder demons already wage war against my father."

"But Pazuzu hates all Hell demons. After he defeated your father, he would turn against us."

"Not necessarily. There is one that can protect us from Pazuzu—one who is invulnerable to his attacks."

"Who?"

"Lamashtu."

"That ancient hag? She is worse than Pazuzu. We cannot control her!"

"We need not control her. The ancient gods created Pazuzu to thwart Lamashtu. She hates him above all others but cannot destroy him. If freed, she will pursue and fight him for eternity. Fate bound them together in an endless cycle of hatred. Love and hate are comparable emotions and come within our sphere of influence."

"Hate, I understand, but how can you even consider—the other—part of our remit?"

"You disappoint me, Asmodeus. You of all demons should know that love often transforms into hatred. Mortals are prone to detest former lovers that spurned or abandoned them. Therefore, as demons we should encourage humans to love, because Love is ephemeral, transient, and invariably results in hatred or loathing. When I am empress, we shall exploit this human weakness to our benefit and fill our pits with even more souls."

Asmodeus scowled. This heretical talk of the unmentionable emotion brought back disturbing memories he preferred to keep repressed.

"So you reason if you free this cadaverous hag she and Pazuzu will be too preoccupied to attack us?"

"Just so. But we will not release Lamashtu until Pazuzu has defeated my father."

"And what do we do with him then?"

"Why, banish him to the Lower Depths, of course," Naamah replied, grinning.

"Why do you wish to usurp your father?" Asmodeus asked. "I thought you craved his attention and lustful advances?"

"Who told you that?" she retorted angrily.

"It is common knowledge."

"Then they are fools! Once I did, but no longer. He used and discarded me as he does all his conquests. Now I just seek his destruction."

Asmodeus did not fully believe her, but put the matter aside for the moment.

"How do I know that you will not plot my destruction once you are empress?"

"Why should I? You were loyal to Lilith and stayed with her for millennia. In Hell, that is very unusual."

"I gave her everything she desired, and yet she still betrayed me," Asmodeus bemoaned.

"Then have no fear. You will find me an entirely different consort. If you are loyal to me, I shall be loyal to you. Of course, you may have as many dalliances as you wish with other females. That is your nature, and I would not seek to change it. But I shall never betray you."

"I believe you," he said.

But he did not. Naamah would be a much harder taskmaster than Lilith had ever been, and her smooth talk of permitting him boundless frisky romps did not fool him in the slightest. She was jealous, scheming and spiteful. Her venomous relationship with her father revealed her true nature.

Although he now hated Lilith with all his heart, he had to admit that she had given him as much leeway as he desired. She had never complained about his constant coupling with other females and had asked for nothing. And when he had summoned her, she had appeared and satisfied his every deviant desire without hesitation or complaint.

Part of him now regretted usurping her. If he had turned a blind eye to her infatuation with her Revenant, things could have been much simpler and continued as they had always had.

However, Naamah was a completely different kettle of rotten fish. He would have to watch his back all the time, waiting for her to strike like a coiled viper. But that worried him not. He would strike first. That was *his* nature. However, he then recalled something that very much worried him.

"Has your father created the Antichrist?"

"He has."

"Did he tell you?"

"No."

"Then how do you know?"

Naamah looked uneasy. "Once upon leaving my father's inner sanctum, I chanced upon a being that I had never seen before. I demanded to know his name, but he refused to answer and just grinned at me. I made to strike his face, but he caught my wrist in an iron grip and stayed my hand. I felt his power, Asmodeus, and it frightened me."

The King of Demons raised an eyebrow. He could not imagine Naamah being afraid of anything, but let her dubious assertion pass unchallenged.

"What happened then?" he asked.

"He stared into my eyes for a moment and I saw the fires of Hell burn in them. He released me, bowed, and sauntered off as if nothing had happened. It was then, I knew without a shadow of a doubt that I had inadvertently met the Antichrist."

"What was his appearance?"

"An angel."

"An angel?" Asmodeus exclaimed.

"Tall, dark, beautiful, with feathered wings of ebony."

"The Angel of Death," Asmodeus muttered.

"Aye, and he will be the death of us all if we do not stop my father. Well, Asmodeus, are you ready to fight to become the new emperor of Hell?"

The King of Demons considered her offer and thought it worth the risk. If things went awry, he could always tell Satan that he had joined the plot to discover the names of the conspirators and their plan. Naamah thought she was unassailable because she was Satan's daughter. But she was Hellborn, and there was one factor she did not and could never comprehend–divine loyalty. Asmodeus had been her father's closest friend in Heaven and had fought alongside him during the Great Rebellion. They were part of the Fallen, and loyalty to their unholy order would always supersede mere flesh and blood. When it came to the executioner's block, Satan would always believe him over her–or so he chose to believe. With that comforting thought in mind, he agreed to her pact.

"I am, my lady. Let the great game commence."

"Excellent! I will leave you to set in motion your plan for destroying the Revenant. And remember, instruct your mysterious assassin to make him suffer."

"He will die the most excruciatingly painful death ever seen in Hell," Asmodeus growled.

CHAPTER XV

With the Valley of Moloch far behind them, Longinus and Armilus arrived at the foot of a high mountain. The cambion showed little enthusiasm for climbing, but as that was their only way forward–and after some gentle persuasion to his backside from the toe of Longinus' sandal–he relented and swore to make the best of it.

The centurion slung his spear on his back, transformed his hands into claws, and climbed after the half-demon. It was slow, perilous work, and occasional gusts of sweltry wind threatened to pry them loose. As the cambion had only one good claw, Longinus assisted him during the ascent. When they were about halfway up, a rock came loose and Armilus slid down over a ledge. Longinus grabbed the cambion's stump and was well nigh wrenched from the mountain for his trouble. Fortunately, the centurion had his right claw wedged into a crack and held fast until his screaming guide found new holds.

"Thank you!" the cambion gasped.

Longinus scowled and grunted. It amazed him how much the little runt weighed. His arms felt as if they had been wrenched from their sockets.

After a few tortuous hours, they dragged themselves up the final scree slope and stood like exhausted but victorious climbers on the wind-swept summit. Below them, stretching into the distance, was a plain of volcanic black rock, orange lava flows and towering columns of basalt.

They worked their way down. The leeward side of the mountain was less steep, and they could descend the jagged incline with little difficulty. Near the bottom, they reached a small plateau and started as they heard a terrible, piercing scream. They crawled forward and peered over the edge. Armilus groaned with fear and Longinus gaped in disbelief.

A gigantic horned figure sat in a gorge a hundred feet below them. Its limbs were as thick as oaks and its misshapen skull larger than two oxen. The single eye in the centre of his forehead gleamed with a red malevolence. Longinus calculated the demonic colossus was some twenty feet in height, and the top of his head would only reach the lower part of its knees.

The monstrosity sat before a large fire and hanging over the hungry flames was a large pot that bubbled and spat forth a vile reddish liquid. In its enormous claws, it held a twitching succubus, skewered from anus to mouth on a spit. Longinus now knew what had uttered the unearthly scream.

Behind the cyclopean was a metal cage containing another succubus. She had a pale, pretty countenance and shoulder-length raven hair. Two curved ebony horns protruded from her forehead, and a long red tail complimented her rear. Her black wings lay folded behind her naked body.

Longinus gazed at the succubus for a moment and then back at the giant. "What manner of demon is that?"

"It one of the Nephilim," Armilus whispered. "This is their domain. They are very territorial and destroy any trespassers. Come, we must skirt around this monster so it does not see us. To invite its wrath is certain death."

Longinus raised an eyebrow. "And the female?"

The cambion gave a snort of derision. "She is naught but a succubus: a lying, mischievous creature like all of her kind. Do not concern yourself with her. We must leave her to her fate and move on."

"And what fate is that?" asked Longinus.

"Why, to provide sustenance for the giant, of course! These Nephilim consume anything they catch. They are cannibals and very partial to demon flesh."

"These Nephilim are the abominations spawned by human women after they mated with fallen angels?" asked Longinus.

"Yes. Long after the fall of the Garden of Eden, mankind populated the earth. Satan and the other archdemons consorted with earthly women and gave them forbidden knowledge in exchange for carnal pleasures. From these demonic couplings, the Nephilim were born. As you can well observe, they grew to a prodigious size.

"At first, the Nephilim were content to hunt and consume the wild animals of the earth, but they grew lazy and compelled humans to provide them with livestock to eat. After a while, there was no livestock left, and the Nephilim devoured humans and each other.

"It is said the Great Tyrant was so angered by the Nephilim—or 'demons' as He called them—and wickedness of mankind that He sent a great deluge to destroy all life on earth. And thus the human sinners and the Nephilim died and their souls sent to Hell."

"But He did not destroy all life," said Longinus. "He commanded one man to build an ark so he could escape the flood."

"Yes, legends tell that one human and his family escaped the flood. They say he also took two animals of every kind upon the earth into the ark. Do you know why he only took two?"

"No."

"Because the Nephilim devoured everything else!" Armilus said pointedly.

"Do you believe the story?" asked Longinus.

"No! It is preposterous. How could such a small vessel contain so many? But I do believe the Nephilim consumed everything in their path. Look at that monstrosity and tell me you doubt my word. We must leave this place!"

Longinus smiled at Armilus' incredulity. They were in Hell, travelling through inter-dimensional portals, trying to escape from Satan and Asmodeus, and yet the cambion still believed that some things were impossible. It seemed to Longinus that any god powerful enough to create the universe would have little trouble in filling an ark–nay, even a thimble– with a multitude of animals if He so desired.

He glanced at the pot. As the giant stirred it with the haft of its battleaxe, the centurion could see parts of limbs and heads appearing and disappearing in the thick, viscous mixture. He looked back at the succubus and felt pity for her. Of course, he well knew she was a temptress, an evil thing that preyed on men as they slept; however, to his mind, there were worse demons than her kind in Hell. Seducing men and stealing their seed seemed a rather minor indiscretion compared to the abominable evils perpetrated by other archfiends. In any case, he had never seen men lining up to complain about being abused by succubi. He suspected most of them thought the encounter had been an erotic dream and awoke with contented smiles on their faces. Lilith's sultry vixens went about their work in a commendably scrupulous manner and left not a drop of incriminating evidence behind them: which is more than could be said for Asmodeus' disgusting incubi.

As Longinus stared at the fetching prisoner, the adventurous little devil within him reared its head.

"What is the singular of Nephilim," he asked.

"Eh?"

"What is the singular form? What do you call one of these giants–a Nephil, Nephus?"

Armilus snorted at the Revenant's ignorance. "No! In Hell, the word Nephilim can mean one or many."

"Good," Longinus replied nonchalantly. "Then keep your eyes on yonder Nephilim and shout and wave your arms to distract it if it turns in my direction."

The cambion gaped in horror as Longinus climbed down into the gorge.

"What are you doing?" he whispered hysterically. "It will tear you apart!"

Longinus looked over his shoulder and grinned. "If it catches me."

Armilus stared in disbelief as Longinus crawled headfirst like a lizard down the rocky slope. Every so often, he paused and glanced at the giant to ensure that it had not seen him.

The cambion gripped his head in his hands and rocked backwards and forwards.

"No! No! The stupid creature is mad! This will not end well for us!" he moaned.

On reaching the bottom of the gorge, Longinus removed the spear from his back and crept towards the cage. The Nephilim sat with its back to him, and he could see its muscles rippling as it stirred the pot. For a fleeting moment, the centurion regretted the folly of his action. The succubus meant nothing to him, and he could have abandoned her to her fate. His primary aim was to escape from Hell and save Rachel. This diversion was an act of lunacy, but such insanity was part of his nature. He could never resist a challenge—or a pretty face—when dangled in front of his eyes.

The succubus noticed him and started in surprise. Longinus gave her a stern look and put a finger to his lips, warning her to keep silent. He was uncertain whether she would understand his human gesture. Fortunately, she did, and nodded grimly in reply.

Keeping his eyes on the back of the giant, he moved to the front of the cage and pulled the large metal bolt back very slowly to make as little noise as possible. Everything went well until the bolt reached the last six inches of its length—then it emitted a high-pitched grating sound. Longinus froze as the Nephilim ceased stirring the pot and cocked its mammoth head to one side. However, after a few worrying seconds, it shrugged its shoulders and started stirring again.

Longinus lay down his spear and used both hands to coax the last few inches of the bolt silently from the hasp. He opened the door to the cage gingerly and gestured to the demoness to escape. A look of terror appeared on her face. Longinus spun around and an enormous pair of hairy legs confronted him. Glancing up, he saw the glint of a massive axe head. He dived to the left. The gargantuan blade narrowly missed him and sliced several feet into the ground.

The giant uttered a deafening roar and glared down at him. It pulled the axe head free and lifted it to strike again. Longinus reached out and grabbed his spear. The axe blade flashed, and he rolled to one side as it struck the ground beside him like thunder. He sprang to his feet and ran. The Nephilim raised its massive foot and tried to stomp on him, but the centurion was too nimble for the ponderous Goliath. He sprinted to the fire and turned to face his monstrous opponent.

The Nephilim trundled after him and swiped the axe at Longinus' head. The centurion ducked under the scything blade and kicked over the pot. Scalding liquid spilled over the cyclops' toes. Roaring in pain, the giant kicked the pot. Longinus dived out of the way as the heavy cauldron flew past him and bounced along the gorge floor with a series of resounding clangs.

The Nephilim charged with a surprising burst of speed and swung the axe down at him. Longinus raised the spear above his head to block the deadly blow. The axe blade struck the spear with a shower of sparks, and the centurion's feet sank an inch into the ground with the force of the awful impact. A burst of blinding pain shot through his body as every joint and muscle screamed in protest. His shoulders felt dislocated, his spine crushed. He grunted and tried to clear his vision.

The giant retracted the axe and swung it at the centurion's unprotected chest. Through the shock and pain, his long years of practice and battle experience saved him. His muscle memory responded to the threat, and he shifted the spear into a vertical position to cover his right side. He blocked the savage attack, but the force of the blow sent him flying, and he landed on his back some twenty feet away. For a moment, he felt dazed, but he gritted his teeth, shook his head and regained his senses. He emitted a throaty growl as a surge of rage flowed through his body.

Springing to his feet, he roared in defiance. The Nephilim's attack had caught him on the back foot and put him on the defensive. But now he had the measure of his towering opponent and went on the offensive. There was only one thought burning like red-hot iron in his mind: make it suffer—and in the worse way. As the giant charged again, he raced towards it and rolled under its legs. The Nephilim looked surprised. No prey had ever run *at it* before; everything ran away.

Longinus sprang to his feet and threw his spear. It struck deep into the Nephilim's neck–to no effect. Like Leviathan, the demon was too large for the spear to consume quickly. He knew he had to find a vulnerable part of the demon's body. Cursing, he transformed his hands into claws. Before the giant could turn around, he jumped onto its leg and started climbing. The Nephilim roared and tried to shake him off, but Longinus dug his claws deep into its flesh and held on for grim death. As he reached its back, the giant dropped the axe and reached behind it, trying to grab Longinus and crush him. It spun around, trying to dislodge him, but the centurion grabbed its long, dirty hair and heaved himself onto its shoulders. It tried to swat him with its claw, but Longinus dropped, hung by its thatch until it had stopped, and then pulled himself up again. Holding onto the Nephilim's head with one claw, he tore the spear free and stood on the giant's shoulders. The colossus stopped rotating and reached up. As its enormous claws sped towards him, Longinus raised the spear above his head, uttered a terrible battle roar, and plunged the weapon deep into the Nephilim's thick skull.

The cyclops froze, its lethal claws mere inches from the centurion's body. Longinus felt the spear vibrating and power surging up his arms. The Nephilim howled as its vast frame withered, and Longinus jumped from its shoulders as it collapsed onto its knees. He stood watching impassively as the Nephilim gave a final groan, fell forward, and buried its face in the fire; a hollow husk of the colossus it once had been.

He walked around the bonfire and wrenched the spear from its head.

"You have served me well again, old friend," he said, wiping dark brain tissue from the shaft.

Longinus looked over at the cage. The raven-haired beauty had vanished.

"Not even a farewell? Parting is such sweet sorrow," he muttered wryly.

Longinus started as the ground trembled beneath his feet and deafening roars filled the air. He spun around and saw a score of Nephilim thundering towards him. Their enormous figures blocked the exit from the gorge. They had heard the death knell of their fallen kin and were eager to avenge its death.

He glanced at the surrounding cliffs and knew there was no time to reach them and climb out of harm's way. The bellicose giants would pluck him from the rock face and squash him like a fly. He stuck his spear in the ground and wrenched the shield from his back. Thrusting his arm through the leather straps, he whispered the words of ancient Spartan mothers to their sons: "With shield or on it."

It meant they considered it dishonourable for a warrior to return to Sparta without his shield. A Spartan could only come home victorious, bearing his shield, or with his dead body carried upon it.

Longinus grabbed his spear and adopted a defensive stance. As the fearsome giants drew closer, he knew that this would be his last battle.

"Death and glory!" he whispered to Naram-Sin.

"Death and glory, centurion!" Naram-Sin cried proudly.

Something bumped against his back. Before he had time to react, two pale, slender arms wrapped around his waist and lifted him into the air. Glancing over his shoulder, he saw black wings and knew it had to be the succubus. He looked back, and his eyes widened in alarm. They were flying straight at the furious, gargantuan horde.

The demoness was going to drop him at the feet of the Nephilim!

CHAPTER XVI

The Stygian cavern was over a mile wide and half as much in height. A lake of molten lava churned at its base and arising from the belching smoke and flames was a lofty pillar of dark basalt. Atop the immense pinnacle lay an ominous, domed, circular temple supported by dozens of thick buttresses and obsidian columns. The circumference of gloomy interior boasted twelve enormous statues, arranged like the hour marks on an earthly timepiece, of malevolent creatures with bat-like wings and fearsome claws.

No demonic legions guarded this dread and unhallowed place; none were needed. This sanctuary was under Asmodeus' protection, and although many archdemons drooled at the thought of the sensual delights that lay hidden within, they were unwilling to incur his wrath. Even in Hell, some sinful pleasures bore too high a price and were best left to depraved imaginings.

In the centre of the temple, twelve stone thrones stood in a circle. Three were empty, but nine ravishingly beautiful women occupied the others. Luxuriant curls of bewitching hues tumbled around slim waists, and diaphanous, silken black robes gave tantalising glimpses of voluptuous charms. Any mortal man beholding these exquisite creatures would gasp and believe he had entered his own personal paradise, but that delightful first impression would soon crack and shatter. On closer inspection, he would notice their pointed ears, abnormally long nails, and cold predatory eyes. His knees would tremble as he felt their cruel and malevolent presence and realise to his alarm that these most alluring visions of pulchritude were not menial playthings employed to purr, pander and satisfy any man's selfish desires–but powerful and voracious dispensers of death. For they were the Lilitu, Lilith's daughters, her handmaidens of destruction.

At the peak of their standing in the Abyss, they had numbered twelve, but now they were nine. Agrat Bat Mahlat had slain Eldora, their eldest sister, because she had refused to betray her mother, and Longinus had destroyed their youngest siblings, Miriam and Marika, in Purgatory.

Under their mother's rule, they had been princesses of the Abyss, but they had become greedy, dissatisfied, and desired more. Agrat Bat Mahlat had promised them when she slew Lilith and became Queen of the Night, she would grant them greater power and their own dominions in Hell. But now Agrat Bat was dead, and without their mother to protect them, Asmodeus had moved swiftly and made them his concubines.

Each night, he commanded them to attend him in his basilica, and they complied to his demands with much wailing and gnashing of teeth. To couple with the King of Demons was a lesson in extreme pain and degradation. He had split in twain or torn apart lesser female demons in the ultimate throes of his demonic ecstasy. However, fortunately—or unfortunately, depending on one's view on being the recipient of savage ravishing—the Lilitu were more resilient and could survive his cruel advances, but, even so, they found the shame of their new demeaning roles much harder to bear.

It was only now they fully realised the immense power, prowess, and strength of their mother. Even working together feverishly and incessantly, they struggled to slake Asmodeus' prodigious lust, while Lilith had been more than capable of satisfying his every desire on her own.

And yea, their mother had warned them. She had cautioned her offspring not to betray her and side with Agrat Bat. She had begged them to reconsider, saying that it was only her power that protected them from the lust of Asmodeus. But true to their ruthless and haughty natures, they had gleefully ignored her heartfelt and prophetic admonitions.

And so, by some sublime retribution of Fate, they spent their abysmal time bickering about whom or what was to blame for their downfall and bemoaning their outcast state. For it would never occur to any of them, even now, that they were the scheming progenitors of their suffering.

"The Revenant deceived our mother and turned him against us!" screamed Sarai.

"She thought she loved him," Rebekna said angrily. "But a demon cannot feel love. He bewitched her!"

"And she has betrayed us again by accepting the Great Tyrant's salvation," moaned Oholibamah. "How is such a thing possible? It is beyond belief. The Tyrant does not forgive demons."

"Our mother's treachery has ruined us," screeched Bilhah.

"Asmodeus promised he would make us queens of Hell! We never should have trusted him," growled Leah.

"Nor Agrat Bat Mahlat," added Shelomith. "She promised us castles of gold but deceived us. It is her fault."

"Once we were princesses, but now we are reduced to being Asmodeus' harlots," hissed Leah.

Nashiram, the eldest of the nine, called a halt to their infernal bickering.

"Enough! What good is there in sitting here and complaining? We chose sides and lost. Now we must suffer the consequences! But never forget that things were perfect in our realm until our mother created her last Revenant. He is to blame for all that has happened. No one else but him!"

"Our sister speaks the truth!" hissed Basemath.

"The Revenant is the cause of all our woes!" agreed Baileet.

"If only I could sink my claws into his flesh!" Sarai growled, clenching her fist.

"If only I could sink my fangs into his throat!" Bilhah spat.

"Asmodeus rips him apart each night. That provides us with some solace," said Nashiram.

"But he will not let us touch him! Even a little!" complained Rebekna.

"He fears what we would do to his little plaything," Shelomith laughed coldly.

"No," said Nashiram. "Asmodeus denies us our just vengeance because it gives him leverage over us. The Revenant knows that we plotted with Agrat Bat to destroy our mother. As long as the pathetic creature lives, the King of Demons has us in his power and will never let us go. But we shall have our revenge–one day. This I promise you."

"We shall have our revenge," the other sisters said in unison.

They sat brooding for a moment. Soon the King of Demons would call for them, and they would have to satiate his lust and deviant fantasies.

A chill wind arose and blew through the pillars of the temple, ruffling their hair and robes. They looked up and peered around them. Something was coming; something of great power. They could feel it. Their eyes narrowed as a dark spot appeared at the temple entrance and grew larger.

A large claw appeared, followed by a tentacle, and to their astonishment, the vast bulk of Asmodeus materialised.

The Lilitu scrambled apprehensively from their thrones and gathered in the centre of the floor.

"Well, whores?" he boomed. "Is this the greeting you give your lord and master?"

"You dare intrude upon the sanctity of our temple? This place is inviolate!" Nashiram protested.

"Sanctity?" the King of Demons chortled. "That sounds like Heavenspeak to me. You had better not let the Grand Inquisitors hear you utter that word. They may consider you heretics. Our satanic master has commanded them to seek out all snivelling apostates and dissenters."

"We are no heretics," Nashiram responded angrily. "But you promised us you would treat our temple with the respect it has always received–a place where only the Lilitu may gather–a sanctuary that protects us and where no archdemon may enter."

Asmodeus' great swirling face of darkened. "When your mother was my consort, it was protected by her power. But you rebelled against her, and she removed her protection. But I saved you. I, Asmodeus, King of Demons! It my authority that shields you from the obscene indignities of other archdemons. Even as we speak, Lilith's succubi legions are being rounded up and sent to the Dungeons of Hell for torture and interrogation. But I would not let the inquisitors take you. I assured our satanic master of your innocence in the matter of your mother's defection. It is I who defends you–and only I. Would you rather I let them take you to the dungeons or gave you to Moloch or Azazel?"

Lilith's daughters looked aghast. Being Asmodeus' concubines was bad enough, but being a slave of Moloch or Azazel was even worse. They could just about cope with Asmodeus' lust, but the other two archdemons took pleasure in subjecting others to pain, extreme pain, an agonising, soul-destroying pain that could only exist in Hell. And while the Lilitu enjoyed inflicting pain on others, they took no pleasure in receiving it.

They rushed forward, mewling and shrieking, and knelt in homage before Asmodeus.

"Great king and lord, forgive our arrogance," they cried as one. "We are grateful for your protection and will do anything to prove our loyalty to you."

Asmodeus smiled lustily. "Anything?"

They hesitated for a moment before replying, wondering what new indignities Asmodeus had in store for them.

"Yes, *anything*, our king!" they cried.

Asmodeus gazed down at the cowering Lilitu and shuddered as he ran his multitude of phalluses over their firm bodies. That was why he enjoyed adopting his strange, amorphous form: it increased his sexual gratification a thousandfold. Not one of the Lilitu could equal their mother in satisfying his enormous carnal desires–but together, these beautiful little strumpets danced a merry jig on his tentacles and had even come close to milking him dry on several memorable occasions. But he would never admit that to them. It was much better to make them feel inadequate. They would work so much harder to attain his praise and thereby continually increase his sensual pleasure.

He sighed regretfully and withdrew his appendages; he was not here to satisfy his lust and had a more urgent chore for his nubile thralls. However, he decided to couch it terms that made him seem magnanimous and appreciative of their efforts.

"I have a little gift for you, my beauteous ones. A boon that you shall treasure for aeons to come."

The Lilitu looked surprised at his benevolence and whispered excitedly to each other.

"What gift, oh most powerful lord! Tell us!" they gushed in concordance.

"The Revenant has escaped," he said casually.

Asmodeus smiled inwardly as the Lilitu ceased being subservient and their expressions became as hard as flint. He knew they hated Longinus with demonic passion and would not be satisfied until they had destroyed him.

"I released him so I could hunt him for sport, but he has evaded me. As a reward for your loyal and obedient service, I wish you to find—and destroy him."

Lilith's daughters gaped at him for a moment and then shrieked and cavorted with hellish delight.

"We shall tear him limb from limb!" screeched Nashiram.

"Rip out his heart!" cried Baileet.

"Gouge out his eyes and disembowel him!" Sarai hissed gleefully.

Asmodeus laughed in pleasure at their antics. "Yes, yes, my vindictive, little stepbrood! Do whatever you desire with him, but his physical remains and mortal soul must never be found. Our imperial master has commanded me to fetch the Revenant to him for interrogation, but this we cannot permit. He would lay the blame for Lilith's defection squarely at your door, and that would grieve me."

The Lilitu stopped dancing and looked pensive as they considered the repercussions of Satan finding out their part in their mother's downfall.

"Worry not, my little ones," Asmodeus said in a honeyed tone. "Your wellbeing is my major concern. I have grown very fond of you and wish to increase your powers and ranks. You will be my royal consorts—my infernal queens of the Abyss!"

The Lilitu screamed in delight, rushed to him and covered his various appendages with grateful kisses. Asmodeus grinned and made a mental note to act benevolently more often.

After a few moments, Nashiram frowned and looked up at him. "My lord, disposing of his remains will be simple, but what of his immortal soul? We cannot destroy that."

The King of Demons smiled indulgently at her and stroked her chin with a claw. The harlot was ill tempered but had a mouth like a suction pump.

"You are correct, my sweet strumpet, but your lord has already thought of that."

Asmodeus waved a tentacle and a gold finger ring and leather pouch appeared in his claw.

"Take these," he said.

Nashiram took the ring and pouch and stared in bewilderment at them. "For what purpose?" she asked.

"Look closer at the ring," he said grinning.

She peered at it, screamed, and dropped it onto the temple floor as though it was red hot.

"It has the Pentagram, the seal of Great Tyrant engraved on it!" she screeched.

Her sisters sprang to their feet, and withdrew ten paces away, crouching and hissing.

"It will do you no harm," Asmodeus laughed, greatly amused by their expressions. "His symbols have no power in the Abyss."

"But why did you give it to me?" she shrieked angrily.

Asmodeus raised an eyebrow and sighed. It was growing very apparent to him that Lilith had been the only demoness in Hell who had appreciated a good jest. All the others, like Naamah and the Lilitu, were as humourless as a bag of dried bones.

"This once belonged to a mighty king," he said, picking up the ring and toying with it. "His name was Solomon."

"We know of this vile ruler. He enslaved demons and compelled them to build his odious Temple of Jerusalem," Rebekna growled.

"And this is the very ring he used to enslave them!" Asmodeus announced with a dramatic flourish.

You could exorcise the demon from the actor, but you could never rid the demon of the player. He had once joined a troupe of professional actors in 16th Century Italy and played the character of Scarramuccia in their Commedia dell'arte. He had enjoyed watching bosoms heave and quims quiver as he, Scarramuccia, the handsome adventurer; master swordsman; and lover; had strutted the boards, robbing the rich, giving alms to the poor, and slapping his thigh and codpiece provocatively. Many maidens and matrons had fainted during his performances and had sought holy forgiveness in their confessionals. But they had always returned to see their gallant prince and dream of one blissful night where they were free from their stern and dusty moral constraints. It had been a dark wish that Asmodeus had been only too happy to grant them.

The Lilitu stared apprehensively at the gold band.

"Where did he get it?" asked Sarai.

"From the Great Tyrant," purred Asmodeus. "Archdemon Ornias was tormenting a handsome youth by making him suck his thumb—among other things—and Solomon prayed to the Great Tyrant for help. The accursed Archangel Michael appeared and gave this ring to him saying it would allow him to command demons. It did, and he did, and thus the holy temple was built through the back breaking toil of the unholy."

"But how does this help us with the Revenant's soul?" demanded Nashiram.

"Ah, the young of Hell have so little interest in the history of mankind," bemoaned Asmodeus. "You should study it well. It provides us with no shortage of arcane information that we can use to our advantage."

"Then educate us, my king," Baileet whispered seductively.

Asmodeus smiled. He had promised but a few minutes ago to make them his queens, and some were already scheming how to improve their position in the royal connubial pecking and poking order. Last night, none of them had seemed eager to dangle on his crowned heads, but now they were competing for that regal honour. "Ah," he mused to himself, "how easily the female mind is swayed by rank and privilege."

This, he had learned from mortals and therefore knew it to be true. How else could one explain the inexplicable human phenomenon of pretty young things allowing rich, powerful, ugly men–adopting strange, unearthly hairstyles to disguise their balding pates–to grope and mount them? Mammon maintained that money talked, but Asmodeus knew that power and lust screamed.

"A cornerstone of the temple," he continued suavely, "proved too heavy or holy for the enslaved demons to lift, and they informed him that only a wind demon in Arabia had the power to put the stone in place."

"Who was this wind demon, my lord?" asked Shelomith.

She was quieter than the others were and never complained or shed mock tears. During his debaucheries, he had favoured her stoical attitude of gritting her teeth and getting on with it. Under his paternal protection and tutelage, this somewhat reserved princess of Hell had found her true calling: a hard working whore. As business mortals bleated in their irritating gobbledegook–an excellent master must always strive to further the personal development of his slaves. Asmodeus had taken this blithe pronouncement to heart and was rather proud of the fact that no archdemon took more of an interest in 'personally developing' his thralls than he.

"Archdemon Ephippas," he replied nostalgically. "He was always an incompetent blowhard, but on this occasion his hot air would be put to good use."

The Lilitu giggled girlishly, as they thought required of them, and sat on the floor seemingly enraptured by his long-winded tale. They were impatient to hunt the Revenant, but Asmodeus' promise of making them his queens compelled them to humour their potential benefactor. Anything was preferable to being pounded like cold slabs of meat into insensibility.

"Solomon gave a servant boy the ring and a wineskin. The child held the band in front of the bag and faced into Ephippas' wind. Not a pleasant task, I assure you. Ephippas does not produce wind from his mouth—but from his hinder end."

The Lilitu cackled dutifully.

"The ring sucked the archflatulent into the bag, and the servant tied it tight. Thus did Solomon capture him and compel Ephippas' back passage to do his bidding."

"And did Ephippas succeed in moving the cornerstone into place?" asked Basemath, widening her eyes and batting her long lashes at him.

"Indeed, he did!" Asmodeus laughed. "But they had to cease construction for three days because of the stench! That taught Solomon that the denizens of the Bottomless Pit were not without bottoms!"

Lilith's daughters fell about shrieking with laughter, each one competing with the other to exceed in appreciation of their master's tasteless, yet not odourless, jest.

"And speaking of buttocks," Asmodeus murmured, reaching out with his dripping appendages.

"But what has this to do with the Revenant's soul?" Nashiram asked quickly, eager to distract him from his lecherous intent.

"Ah, quite so," Asmodeus replied regretfully, remembering the principal purpose of his didactic tale. "When the Revenant dies, capture his soul by holding the ring against the mouth of the wineskin. Tie it tight and bring it to me. I shall bury it in a deep, dark place where even our illustrious master cannot find it. Then, your secret will be safe for eternity."

"You are certain the ring can do us no harm?" asked Nashiram.

"You have my word on it."

She looked doubtful and stared at the band. Before she could make up her mind, Shelomith strode forward and picked up the gold band.

"There!" she cried scornfully. "You take the wineskin, and I shall carry the ring. Time is wasting and our satanic master's gaze is upon us. Shall we proceed immediately, my lord, or do you wish to have us first?"

The quiet one's impertinence surprised him, but he could not fault her pragmatism. He had always found the fuck, fight, or flight response a hard decision to make and often wished he could have done at least two of the aforementioned simultaneously. However, such a voyage of discovery would have to wait until a more convenient moment. As his grim little strumpet had so rightly pointed out, one of the Great Dragon's malevolent heads had twisted in their direction.

"Nothing would give me greater satisfaction," he growled. "But what you say is true. Time is of the essence and my—our—pleasures must await."

"Where did you last see him?" asked Nashiram.

Asmodeus pursed his thick, blubbery lips. He did not consider it wise to reveal to them he had become entangled with Lady Naamah.

"He escaped the river Styx and fled into Leviathan's domain."

"Then he may already be dead."

"I suspect not. You know the Revenant. He is as slippery as a barrel of eels. Pick up his scent in Leviathan's kingdom but use stealth and let no one observe you. I desire to remain on peaceful terms with the lord of the watery chasm."

"We shall take the utmost care," replied Nashiram.

"Excellent! Go now. Hunt him down and make him suffer. Let no one stand in your way. If you succeed, your rewards will be great—but if you fail me, I shall be merciless!"

"We will do as you command, our king!" they vowed in unison.

Shrieking with malignant laughter, the Lilitu transformed into their demonic forms: pale skin turned obsidian, hands and feet became deadly talons, and bat-like wings erupted from backs.

With high-pitched shrieks of gleeful anticipation, they scrambled out of the temple and soared into the inky void of the Abyss.

Asmodeus grinned as he watched them depart. It was done. The Lilitu would not cease until they found and destroyed the Revenant. He had set the first part of his plan in motion; now it was time to proceed with the second phase. Although it would inconvenience him greatly to lose his succulent little whores, he had concluded they knew too much.

Like Solomon's wineskin, the loose ends needed tying; and he would eliminate all witnesses who could testify to his part in Lilith's downfall.

It was time for him to meet with the Hunter of Souls.

CHAPTER XVII

They were flying straight at the Nephilim. He smelt their foul breath, and their insane bellowing deafened him. Longinus struggled to break free, but the succubus' grip was as strong as iron. Just when he thought his fate was sealed, they soared up like an eagle and flew over the heads of the titans. The Nephilim struck wildly at them with their axes, but she darted between their savage blows and kept ascending. She rolled into a graceful, shallow turn and carried him back to the ledge where Armilus crouched. The centurion grunted with relief as she released him, and his feet landed on firm ground. He peered down into the gorge, and it gladdened him to observe the Nephilim showed no interest in climbing the cliff. They gathered around their fallen kin and poked its shrivelled corpse with their axes, apparently perplexed by the manner of its death.

"Well, that was invigorating," Longinus said dryly.

The succubus frowned and stared at him as though he had just grown a second head.

Armilus ran across to them crying, "Begone! Begone, harpy!"

She glared contemptuously at him for a moment, and after a curious glance at Longinus, she turned around and flew back down into the gorge.

"What is she doing?" said Longinus.

"The harridan is insane!" exclaimed Armilus. "You have just saved her and yet she returns to her doom!"

As they stood watching, she landed in the gorge and ran towards an immense pile of weapons and armour near the cage. Longinus surmised that these had belonged to the previous victims of the giants. The Nephilim noticed her and charged. She found what she was searching for and extracted a long black trident from the arms cache.

The roaring, slavering goliaths were nearly upon her when she calmly spread her wings and sailed into the air. The centurion and Armilus gazed on in amazement as she darted out of the gorge with the horde of angry Nephilim in hot pursuit. It appeared to Longinus that she was encouraging the giants to chase her.

"What is so important about the weapon?" he asked.

"It is her trident," said Armilus, shaking his head. "Each succubus carries one and considers it shameful to lose it. All succubi are mad!"

Longinus rubbed his chin. "How many Nephilim dwell here?"

"Thousands," the cambion replied glumly.

"Where is the next Hellmouth?"

Armilus grimaced. "It lies yonder–beyond the domain of the Nephilim."

"We would not last five minutes down there. Is there a way around the giants?"

As he spoke, the succubus flew into the gorge and landed at the arms cache below them. She had led the Nephilim on a merry chase and then doubled back on them. Longinus watched as she rummaged through the pile and found a shield, breastplate, kilt, bracers, and greaves. Holding them in her arms, she flew up to the ledge. She alighted beside them, dropped the armour onto the ground with a clatter and pointed her trident at them. The sharp tips glistened like a three-eyed rat in the crimson light.

In Roman gladiatorial games, the retiarius or 'net man', armed with a trident and net, had been considered the lowliest rank of fighter. But Longinus had always held a grudging respect for the retiarius. The gladiator had worn light armour and relied on his speed, agility and skill to defeat his traditional heavily armoured opponent–the secutor. The trident was a formidable weapon in the hands of a trained warrior, and its lethal points could inflict thrice as much damage as a spear.

"Who are you?" she demanded, her long tail swaying behind her like a snake preparing to strike.

Longinus arched an eyebrow and a small smile hovered on his lips. He found it rather amusing that she threatened his life while wearing naught but the robe of Eve.

She was not as beautiful as Lilith–no demoness could be–but there was something about her he found enticing. He had often found during his long existence that beauty was not the key attribute that attracted him to a female. Sometimes it was a smile or a look, and on other occasions it was a voice, manner or the eyes. Often it would be wit and intelligence. But, occasionally, there was just an indefinable quality about a woman's face that attracted him like a bee to nectar. And he found this succubus' countenance very pleasing to his eye.

He took his time to savour every curve of her athletic physique before replying. It had been a long time since he had beheld an attractive female. All the vindictive she-devils in Asmodeus' basilica had been emaciated hags. If the King of Demons had any beauteous vassals serving him, he had not deigned to reveal them to Longinus.

She noticed his eyes straying over her body and seemed disconcerted by it. If he did not know better, he could almost have mistaken her reaction as one of embarrassment. It was hardly the reaction he would expect from a demonic mistress of seduction.

"My name is Longinus, and he is called Armilus. We are not related," he said amiably.

She frowned and sniffed the air suspiciously. "You are neither living nor dead. What manner of being are you?"

"A vampire."

"Vam-pire," she said thoughtfully, rolling the word around her tongue. "I have heard of your kind. They exist on the mortal plane. Why are you in Hell, and why do you travel with a half-demon? Are you spies? Who sent you?"

"I warned you not to save the harpy," Armilus said worriedly. "You cannot trust a succubus."

"Silence, cambion, or I shall skewer you where you stand!" the demoness hissed, pointing her trident at him.

Armilus looked shocked and took a few steps back so he was behind Longinus. The centurion noticed his ploy and smiled to himself. The cambion was obviously going to be a great asset in combat.

"Is this the way you treat those who help you?" Longinus said nonchalantly, trying to diffuse the situation.

"Why *did* you rescue me? I do not understand?" she said angrily.

"Why did you rescue me?" he countered.

"Why do you answer a question with a question?" she screamed. "I think you are spies, and I should destroy you!"

"You can certainly try," Longinus replied quietly. "I saved you because I felt pity for you, but now I am beginning to regret my decision. Perhaps I should have left you to the Nephilim?"

Armilus poked his head out and cried, "Begone, vicious shrew! We do not fear your kind. This is Lilith's Revenant! He is a fearsome warrior and has destroyed demons more powerful than you."

Longinus arched an eyebrow and gave the cambion a withering look.

"Do you mind? I am trying to settle this matter peacefully."

The succubus looked startled by Armilus' revelation.

"*You* are Lilith's Revenant?"

"I am—was. Who are you?"

The succubus regarded him suspiciously for a moment and then intoned, "I am Onoskelis. I was the commander of Lilith's legions."

"Commander of Lilith's legions?" Longinus asked, somewhat dubiously.

"Yes!" Onoskelis replied sternly.

"You look very young to command legions."

She laughed scornfully. "This is Hell. I am much older than I appear, that I can assure you."

"I know the feeling," Longinus murmured.

Bruises covered his body, and his lower back ached. For the first time in his existence, he felt old. It was no fun being a millenniagenarian.

"You say you were commander of Lilith's legions. I assume you no longer lead them?"

Onoskelis relaxed slightly and lowered her trident a few inches. "No."

"What happened?"

"After Lilith's desertion to Heaven, Satan had all of her legions disarmed and conducted a purge. The archdemons routed out and destroyed Lilith's commanders and sent all remaining succubi to the Dungeons of Hell for interrogation. I was one of the few to escape. Since then, I have been trying to find somewhere I can be safe, but it is proving an impossible task."

"How came you to be captured by the Nephilim?" asked Longinus.

"I was flying over these accursed mountains when I was ensnared by a thrown net. I now know it is a method employed by the Nephilim to catch unwary demons. They are very partial to incubus and succubus flesh."

"The Nephilim will eat anything," Armilus said tartly.

"Quiet, cambion, or I shall send you to oblivion!" Onoskelis retorted angrily.

Longinus studied her for a moment and then nodded at her trident. "Can you use that thing?"

"Use?" she asked, frowning.

"Against your enemies."

Onoskelis smiled grimly and exploded into a powerful demonstration of her skill. She leapt, spun, dived, parried and thrust her weapon into over a dozen imaginary enemies before halting the sharp points an inch from Longinus' throat.

"Does my *use* of it please you?" she asked.

Longinus pursed his lips appreciatively. "Very impressive. You are obviously an expert with your weapon."

She nodded and lowered the trident. "I was bred for war and have trained assiduously every moment I could."

Then her shoulders slumped, and she looked weary. "I cannot understand why Lilith did this to us; it is beyond belief. She was Queen of the Night. How could she join the accursed angels?"

"It was Asmodeus' doing," said Longinus. "He became jealous of her relationship with me and decided to usurp her. He formed an alliance with Agrat Bat Mahlat and tried to destroy Lilith. Agrat Bat even managed to turn Lilith's daughters against her."

"But why did not Lilith seek the help of our Satanic Majesty?" she protested. "He has always favoured her and would have put a stop to Asmodeus' plot."

"Because Lilith had changed," said Longinus.

"Changed? How? I do not understand."

Longinus chose his words carefully. He wanted to see what her reaction was to the concept of love.

"She committed the cardinal sin for any demon. I loved her—and she loved me."

Onoskelis looked dumfounded. "No, I cannot believe it! She was the Mother of Demons! Demons cannot love!"

"Well, apparently things have changed."

Onoskelis thought for a moment and said, "That would explain why she did not seek Satan's protection. He would have detected this weakness in her."

Longinus shrugged his shoulders. "I will take your word for it."

"And where is Agrat Bat Mahlat? Satan has turned Hell upside down trying to find her."

"I destroyed her in Purgatory," Longinus said coldly.

"You? But Agrat Bat was a powerful demoness. How could you, a mere vampire, destroy her?"

"I am part vampire and part demon. Just as she was about to destroy me, I transformed into my demon form and decapitated her. Lilith and I thought it was over, but Asmodeus appeared and threatened to drag both of us to Hell."

"But how did Lilith escape from Asmodeus? No one has escaped from the King of Demons. Once he has you in his clutches, your fate is sealed."

Longinus paused before continuing. There was an element of child-like innocence in Onoskelis' manner he found surprising. It seemed most unusual for a hardened demon commander such as her.

"Archangel Michael appeared and told Asmodeus that he could only take one of us. Asmodeus hatred for me is so great that it did not take much persuasion for me to convince him to take me instead of her. He dragged me to Hell, and I never saw Lilith again."

"The archangel must have offered Lilith salvation," replied Onoskelis.

"I can only assume that is what happened. After all, she could not return to Hell. What other choice did she have?"

"None," said Onoskelis. "I can see that now. Your revelation has allowed me to make sense of these inexplicable events."

He watched as she strapped on her armour. She did not turn away or try to conceal her nakedness from him; indeed, he rather sensed that part of her enjoyed displaying her magnificently sculptured body to him. Or was it just his suppressed demon carnal desires tainting his imagination? He did not know and rubbed the back of his neck to clear his mind of such thoughts. He had enough troubles on his meagre plate.

She spread her bat-like wings to put on her cuirass, and it surprised him to observe she had a hump on her upper back. He had never met a succubus with any form of deformity and wondered what had caused it.

When she had finished dressing, Onoskelis no longer appeared like an innocent young succubus; she now looked like a formidable warrior of Hell.

"Slay her now, Revenant!" Armilus whispered in his ear. "I do not trust her. She will betray us!"

Onoskelis' hearing was very acute, and she glared at Armilus' satanic cuirass.

"Why do you travel with this pathetic creature? He is an informer."

"I was an imperial messenger!" Armilus retorted indignantly.

"Imperial calumniator, more like! All in the Abyss know that Satan's emissaries act as spies and take pleasure in whispering false allegations into the ears of the inquisitors."

"Lying harlot! I reported none to the tormentors!" Armilus screeched.

"The past is the past," Longinus interjected diplomatically. "We must move forward. Like you, we seek to escape Satan's power."

The succubus shook her head at his naivete. "You cannot hide from the Emperor of Hell. It is just a matter of time before his vassals find us."

"The cambion knows the way to the Lower Depths."

Onoskelis looked truly shocked.

"Are you as simple as you look? Why do you wish to travel to that accursed place? It is worse than the Abyss!"

Longinus grinned and scratched his head. His little succubus certainly did not believe in mincing her words.

"For that very reason," he explained with the patience of Job. "Even Satan and Asmodeus fear treading there. You should join us. We could do with another experienced warrior."

"But she may be a spy and betray us!" Armilus cried.

"No! You are the spy!" she snarled.

"Oh, joy," Longinus sighed, holding up his hand to silence their infernal bickering. "Enough! I trust neither of you, but we have a common goal. Let us declare a truce and work together for a brief time. Once we arrive in the Lower Depths, we can go our separate ways."

"But she may inform Asmodeus of our whereabouts!" Armilus whined.

"Then why did she rescue me from the Nephilim? She could have left me to my fate."

Armilus gurned, and the centurion could see the tiny cogs of his brain turning as he tried to offer a rational explanation for Onoskelis' strange intervention.

"Anyhow," added Longinus, "look on the bright side. You would have two seasoned warriors to protect you. I thought that would please you?"

Armilus glared at succubus and said grudgingly, "Well, I suppose our path is fraught with dangers, and two is most certainly better than one."

"Yes," replied Onoskelis. "You would have two skirts to hide behind."

Armilus scowled but said nothing. He seemed reconciled to making the best of a bad lot.

Onoskelis stared at Longinus for a moment and said, "I detect no deceit in you, but I must decline your offer."

"Why?"

"I have heard tales of the monstrosities that dwell there and have no wish to encounter them. I shall find some other means of escape. But–I thank you for saving me from the Nephilim–and wish you a safe journey."

"Good!" Armilus muttered.

"Farewell," said Longinus. "I hope you find a haven."

She was about to fly away but stopped. He thought she had changed her mind.

"In which direction do you travel?" she asked.

"We need to reach the Hellmouth on the other side of the Nephilim's domain," he replied.

"There is a ridge yonder," she said, pointing with her trident. "That will take you over the mountains and beyond the reach of the Nephilim. I saw the way when I flew over there."

Longinus smiled. "Thank you, Onoskelis. Seek us out if you change your mind. My offer will still stand."

Onoskelis frowned and stared at him for an instant. Then, without another word, she took to the air and flew back into the domain of the Nephilim.

"You told her too much!" complained Armilus. "Now she knows where we are heading and may betray our position!"

"I do not think so."

"And why not? Pray tell what mysterious power allows you to discern such a thing?" Armilus replied sarcastically.

"Because I like her, and I have never been wrong about anyone I liked."

"Never?" Armilus asked, incredulously.

"Well–most of the time," Longinus said with mock thoughtfulness, keen to rile his irascible companion.

Armilus stared at him as though he was insane. "There is a self-destructive aspect to your nature that I do not welcome, Revenant. If you are so keen to be recaptured by Asmodeus, then go, but please do not endanger my freedom! I have worked very hard for a long time to plan my escape, and I have no intention of returning to Infernus. I would rather destroy myself!"

Longinus was about to utter a sarcastic reply, but bit his tongue. There was truth in what the demon had said. He very much wanted to die. It was only his sense of honour and desire to save his friends that prevented him from taking that path.

The cambion's passionate outburst had surprised him. For once, the half-demon had shown some backbone. He had considered him a rather pathetic figure, but now realised how strongly Armilus felt about his bid for freedom. And as Longinus well knew, Liberty was not an ideal to be scorned or taken lightly: it should be nourished and encouraged.

"You are correct, and I apologise if I have placed you in peril. I shall try to be more circumspect in my actions."

"Good!" Armilus grumbled. "It is in our best interest. We must look to our own survival."

Longinus grimaced at the cambion's selfish attitude.

"Right! Let us head to the ridge. I assume you trust the succubus enough for that—or do you wish to take your chances down there?"

Armilus peered down and saw more Nephilim gathering in the gorge. Their roars and screams made him jittery.

"No," he declared, "the harpy's directions may have some merit to them. We should follow the high mountain route."

"After you, your lordship," Longinus said, bowing.

The cambions muttered an unintelligible obscenity and proceeded cautiously along the side of the mountain. Longinus hitched up his sword belt and followed him.

As he viewed the decidedly unattractive figure shamble along in front of him, he regretted the fiery succubus had declined to accompany them. He would much rather be watching her swaying hips than the cambion's hairy backside.

There was something about her he found captivating. Even her horns and tail had not dampened his interest; and he wondered darkly if this was a sign that the demon part of him was growing stronger.

Lilith had never made love to him in her demonic form. She had always adopted the appearance she had when she lived in the Garden of Eden, and he was very glad of that. Her infernal manifestation was extremely intimidating; however, over the years, he had grown accustomed to it. It was like having a lover with a physical disfigurement: true love makes all imperfections invisible to the devoted eye, and one sees only the beauty of a Venus or Adonis.

She had never revealed to him how she had become a demoness. He had broached the subject with her frequently, but she had deftly avoided answering his question and stopped his lips with a kiss. Not wishing to antagonise her, he had let the matter lie. Even the profane *Book of Lilith* did not supply a full account of her fall from grace. There were rumours about Satan, Asmodeus and even God, but her unholy conversion was shrouded in mystery.

He had regarded her as two separate beings, a split personality: the woman he loved, and the Mother of Demons whom he feared. In ancient times, the demoness in her had been more dominant, but as the centuries had passed, the woman, the human, in her had blossomed and come to the fore. This did not surprise him. He had always known she had good in her. Lilith's existence had been a constant struggle between the good and evil that coexisted within her. They were unwilling and hostile bedfellows who battled for supremacy. But God had created her to be Adam's wife, and despite how viciously the demonic side of her tried to take control, it could never quite extinguish the divine spark of her rebellious spirit. It was part of her for eternity.

That was why she protected her daughters. In a ghastly realm where most fiends abused their offspring, her motherly concern was considered unnatural and treated with suspicion. Even her own children regarded it as a weakness and betrayed her. He hoped they were enjoying their new life with Asmodeus. He would soon prove to them that life under their mother's stern but fair rule was not as bad as they had thought.

She had committed many heinous crimes, but unbeknown to her demon counterparts, she had frequently shown compassion or granted mercy to humans. He believed that is why God had forgiven her; she was His prodigal daughter, His rebellious creation, and after centuries of exile, He had allowed her to return to the fold.

Yet her apparent salvation stirred conflicting emotions within him. It was like losing a lover who had endured a long, painful illness but was now at peace. While thankful she no longer suffered, it broke his heart to lose her.

"Yes, you loved her so much that you honour her memory by lusting after a little succubus!" he muttered angrily to himself.

Shaking his head in morose disbelief at his hypocrisy, he decided that accompanying the irascible cambion was a fitting penance for him.

Clearing his mind of sinful thoughts, he rapped his forehead with his knuckles and whispered, "Stupid bastard."

CHAPTER XVIII

The treasury of Hell was a vast, rectangular fortress made of granite and gilded with gold and silver leaf. A towering aureate statue of an obese demon sat atop the roof of the glistening yet foreboding structure. For this was Mammon's demesne, and the cunning archdemon of avarice wielded absolute power as far as the eye could see.

For hundreds of leagues around the stronghold, human souls demons toiled perpetually at enormous blast furnaces that belched acrid smoke and flames into the fiery vault. Large kilns glowed and vast grinders and tumblers rumbled as they spat out crushed gold and silver ores. Cluttered workshops rang with the sounds of eldritch screams and hammers as Mammon's vassals processed the precious metals and gems of the Abyss and transformed them into artifacts of demonic beauty or objects of earthly greed.

From Mammon's fortress spewed the hellish, unlimited wealth that funded evil humans, corporations, and regimes around the mortal world and bound them to the Evil One's cause. Despots, politicians, bankers, terrorists, fundamentalists, false prophets, celebrities, and many Christian sects and churches sucked greedily on Mammon's dripping teats, and he was only to happy to provide their slobbering mouths with sustenance. Money, bribery, corruption, and contempt for the planet, the other, the sick, the elderly, the destitute, and the poor ruled. Mammon was mankind's new god—their golden goose and calf.

In the innermost chamber of the devilish bastion of opulence, a most unsightly spectacle was taking place.

"Does he trust you?" asked Naamah.

"No, my lady," Mammon replied, irritated she had put him off his stride.

She lowered her serpentine body to accommodate him. He was standing on a stack of gold ingots and hanging onto her hips like a bloated, randy leech.

"Then why has he joined our cause?"

Mammon grunted, grabbed her scaly buttocks in his claws, and pulled. The added depth increased his pleasure.

"Because he has the scent of power and your exquisite orifice in his nostrils," he gasped, intoxicated by the seductive odour of her musk.

"Will he will betray us?"

"No, but he will do everything in his power to deceive us."

"Do you wish me to tighten?"

"That would be most welcome, my lady."

Mammon winced as she closed like a vice.

"Not too much!" he squealed.

"As you wish," she replied, easing off some fifty pounds per square inch.

Her father had taken all she could give him and demanded more.

"How does that feel?" she enquired impatiently.

"Much better, thank you, my lady," he puffed, his yellow eyes popping.

"And I thought Asmodeus was the archdemon of lust," she laughed, examining the nails of one talon.

"Your enticing beauty makes all demons lustful," he growled, leering at the towering mountains of gold that lay behind her.

It was so smooth and beautiful to touch. He could spend hours lying in it, rubbing his naked body with it. It was like an enormous, warm, yellow womb.

"Especially, the fat ones," she murmured as he shrieked, wobbled, and spent his seed inside her for the tenth time.

However, his meagre offerings at her magnificent altar of pleasure satisfied Naamah. It strengthened their alliance and allowed her to conceive new nehushtan. She could already feel the foetuses stirring in her womb. In but a few hours, they would slither out and please her with their delightful snarls and howls.

And with her new hounds, she would hunt the Revenant to the ends of Hell and back.

CHAPTER XIX

Longinus and the cambion trudged along a high track that wound its way between the summits of a chain of dormant, leaden volcanic mountains. Lines of huge, jagged rocks tilted at bizarre angles and reminded the centurion of a mythical dragon's back. Ever present above them, dense black clouds billowed in a churning sea of carmine and occasional peals of thunder reverberated through the dismal heights.

"Where is the next Hellmouth?" Longinus asked.

"On the great plain beyond those two peaks."

Longinus grunted. It would take many hours of slow, hard climbing to ascend the summits. He sat on a rock, removed a sandal and shook the grit from it. Sharp stinging sensations like a band of miniscule pirates stabbing his foot with tiny daggers had been annoying him for some time, but he had not wanted to stop. However, as one little bugger now appeared to be using a cutlass on the underside of his big toe, the centurion had decided it was time to throw the impudent offender and his mutinous shipmates overboard.

"Is there no way around them?" he asked, slapping his sandal against the rock to dislodge any stowaways.

The half-demon stopped and scratched his head. "There is another route, but we would be wise to avoid it."

"Why?"

"It leads to the Dungeons of Hell. I have delivered imperial messages to it on three occasions, and that is three times too many. It is not a place I desire to visit again. They torture human souls and demons there," he replied, his mismatched eyes widening with dread.

"Why do they punish demons?"

"For heresy."

"Heresy! What could possibly be heretical in Hell?" Longinus laughed.

Armilus looked uneasy. "Being suspected or accused of being disloyal to Satan. After Lilith defected to Heaven, Satan has become paranoid and sees traitors and defectors everywhere. He has commanded the archdemons to rout out any they suspect of treachery."

"Like Lilith's succubi? Onoskelis said they were being interrogated."

"Yes."

"Why take them to these dungeons? Cannot the archdemons 'question' them?"

"Satan does not trust his vassals. He knows they would lie to cover their own hides. However, the inquisitors are fanatically loyal to the Evil One. It is their task to extract information and confessions from their victims, and they seldom fail. Once the inquisitors have you in their grasp, you would confess to anything."

"Just like their counterparts on earth," replied Longinus. "Deny your guilt and be burned at the stake for lying, or admit your guilt and be burned at the stake to purify your soul."

"Well put. It is a very efficient method of disposing of enemies, or those who stand in your way."

"They call that a witch-hunt on earth. Is that why you seek to escape? Were you disloyal to Satan?"

Armilus sighed. "That is one reason. I have said many things in the past that could be used against me by those jealous of my position and influence. I once mentioned injudiciously to a fellow messenger that our purpose in Hell was to punish human souls and not fellow demons."

"And did he, she, or it, report your words back to Satan?"

"No, to Baal Zebub. He supervises the satanic messengers and the flow of information in Hell."

"I thought Baal Zebub was just another name for Satan?"

"That is a common misconception held by humans," said Armilus. "Baal Zebub is Satan's mouthpiece, and one of his most trusted advisors. In Hell, he is known as 'Lord of the Flies' or the 'Silver Tongued One.' He is a master of political scheming, and also takes special pleasure in possessing the bodies of prepubescent girls. That is why flies often appear during human possessions and exorcisms."

"And poor old Pazuzu got the blame," Longinus replied dryly.

Armilus did not understand that Longinus was jesting and considered his remark very seriously.

"To my knowledge, Pazuzu never possessed mortals. In ancient times, humans used his image to protect themselves from other malicious demons."

"I know—like Lamashtu."

Armilus shivered and whispered, "Do not even mention her name. She is worse than ten archdemons!"

"Where is she now—part of Satan's legions?"

Armilus gave a mirthless laugh. "No! She was too insane and powerful for even Satan to bend to his will. After a great battle, he and the other archdemons managed to bind her with satanic chains and entomb her for eternity."

"In Hell?"

"No, somewhere in the Lower Depths."

Longinus raised an eyebrow. "The Lower Depths—as in—where we are heading?"

"Yes."

"Oh, joy! This day just keeps getting better and better!"

"Now you can understand why I asked you to accompany me," Armilus said glumly.

"Oh, yes, I understand completely," Longinus replied with sardonic cheerfulness. "You need me to distract the most vicious, demented night-hag that ever existed while you scuttle into the distance like a bat out of Hell."

"There are no *chiroptera* in the Abyss," the cambion retorted disdainfully.

"Shut up."

Armilus gave Longinus a sullen look and starting walking again. He did not appreciate the centurion's lack of sympathy with his current situation.

"Wait for your bodyguard," Longinus called after him.

The half-demon hunched his shoulders and muttered obscenities about his protector's parentage under his breath.

Longinus strapped on his sandal and grinned. Teasing the cambion was becoming one of his favourite pastimes. It broke the monotony of their dreary journey together. There had always been a little devil in him that had relished stirring things up. As Marcus, his old centurion and mentor, had often said about him, "Gaius, with a look of youthful innocence on his countenance, can start an uproar in any taberna and thoroughly enjoy the ensuing fisticuffs."

Most of his drunken brawls had been with members of the haughty Praetorian Guard who had considered themselves superior to common legionaries. In Longinus' humble opinion, the strutting imperial peacocks had always looked much better when sporting a broken nose, thick lip or black eye.

He started after the cambion and began humming a heavy metal song that had popped in to his head. His musical tastes had changed substantially over the centuries, but latterly he had favoured classical and highly amplified, harsh-sounding rock music. Classical music was excellent for relaxing or bathing. His favourite piece while showering—as Naram-Sin had so aptly put it, they were a living corpse, but that was no excuse for smelling like one—was Beethoven's 9th Symphony. He found it invigorating to scrub his bits while singing along in 19th century New High German to the choral sections. But heavy metal was an absolute necessity while riding a motorcycle. Some things, he mused, just went together: a sword and shield, a tavern and wench, his spear and a demon's hairy arse, and heavy metal and motorcycles. There was no better feeling than hitting the road on a powerful machine with a virtuosic guitar solo perforating your eardrums.

After three hours of hard climbing, they reached a small ravine that ran between the two summits. One peak towered above them like a giant spike, whereas the other was dome shaped. Armilus scuttled ahead of him like a mountain goat, and Longinus increased his pace to keep up with him. But then he stopped as the hairs on the back of his neck stood up. He spun around and scoured the mountainsides in all directions but could see nothing. Then, very slowly, he looked up and muttered a curse.

"Armilus!" he hissed.

The cambion turned around and regarded him with a surly expression. "What is it? More humour at my expense?"

Longinus put his forefinger to his lips and looked up. The cambion followed his gaze, and his face turned from ashen to white. He scrambled behind a large rock and hid. Longinus followed and crouched down beside him.

High above them, thousands upon thousands of winged incubi were flying over their position. They were in strict formations and heading in the same direction as Longinus and the cambion.

"What is happening?" Longinus whispered.

"It is a Conventicle!" Armilus gasped fearfully.

"What? An unlawful religious meeting?"

"No—an unholy one. Satan is assembling the armies of Hell for his attack on Purgatory."

Longinus moved further behind the rock to obtain more cover. The cambion's larger eye seemed more watery than usual, and he rubbed the back of his bald dome nervously.

"Why, Purgatory?"

"To capture the human souls that languish there."

"I saw no souls when I was in Purgatory."

"Purgatory is vast and has many parts."

"Agrat Bat called it the Plain of Souls."

"That is a no-man's-land between Heaven and Hell. If you had travelled further into Purgatory, you would have seen millions of souls being purified."

"Why do they need to be purified?"

"They are the souls who committed sins but were granted salvation by the Great Tyrant. They are not pure enough to enter Heaven."

"How long does it take?"

"Months, years, centuries, I know not."

They sat in silence as a never-ending stream of demons filled the blazing sky above them. Longinus spent the time by rubbing more dirt on his face and body to camouflage himself. After twenty minutes, the last group of incubi passed over them.

Longinus peeked out from behind the rock and grinned. The coast was clear. He stood up and was about to speak to Armilus when he noticed something out of the corner of his eye. He froze. A solitary straggler was looking down upon him. Longinus cursed himself for failing to see it. The scarlet empyrean glare had hidden the incubi's figure.

Armilus made to crawl out from behind the rock.

"Stay there!" Longinus hissed, glancing up with his eyes.

The cambion followed his gaze, gasped in horror, and retreated back into his hiding place.

The demon was hovering some two hundred feet above him. At that distance, the centurion hoped that the incubus would think he was another demon, but if it ventured closer, his disguise would most certainly be detected. It would call other incubi to its aid, and they would capture him and the cambion. He had to think of something quickly. Then he remembered how his demon guards had saluted Asmodeus, and that gave him an idea. He drew his sword and held it in front of his face with the blade pointing upwards.

Longinus gritted his teeth and whispered, "Come on, you bastard, come on!"

Seconds seemed like minutes as he stood there helpless and exposed, but finally the incubi drew its sword and saluted back to him. Longinus watched in relief as it sheathed its blade and flew on.

"It has gone. Let us climb up and see what is happening."

Armilus reached out and grabbed his arm. "No, please! They shall see us!"

The centurion could see that the cambion was beside himself with fear.

"Very well. Stay here, and I shall return."

The half-demon rocked back and forth and muttered incoherently.

"Armilus! Did you hear what I said?"

The cambion nodded. The centurion did not understand why Armilus was such a coward. He had assumed that all demons were violent and fearless, but he obviously still had a great deal to learn about the lesser denizens of Hell. After waiting for a moment to ensure the cambion would be all right on his own, Longinus stole his way to the summit of the domed mountain.

It was slow going. Broken rock fragments, different from the cap or base rock, littered the mountaintop, as though a subterranean storm had scattered them there. At one point where the scree was thinner, he detected a glint of metal and kicked the surrounding stones away with his foot. He uncovered part of a large reddish-black metal plate. He thought it was a buried shield and cleared away more debris. The area grew larger until it was at least twelve feet wide. The plate was evidently part of a larger structure, and he suspected that something lay buried beneath his feet. He was curious to know what it was, but as this was neither the time nor the place to investigate such a mystery, he shook his head in puzzlement and continued upward.

Finally, he hauled himself to the pinnacle, slipped behind a crag and looked down. He stifled an involuntary gasp as he viewed the monstrous scene before him. Below him was a vast plain stretching into the distance. Arrayed on the flatland were millions of demons assembled in legions, and vast swarms continued to arrive by air and on foot. Thousands of giant Nephilim bellowed and argued as they trundled to join the awaiting army.

There were demons of all shapes and sizes, from small, naked hobgoblins to large semi armoured monstrosities. He recognised many of the types such as the menial skeletons, Leviathan's reptilian vassals, and Asmodeus' loathsome incubi, but there were hundreds of other fiends he had never witnessed before. Some were fleshless, perverse parodies of animals or insects, while others were beyond the comprehension of sanity: large amorphous bulks of quivering flesh, claws, and teeth that slithered or crawled.

The ground shook beneath them, and the noise was unearthly and appalling to his ears. Unholy shrieks, howls, roars, titters, and eldritch screeches filled the air and cut like daggers into his mind and soul. Swarms of odious flies surrounded the hellish host, and the foul stench of excrement and rotten meat hung over the plain like a noxious cloud.

Hideous archdemons adorned in elaborate Hell armour bellowed to lesser demons who then scuttled about conveying their masters' commands to the infernal assemblage. It seemed to Longinus that the archdemons were trying to impose some order on the demonic ranks, but such discipline did not come easily to the inhabitants of Hell. They appeared more like the disorganised barbarian hordes he had fought in the past rather than the structured formations of the Roman legions.

He sensed movement behind him and glanced over his shoulder. Armilus was crawling up to join him.

"I thought you were worried about being seen?" he whispered.

"I was more concerned about being caught on my own," the cambion grumbled.

Longinus gave him a wry smile and turned back to watch the demon horde. He noticed some legions composed of male and female demons that bore a striking resemblance to Armilus; however, unlike him, they were not deformed.

"Relatives of yours?" he asked, pointing.

Armilus squinted at them. "Yes, they are cambions."

Longinus watched them snarling, cursing and pushing each other. "They look quite warlike. Why are you not like them?"

"I am a thinker, not a warrior." the cambion said quietly. "I prefer to use my brain instead of my brawn."

Longinus glanced at him. He suspected that the cambion's deformities had influenced his nature. He looked smaller and weaker than his kin, and perhaps they had mocked and ostracised him. He had seen humans treat those who looked different or had a disability with contempt and cruelty, and he imagined that such base and ignorant behaviour was worse in Hell. But, in any case, the cambion had had the last laugh on his tormenters. He had become one of Satan's messengers, and that was a powerful position. The Evil One had obviously seen something special in him, and Longinus could but wonder what it was.

"There is no shame in that," he murmured. "Intelligence and strength of character are more important qualities."

Armilus' big eye widened in surprise. He was unused to receiving compliments from his gruff and intimidating companion.

Longinus smiled inwardly at the cambion's expression and looked back to the plain below. In the centre of the horde was a large metal tower over two hundred cubits in height. Standing on the platform was a large, imposing-looking demon clad in red armour. Upon its bull-like head, it wore a helmet with two long horns. Longinus assumed the horns were decorative, but at that very moment the demon commander removed its helmet and revealed the metal covered similar horns protruding from its head. It started bellowing at the legions. The commander's voice was so deep and thunderous that the centurion could hear it above the cacophony of madness issuing from the obscene multitude.

"Is that Satan?" he asked.

Armilus peered at the demon on the platform.

"No, that is Moloch, commander of Satan's armies, and the champion of Hell. Most other demons fear him."

Longinus narrowed his eyes and took a keener interest in the bullish archdemon. He remembered the lost souls of the infants they had encountered in the Valley of Moloch and wished he was close enough to thrust his spear down the demon's throat. That would shut its big, gaping mouth and repay it for all the children it had made suffer. Longinus envisaged in his mind's eye the demon screaming in agony as its body withered and died. He smiled grimly at this most satisfying of visions.

Another demon commander appeared on the platform. It was tall and thin with a goat's head and legs. Its slow and deliberate movements oozed with malevolent intelligence, and it reminded him of representations of the Devil he had seen over the centuries in art and in books.

"Surely, that is Satan?"

"No. That is Azazel, the demon god of the desert."

"And Aaron shall cast lots over two goats, one lot for the Lord and the other lot for Azazel," Naram-Sin murmured.

"Sorry?" asked Longinus.

"That is what is written in the Jewish Torah and Christian Bible," replied Naram-Sin. *"Azazel is one the few demons named by God in the Bible. And therein lies a sign of the power of that archdemon. Even the Judeo-Christian god refers to him by name."*

"Yes," replied Longinus, *"I remember now. It was something about a scapegoat, was it not?"*

"You are correct, centurion. Like many archdemons, Azazel convinced humans to worship him as a god. The Jews would take two goats before God. They sacrificed one animal to Him and confessed all their sins upon the other before casting it into the wilderness where dwelt Azazel."

"But why did God even bother to mention Azazel?" asked Longinus. *"I thought He did not acknowledge false gods?"*

"I think by sending Azazel a live scapegoat, God was telling the Jews that they should not make sacrifices to any other god but Him. God knew Azazel. Like Moloch and Asmodeus, he was a fallen angel. It was Azazel who taught mortals how to make weapons, shields, jewellery and colouring tinctures for beautifying their eyes and bodies."

"He must be popular with the ladies," Longinus murmured.

Ignoring the centurion's all too familiar levity, Naram-Sin continued, *"These discoveries made humans wicked and caused them to wage wars, murder and fornicate wantonly. Both Azazel and Asmodeus helped Satan to lead humans astray and corrupt them."*

"It is amazing what a touch of eye shadow can do," quipped Longinus.

Their secret conversation was interrupted as deep, discordant horns echoed across the plain. A huge dark rift appeared in the air far below them, and a never-ending stream of new demons emerged from it, marching and wheeling in vast formations. The newcomers were horned, red skinned, humanoid creatures with fiery eyes. For some unfathomable reason, these demons troubled the centurion more than the other grotesque monstrosities he had witnessed.

"What are they?" he whispered to Armilus.

"A mere fraction of the evil human souls that Satan has converted into demons."

"Human souls!" Longinus exclaimed. "Asmodeus had some converts serving him, but I thought he had only done that to torment me. How many of those things are there?"

"Millions—and Satan rewards them well."

"How?"

"He gives the wicked power to influence or possess the bodies of weak or evil humans. In this way, they can continue to practise the turpitude of their mortal existences; murderers can kill, rapists can ravish, thieves can swindle and steal, and perverted ones abuse others. The converts can do anything they desire and cannot be punished. Once their hosts are captured or slain, they move on and possess other victims. Thus, these wicked ones continue to enjoy the fruits of their depravity for eternity."

"I thought the whole purpose of Hell was to punish sinners?"

"In the beginning, it was. There was an agreement between the Evil One and the Great Tyrant called the Old Laws, which defined their roles in the cosmos."

"Hmm. Archangel Michael mentioned something about the Old Laws when he confronted Asmodeus in Purgatory."

"There has always been a channel of communication between Heaven and Hell. Satan has spoken to the Great Tyrant many times since he was cast out of Heaven."

"The trials of Job being one such occasion."

"Who is Job?"

"A righteous man whom God offered up as an exemplar to Satan. But the Devil scoffed and said Job was only devout because God had blessed him with material wealth. Satan maintained that if God took away his blessings, then Job would curse his Creator. God allowed Satan to test Job. The devout man suffered pain, poverty, and a lapse of faith, but he persevered, proved Satan wrong and was rewarded by God."

"So it was a wager between the Great Tyrant and Satan?"

"Yes, I suppose it was," Longinus mused. "The relationship between Satan and God is not as straightforward as many of the righteous believe."

"That is true," replied Armilus. "The exact nature of their accord is unknown to any man, demon or angel. The Great Tyrant permitted Satan and the other fallen angels to escape the Lake of Fire so they could tempt man and punish sinners.

"But after the Creator's Son sacrificed his life to save mankind, Satan was furious. He felt that the Great Tyrant had tricked him and therefore pursued a new stratagem. He realised that by punishing souls, he was still obeying the Tyrant's will. So now he offers evil souls redemption."

"Redemption?"

"Yes, evil souls can choose to be punished or transformed into demons. As you may well imagine, most take the latter option. Using this stratagem, Satan has increased Hell's legions beyond imagination."

"That explains why Hell appeared so empty. I expected it to be brimming with the damned."

"Satan has imprisoned all the unconverted souls in the dungeons where there is less chance of them escaping."

"Have many escaped?"

"Yes, a surprising amount, much to the Evil One's annoyance. He gloats over his flock like a miser with a hoard of gold. The laziness and complacency of his archdemons allowed many souls to break free. Most were recaptured swiftly; however, a few have evaded the Hunter of Lost Souls for millennia. A remarkable feat, I can assure you."

"Who or what is this hunter?"

"Archdemon Eligos," the cambion replied uneasily, making the sign of the satanic inverted cross—stomach, forehead, and both shoulders—on his breastplate. "Pray that you never meet him."

"You said evil souls are the best converts. Are not all souls in the Abyss considered evil?"

"No. They are all sinners, but most are not evil. There is still good in them, and that virtue must be purged before we can convert them into demons. Centuries of incessant torture drives them insane, and they hunger for revenge against the Great Tyrant."

"Does Satan intend to use these new legions in Purgatory?"

"Yes."

Longinus shook his head and sighed. "The Evil One must truly hate God and His Son."

"With all the fury of the Abyss. Yet, there is one he despises more."

"You?" Longinus quipped.

The cambion gave him the filthiest of looks. "No! Archangel Michael."

"Why?"

"He defeated Lucifer in Heaven and quashed his rebellion against the Great Tyrant. Satan would do anything to have his revenge on the accursed archangel."

Armilus had barely finished speaking when the peak shook and enormous slabs of rock tumbled down the slopes and crashed upon the plain below. Longinus looked around in alarm. Sections of metal plates, similar to the one he had uncovered before, appeared all over the mountain.

"What is happening?" Longinus yelled.

The cambion gaped at the reddish-black panels and sprang to his feet like a frightened rabbit.

"We must flee to the other summit! Quickly!"

Armilus scrambled back down the escarpment with Longinus in hot pursuit. Gigantic tremors ran through the mountain, and they barely avoided being swept away in tumultuous landslides of scree and rocks. The centurion cursed as a shower of stones pelted his back and legs. He glimpsed a large rock strike Armilus' head, but the half-demon ran on, seemingly too petrified to feel the savage blow. More by luck than courage or skill, they arrived relatively unharmed at the ravine that ran between the summits. Longinus skidded to a halt as the ground in front of them collapsed, revealing a yawning chasm. Grabbing Armilus by the breastplate, he took a flying leap, and they landed on the opposite slope. They kept climbing and dodging falling boulders until they arrived at the top of the adjacent peak.

Longinus stared in awe as a gigantic beast emerged from under the other mountain. He had never seen a creature so large or monstrous. It had four legs and a long tail and snout. Huge metal plates covered its body like scales, and along the ridge of its back were enormous crimson spines. As it shook itself, hundreds of tons of rock and debris slid off its massive frame. It was then Longinus realised that the summit they had crouched on had been the back of a gargantuan beast.

The creature opened its cavernous jaws and roared; and the sound was so thunderous that Longinus and Armilus covered their ears and slumped to their knees. The mountain shook as the monster strode slowly across the plain to join the gathering demons.

"What—is that?" Longinus gasped.

Ashen-faced, the cambion wiped his brow with the back of his claw.

"Behemoth."

"Bloody hell!" Longinus exclaimed. He was so engrossed by the creature, he did not see the irony of his utterance. "Is that the biblical beast the righteous will eat at the feast on Judgment Day?"

"Yes, along with the other chaos monsters, Leviathan and Ziz," Armilus whimpered.

"Ziz?" Longinus yelled, trying to clear his ears.

"A giant bird that exists in the bowels of the earth. Demons whisper she is so tall that her head reaches the heavens."

"I thought Leviathan and Behemoth were archdemons?"

"No, they are monsters from the Realm of Chaos. The Great Tyrant defeated them before He created the universe and cast them into the underworld. He shall release them again at End Times and slay them with His sword. From the skin of Leviathan, He will create canopies to shelter the righteous as they feast upon the flesh of the great fish lord and Behemoth."

"What is Chaos?"

"A terrible place of ravenous beasts ruled by gigantic monstrosities called the Lords of Chaos. Only the Great Tyrant's power holds them in check. If His power should ever falter, the chaos-monsters would return to this universe and devour and destroy everything in their path: demons, angels, souls and mortals. Heaven, earth, and Hell would fall. It would mean oblivion."

"Life began in chaos and shall end in oblivion," Longinus muttered, remembering an enigmatic prophecy in the *Book of Lilith*.

"Oblivion is the ultimate death, extinction—a state of nothingness. In oblivion there is no life or afterlife, salvation or damnation, escape or rebirth. It is the end of all things. We return to the dust of the cosmos."

They both jumped as Behemoth uttered another deafening roar and its foul breath filled the plain.

"The righteous are actually going to eat Leviathan and that 'thing' at End Times?" Longinus asked, increduously.

"So it is written."

The centurion recalled the putrid stench inside Leviathan's mouth. The very thought of eating its stinking flesh almost made him retch.

"Well, good luck to them!" he growled. "I am happy being unrighteous! We cannot go this way. We must take the other path you spoke of."

"But that leads to the Dungeons of Hell!" Armilus whined.

"Have you a better idea?"

"No," Armilus sighed resignedly.

"Is there a passage through the dungeons to the next Hellmouth?"

"Yes—but the Grand Inquisitor sits upon it."

"Then he must have cheeks large enough to match his title. Our path is set. Let us travel to these foul dungeons. I am most curious to see them. They cannot be worse than Behemoth."

"As you wish," the cambion groaned, almost tearfully. "But they may be the last thing you ever see."

CHAPTER XX

Longinus and the cambion stood before enormous metal double doors, which bore the pentacle and triple-headed beast symbol of Satan.

"This is the main entrance to the dungeons," Armilus whispered. "Are you certain you wish to proceed inside? It is dangerous."

Longinus shrugged his broad shoulders. "We have no other choice. We cannot go back. What form do these torture chambers take?"

"There are twelve principal dungeons and many smaller ones. Each chamber is limitless and administered by demon inquisitors. An overlord called the Grand Inquisitor rules over them. Appointed by satanic decree, they exercise absolute power in their domain. All were once men, but are now among the Evil One's most devoted and fanatical servants. Do not speak unless spoken to. Let me converse with them, and we may just survive."

Longinus nodded and girded his loins for whatever fresh horrors would assault his senses.

"Play your part well, messenger," he hissed.

Armilus winced. "I will do my best—for both our sakes."

The cambion pushed against the immense doors with one claw, and they creaked open with little effort. A blast of hot, putrid air greeted them. Stepping over the threshold, they entered a huge domed chamber hewn from solid rock. In the centre of the area was a circular dais over one hundred cubits—the distance from the elbow to the tip of the middle finger—in diameter.

"Who dares enter the Dungeons of Hell without invitation?" a deep, sepulchral voice intoned.

Longinus started and peered around. He could not see the demon but felt its baleful presence.

The cambion reached into his breastplate, pulled out his medallion and held it aloft.

"Salutate Satanam! I am Armilus, a herald for our omnipotent and magnificent satanic majesty!" he announced grandly.

Longinus saw a crimson glimmer in the air fifty paces away. A tall, hooded shape in a black robe materialised. The ether flickered again, and the figure appeared in front of them. The demon guardian possessed no legs and floated like a wraith. Its black, shrivelled face had no lips or nose, and its deep-set ruby eyes gleamed with a malignant intensity.

The wraith glared at the cambion and studied the medallion.

"Salutate Satanam! You bear the symbol of protection from our omnificent emperor. No harm will befall you here," it said regretfully.

It turned its attention to Longinus.

"But what of this one? He carries no medallion!" it hissed excitedly, flexing its large claws.

"Leave him be!" Armilus commanded. "He is under my protection. Our master wishes him to see the dungeons."

"For what purpose?" the spectre asked, suspiciously.

"That is not for you to know!" Armilus snapped. "Our imperial master commands, and we obey without question!"

The wraith cocked its head and regarded him silently for a moment.

It spread its long, bony arms and hissed, "Then I bid thee welcome to the Dungeons of Hell!"

There sounded a tremendous clanking of great chains, and the dais beneath their feet jolted and descended slowly. The platform was a giant lift, and they were sinking into the bowels of Hell.

Longinus grimaced. The shaft was as soft and bloody as raw flesh. Embedded in the wall were thousands of human souls fused together into a horrific amorphous mass that heaved and throbbed as they moaned and begged for mercy. After a few minutes, Longinus looked up and saw only a small circle of light coming from the chamber high above them. He noticed the wraith was studying him. Disregarding Armilus' advice, he engaged it in conversation to judge its intent.

"How far is it to the dungeons?"

The wraith turned its head languidly to one side and laughed. It was sounded like the last rasps of life escaping from a corpse.

"Distance and time have no meaning here, but you shall reach your destination soon enough. Be ye certain of that."

Longinus detected an implied threat in its mocking tone, but chose to ignore it. Armilus glared at him and shook his head, warning him to keep quiet. The centurion shrugged and stared at the blood-soaked wall.

Deeper and deeper the platform descended. They stood in silence as the continuous stream of souls appeared and then vanished into the Stygian darkness above them. Longinus knew they were sinners, but he could not help feeling pity for them. It was a terrible way to spend eternity. He glanced at Armilus. The cambion was standing with his back erect and his head held proudly. He had a confident, disdainful look on his face. For the first time since they had met, the half-demon exuded the dignity and authority, which Longinus assumed that a true messenger of Hell would display. This was a side of Armilus he had never seen before, and he hoped the cambion could maintain his performance until they escaped the dungeons. Their survival and freedom depended upon him now.

The amber flickering lights of flambeaux broke his reverie. He steadied himself as the dais jolted to a halt with a deafening boom and rattle of chains.

He beheld a titanic dome-shaped chamber with twelve massive portcullis gates arranged like a clock face around the wall. Between each gate was the entrance to a tunnel. The chamber floor was strewn with hundreds of obscene devices operated by obese demon torturers. The tormentors' red, sweaty bodies were clad in bloodstained leather aprons that amply displayed their disgusting naked backsides and tails. Slits in their black hoods revealed their leering, sadistic eyes and grinning mouths. Beside them stood horned fiends, adorned in monks' habits, who supervised the excruciation of the victims with fanatical glee and fervour.

"Confess! Confess and I shall end thy torture!" shrieked one diabolical zealot at a naked succubus tied to the rack before it.

The monk signalled to the burly torturer to activate the handle and ratchet mechanism. Longinus winced at the succubus's high-pitched screams as her cartilage popped and bones snapped.

At another rack, the fiendish interrogator took a quieter yet more abhorrent approach.

"Tell me and I shall, and I shall end thy suffering," he said soothingly, stroking the she-devil's brow as a torturer nipped her breasts with metal pincers.

Next to them, a small cage containing another succubus hung from the high, vaulted ceiling. Below the cage was a large brazier belching Hellfire. The demoness howled in agony as a torturer prodded her with red-hot irons and flames licked her burnt, blackened body.

Another female demon was bound to a giant spiked wheel that broke her bones as it revolved.

On a table lay yet another succubus tied spread-eagled. A torturer with a licentious protruding tongue had just finished inserting a pear-shaped metal object into her vagina. It screwed the 'holy pear of anguish' open, and she shrieked as the serrated blades ripped her cervix apart.

Longinus stared in horror. The chamber was an obscene recreation of the Tribunal of the Holy Office of the Inquisition—more commonly known as the Spanish Inquisition. In his dark past, he had stormed one of their strongholds to rescue a blacksmith and his family. He had been too late to save the kindly couple and their children, but he had freed those who were still alive and sane. The inquisitors and torturers, he had slaughtered with impunity.

"But I do the work of God!" one inquisitor had screamed as Longinus thrust him, trembling and urinating with fear, into an Iron Maiden.

"Then go and join your God!" Longinus had roared, kicking the door shut and plunging the lethal spikes into the inquisitor's flesh. The monk's dying screams had been most gratifying to hear.

He had stumbled upon the loathsome cleric ordering his torturers to add extra weights to the ankles of a heavily pregnant woman they had strung from a beam. The innocent and devout mother had confounded the expectations of her tormentors by lasting over a week without confessing to be a witch. She and her unborn child had died in Longinus' arms after he cut her down. Her last words to him were, "I forgive them. My child will be born in the arms of the Lord." However, the centurion had not been as forgiving as she. He had cursed the Christian God and killed every guard, torturer, monk, and sadistic voyeur he found.

Many years later, he had discovered that her death, and the demise of hundreds of thousands of innocents like her, had served as a rallying cry among brave, enlightened men and women—for behind every enlightened man there was an enlightened woman urging her husband on and guiding his Christian conscience—in their fight for reason to prevail and to put an end to the horrors, superstitions and gross injustices of the Holy Inquisitions.

But as Longinus well knew, it had taken a very long time to stop the madness. Rooting out witches and heretics was a very profitable business. In Europe, the Middle Ages diseases of superstition, ignorance, and hysteria continued well into the late 18th century; and the Spanish Inquisition continued to do 'God's work' until Queen Isabella II abolished it in 1834.

As Longinus and Armilus stood transfixed by the hideous scenes, the wraith glided away and approached a tall, horned demon sitting on a throne constructed from human bones. It was an ugly fiend attired in a scarlet robe and fish head mitre cap similar to those worn by ancient Babylonian priests and modern pontiffs.

"That is the Grand Inquisitor," Armilus whispered.

"He would make Vatican tours less popular," Longinus murmured.

"What?"

"Never mind."

The wraith and the Grand Inquisitor exchanged some words, and the Pontifex glared suspiciously at them. The wraith bowed and vanished. In the blink of an eye, it appeared before Longinus and the cambion.

"Follow me. My master has deigned to grant you an audience."

"He honours us," Armilus said.

"Indeed, he does," the wraith replied, somewhat enigmatically.

They accompanied the loathsome spectre through the gruesome scenes of torture, screams and dismemberment. Longinus noticed huge piles of succubi armour and tridents lying around the circumference of the chamber. He tightened his grip on his spear and kept a wary eye on the ranting, fervid monks and bared-arsed torturers.

After a few minutes, they arrived at the throne, and the Grand Inquisitor stared balefully at them. The fiend was gaunt with a colossal head, wide mouth, and bulging yellow eyes with slitted red pupils. As the unholy pontiff scrutinised them, Longinus felt he was being dissected with the same dispassionate coldness as a scientist cutting up a frog. He suspected the hellish cleric was assessing which forms of torture would be most effective on them.

"Salutate Satanam!" Armilus said, bowing.

"Salutate Satanam, dominum obscurum magistrumque!" the Grand Inquisitor corrected him irritably. "You failed to address me using the full salutation that both honours and pledges eternal loyalty to our satanic majesty. Are you a heretic, messenger?"

"I am no dissenter, my lord."

"So say you," the inquisitor replied with a thin smile.

"No, so sayeth Archdemon Baal Zebub, my lord," the cambion replied calmly. "It is he who determines imperial protocol on behalf of our satanic emperor, and it is he who has instructed heralds such as myself on how to address the archdemons and lords of Hell. Only archdemons are permitted to give the full greeting, and I am but a lowly herald. Do you wish me to return to Archdemon Baal Zebub and inform him you request all imperial heralds to honour you with the full salutation?"

The demon lord's eyes narrowed as he tried to discern if the herald was being impertinent or merely stating the facts. However, the cambion's face and manner betrayed no evidence of disrespect. In any case, the inquisitor had no desire to offend Baal Zebub who had the ear of Satan.

"That will not be necessary," he said quickly. "Your salutation was proper. I sought merely to test your knowledge."

"I understand, my lord."

Longinus also understood. If the sly inquisitor had succeeded in tricking the cambion into using the full greeting, he would have accused the messenger of heresy. Armilus had handled it well.

"These are dangerous times, herald. Traitors and heretics are everywhere. We must all be vigilant and show resolve in exposing our master's enemies."

"I could not agree more, my lord," Armilus replied.

The Grand Inquisitor arose and glided down the throne steps. He was over ten feet in height and clasped his bony claws on his chest. He reminded Longinus of a Praying Mantis.

"Your face seems familiar to me. Have you have visited the dungeons before?"

"I have, my lord."

"You bear another message from our satanic master?"

"Yes, your Excellency," Armilus lied. "Our emperor wishes to ascertain your progress."

The Grand Inquisitor grinned, revealing long, pointed teeth.

"It is most gratifying to know that our emperor takes such a personal interest in our work. As you can observe, we are working tirelessly to root out the traitors and heretics."

"Why do all the demons here dress like monks?" Longinus asked.

The Grand Inquisitor glared at the centurion. "Have you not taught your servant to be silent in the presence of his betters?"

Armilus gave the centurion a scathing look. "Apologies, my lord. He is not my servant, but a messenger in training. Archdemon Baal Zebub commanded him to accompany me so he may learn the locations of Hell's dominions."

The unholy pontiff gave Longinus a curious look. "You are neither a demon nor a human soul. Yet, there is still life in you—I can sense it. What manner of being are you?"

"A vampire," Longinus sighed.

He was getting tired with having to explain himself to demons. The little devil in him whispered he should call himself a shit stirrer next time and see what infernal confusion that caused among the horntails.

"Hah! You are naught but one of our minor servants who straddle the realm between the mortal coil and Hell," the demon lord said disdainfully.

"Yes—I do much straddling," the centurion replied innocently.

The Grand Inquisitor's ocherous slits narrowed, but he could see no trace of insolence on Longinus' face.

He smiled and said to Armilus, "A most unusual choice of being to serve as a messenger of Hell."

The Grand Inquisitor's apparently innocuous comment did not deceive the cambion. He knew that his loyalty was being tested. If he agreed with the remark, he would be accused of doubting Satan's wisdom and therefore heresy.

"I do not question," he replied tersely. "I do as my master commands."

The pontiff nodded in approval. "Well said! As do we all! We must obey our emperor's will and pledge our eternal obedience and loyalty to him."

The Grand Inquisitor then fixed Longinus with a penetrating stare. "In answer to your question—straddler—like you, we were once mortal men. We were Dominican and Franciscan monks. The church appointed us as inquisitors and gave us the title of *Dogs of the Lord*. Our popes ordered us to seek out and punish witches, apostates and heretics. However, for the agonies we inflicted on mortals, the Great Tyrant damned us to eternal punishment in Hell. But He made saints of the very pontiff's who directed us on our holy quests and granted them everlasting life in Heaven!"

"Perhaps you pursued your mission with too much zeal?" Longinus suggested coldly.

The demon growled. "Our only mistake was believing in the Great Tyrant. But our satanic master is merciful. Instead of condemning us to the tortures of Hell, he empowered us to carry on our work. Only now, instead of seeking out those who reject the Word of the Tyrant, we pursue those who betray our true lord and saviour, Satan!"

"Are there many who are disloyal?" asked Longinus.

The Grand Inquisitor regarded him incredulously.

"We are surrounded by traitor and dissenters! After the defection of the whore, Lilith, and the rebellion of the accursed Pazuzu, all are suspect. Our most Satanic Majesty has given us unlimited power in rooting out the traitors and making them confess."

Longinus' ears pricked up at the mention of Lilith's name.

"Do you know why she defected?"

"Not as yet, but we are confident that her succubi whores will shed some light on the matter. We shall not rest until we have uncovered the truth," the demon said with an icy grin.

"What was your mortal name?" Longinus asked.

"Why do you wish to know? It has no meaning in Hell."

"I am curious. Our paths may have crossed."

The demon pontiff gave a mirthless laugh. "If we had met, you would remember me. All mortals feared my name."

"Which was?" Longinus asked, nonchalantly.

"It is of no importance," Armilus blurted.

"Oh, but it is, messenger!" the demon lord insisted. "Your neophyte shows his ignorance and must be educated. My mortal name was—Tomas de Torquemada, Grand Inquisitor General for all of Spain! I was a man of substantial power and reputation."

Longinus bristled with indignation. This monster had sent thousands of people to torture chambers and the stake in the name of the papal *auto-de-fe* —the act of faith.

The torturing of the victim's children had been prevalent, as the inquisitors knew infants had a lower resistance to pain. 'Glory be only to God!' the torture devices had inscribed on them. After crushed ankles, broken ribs or pulled fingernails, most children screamed that their parents, brothers, sisters and everyone they knew were heretics and in league with the Devil. After the children's parents were burned at the stake, the orphans, now crippled in body and mind by the cruelty of the inquisition, were left to starve on the streets. No relative or good Samaritan dared feeding or sheltering them for fear of being accused of heresy or witchcraft by association.

Many inquisitors later admitted regretting their 'leniency' towards the offspring of heretics and witches, believing the Devil had clouded their judgement. Therefore, instead of just having infants flogged as they watched their parents burn, these devout men of God wished they had also cast the foul progeny of the offenders into the holy fires.

The land and possessions of executed apostates, heretics and witches were divided between the church and the state. Many prelates, torturers, officials, aristocrats and sovereigns became wealthy beyond their wildest dreams by enforcing the Word of God. Such was the power, bigotry, greed and hypocrisy of the papal and Spanish inquisitions.

Longinus never had the pleasure of killing Torquemada, but years after the inquisitor's death, the centurion had disinterred his bones and incinerated them. In those dark days, he had believed that destroying the friar's physical remains would prevent him from receiving a new glorified body at the Resurrection. He now realised he should not have bothered; Torquemada's soul had been sent to Hell. However, he was determined to wipe the smug look off the hideous pontiff's face.

"Yes, your reputation is indeed great. You are one of the most reviled men in history," Longinus retorted.

"Excellent!" hissed Torquemada. "Let them fear me and pray that they do not meet me in Hell. There is nothing I enjoy more than watching a human soul squirm in agony."

"Yes, but you were not always so immune to the suffering of others."

Torquemada glanced sharply at him. "What do you mean?"

"Many people said that you could not bear to watch your victims being tortured and often left the chamber in tears."

Torquemada looked taken aback and glared around to see who might be listening. He noticed two demon inquisitors staring at him.

"What are you gawking at? Get back to work!" he bellowed.

"Is it not true?" Longinus asked with an insolent smile.

Torquemada flexed his claws and regarded him with a baleful expression. What Longinus said was true, but he had no desire to have it made known to his fellow inquisitors. It would damage his prestige and status as Grand Inquisitor of Hell.

"Lies!" he growled. "It was a foul rumour spread by my enemies to undermine my position. I enjoyed watching the accused suffer!"

"Then it is a pity that humans have branded you as weak, insane sadist," Longinus said regretfully. "History is so unkind sometimes."

Torquemada hissed with displeasure.

Armilus' bigger eye widened imperceptibly as he saw more inquisitors emerging from the tunnels. They were whispering to each other and staring in his direction. He was getting a very uncomfortable feeling about this insane adventure and cursed Longinus for persuading him to take part in it.

"We shall take our leave, my lord," he said casually to Torquemada. "We do not wish to interrupt your important work for any longer than necessary."

The Grand Inquisitor's mood became more affable.

"But you have travelled such a long way!" he protested. "You must at least look through the gates to the dungeons before you depart. Only then can you give our esteemed satanic master a fair and detailed report of our progress."

"Very well, your excellency," Armilus said reluctantly. "But we must not tarry too long. Archdemon Baal Zebub has entrusted us with other important messages to deliver. One is for the King of Demons, and he frowns upon being kept waiting."

Longinus raised an eyebrow and smiled to himself. The cambion's bluff was a good one. Surely even the Grand Inquisitor of Hell would seek to avoid angering the mighty Asmodeus.

"Of course, of course!" Torquemada said worriedly. "We would not wish to delay an important imperial message to the Prince of Lust and Revenge! After you inspect the gates, I shall grant you access again to the underground passage that leads to the Hellmouth on the other side of the dungeons. That will facilitate your haste and make good any time lost."

Armilus breathed a huge, secret sigh of relief. This is exactly what he wanted! Perhaps the Revenant's plan was not as harebrained as he had thought.

"Thank you, my lord," he replied. "It will delight us to observe and record your labours."

"Excellent! Follow me!" the Grand Inquisitor gushed, eager to have proof of his loyalty and fanatical zeal relayed to his unholy master.

They wound their way through the horrendous scenes of excruciation and stopped before one of the portcullis gates. It comprised a metal lattice grille some fifty cubits in width and one hundred cubits in height. Attached to the front of the gate was a large, round, pulsing satanic seal of polished obsidian.

"What is the purpose of the seal?" Longinus asked.

"The souls of the damned are held captive by the symbol of our master," answered Torquemada. "Through the power of these seals, we may administer punishments as we see fit. Observe how they writhe and squirm! Their cries are like a symphony of pleasure to my ears and send shivers of ecstasy down my spine!"

"What would happen if you released the souls?" Longinus enquired.

"We will never free them," Torquemada laughed.

"But what if they were? Where would they go? Would they just drift aimlessly in Hell?"

"You ask the most curious questions," Torquemada said irritably. "Of course they would not remain in Hell. Any soul not imprisoned here would be drawn to Limbo and languish until End Times for its immortal fate to be decided. But as you already know, our satanic master does not want that. He wishes to convert them to his cause."

Longinus stared through the gaps in the grille and saw naked men and women hanging by their tongues from metal beams as fiery-eyed skeletons prodded them with pitchforks and hot irons. The moans of the damned were most pitiful to hear. The gruesome scene extended as far as the eye could see, and Longinus realised the portcullises were not gates to cells; they were portals to vast and separate realms of torture.

"Who are these people?" he asked.

"These are the Blasphemers. Is it not apt that the same organ that condemned them to Hell should provide the instrument of their suffering?" Torquemada replied gleefully.

"It is truly a work of art," said Armilus. "Our emperor will be most pleased to hear of this."

The Grand Inquisitor's eyes glowed with sadistic pleasure, and Armilus' compliment seemed to warm him to his task.

They followed him to the second gate and saw those who had perverted justice burning in large pits. Adulterous men dangled from meat hooks by their genitals and unfaithful women hung by their breasts.

In the third vault, they beheld souls who had persecuted the righteous and surrendered them to be tried, tortured or put to death. They lay writhing in pits while large, vicious-looking tapeworms devoured their bowels.

Those who had born false witness against others lay in the fourth keep. Some had their mouths stuffed with burning coals, while others were forced to bite off and swallow their tongues in an endless bloody cycle.

In the fifth dungeon were the rich and selfish who had not helped or shown compassion to the poor, sick and destitute. They walked on red-hot flints that cut like razors while carrying heavy sacks of gold on their backs.

The next realm held the moneylenders, who had charged interest and interest on interest, driving their victims to despair or death. They counted burning silver coins while being scourged by skeletons. It appeared to Longinus that the fiery-eyed, skeletal torturers were the infernal worker drones of Hell.

At the seventh gate, Longinus saw men and women being pushed off high cliffs by skeletons. After they fell, imps forced them to drag their broken bodies back up the slope to begin again. Some male souls were being castrated, while many souls of both sexes were having hot pokers forced into their writhing bodies.

"These are the ones who polluted their bodies through masturbation, fellatio, cunnilingus, sodomy, homosexuality, incest, bestiality, having intercourse with a woman when she is ritually unclean, and other unnatural acts!" Torquemada shrieked. "See how they burn, break and bleed!"

He ushered them to the eighth dungeon. There they beheld multitudes of souls dragging grotesque statues through a foul-smelling sea of excrement.

"Let me guess," Longinus said. "They worshipped false gods and idols?"

Torquemada gave a high-pitched squeal of delight. "Yes, yes! That is so! You are learning swiftly, neophyte. We obtain many willing converts from this dungeon."

Longinus sighed. He was tired of this hellish tour but held his peace. Torquemada was obviously relishing showing them his handiwork, and he knew it would be unwise to further antagonise their disgusting host. The sooner they finished, the quicker they could leave this accursed place.

The ninth dungeon held people skewered and turning on spits over furious fires. They were the apostates who had left the path of God.

At the tenth gate, Longinus gazed through the lattice and saw a myriad of souls tied to the stinking ground and consumed by large, poisonous, spider-like insects. Other souls were impaled on stakes that entered their rectums and emerged through their mouths. The noise of the feeding; and screams and moans of the victims were deafening.

"This is by far our largest dungeon," Torquemada announced grandly.

"And what foul sins did these souls commit?" Longinus asked.

"These are the atheists and agnostics! They were too clever to believe in Heaven and too stupid to believe in Hell. This is my favoured dungeon. Can you guess why?"

"Because they have goodness left in them, and nothing brings you more pleasure than torturing a soul that has some good in it?" Longinus answered wearily.

"Yes!" the Grand Inquisitor, exclaimed. "How did you know?"

"I had a good tutor," the centurion replied grimly, thinking of Asmodeus.

Torquemada grinned at him. The thin black lips stretched over bared teeth looked manic and ready to snap.

"He taught you well. Many of these souls have goodness in them. Their only sin was failing to believe in the Great Tyrant, but in all other ways they led exemplary lives. Most spirits in the twelve dungeons are not evil and that heightens my enjoyment as I watch them suffer."

"Do you obtain many converts from the non-believers?" Armilus interjected, eager to divert Torquemada's attention away from Longinus.

"Indeed! Along with the idolaters, it is our largest source of converts. Of course, many are still too virtuous for us to mould into demons, but in time their goodness will fade. No one can endure the agonies of the dungeons forever. We speed the process by making the weakest souls supervise the punishments of the strongest. It has proven to be very successful stratagem. More and more seek to impress us with their cruelty and become overseers."

"Remarkable, my lord!" replied the cambion. "I am certain your devotion and guile will please our imperial master."

"Your praise is most gratifying to hear. Most demons, indeed even archdemons, do not appreciate the work we undertake here. They fear and despise us. Do they not understand that it is through our zealous efforts, the satanic legions have increased tenfold?"

"That is very true, your excellency," Armilus replied sympathetically. "But rest assured that I will make Archdemon Baal Zebub and our satanic master aware of your continued diligence and outstanding successes!"

Torquemada clasped his bony claws and bowed his head. Some grubs wriggled out from beneath his mitre.

"You are too kind," he said with a self-satisfied smile.

Armilus bowed in return, but a warning bell tolled in his head. Demons never used the word 'kind' as a compliment.

At the eleventh dungeon, Longinus grunted in horror. He had seen many terrible sights in Hell, but this one was beyond belief. Female souls stood chained and up to their waists in blood, and babies hovered and screeched above them. Fiery rays issued from the hellish neonates' eyes, blinding and scorching the flesh of the women.

"They are the cursed ones who made abortions!" See how the murdered fruit of their own wombs tortures them!" Torquemada said triumphantly.

It shocked Longinus to see the innocent children were also in Hell, and he hoped it was an illusion, some form of devilish trickery. But he then remembered that Saint Peter had described a similar fate for the unborn in his Apocalypse of Peter. For some demented, inexplicable reason, God cast them into the Bottomless Pit to torture their mothers.

"Why are the men who impregnated these women not suffering alongside them?" Longinus demanded.

Torquemada looked at him in amazement. "Because women have cold wombs that need filling to warm them, and it is in their sinful nature to tempt men from the path of righteousness! Men are the victims of this outrage and entirely blameless in the matter."

"Perhaps such grovelling weaklings should learn to keep their cocks in their loincloths or marry the poor girls," Longinus growled.

The Grand Inquisitor hissed in annoyance at such rude language. Although a demon lord, the twisted Dominican in him still took offence at matters of—as Pope Innocent III had so amply described it—the 'most filthy sperm' being discussed. Coupling was for procreation and not pleasure. He still adhered to the view of the church in his time—any woman, married or not, who enjoyed such licentious practices was a harlot, a witch and beyond salvation. A truly virtuous woman would feel interminable shame and pray for forgiveness before, during, and after the disgusting act.

Satan had chosen his inquisitors well, and it amused him that such formerly pious men used the primitive laws of the Great Tyrant as excuses for the sadistic tortures they inflicted on the screaming souls in the Abyss. Fervent righteousness and blind obedience to a religion was a two-edged sword that could be wielded for good or evil. Unfortunately, in the dark history of mankind, wickedness had prevailed and millions of innocent and falsely accused human souls had poured into the leering, avaricious, and blazing coffers of Hell.

They moved on to the last dungeon. Torquemada gazed through the lattice with wild, staring eyes and rubbed his claws together.

"This realm once contained the thieves, pedophiles, rapists, sadists and murderers—but no longer. Our imperial majesty has seen fit to grant an amnesty to all such souls, and they have joined our ranks. Therefore, we now imprison Lilith's legions here."

Longinus stared in amazement. The dungeon was brimming with thousands of succubi. Most sat with their eyes downcast and awaited their torture, but a few stood and glared at their jailers. One caught Longinus' eye. This succubus differed from the others. She was fair and had the legs of a mule. She gazed defiantly at him, and he averted his eyes. His burning desire to punish all demons faltered. He felt guilty that they would torture her when she was blameless. Only he, Asmodeus, and Lilith's daughters knew the truth behind Lilith's defection. It had involved none of the succubi.

He looked back at her, and their eyes locked. He gave her a slight nod, which he hoped she would interpret as a sign of his empathy, his irrational desire not to be construed as one of her torturers, but she showed no response. Longinus did not blame her. She did not know who he was and why he was here. She did not know that he had loved, worshipped, and died countless times for her queen. For the first time in his existence, he felt cowardly. He could free her if he told the truth, but he knew that honesty was not welcome in Hell. Truthfulness would only lead to him being tortured alongside the brave and truculent succubus.

"Ah, there is no greater pleasure than seeing a beautiful face contorted in agony," Torquemada said gleefully.

Two demon monks glided across to them and whispered in the Grand Inquisitor's ear. He listened for a moment and stared at Longinus.

"Any god who punishes souls in these ways is a madman or psychopath," Longinus murmured.

"I agree with you," Torquemada said smoothly. "All the things you have seen here are done, and can only be done, with the Great Tyrant's permission. This was agreed under the Old Laws of Heaven and Hell. However, your display of outrage betrays your genuine feelings—and your identity."

"What do you mean?" asked Longinus.

One of the inquisitors standing beside Torquemada said to Longinus, "My mortal name was Heinrich Kramer. Is it familiar to you?"

Longinus frowned. "No. Should it be?"

The monk scowled. "My Latin name was Henricus Institoris, and I wrote the *Malleus Maleficarum*. Do you know what that is?"

"I do. It is the *Hammer of Witches*—a guide for witch finders and the inquisition."

"I drowned in the Morava river in the town of Kromeriz in 1505."

"How very unfortunate for you."

"My fellow Dominicans believed I fell into the river by accident—but someone murdered me."

"Oh?"

"A knight threw me into the water while crying, 'Let us see whether you sink or float!' "

"It seems an ironic end for the man whose treatise caused the deaths of eighty thousand women and led to eight million being killed in the church's name during the Thirty Years' War," Longinus replied dryly.

The second monk glided forward. "My name was Conrad of Marburg."

Longinus shrugged. "And?"

"I was an inquisitor sent by Pope Gregory the IX to Germany to seek out witches and heretics. I excelled in my task and sent thousands to the faggot to burn."

"Yes, thousands of innocent people."

"Ah, you do remember me," replied the monk.

The centurion grimaced. More ghosts from his past had returned to gnaw on his bones. He glanced at the cambion and saw his face was ashen with fear.

"I do," Longinus replied. "Because of your inquisitions, brothers accused brothers, wives accused husbands, and children accused parents. Tell me, monk, how much torture did it require to force a child to lie about their mother and father?"

"Oh, very little," Conrad replied grinning. "However, I always took my time. The screams of children were like the harps of angels to my ears."

"Indeed!" the centurion growled.

"But," continued the monk, "a local count resisted my mission and even rallied the local clergy behind him. His adviser was a knight. He always stood in the shadows, and I never saw his face. They drove us out of Sayn, and we vowed to return with increased numbers to enforce the Pope's will. But when we reached the crossroads near Marburg, the knight overtook us, with visor down, and slew us with his spear. He said it was a just fate for the pain and suffering we had caused to others. Does that tale mean anything to you?"

"No. Should it?"

"As I have said," Conrad continued with an evil smile, "I never saw the knight's countenance–but I have always remembered his deep, melodious voice."

"Is there a point to your endless prattle?" asked Longinus.

"Oh, there is indeed, straddler!" the Grand Inquisitor shrieked. "You killed them! *You* were the mysterious scourge of our order. How many Dominican inquisitors died at your hands?"

Longinus knew the game was up and spat on the ground at Torquemada's feet.

"Not enough!"

Torquemada gave a hollow laugh. "Did you and this pathetic cripple believe you could deceive us? Our imperial master warned us to be on the lookout for a renegade messenger and Lilith's Revenant. Our satanic emperor will be most pleased to hear that we, his loyal inquisitors, have apprehended you. But first–we shall let you enjoy the full delights of our torture chambers."

The air in front of Longinus warped, and the wraith appeared. He thrust his spear at the guardian's chest, but it passed through its body and caused it no harm.

"Your spear is useless against me, Revenant," the apparition hissed. "I am incorporeal and have no flesh or bones. But I can inflict pain upon you."

It lunged at Longinus, gripped his face in its claws and threw him to the ground. Institoris and Conrad grabbed the cambion and held him in their vice-like grips.

"Unhand me!" Armilus shrieked. "I am a satanic messenger!"

"You are a snivelling traitor!" Torquemada roared. "You helped the Revenant escape and betrayed our master!"

Longinus jumped up and swung the spear at the spectre's head. He grunted in pain as the wraith struck him on the jaw and sent him reeling. The impalpable guardian grabbed him by the hair, dragged him along the floor and threw him against the dungeon gate.

The centurion spat blood and struggled to his feet. Hundreds of demon monks were pouring into the chamber like rats.

The wraith gave a low, malevolent laugh. "Throw down your weapon,

Revenant."

Longinus wiped his bloody lips with the back of his hand and tried desperately to think of a way to defeat an opponent whom he could not touch.

Then he heard Naram-Sin screaming in his mind.

"The seal on the gate! Destroy it and free the succubi!"

Longinus smiled grimly. He knew not whether Naram-Sin's suggestion would work, but it was worth a try. At this precise moment, anything was worth a try. Readying his spear, he faced the wraith and the army of inquisitors that surrounded him.

"You cannot defeat us, Revenant. We are the masters here!" Torquemada cried triumphantly.

Longinus grinned savagely, his eyes as fierce as a cornered lion.

"Then it time for the slaves to have revenge upon their masters," he hissed.

With a swiftness that surprised his opponents, he spun around and struck the gate seal with his spear. His eyes widened as arcs of red lighting flashed from his weapon. With a thunderous boom, the satanic emblem smashed into thousands of pieces, and the great gate rumbled open. The Evil One's spell of binding holding the dungeon's captives in a state of submissiveness was broken. The succubus with the mule's legs gave an ear-splitting battle cry, and thousands of her kin sprang to their feet and attacked the skeleton guards.

"Noooo!" screamed Torquemada.

The wraith flew at Longinus, but he ducked under its claws and ran for the eleventh gate.

Torquemada, Conrad and Institoris shrieked in terror as a flood of angry succubi swarmed through the gate and enveloped them.

"I am the Grand Inquisitor!" Torquemada screeched as they ripped his head from his shoulders. Conrad and Kramer's heads soon followed and bounced across the floor to join their foul master's.

The succubus with the mule's legs was in command and issued orders. At her bidding, most of the succubi grabbed their armour and weapons and escaped up through the lift shaft. However, they left a substantial rearguard behind them to mete out punishment to their torturers.

Longinus smashed the seal of the eleventh gate and watched it open.

The wraith ignored Longinus and turned to rescue its master. It ploughed a path through the succubi, tearing at them with its claws. The female demons tried to strike the wraith, but their tridents passed through its body and could not injure it. The guardian howled in rage when it found Torquemada's decapitated corpse.

Taking advantage of the mayhem, Longinus started breaking the seals on the other gates. Monks tried to stop him, but armed succubi cut them down.

The souls were flying towards the open gates. Satan no longer had power over them, and soon they would be free.

He turned to see the angry wraith bearing down on him.

"I will tear thee limb from limb!" it roared.

Longinus pointed his spear at it.

"Fool! Your puny weapon cannot harm me!"

"No–but they can," Longinus retorted grimly, shoulder rolling clear of the gate.

The wraith's eyes bulged as an ocean of vengeful human souls engulfed it. They too were incorporeal and could inflict damage upon its body. The wraith shrieked in agony as the multitude of the damned took pleasure in ripping it apart.

A monk wielding an axe ran screaming at Longinus. He stood motionless until it was with range, then lunged and thrust his spear through its chest. He sensed movement behind him and turned to see another deranged cleric with a raised axe in its claw gaping at him. Three sharp-looking metal points protruded from its face. The mule legged succubus kicked the monk to its knees and wrenched her trident free from its bloody skull.

"Watch your back, warrior!" she said with an icy grin.

Before he could reply, she spread her wings and flew off to join her kin who were pursuing the monks and torturers down the tunnels leading from the main chamber

Longinus walked over to the dungeon containing the mothers and children. The centurion was in two minds whether to break the seal. He was uncertain whether the unborn would allow their mothers to escape or take kindly to him releasing them. As in the Valley of Moloch, the last thing he wanted was to fight little children. In fact, deep down, he knew he could never bring himself to do it.

"Naram-Sin?"

"I do not know, centurion. Do what you think is right."

Longinus gave a deep sigh and then shattered the seal with his spear.

The gate rattled open. As he watched in trepidation, the infants ceased torturing their mothers and began wailing. Slowly, each unborn drifted into their mother's waiting arms and was comforted by her.

Armilus hobbled up and stood beside him. It surprised the centurion to realise he felt glad his surly demon companion had survived.

"I have never beheld such a sight," the cambion whispered.

Longinus smiled. "Yes–it is most pleasing."

One mother and child drifted out of the gate and floated above them.

"You have freed us from the torments of Hell, and for that we are eternally grateful. We are reunited with the children we lost."

"I am happy for you," Longinus replied. "Now, flee. You must travel to Limbo. There you will be safe. No demons can enter there."

"But it was God who sent us to Hell. Will He not send us back here?"

"I hope not. I think you have suffered enough. Can you find your way to Limbo?"

"Fear not. I can feel it calling. When we arrive there, I shall tell my people what you did for us."

"Who are your people?" asked Longinus.

"I am Donatiya of the Canaanites."

A young male soul joined her. "And I shall tell my people. I am Alexandro of the Athenians."

Then many souls from the other dungeons joined them and told Longinus their names and the lands of their peoples. There were shades from throughout history and from all nations.

After a few minutes, Longinus said, "You must go now before Satan realises what is happening. Go quickly and do not stop until you reach Limbo. I hope the God of the Jews and Christians will grant you mercy and give you peace."

"Farewell, Longinus," said Donatiya. "We shall never forget you."

"Nor I you, Donatiya of the Canaanites," Longinus said kindly.

As the centurion and cambion stared in wonderment, millions upon millions of glowing souls entered the lift shaft. They travelled slowly at first but soon gathered speed until the great exodus of incorporeal bodies became a beauteous and fantastical blur of motion.

In less than a hundred heartbeats, the dungeons were empty, and all that remained were the torn and bloody corpses of the inquisitors and torturers.

"Well—that was harrowing," Longinus quipped.

"How did they know your name?" Armilus asked.

Longinus frowned. "I must have told them."

"You did not."

The centurion shrugged. "What does it matter? We have done a good day's work."

"Satan's wrath will be great!" warned Armilus.

"Aye, I am sure it will—and so will God's," Longinus added cheerfully. "We are now at the top of both their lists. I am certain the Creator will reserve an especially warm place for us in the Lake of Fire."

The cambion rolled his eyes in horror at the prospect of doubled toil and trouble.

Longinus patted him on the shoulder. "Never mind, Armilus, look on the bright side. You will be infamous throughout Heaven and Hell. Demons and angels will curse your name for eternity."

"I am in the company of a madman," Armilus moaned.

Longinus grinned. "Keep calm, your heraldship. Now how do we get out of this satanic shithole?"

"The entrance to the hidden passageway lies under the Grand Inquisitor's throne. I used it the last time I visited the dungeons."

"Excellent!" Longinus replied.

They walked over to the throne, and Armilus searched for the concealed lever.

"I am certain it was just about here," he muttered.

"Let me see," Longinus said, kneeling. "Ah, here it is. You were looking on the wrong side."

He pulled a lever made from a human thighbone, and the throne slid back silently to reveal slimy steps cut into the rock.

"There we are!" Longinus said cheerily, peering into the darkness. A large rat with beady, red eyes stood on the bottom step, twitching its nose, and stared back at him.

"Hmm. We travel from one delightful shithole to another," he added.

His eyes narrowed as he heard Armilus moan in terror.

He arose slowly and looked around. Fifty or more armed succubi surrounded them. The sultry ones regarded him with expressions ranging from icy indifference to open hostility.

Armilus licked his lips and squawked, "This is Lilith's Revenant. He came to free you."

Longinus could see the cambion's knees shaking.

The succubus with the mule's legs appeared from one tunnel. She was wiping dark blood off her trident with a monk's habit.

"Is that true, Revenant?" she said, casually. "Did you come all this way to save us?"

A smile hovered on his lips as the little suicidal devil within him reared its head.

"No," he said.

Armilus groaned as the succubi hissed and growled.

The mule-legged one stopped cleaning her weapon and stared at him.

"Then why did you free us?"

"The inquisitors outnumbered us, and I thought you would provide a distraction."

"So it was a mere stratagem to cover your escape?"

"More of a tactic," he replied nonchalantly.

The succubus smiled. She had recognised him as soon as she had seen him, and how he had looked at her through the grille had given her hope. He did not remember her, but she had seen him in the company of Lilith many times in the past.

"Then it was an excellent tactic," she replied. "*You* may leave."

"And my companion?"

"He is a filthy cambion informer. We shall deal with him as we did our torturers."

Longinus showed no outward reaction, but steeled himself for combat. He had no intention of letting the succubi tear Armilus apart. He may be a filthy cambion, but he was *his* filthy cambion, and the centurion would do everything in his power to protect him. But before taking that most violent of irrevocable steps, he would try diplomacy and follow his own Revenant version of Churchill's famous quote: "Meeting jaw to jaw is sometimes—but not often—better than claw to claw."

"I need him," he said amiably.

"What for—to slit your throat while you sleep?" she said with a mocking laugh.

"He is my guide to the Lower Depths."

She frowned, and the other succubi whispered to each other.

"Why do you wish to travel there?"

"We are fleeing from Asmodeus. It is the only place we can go."

Mentioning the King of Demons caused quite a stir among the female demons. They cursed Asmodeus' name and spat and hissed.

"We saved one of your kind from the Nephilim!" Armilus whined.

"Is that true?" the succubus asked Longinus.

"Yes, her name was Onoskelis."

The appellation stirred up a greater hornet's nest of growls, hisses, glares and unintelligible tongue wagging among the irascible she-devils, and they looked at their leader.

"Describe her appearance to me," the mule-legged one said.

Longinus recounted Onoskelis' appearance to the best of his ability.

The succubi murmured among themselves, and some even displayed the semblance of a smile.

"Where is she now?"

"I do not know. She left us there."

She stared at Longinus. "Well, sisters? Do you believe him?"

"I believe *him*—but not the ugly one," a blonde vixen said, eyeing Longinus, seductively.

A short, dark-haired, buxom demoness noticed the fair one's gaze and seemed quite jealous.

"We should cut out his tongue, poke out his eyes and roast him slowly over a lava pool," she growled.

"Would you like me well done or rare?" Longinus asked, suavely.

"Just hot," murmured the blonde, licking her lips.

Many of the succubi shrieked with laughter as the jealous one bristled with rage.

"I say, let them go," an older and extremely attractive one sighed impatiently. "Without their help, we would never have escaped this place. They are no threat to us and appear to hate Asmodeus as much as we do."

"It is true! I spit thrice upon his name!" Armilus exclaimed, expectorating loudly three times.

The monstrous regiment laughed at his pathetic attempt to save his skin.

"And do you also spit upon his name, Revenant?" the leader asked.

"No—I just want to destroy him," Longinus replied grimly.

"A sentiment upon which we can all agree. You and your cowardly companion may leave. But if we discover you lied and harmed our sister, we will hunt you down and slay you."

"I would expect no less. But I can assure you that she left us in good health and with her rebellious spirit intact."

His answer seemed to satisfy her and the majority of the other succubi. They saw no trace of deceit in his strange blue eyes, and that further reassured them that their demonic sister was safe.

"Go," said the leader, pointing her trident at the throne.

"Thank you," said Longinus. "And what is your name?"

She frowned and stared suspiciously at him.

"Why do you wish to learn my name?"

"In case we should ever meet again," he said charmingly.

Armilus nearly sobbed in disbelief, and he rued the day he had met this king of fools.

She laughed and a mischievous twinkle appeared in her eyes. "You may call me—Satrinah."

"Then, until we meet again, Satrinah," he said with the roguish, confident air of an adventurer.

The succubi cackled and whooped as he bowed to her, but their amusement abated somewhat when he added, "Safe journey to all loyal sisters of Lilith's legions."

"And safe journey to you, Revenant," Satrinah replied grimly.

The short, jealous succubus, who seemed to favour the passions of Sappho, kicked Armilus on the backside and sent him scampering down the stairs.

"Leave them!" Satrinah commanded.

The unruly one glared at Satrinah and then back at Longinus. He glanced at the abundant cleavage straining to escape from the confines of her breastplate with an appreciative smile. She raised her trident, and he saw raw bloody murder in her eyes.

"I said, leave them be!" Satrinah roared.

The dark-haired beauty lowered her weapon reluctantly, and the centurion gave her an insolent wink as he sauntered past and entered the dank and dingy tunnel.

"Your demon charm worked wonders on them, old boy!" Longinus remarked in woefully unconvincing upper class English accent to Armilus. "But tell me—how many times would you spit on my name?"

The cambion pulled one of his grotesque faces, rubbed his buttocks and muttered an uncouth reply as he slipped and slid along the clammy passageway leading to the next Hellmouth. Longinus grinned, but then stopped and frowned as he noticed something carved upon the tunnel wall. He scraped away the lichen and revealed a small symbol comprising two intersecting arcs. It was the ichthys or sign of the fish. Longinus raised an eyebrow. The design was not carved; it was scorched into the rock as if by lightning.

Someone or something of great power had once trodden this path many, many centuries before him.

CHAPTER XXI

After escaping from the Dungeons of Hell, Longinus and the cambion spent many hours tripping and sliding through the dark and clammy passage. They did not converse, each content to brood over their dark pasts and even darker futures. The centurion was the first to break the deep and gloomy silence.

"What does Satan look like?"

"Eh?"

"I said–what does Satan look like?"

"I know not. I have never seen him."

"But you were his messenger."

"I was but one of hundreds of imperial couriers."

"And you never saw him?"

"No."

"Then how did he impart his messages to you?"

"Through Baal Zebub."

"Were the memoranda written or oral?"

"They were scribed in blood on parchments of human skin."

"You are jesting."

"I never jest."

"And you never saw Satan even once?"

"No! How many times must I tell you?"

"It just seems strange."

Armilus gave a scornful laugh. "Satan would never reveal himself to a lesser demon such as I. He only appears in physical form to archdemons, but it has been centuries since any of them have beheld him. In any case, I am very glad that I have not seen him."

"Why is that?"

"Because his sheer power and magnificence would scorch your eyeballs in their sockets and roast your brain. It would leave you a screaming, blind imbecile. They say you cannot behold the Great Tyrant in Heaven, and the same holds true for Satan in Hell."

"Well, what is he rumoured to look like? Demons must speak about it. What do they say?"

"They who dare to mention his name only do so in whispers. Satan can take many forms. They suspect that he sometimes appears as a lesser demon so he can spy on his vassals."

"So—you could be Satan?" Longinus observed with a twinkle in his eye.

"I wish I were!" Armilus said testily. "I would not have to trudge through this stinking tunnel and answer your puerile questions!"

"Please forgive me, your imperial majesty. Pray continue with your fascinating and illuminating disquisition."

"Some say he can appear as beautiful dark angel, and others maintain that he is a horned, two-legged beast with three heads and a second face on his belly that devours the souls of the wicked. But his most fearsome manifestation is that of the Great Dragon."

"I dreamed I met a dragon in ancient Babylon. He was quite a charming and cultivated creature," Longinus mused.

"Well, you would not enjoy meeting this dragon. Satan is reputed to belch Hellfire hotter than lava that can incinerate both angels and demons."

"Impressive! The *Book of Lilith* implied that Hell exists within the body of a great dragon, and it opens its jaws to swallow the damned."

Armilus frowned. "What is the *Book of Lilith*?"

"An ancient tome of spells and incantations in which the author claimed to record the history of Lilith, Heaven and Hell."

"What type of spells?"

"Travelling back in time, for one."

"Astounding!" exclaimed the cambion. "Does it work?"

"Oh, yes, but it proved utterly useless."

"Why so?"

"Because I could find no means of specifying the year and destination. It was like shooting arrows in the dark; you could end up anywhere."

"Who scribed the book?"

"No one knows."

"Most curious. Only Lilith or one of the Fallen could have imparted such knowledge to the amanuensis."

"Lilith maintained she had no part in it."

"Then it must have been an archdemon."

"But not Asmodeus," Longinus replied grimly. "He holds onto secrets tighter than a squirrel gripping its nuts.

"What is a squirrel?"

"A earthly tree-dwelling rodent that eats nuts."

"Nuts?"

"A fruit with a hard shell or male testes," Longinus sighed wearily, peeved the cambion's tiresome lexicography had blunted his wit.

"Hah!" the cambion snorted. "I now understand your meaning. It was a childish attempt at levity. But returning to your original point concerning the dragon, that is also the view of many demons. They believe we reside inside Satan's body. According to them, Satan does not just rule Hell–he is Hell!"

"Then we are truly in the belly of the beast," Longinus murmured.

"Your mocking words may be more accurate than you think. I have seen the gates of Hell, and they resemble a dragon's jaws."

Longinus considered this gruesome concept for a moment. The realm of the Abyss was so utterly fantastical that anything may be true.

"Where do you think Satan goes?"

"Goes?" the cambion replied while kicking at a rat and missing it by a foot.

"Well, you have said that the archdemons have not seen Satan for centuries, so what do you think the Evil One has been doing all this time? Let us assume that he has not been sitting on his imperial backside and twiddling his tail."

Armilus considered his question with the gravitas of a dusty, pipe-smoking scholar ensconced in an Oxbridge ivory tower.

"In my opinion, he spends much of his time ruling his other kingdom."

"Other kingdom?"

"Why, the material plane of earth, of course. He is emperor of Hell and prince of that world. He has left the day-to-day running of Hell to the archdemons, and that has freed him to do what he enjoys most."

"Which is?"

"Walking as a man in the world and tempting mortals with promises of wealth, power, fame or carnal pleasures."

"Be sober, be vigilant; because your adversary the devil, as a roaring lion, walketh about, seeking whom he may devour!" Longinus intoned in his best Bible-thumper voice.

"Hah! Satan's days of tempting individuals are long past. He can now recruit and deceive entire communities, cities, and nations at the press of a button. He uses mankind's own technology against them. Satan now wears a business suit and adopts the guise of a billionaire. Business people, politicians, celebrities and governments vie for his clandestine support."

Longinus viewed the back of the cambion's bald pate suspiciously and resisted the urge to smack it. For someone who purported not to know what a nut was, the half-demon seemed to know a hell of a lot about the current mortal world. The centurion wondered if the jester had been made the fool.

"Does no one suspect who he is?"

"Why would they? Most mortals do not believe in Heaven and Hell. They think it is an old wife's tale used to frighten children."

"Vampires have used scientific skepticism to conceal their existence from mortals for centuries," Longinus conceded. "Humans used to fear, hunt and stake the stalkers of the night, but now they mock and disregard the hard earned knowledge of their ancestors."

"Precisely!" said Armilus. "The greatest danger Satan faced in the twentieth century was mankind forming organisations that prevented wars and promoted the common good of the earth; and he has been doing everything in his power to discredit and destroy such institutions. He encourages skepticism, selfishness, fervent nationalism, racism, and intolerance. Even the so-called righteous ones are deceived by his plausible ideologies. Divide and conquer—that is his great aim. And as Satan strengthens his grip on the world, the temperature increases, the seas rise and fires and new diseases spread throughout the lands."

"Mhmm," Longinus muttered, more convinced than ever the little bugger *did* know what a nut was.

"Mankind," Armilus ranted, "has the power, will, and determination to solve many of the problems they face in their dying world. However, as long as Satan and his disciples can recruit greedy mortals with the financial rewards gained by promoting distrust and disunity, humans will experience untold suffering and march blindly towards the Evil One's ultimate goal of establishing Hell on earth."

Longinus stopped and gave the cambion a slow clap.

"That was an eloquent diatribe. I had no idea that you cared so much about mankind!" he said sarcastically.

Armilus screwed up his face in disgust. "I care not a demon crack hair about them! But their stupidity and naivete never ceases to astound and annoy me. He gave them the Garden of Eden, and they betrayed Him. He gave them a *second paradise*, and they are destroying that. The Great Tyrant should have made sheep His most perfect creation. Humans are like sheep in all but name: they follow each other without thinking and go to slaughter as meekly as other even-toed ungulates. Even if the Son of the Great Tyrant returned tomorrow and offered them eternal life, the bleating herd is too ignorant to hear Him. The Fallen were granted no second chance to learn from the folly of their arrogance and stupidity, but mankind receives interminable forgiveness for its sins."

Longinus gave a non-committal Gallic shrug. "Humans are the thorns in the Almighty's backside. Anyway, Plato, keep moving."

Armilus grunted in anger and turned on his heel. After a few minutes, he asked, "What is a Plato?"

"Something to put your *mealo* on," Longinus growled impatiently. "How long is this damn tunnel?"

"We are nearly there," Armilus snapped.

Two hours and much bickering later, they emerged from the passage and blinked around them. They were standing on a hillside overlooking a pass. At the end of the gap was a reddish black metal cantilever bridge that spanned a chasm a mile in width. The bridge appeared to be constructed in a box girder design, with the deck built of thick metal plates. Two lofty supporting towers stood on either side of it.

"The next Hellmouth is on the other side of that bridge," Armilus said.

"Kneel down, keep still, and wait a moment," Longinus replied. "I want to check for threats."

They both knelt, and the cambion watched as the centurion narrowed his eyes, listened attentively, and scanned the landscape from right to left for enemies.

"What are you looking for?" Armilus whispered, fascinated despite himself.

"Movement, shapes, shadows, silhouettes, or anything that catches my eye and seems out of place," Longinus murmured.

After a few more minutes and passes, Longinus stood up.

"All right. Let us make our way down. Keep low, move slowly, and make as little noise as you can. "

They descended to the pass and reached the support towers. Longinus held onto a beam and looked over the edge. The chasm was at least a mile deep, and its bottom shrouded in darkness. A mournful, fetid wind emanated from the depth and tugged at his body. He looked at the bridge and shook his head in disbelief. On earth, such an impossible structure would collapse under its own weight, but like all things in Hell, the bridge defied the normal laws of physics, reason and sanity.

There were no guardrails, so they kept to the centre of the deck as they crossed. The wind was picking up, and they were concerned about being blown over the side by a freak gust. After thirty minutes, they sighed in relief as they arrived, windswept but safe, on the other side.

"Look!" Armilus said excitedly. "You can see the Hellmouth arch from here."

Beyond the bridge was a vast flat-bottomed canyon. Between the valley's towering cliffs of solidified crimson lava falls lay an inert red and brown volcanic field. The canyon ran straight for a mile before winding right behind a peak. Above the outline of the summit, Longinus could see the turret of a lofty tower.

"What lies yonder?" he asked.

"Archdemon Azazel's fortress. We must stay well away from it," the cambion replied warily.

"Where is the Hellmouth?"

"There!" Armilus answered, pointing.

Longinus shielded his eyes from the fiery overhead glare and spotted the vacant metal span a quarter of a mile away. He frowned.

"A mouth has appeared in the arch," he said.

"What?" Armilus squawked.

"It is opening!"

They both stood peering as the enormous jaws parted. Nothing happened for a moment, then armed demons spewed from the portal.

"Damn! Get down!" Longinus hissed.

They hit the ground, lay on their stomachs and watched as more fiends arrived. The horde gathered in front of the Hellmouth and formed into loose, obstreperous ranks.

"There must be at least a hundred of them," the centurion growled.

"Let us hope they are travelling to Azazel's fortress," whispered Armilus.

"I thought only archdemons and messengers can use the Hellmouths?"

"That is true."

"Then how are they getting through?"

"I do not know," whined Armilus.

"Oh, joy," Longinus groaned as he saw a tall, familiar shape slither from the portal.

"Naamah!" Armilus gasped.

"Yes!" Longinus said tersely. "You forgot to add her to your list of hellish commuters. Is there anyone else you forgot to mention—the New York Yankees, or the Pitlochry Pipe Band?"

"I do not know what you speak of," Armilus protested angrily. "I have never seen Naamah use a Hellmouth before!"

"Perhaps she heard about our little visit to the dungeons."

Armilus' bigger eye became perceptibly wider and more watery.

They gawked as four large hounds appeared beside Naamah.

"She must have pumped out a few new ones," murmured Longinus.

"New ones?"

"I inadvertently helped to destroy her old hounds."

"So now Satan's daughter pursues us as well?" the cambion moaned.

"It could be worse," Longinus replied dryly. "You should see her snakes."

"Snakes!"

He was not overly fond of Hell's reptiles. They had the habit of swallowing unwary satanic messengers.

"Yes, larger than a hundred of you. They chased me into the river Styx and Leviathan devoured them."

The cambion gulped and stared fearfully at Naamah. Hell-life was so unfair! By heroically saving his brutish and unsympathetic guardian, he had unwittingly put a Leviathan-sized target on his own poor back.

Naamah raised her sword above her head, and the nehushtan started sniffing the ground.

"Thank the gods we did not pass that way," said Longinus.

They stiffened as one hound reared its head, uttered a piercing, spine-chilling howl and raced toward the bridge. The other beasts joined it, with

Naamah and her demon cohort following swiftly behind.

Armilus seized the centurion's arm. "What shall we do? They will be here in minutes!"

Longinus looked around. The land was flat, and there was no place to hide. They could try making a run for it to the opposite side of the bridge, but the demons would spot them.

"Under the bridge!" he said.

"What?" Armilus exclaimed in horror.

"There are girders under the bridge. We can conceal ourselves there until they pass over us."

Longinus slung his spear on his back, and they crawled to the edge of the deck.

"I fear heights!" Armilus whined, gripping the metal with white knuckles.

"Here, take my hand. Get your legs over and feel with your feet for the crossbeams. Do not look down. Just concentrate on holding on."

The half-demon put his trembling legs over and after a few frantic moments of air paddling, found a girder. Gripping the beam that supported the deck and cursing vociferously, he swung himself under. Longinus slid his legs over the edge, and with the swiftness and confidence of a lizard, dropped down to join him.

They worked their way cautiously to the nearest intersecting struts and hung on for grim death. The wind was stronger under the bridge and threatened to wrench them free and send them tumbling into the incalculable depths of the chasm.

"Do not look down. Keep your eyes on me," Longinus whispered.

The cambion gasped, nodded and stared like a maniac at him.

Soon afterwards, snarls, howls, and the awful clatter of scores of heavy hooves pounding on the metal plates above their heads deafened them. Longinus put his finger to his lips and bid the cambion to remain as still and silent as the grave.

As they waited, Longinus glanced down into the chasm. He frowned. The bottom of the abyss had turned white. He squinted and peered closer, trying to discern what was happening. His eyes widened as he saw a vast translucent shape arising. It looked like an enormous amoeba with hundreds of arms. Its long appendages were gripping the sides of the chasm and propelling it upward at great speed. Its gaping jaws and irregular teeth reminded him of grotesque, luminous predators that dwelt in the Stygian depths of earth's oceans. As it drew nearer, an icy shiver ran down his spine. They were not arms—but tendrils. It was the monstrosity from the pool, and it had discovered a fissure large enough for it to squeeze its entire loathsome body through. He had suspected that the avaricious cirri had been part of a much larger creature, and now he had the inviolable and ghastly proof.

With his heart in his mouth, he looked up at the bridge deck. The demons were still crossing. The centurion wiped his lips with the back of his hand and noticed it was shaking. He had to do something, or the odious abomination would suck them dry like fat, juicy flies in a spider's web.

He leaned out from the edge, trying to view the end of the bridge so he could judge how many more were still to come. All he could see were demon horns. But then the gods smiled on him. A gap appeared. He looked down. The thing was getting closer; it was now the size of a large ship.

"We need to climb up now!" he said in a low voice, grabbing Armilus by the elbow.

"But they are still on the bridge!" Armilus whispered hysterically.

"Look down!" Longinus hissed.

Armilus glanced down, and his eyes bulged out of his head.

To Longinus' amazement, the half-demon brushed past him, scuttled up the girders like a champion of free climbing and disappeared over the top. Longinus cursed and followed him. As he hauled himself onto the deck, he saw Armilus cowering before him and the rear of the demon cohort halfway across the bridge. He pulled Armilus to his feet, and they ran for the Hellmouth.

A thin, wiry fiend at the rear of the echelon spotted them and roared to alert the others. The unholy cohort turned around, emitted eldritch screams and chased after them. Some threw bolas weapons constructed with thin chains and metal balls. One hit Longinus on the back. Another struck his leg, but he jumped to avoid being ensnared by its chains and kept running. He heard Armilus cry out. Glancing behind him, he saw the cambion fall to the ground with a bolas wrapped around his ankles.

The voice of reason in his mind screamed at him to flee, but the warrior spirit in his heart ignored it. Ripping the shield and spear from his back, he turned and stood over Armilus. His face was grim, his eyes hooded. There was no time to think. All he could see was the solid wall of hounds and demons charging at him. Naamah towered behind them, her mouth gaping wide enough to swallow a horse. Longinus unconsciously decided which hound he would destroy before the others brought him down. The front ranks were reaching the end of the bridge. He readied his spear and braced his shield for impact. His lips curled into a snarl.

There was a deafening boom, and the ground shook beneath his feet. He stumbled back as the centre of the bridge rose fifty feet. Hundreds of lucent tendrils lashed over the deck. The bridge heaved and there was a thunderous groan of metal buckling. Longinus ducked as a long, heavy girder flew past him and clattered end for end down the hill. He looked up and saw Naamah and a hundred screaming, writhing bodies held in ravenous embraces, before the bridge cracked like thunder, throwing massive beams and plates into the air, and sank with a despairing moan like a dying dreadnought of the sea.

Longinus staggered to the precipice and looked down. He saw the disgusting bulk and bridge falling into the chasm. Scores of demons that had avoided the creature's grasp were tumbling through the air behind it. Just before the translucent horror disappeared back into the darkness, its tendrils lashed out and snapped their bodies into its jagged, cavernous jaws.

"Buon appetito," the centurion muttered.

Then all was quiet. He gazed around in stunned silence. None of the demons on the bridge had survived. Slinging his shield on his back, he walked back to Armilus. The half-demon was untangling the chains around his ankles.

"Is it gone?" he gasped.

"Yes. What was it? A demon?"

Armilus winced in pain. "No. It is something that has escaped from the Lower Depths."

Longinus arched an eyebrow. "The Lower Depths—where we are going?"

The question was fast becoming a grim jest between them.

"Yes," said Armilus.

"We will have quite a reception committee waiting for us down there. How are your legs?"

"I jarred my hip when I fell."

"Can you walk?"

Armilus struggled to his feet and hopped around for a bit. "I cannot put any weight on it."

"Does your body heal quickly?"

"Yes, given a little time."

"We do not have time. The sound of the bridge collapsing was enough to waken the dead."

"The dead are already awake in Hell," Armilus observed.

"Thank you, Descartes."

"What is a day cart?" Armilus asked, frowning.

"A French wagon," Longinus growled. "I wish I had one. I could throw you under it."

"But what shall we do? I cannot walk."

"I will carry you. Then we can be free of this terrible place."

"I refuse to be carried like a mewling bantling!"

"Shut up," Longinus sighed.

Longinus pulled the protesting half-demon onto his shoulders in the manner that soldiers from time immemorial had carried injured comrades from battlefields. He grunted and adjusted his grip. The cambion was surprisingly heavy for such a little runt. As he strode down the hill, he had the eeriest feeling that he was being watched. He spun around and stared at the chasm. A lone tendril swayed in the air.

"Still hungry, you greedy bastard?" he whispered.

"What?" asked Armilus.

"I was just speaking to myself."

"I do that from time to time."

"Really?" Longinus answered dryly. "I would never have known."

He turned on his heel and began humming a cheerful little ditty composed by an ensemble of human rock musicians called the Iron Maidens, or some such name.

The centurion favoured iron maidens.

He had loved and worshipped one.

CHAPTER XXII

They emerged from the Hellmouth and entered the forbidding domain of Belial. It was a black volcanic landscape with rivers of bubbling lava and giant geysers that blasted steam and thousands of gallons of scalding water hundreds of feet into the fetid air. After travelling through the sweltering and deadly terrain for hours, they came upon a clearing where stood twelve, towering obsidian standing stones.

Longinus did not sweat, but he felt hot and sticky. His armour clung to his skin, chafing him, and rivulets of condensation streamed down his body. The humidity was intolerable and drained his energy, leaving him exhausted and lethargic.

"Let us rest here for a moment," he grunted, wiping his brow.

He lowered Armilus off his shoulders and helped him stand.

"How does your hip feel?" he asked.

"My hip is the least of my problems," Armilus groaned, clutching his groin. "It is extremely uncomfortable being carried that way."

"You weigh more than an ox," Longinus grumbled, stretching his aching back and shoulders.

Armilus tried putting some weight onto his right leg.

"Can you walk?"

The cambion's face twisted in pain, and he stumbled.

Longinus grabbed him. "Not yet, it would seem."

The centurion helped him sit with his back against a monolith.

"How does that feel?"

"Good!" Armilus sighed in relief.

Longinus removed the shield from his back and placed it and his spear against the standing stone. He took a moment to wipe the streams of moisture off his face and body, but it was a useless task. He felt like a dripping sponge. The abrasions under his arms caused by the armour stung like wasp bites, but he could not be bothered removing his breastplate. With a weary sigh, he slumped down beside the cambion and stared blankly at the ground.

"How many Hellmouths before we reach the Lower Depths?"

"One."

"Thank the gods."

After a few minutes, his eyes strayed over the standing stones. "What are these monoliths?"

"I know not," Armilus replied, too absorbed in his own suffering to care.

Longinus dragged himself to his feet and wandered over to the slab on their left. He wiped away the grime from a small section on its face and uncovered faint markings. They comprised unintelligible demonic writing and hieroglyphs depicting strange demons with tentacles for legs.

"What demons are these?"

The cambion squinted at the graven images for a moment and sat bolt upright.

"Howlers! We must flee!"

"What?"

Longinus narrowed his eyes and peered around. The stone circle was becoming darker.

High-pitched, ear-splitting, unearthly screams filled the air.

"Too late, too late! They are here!" the cambion gibbered, crawling on his hands and knees into the centre of the circle.

Longinus spun around and saw large, hideous shapes rising slowly from the ground between each stone. He grabbed his spear and shield and ran to join Armilus.

"Stay behind me!" he barked.

The saucer-eyed monstrosities had enormous heads, short torsos, stubby arms, and moved on long, thick tentacles. Their three-fingered claws were almost as large as their skulls, and their gaping jaws exposed short, pointed teeth like saw blades.

Armilus spun around in the dirt, looking frantically for some means of escape. But there was no place to crawl to, and nowhere to hide; the howlers were attacking from every direction. Burying his face in his claws, he cursed ever meeting the Revenant and bewailed his miserable fate.

As the demons slithered closer, Longinus wished he had a braver companion. His first instinct was to break out of the circle and find a choke point where he could hold off his attackers. But he could not do that, as he had to protect the cambion. The half-demon was the only one who could guide him out of Hell. He could not let the cambion die or all was lost.

He crouched and started circling, trying to gauge which fiend would attack first. Their movement was slow and coordinated. They were covering all means of escape and determined to catch their prey.

His answer was not long in coming. One emitted a deafening screech and charged at him. He thrust his spear into its yawning jaws. The weight of the fiend drove him back as the weapon consumed it, and its scream of rage transformed into a deflating wail of agony.

The other howlers stopped and glared at him with baleful intent, but none made a move to get within the range of his spear. It was a standoff. They were intelligent enough to understand the centurion could destroy them, and although they suspected they could defeat him if they all attacked at once, none wished to sacrifice itself on behalf of the others.

Longinus started as a spear tip erupted from a howler's face, and it collapsed to the ground. The other demons howled and peered into the surrounding darkness for their new opponent. A few moments later, another howler screeched and fell as a spear burst through its chest.

A tall, bearded man leapt over the demon's body and landed in the circle. He was garbed in Greek armour with a Corinthian helmet.

"You appear to be outnumbered," the stranger announced.

"Who are you?" Longinus growled, pointing his spear at him.

"Aeneas," the man replied, readying his spear and shield as he turned to face their malevolent attackers. "Who are you?"

"Longinus," the centurion replied suspiciously.

The man grinned. "Well met, Longinus. Let us see if the gods' favour or curse us."

Longinus grimaced. Although the unexpected intervention of this unknown warrior had improved their chances, the grotesque monstrosities still held the upper hand.

One howler sniffed the air and shrieked to the others. To Longinus' surprise, the demons retreated and sank back into the earth. Within a few seconds, they had vanished as quickly as they had appeared.

"Why did they stop attacking?" asked Longinus.

"Hah! The fiends realised that we were more than a match for them," Aeneas replied triumphantly.

"Perhaps," Longinus muttered.

The cambion removed his hands from his face and gaped in disbelief. The howlers had vanished, and he, Armilus, had survived again! He now regretted cursing Longinus. Lilith's Revenant was the very best bodyguard in Hell! However, his joy was short-lived when he noticed the tall, warlike stranger. Muttering obscenities, he crawled behind the centurion for protection.

Longinus looked around, and the hairs on the back of his neck stood up as he spied nine dark, winged shapes flying towards them.

"No!" he whispered.

"What is the matter?" asked Aeneas.

"Run and do not look back! This is a fight we cannot win!" Longinus hissed.

Aeneas followed his gaze and saw the hideous black figures approaching.

"What in the name of Zeus are they?"

"It is the Lilitu!" Armilus screamed.

"What?" asked Aeneas.

"Lilith's handmaidens of destruction," said Longinus. "They have no interest in you or Armilus. It is me they want. Take my companion and flee now before it too late. I will distract them and give you a chance to escape."

Armilus stared at him for a moment and started crawling back the way they had come.

Aeneas watched him go and rubbed the back of his hand across his chin. "I have only fled twice in my life, and I will not run away again."

"Then you will die," said Longinus.

"I am already dead," said Aeneas. "I have no fear of death."

"Then fear pain. Those harpies can inflict unimaginable agony on both the living and the dead."

"So be it!" Aeneas said. "I am tired of running and hiding. Let it end here."

Longinus shook his head and sighed. The hunt was over. It was inconceivable that he and Aeneas could defeat nine of Lilith's daughters. He had seen them destroy an army of the undead in Babylon. They had no chance of surviving this fight. He only hoped he could destroy one or two of them before he died.

With whoops of triumph and malevolent delight, the Lilitu landed and surrounded them. They were in their demon forms and no longer disguised themselves as beautiful women. Their black sinewy bodies, bat-like wings, and sharp talons glistened in the flickering vermilion hue.

"Did you think you could escape our vengeance, Revenant?" screeched Nashiram, throwing a wailing Armilus back into the circle.

The other eight shrieked with deranged laughter.

"Who are your companions—a little half-demon and a human soul? How pathetic!" sneered Sarai.

"Where are your Knights of St. John to protect you this time?" screeched Rebekna.

"You forget, sister," cackled Bilhah. "The accursed knights cannot enter Hell."

"Yes, this is our realm, and no one can save him," howled Basemath.

"What do you want?" Longinus asked.

But he already knew the answer. He was just delaying the inevitable and playing for time in case there was a slightest glimmer of hope.

"Want?" Shelomith cried. "We want you, Revenant!"

"You destroyed three of our sisters and made us Asmodeus' playthings," hissed Leah.

"And we will feast on your entrails," Bilhah added coldly.

"Let the others go. They have no part in this. Take me," Longinus said.

Nashiram grinned. "Why? Do they mean something to you?"

"Are they your friends, Revenant?" asked Oholibamah, her bottom lip trembling in a perverse parody of concern.

"Good!" Rebekna cried exultantly. "You will die knowing that they suffered the same fate as you."

"But this time there will be no rebirth," growled Nashiram "and our mother will not be here to protect you."

Armilus moaned and buried his head in his hands.

"You keep charming company," murmured Aeneas. "What harm did you do them?"

"Long story, no time," Longinus grunted, raising his shield and levelling his spear.

"Well said. Talking is for priests and philosophers," Aeneas grunted. "Let us die again with honour."

"With honour, brother," Longinus replied.

"Well, well, sisters," Nashiram laughed, "it would seem our prey yearn for a hero's death. Let us not disappoint them."

The Lilitu grinned and moved in for the kill. Their moment, the moment they had been dreaming of for so long, was at hand. Their revenge on the puny insect that had turned their mother against them and foiled their grand design for power would soon be realised.

"Come, foul hags! Who wants to be first to join their sisters in oblivion?" Longinus sneered.

The Lilitu screamed in rage and crept closer. Even in his last moments, Longinus could not help but find them fascinating and even admire them. Their eyes were cold and motions honed to perfection. There was no wasted energy, and every movement was measured and balanced. They had perfected killing into a fine art, and that he could respect. They were a fitting tribute to their mother: the ultimate predators.

He could see four readying to pounce on Aeneas while the remaining five attacked him. When assault came, it was swift, powerful and devastating. Longinus thrust his spear at Nashiram, but she deflected it with a claw and wrenched the weapon from his grasp. Bilhah kicked his shield. The blow stunned him, and he staggered back. The others sprang forward, throwing him to the ground. Four held him spread-eagled as Nashiram stood gloating. She sat slowly and sensuously on him, savouring the moment, straddling his abdomen.

"Did not your mother teach you better manners?" he grunted defiantly, as her sharp claws dug deep into his arms.

Nashiram grinned. "She taught us many things—as you will soon learn."

Longinus glanced to his right and saw the other Lilitu had disarmed Aeneas; two held his arms while a third gripped his throat. Armilus screamed as the fourth one dragged him to his feet and slashed his buttocks with her claw.

Nashiram reached beneath her and held Longinus' testicles gently in her claw.

"These are the cause of all our misfortunes," she said, staring at him with a manic grin. "If our mother had castrated you, none of this would have happened. But fear not. I shall complete what my dear mother failed to do."

She gripped hard and twisted. The pain was sickening, excruciating. He groaned, screwed up his eyes, and tried to concentrate on dislocating his mind from his screaming nerve endings. Then, inexplicably, the gut wrenching agony ceased. Gasping, Longinus opened his eyes and looked up. Nashiram was glaring at something behind him. He twisted his head and saw a glimpse of black wings.

"Leave him be!" Onoskelis cried, brandishing her trident.

Nashiram gave an incredulous laugh. "Look, sisters. A juicy little succubus dares to defy us."

"More flesh to rip and tear!" cried Oholibamah.

"Now there is enough for all to share!" Baileet hissed. "Let me take her."

"Go on, sister," jeered Nashiram. "But be not too greedy and leave some for us."

Longinus watched as Baileet stalked past him, flexing her claws. Her face was the cruelest he had ever seen on earth or in Hell.

"Onoskelis, flee!" he gasped.

"Debts must be repaid," she replied grimly.

"Come to me, sweet strumpet, and let me gnaw upon thy breasts," Baileet hissed.

Then, to his surprise, Longinus heard a deep male voice speak.

"Sáncte Míchael Archángele, defénde nos in proélio, cóntra nequítiam et insídias diáboli ésto præsídium. Ímperet ílli Déus, súpplices deprecámur: tuque, prínceps milítiæ cæléstis, Sátanam aliósque spíritus malígnos, qui ad perditiónem animárum pervagántur in múndo, divína virtúte, in inférnum detrúde. Ámen."

Baileet screamed in terror and retreated.

"Begone vile obscenities of Hell!" the voice continued. "The power of Archangel Michael and the Divine Spirit commands you. Their light is brighter than a million stars, and you shall burn in the Eternal Lake of Fire when they judge you!"

A dazzling white light appeared and blinded Longinus. The Lilitu released their victims, held their claws in front of their faces, and screeched curses. All nine took flight and their terrible, unearthly, mournful cries faded into the distance.

After a minute, Longinus' vision cleared. Two strong hands reached under his shoulders and helped him up. Bewildered, he turned around and beheld a bearded man adorned in a torn, dirty white robe.

"Who are you?" he asked, hoarsely.

"I am Simon Magus—and our band is now complete," the man replied.

CHAPTER XXIII

Longinus stared blankly at the bearded figure in the white robe.

His head and groin ached, and he felt nauseous. He staggered back and looked around. The Lilitu had fled. Onoskelis, Aeneas and Armilus were struggling to their feet. Their stupefied expressions and lumbering movements reminded him of drunkards in a tavern.

"What did you to them?" he croaked.

"They are stunned but will recover in a short while."

"I feel as though someone beat my head like a drum," said Longinus.

"It will pass," said Simon.

Longinus glanced at the standing stones. "The other demons may return."

"This ground has been cleansed for the present. We are safe for a little while but should leave as soon as possible."

"Are you a saint?"

Simon gave a humourless laugh. "No–I was a sorcerer."

Longinus scowled. He had no liking for shamans. Onoskelis staggered across to him and regarded Simon warily.

"My name is Longinus."

"I know," the bearded one replied enigmatically.

Longinus glowered at him. "How?"

"I had a vision. In this dream, I saw you being attacked by the Lilitu. After I drove them off, you explained to me you wished to reach the Lower Depths and escape Hell."

"And how did you reply in your vision?"

"I said would accompany and assist you in any way I can."

"And will you?"

Simon smiled. "Yes."

"How do I know you are not a demon in disguise?"

"I invoked the protection of the Archangel Michael."

Longinus glared at him but knew it was true. To his knowledge, no demon could utter such an invocation. It would stick in their craw and cause them to vomit–or worse.

The centurion turned to Aeneas. "Say Archangel Michael."

"What?"

"Say Archangel Michael thrice."

"Whatever for?"

"To prove you are not a demon."

"But you travel with two demons!" Aeneas protested.

"I know they are demons, but I do not know what you are," Longinus said grimly.

Aeneas shrugged his broad shoulders. "Oh, very well, if it pleases you. Archangel Michael, Archangel Michael, Arch–aaaaaaargh!"

Longinus and Onoskelis stared in horror as the Greek gripped his throat and put on the most devilish face. The centurion readied his spear to smite him.

"Tis a jest," Aeneas said laughing. "Archangel Michael!"

"Hmm," Longinus grunted angrily, lowering his spear. "Do you always carry on so in the face of death?"

"Only when I have an excellent audience," Aeneas retorted.

Longinus smiled despite himself. He could not but like the Greek's forthright and fearless manner.

"Do not trust him! Do not trust any of them!" cried Armilus.

"And why should he distrust me, demon?" Aeneas said angrily, pointing his spear at the cambion. "Do you doubt my honour?"

Armilus glanced fearfully at the warrior. "No! I–" he stuttered.

Longinus was about to intervene on Armilus' behalf, but Onoskelis surprised him by speaking first.

"Be not offended. He mistrusts everyone."

Aeneas raised an eyebrow and glared at her.

"Even you, demoness?" he asked.

"Especially me, human," she replied, meeting his angry gaze without flinching.

He pursed his lips, grunted, and lowered his spear. "Then I yield to your beauty and wisdom."

She gave a brusque nod in reply to his compliment. Longinus noticed a faint smile play about her lips and felt an irrational pang of jealousy. He shook his head and tried to focus his befuddled head on more important matters.

"What power do you have over demons?" he asked Simon.

"I can cloud their minds and make them afraid."

"He must have used it on the cambion," Onoskelis murmured.

Armilus gave her a foul look but said nothing. He had no wish to further enrage the burly stranger standing beside him.

"Is that what you did to the Lilitu?" asked Longinus.

"No. They are too powerful. That is why I recited the prayer requesting the spiritual aid of Archangel Michael. It worked on this occasion because it caught them by surprise, but next time they may be more prepared to resist it."

"So your sorcery would not work on Asmodeus or Satan?"

"No, alas. I have never had much success with archdemons. And as for Satan, I think it would take a power much greater than mine to affect him."

"Very well," said Longinus. "Your company would be most welcome. What about you, Aeneas? Do you wish to join us?"

"Why not?" Aeneas said jovially. "I will have excellent company and the pleasure of killing foul-stinking demons!"

He frowned as he noticed Onoskelis raise an eyebrow at him.

"Present company excluded, of course," he added with an apologetic grin.

"And what of you, mistress?" Longinus asked Onoskelis, tersely. "Are you with us?"

"Who could resist such an enticing invitation?" the succubus replied dryly. "Yes, Revenant, I shall escort you. Someone needs to keep you and the cambion out of trouble."

"Why did you change your mind and join us?"

"Because I could find no succubi in Hell, and I wish to see if they have fled to the Lower Depths. What other reason could there be?"

"None," said Longinus, avoiding her eyes.

"Our band is growing larger. Soon we will have a horde following us!" Armilus moaned.

"And therefore more warriors to protect you," said Aeneas, slapping him on the shoulder.

"And more skirts for you to hide behind," added Onoskelis.

"Our situation has changed," Longinus explained to the cambion. "The Lilitu know where we are and have probably guessed where we are heading. We have greater safety in numbers now."

Armilus stared at him for a moment, and then his shoulders slumped. "I suppose you are right."

"Then it is decided just as I foresaw," said Simon. "We five shall face the horrors of the Lower Depths together."

"But let us avoid the horrors of Hell first," said Longinus. "Which way, Armilus?"

The cambion pointed dejectedly.

"Very well," said Longinus. "Onoskelis, scout ahead and warn us of any enemies. We will travel as quickly as we can behind you."

"I am not your servant," she replied, scowling.

Longinus sighed. "Onoskelis, would you please be so kind as to peruse the terrain and notify us of any lurking monstrosities that may wish to dismember or devour us? Of course, only if it is not too much trouble and you have no prior engagements?"

The succubus snorted at his sarcasm, unfurled her wings and soared up into the fiery sky.

"She is very wholesome to look upon," said Aeneas, watching her fly. "Is she your paramour?"

"What? No!" Longinus exclaimed.

"Excellent!" said Aeneas, his big face beaming.

"Right, Eros, let us make haste," Longinus growled.

Aeneas looked quizzically at him for a moment and then grinned.

"Ah! You jest with me?" he boomed. "That is good! I have no time for sour-faced companions! Come, little demon, walk with me and I will regale you with the adventures of my youth."

"He has injured his hip and cannot walk," said Longinus.

"Then I shall carry him," said Aeneas.

"That will not be necessary!" Armilus said in alarm, remembering the discomfort caused to his stones when Longinus slung him on his shoulders. "My hip feels much better!"

Longinus smiled and then grimaced as he adjusted his loincloth to ease his own aching bits.

"Welcome to my world," he muttered.

"Are you certain?" Aeneas said, watching Armilus hobble around. "Here, take my spear and use it as a staff."

Armilus grabbed the spear, leaned on it, and sighed with relief.

"You see! That is better, is it not?" said Aeneas.

"Yes, it is. Thank you," said Armilus.

"Excellent! But remember to return it to me hastily if we are attacked," he added confidentially. "I would not wish to see you impaled, dismembered or disembowelled."

Armilus looked aghast at the thought. Aeneas stared at his face and burst into laughter.

"It is only a jest, little demon! I shall protect you. No horror of the Abyss will get its claws into you on my watch."

He clamped a broad hand on Armilus' shoulder and led him from the circle of standing stones.

Longinus grinned and looked at Simon. The sorcerer was gazing intensely at him.

"Are you all right, Simon?" he asked, feeling for some strange reason like a naughty schoolboy caught in the glare of his master's eyes.

"Very much so! I have waited for you for two thousand years and now you have arrived!"

"No pressure, then?" Longinus replied nonchalantly.

Simon frowned and looked embarrassed. "I am sorry, but I do not understand your meaning?"

Longinus smiled. "Never mind. Let us depart before the Lilitu return to finish the job."

Whereupon, the most curious alliance ever beheld in Hell set forth to find the Lower Depths.

CHAPTER XXIV

Longinus and Simon walked behind Aeneas and Armilus as they travelled through the fiery domain of Belial. They remained on their guard, but the Lilitu did not reappear, and Onoskelis reported no sightings of them.

"Your prayer to Archangel Michael was very effective. The Lilitu have stayed away from us," said Longinus.

"It was dangerous, but it was the only thing that I could do. My spells are useless against them."

"Why dangerous?"

"Because we are not Christians. It could have sent us straight into Satan's jaws. Fortunately, it did not."

"Simon Magus," Longinus said thoughtfully. "Are you the sorcerer mentioned in the Christian Bible?"

"I have not read it. It came after my time. What does it say about me?"

"Something about trying to buy the secret of the Holy Ghost."

"Yes," the magus sighed. "The sin of 'Simony', or paying for status and influence in the church, is named after me."

"Why did you intervene to help us?"

"I have no love of demons. Although I am cursed like Aeneas to wander Hell for eternity, I am still faithful to the True God."

"Why were you cursed?"

"As you already know, I was a Samaritan sorcerer. I bewitched my people, and they were in awe of me. After the crucifixion of Jesus Christ, I met Phillip the Evangelist and after seeing the miracles and signs that he performed, I converted to Christianity. With my influence, we soon converted many Samaritans to the faith. When the apostles in Jerusalem heard of our success, they sent Peter and John to join our work, for although we had baptised many people in the name of Christ, they had not yet received the Holy Ghost.

"When Peter and John arrived, they laid their hands upon the people and the converts received the Holy Ghost within them. I was much astonished by this, and in a moment of zeal and temptation, I offered silver to Peter and begged him to impart the secret of this power to me."

"And presumably Peter was not happy with your request?"

"No. He was greatly angered and told me the gift of God could not be bought with money. He said that I was in the gall of bitterness, the bond of iniquity, and that I should pray for forgiveness. But what did I know? I was an innocent in the matters of the Christian God. In other religions, it was customary to pay priests for spells or arcane knowledge. That was the way of things."

"So did Peter's curse and the public humiliation turn you against Christianity?"

"Yes, they cast me out of the apostles. The curse laid upon me reduced me to despair, and I soon relinquished the faith and returned to my previous practice of sorcery. I travelled from country to country performing miracles and arrived in Rome where the emperor Nero took a close personal interest in my powers. It seemed my star was in ascendance.

"But then Peter and Paul arrived in the Eternal City and took every opportunity to denounce me. Finally, Nero commanded all three of us to appear before him so he could judge who was the greatest miracle worker. I asked the emperor to construct a high wooden tower so I could display my power of levitation. The emperor had seen me do this before and was looking forward to another demonstration. I stepped off the platform and floated, but Peter prayed to God and asked Him to intervene. I fell and died.

"The emperor imprisoned Peter and Paul because they were Christians and their fates were sealed. They guarded my body for three days because Nero thought I would rise again–but I never did. Instead, I arrived in Hell to suffer eternal damnation. The feats of the apostles are remembered forever, but mine are forgotten. Yet I performed the greater miracles."

"That is often the way," Longinus mused. "People view supernatural occurrences in the dominant religion as divine miracles but brand similar phenomena in other faiths as sorcery, devil worship or witchcraft. The victors write the history of mankind, and in this case the vanquisher was Christianity."

"Very true," said Simon. "I was a competitor of the apostles, and I lost. Therefore, my life and feats were expunged from the scriptures and history books."

"But how were you able to perform these miracles? If you did not receive your powers from God, then where? The Devil?"

Simon smiled enigmatically. "I did receive them from God–but not God as the Christians understand Him."

Longinus frowned. "What do you mean?"

"After apostles cast me out, I had a revelation on the true nature of God."

"Which was?"

"The world is imperfect and full of pain and suffering. According to Christian teaching, this came about after the fall of perfection in the Garden of Eden. In other words, mankind is to blame for introducing sin into the world."

"So what do you believe?"

"That is not the fault of man—but of the Creator."

"You think it is God's fault?"

"No—the Demiurge. He is the true creator of the universe."

"I do not understand. Are you saying God did not create the cosmos?"

"In a way He did, but not in the manner that you think. Let me explain. There *is* one True God, one Supreme Being, but He did not create the cosmos directly or intentionally. He, she, or it, merely emanated all the matter that is visible and invisible. Everything originated from the Supreme Being but much of this matter is so far removed from its original source, it has less divine qualities and has become corrupted."

"So who created the cosmos?"

"As I have said—the Demiurge."

Longinus rubbed his forehead in exasperation. He was becoming increasingly perplexed by Simon's explanation. "And who or what is that?"

"The True God created the Aeons. They are intermediate divine beings who exist between the True God and us. They and the True God represent the realm of Fullness or Pleroma where true divinity exists. In contrast, all living beings exist in a state that I call Emptiness.

"One of these aeonial beings is called Sophia, which means wisdom. In the course of her celestial journeys, she emanated a flawed consciousness from her own being. This flawed consciousness took many forms, and one of them became the Demiurge. It was the Demiurge, this emanation from Sophia, who created the material and psychic cosmos. It is this Demiurge that much of mankind worships as God."

"But what of the old gods and other religions across the world? Were they just figments of mankind's imagination?"

"No. As I have said, Sophia's emanations took many forms, and humans worshipped them as gods. Some were good and some bad. Some interfered in the affairs of mankind and sought greater power, while others were content to watch man's progress from afar. They fought among themselves, and there was a great celestial war. A few fled into the cosmos, but the others were destroyed. Finally—only the Demiurge remained. After Satan's fall from grace, many of his archdemons impersonated these ancient gods. Most ruled through evil and fear, but a few acted benignly."

"Why would any demon act benignly?" Longinus scoffed.

"Because they were cunning and found they could convert more humans to their cause. They granted their worshippers wealth and success on the field of battle but in return demanded a high price in human sacrifices."

"Does the Demiurge know He is not the True God?"

"No. He is unaware of his origin and believes Himself to be the one and absolute God."

"Why is he called the Demiurge?"

"Because he unwittingly took the divine essence from Sophia and turned it into various forms; therefore, he is known as the Demiurgos or 'Half-maker'. There is a deific component within Creation, one that comes from Sophia and the True God, but that remains hidden from the Demiurge."

Longinus rubbed his chin and tried to make sense of the concept. He had read some versions of this theory of creation many centuries ago. It was called Gnosticism and considered heretical and blasphemous by Jews and Christians.

"So your argument is that the Demiurge is a flawed God, and therefore He created a flawed universe?"

"Yes, and that is why there is so much pain, suffering and natural disasters in the world. The Demiurge can be loving and forgiving—but can also be wrathful and cruel. That is part of His flawed nature."

"Hmm," said Longinus. "I often wondered why God appeared so different in the Old and New Testaments of the Bible. In the Old Testament, He acts like a tyrannical and vengeful psychopath, saying obey and worship Me or I will destroy you and send you to burn in the fires of Hell for eternity. It always seemed to me that a loving, compassionate God would offer humankind a simple choice—a joyful afterlife or oblivion. It is the concept of eternal punishment that I have always struggled to understand. But why did the Demiurge become less wrathful in the New Testament? If He is so flawed, as you contend, why did He change?"

"The Son of God was created to counteract the wrathful nature of the Demiurge. He became mortal and sacrificed his life so the sins of the wicked could be forgiven and offer mankind a last chance to choose the path of righteousness. However, this offer of redemption is in a constant state of flux, a perpetual cycle of punishment or salvation. Sometimes the Demiurge holds sway, and at other times the Son is more dominant."

"But according to your theory, it was the Demiurge who allowed sin into the world. So how can people choose a path of righteousness when the Creator is flawed?"

Simon smiled. "Man comprises two spiritual halves: the part made from the Demiurge, and the part that contains the light of the True God. The half that connects us to the Supreme Being is called the Divine Spark. Most men and women are ignorant of this spark within them, and this spiritual blindness is perpetuated by the influence of the Demiurge.

"When an individual dies, it releases their spark. If the person sought spiritual enlightenment during their life–a process known as gnosis–it joins with the light of the True God. However, if the individual was unenlightened, their divine spark travels to Heaven or Hell depending on the whim of the Demiurge. Mankind can only be saved through understanding the true reality of the cosmos."

"Saved from sin?"

"No–from the ignorance of the spiritual reality of which sin is a consequence. They must understand that they are not responsible for original sin. That was the work of the Demiurge."

Longinus was skeptical but intrigued by Simon's argument. "And how may one find this 'enlightenment'?"

"Through the Messengers of Light."

"And who or what are they?"

"There have been many throughout history: Jesus was one. He was the Logos, or Divine Word, of the True God."

Longinus grimaced. It was bad enough knowing that he had speared the Son of God, but now he had just discovered that he had killed the Logos of the Supreme Being.

"But how could a flawed God, or Demiurge as you call Him, create something as perfect as the Son of God," protested Longinus. "Or is the Nazarene flawed too?"

"Jesus was certainly not perfect when He walked as a man upon the earth, but as the Son of God He is sublime and therefore similar to the True God."

"But how could the Demiurge create him?" Longinus persisted.

"He did not create Him."

"The Nazarene is not the Son of God?" Longinus exclaimed.

"The True God created Jesus through the power of Sophia. She is the Holy Spirit or Ghost of the Trinity. She made the Demiurge believe He had created His Son. Sophia created the Logos to soothe the wrath of the Demiurge. It is through the Nazarene's influence that the God of the New Testament became more patient and forgiving of man's sins. Without the calming and forgiving influence of Jesus, God would have tired of man's sins and enacted Judgment Day. The Son of God begged the Demiurge to give humanity more time, so they could see the errors of their ways and more could be saved from perdition when the Great Day of Wrath comes."

Longinus frowned. The Christian concept of the Trinity–God is one in essence and three in person–had always confused him. To him, the theory had smatterings of the very polytheistic pagan religions that the Christian church had eradicated with fire and sword; and it was the human interpretation of this Triune that had led to the Great Schism that divided the western and eastern churches in 1054 AD.

The Latin church in Rome made a unilateral declaration that the Holy

Spirit proceeded from the Father and Son; whereas, the Greek church in Constantinople maintained the traditional view—as agreed by all churches in the original Nicene Creed—that the Holy Spirit proceeded from the Father alone. Such Christian theological arguments were bewildering enough to a simple Roman centurion, but now Longinus' spiritual waters were further muddied by Simon's own personal brand of Gnosticism.

He suspected that if forced by a mighty hand crushing his stones to choose a religion, the Jewish faith might suit him better. As far as he knew, the Jews believed in one single God. Therefore, in Longinus' mind, all the Christian theological bickering, schisms, wars, and sectarian violence could have been avoided by the simple expedient of whacking haughty pontiffs and patriarchs on their thick domes with the Talmud until they converted to Judaism.

Longinus realised that such a radical measure may have raised a few princely and ecclesiastical eyebrows, but he was a simple man and could only offer simple solutions to the troubles of the world. Anything more complicated was above his centurion pay grade of 6,000 denarii per annum—less food, arms and clothing, of course. Miserly aristocratic bastards! He had called his men scroungernaries instead of legionaries. Whenever they had complained to him about the constant shortage of food or equipment, he had ordered them to saunter forth and scrounge their needs by hook or by crook from other cohorts. It was legend in the Roman army that Longinus' century had some of the most valiant scroungernaries—or thieving arse wipes as the ill-natured bull of a quartermaster had called them—in the legions and wanted for naught.

"So," Longinus said slowly, trying to get his head around Simon's theory, "the Demiurge is the Father, the Nazarene is the Son, and Sophia is the Holy Ghost or Spirit?"

"Yes."

"And the Demiurge does not know that He did not create the Nazarene?"

"No, He does not."

"But if you do not believe in the omnipotence of the Demiurge, then why did you invoke the protection of the Archangel Michael? He was created by the Demiurge and therefore must also be flawed."

"Because the divine spirits of the archangels who remained loyal to the Demiurge are the purest in Heaven. They straddle the material and spiritual worlds and are the guardians of mankind."

"And caused a great deal of death and destruction in the world," grunted Longinus. "The killing of firstborn in Egypt is one of the most horrendous acts in any religion. Even the old gods were not so cruel. The righteous smile, nod their heads sagely, and say the Egyptians deserved it, but what sins did the children commit? None!"

"That was not the archangels. The Demiurge sent his Death Angel–the Destroyer."

"Well, that makes it just," Longinus snorted derisively. "If the Romans had committed such a act, history would have branded us as monsters, but the righteous applaud and give thanks to God for carrying out such atrocities."

"As I have told you–the Demiurge is flawed."

Longinus rubbed the back of his neck and stared doubtfully at Simon. The sorcerer's beliefs made some sense but were heretical in the extreme. Was God the One True God or the Demiurge? Did God, Sophia or a Supreme Being create the Nazarene? He did not know, and, in truth, he did not care. He was not a Christian, and the ways of the gods had always been a mystery to him. However, what he *did* know was that he had to find a way to escape from Hell and save Rachel–and this sorcerer's ability to repel demons would be very useful to him.

"The cambion's leg appears to have healed," Simon observed.

Longinus looked and saw Armilus had returned Aeneas' spear and was hobbling unassisted.

"Yes, it is pity it did not heal sooner. I carried his celestial spheres for twenty miles and now know how poor Atlas felt."

"I once read that cambion flesh is denser than other demons," said Simon.

"Dense makes sense, when speaking about Armilus," Longinus said with a grin. "Anyway, he and the Greek seem to get along well."

"My dear, Longinus," Simon laughed, "please do not let Aeneas hear you say that."

"What? That they are getting along?"

"No! Calling him a Greek!"

"Is he not? I just assumed because of his armour and shield."

"He is no Achaean. He is a Trojan and father of your people, the Romans."

"Aeneas of Troy!" exclaimed Longinus.

"The very same. He was a great leader who led the survivors of his city to the Promised Land, your land, and forged a mighty kingdom."

"But why is King Aeneas wandering around in Hell?"

"Like me, he is cursed, a lost soul. I have met many like us in this terrible place. We are neither of Heaven nor Hell and doomed for eternity to pursue our own long forgotten dreams and destinies."

For once, Longinus was speechless. A bittersweet memory flitted at the edges of his mind. He remembered being a small boy sitting on his mother's knee, wide eyed and sucking his thumb, as she told him stories of the mighty Aeneas, King of the Latins. He could almost hear her soft, sweet voice, but then like so many happy memories from his distant past, it eluded him like a butterfly as he tried to grasp it. He could barely remember her face, and it saddened him he could not honour her memory by reliving the happiness they had once shared. Both he and Aeneas had lost their mothers in savage events and to the cold passing of time.

"We are falling behind. We had better increase our pace," he growled.

Surprised by the abruptness of his tone, Simon glanced at him and wondered what grim echo of the past could bring a tear to the eye of a hardened Roman centurion.

CHAPTER XXV

After many hours spent circumventing a basalt lava field and avoiding some skeleton patrols, Longinus and his party arrived at the foot of towering black cliffs. The centurion wiped the never-ending stream of moisture from his face and eyes. He was tired, wet and sticky. Belial's scorching domain was like a vast steam room, and he longed to escape its sweltering humidity. He glanced up at the blazing firmament. Its tempestuous, fiery hues had transformed from bright yellowish-red to darker shades of scarlet and orange.

"Where is the entrance to the Lower Depths?" he asked Armilus.

"It should be here," the cambion replied, scratching his inflamed, bald pate.

Longinus grimaced as a flake of burnt skin came away under Armilus' claw nail. The cambion looked as though he was suffering from a severe case of eczema. A moment's inattention to the dangerous surroundings had resulted in his dome being splattered with tiny droplets of lava. However, to the centurion's astonishment, the half-demon was so thick skinned he felt no discomfort. In fact, it pained Longinus more to look upon his bright red head.

"Are you certain this is the right place?"

"Yes!" Armilus snapped. "I remember that needle-shaped rock."

Longinus looked behind them. The tall natural pillar was very distinctive and reminded him of an obelisk. There were no other formations similar to it in the vicinity.

"Then it must be here, somewhere," said Longinus. "What does it look like?"

"A stone door in the cliff face. It is well concealed. I only stumbled upon it because it had been left ajar."

They spread out along the cliff face and hunted for the elusive entrance. As they searched, Longinus noticed that the landscape was becoming darker. He looked up and saw ominous black clouds rolling across the flaming sky. Red lightning flashed and was followed swiftly by a tumultuous boom of thunder. Everyone jumped and gawked at the darkening sky.

"It is a Hellstorm," shouted Onoskelis, as the lighting increased in ferocity. "We must find shelter."

"Hellstorm?" Longinus asked.

"Fire and brimstone," replied the succubus. "Uncomfortable for demons, painful for souls–and lethal to you."

"Great! Just what we needed. Armilus! Any sign of that door?"

"Not yet," the cambion whined.

More lightning flashed, thunder rumbled, and it started to rain. Longinus gaped as the first tentative drops struck the ground and burst into flames.

"It is like Greek fire!" he exclaimed.

"Hold your shields above your heads," advised Onoskelis.

"Ow!" Longinus yelped as a tiny blob landed on his head, burning his scalp.

"I warned you," said Onoskelis.

Longinus wrenched his shield free and held it above him. Aeneas ran over to Simon and used his hoplon to protect them.

"Armilus!" Longinus roared.

There was another resounding peal of thunder, and the clouds unleashed their full hellish fury. An incendiary rainstorm hammered down, and the bleak landscape exploded into a raging inferno. The overhang of the cliffs afforded them some protection, but Longinus knew it would not be long before Vulcan's hot piss transformed him into a screaming ball of burning flesh.

"Over here!" cried Simon.

Longinus raced to him.

"What is it?"

"A satanic seal on the rock," gasped Simon. "I think this may be the entrance."

Longinus peered at the cliff face and discerned a barely perceptible rectangular crack surrounding the seal.

"Armilus! We have found something!" Longinus bellowed as the deluge pelted his shield, setting it ablaze.

The cambion stumbled over to them. His head and shoulders were ablaze, and he kept slapping his skin to dowse the flames.

"I do not understand. The door was not sealed when I was last here," he said, frowning.

Longinus grunted and buckled as heavy pieces of exploding Hellfire struck his shield.

"Use your medallion!" Onoskelis screamed, trying to shield the party with her wings.

The cambion extracted his satanic periapt from his breastplate and pressed it against the seal. A small section of the cliff face rumbled and opened inward.

"It is the door!" he shrieked.

"Into the cave!" commanded Onoskelis.

She waited until the others had rushed into the cave and then followed them. Longinus, Aeneas and Simon cavorted like macabre dancers as they extinguished the flames on each other. When finished, they slumped to the floor and gazed out of the door as the Hellstorm erupted into a frenzy of enormous fireballs. Onoskelis sat down beside Longinus.

"We escaped just in time," she murmured.

"Yes. Thank you for shielding us," he said, tentatively exploring the burnt patch on his scalp with a fingertip.

"My wings are very strong."

He glanced at her obsidian pennons and saw red burn marks and splotches of dark blood.

"You are hurt."

"So are you."

"I heal quickly."

"As do I. Demons are born in pain and live in pain. It is our curse. Demons with deformities suffer more. I cannot even begin to imagine what agony the cambion must endure. Everything in Hell comes with a price and must be paid."

Longinus thought of her malformation and wondered how much pain she endured.

"Do demons ostracise those with impairments?" he asked.

"No. Why should they? Many are deformed in Hell. But weakness is not tolerated. I am misshapen, but I am strong. Satan expects all his slaves to be fearless and merciless."

"Then why did he choose Armilus to be a messenger?"

"Cambions are the exception. They are half-demons and therefore inherently weak. But Satan for some unknown reason has always favoured them. He appoints them with more cerebral positions such as intendants and messengers."

Longinus now understood why she had accused Armilus of being a spy. On earth, intendants were temporary royal inspectors appointed by monarchs to root out the crimes, misdemeanours and financial misdealing of corrupt officials. Intendants had served a just function in the mortal world, but he suspected their counterparts in Hell were more interested in searching for accusations of heresy and handing the accused over to the inquisitors.

"I did not know that," he said quietly.

"There are many things about demons you do not know."

"When the Lilitu attacked us, you mentioned something about repaying a debt."

"Did I? I cannot remember."

"Now I am in your debt again."

"Are you?" she said, staring at him.

"Yes."

"Do all of your people have eyes of blue?"

Her question surprised him. "No, most had brown. Although a few of our emperors had blue eyes."

She frowned and thought it over for a moment. "Were you an emperor?"

"No. I was just a common soldier," he laughed.

"Like me?"

"Yes, just like you," he said, smiling.

"Until you met Lilith," she observed.

His smile faded. "Yes—until I met Lilith."

She nodded and seemed satisfied with his explanation.

"I shall demand payment," she said impassively.

"What sort of payment?"

She stood up and adjusted her armour.

"I will think of something."

She walked away before he could think of a reply. Her question about Lilith had thrown him, and he felt somewhat ashamed—like a man trying to cheat on his wife. He knew it was an irrational emotion. Lilith was in Heaven, and there was nothing he could do to bring her back. But he still felt he was betraying her memory and the deep love they had once shared.

He watched as she helped Armilus wipe a splotch of flaming liquid from his back. The half-demon did not complain; he seemed too surprised. The centurion suspected that it was the first time that a fellow demon had shown any compassion for him.

The centurion felt a tinge of guilt for the way he had treated him. He had never mocked the infirm and had always taken a dim view of others that gained a perverse pleasure from such behaviour. His burning desire for revenge had clouded his sense of decency, and he was now forced to concede that he did not hate all demons—most of them—but not all. The cantankerous half-demon had grown on him like an annoying wart, and, despite himself, he rather enjoyed his company. And as for Onoskelis—he did not like to think about her. For some unknown reason, she had got under his skin. She annoyed yet attracted him. He felt like a moth drawn to a flame. But he knew in his heart that he had no time for dalliances and must keep their relationship impersonal and professional.

"Impersonal and professional, stupid!" he whispered angrily, rapping his forehead with his knuckles.

"You practise self-flagellation?"

He looked up and saw Simon staring at him with a puzzled look on his face.

"Yes, it reminds me of my sin, depravity and vileness in the eyes of God," Longinus replied wryly.

"But which God?" asked Simon.

"The Demiurge, knowing my luck."

"There is no need to punish yourself. Sophia is with you."

"Is she?"

"Of course! She has guided our path thus far."

"Really? In what way?" Longinus retorted skeptically.

"She brought us together and allows us to understand each other."

"What do you mean?"

"I articulate in Hebrew and have a smattering of Latin; Aeneas talks in the Hittite dialects of Luwian or Lydian of Troy, Phoenician, and the lingua Latina of ancient Latium; the demons use Hellspeak; and you converse in part Latin and some other vernacular unknown to me."

"English from the land of the Britons," Longinus interjected.

"I do not know that land. Therefore, I ask you, with all our disparate languages, how is it we understand each other?"

"Armilus said that demons can speak in all human tongues."

"But you, Aeneas, and I are not demons."

Longinus glanced sharply at him. Now that he considered the matter, it did seem somewhat strange that he had been able to converse with everyone and thing he had met in Hell. He had always assumed that Asmodeus had spoken to him in Latin, but now he was not so certain. When one was fluent in many languages, one did not think about it while speaking–you just spoke.

"I cannot explain it," he sighed.

Simon smiled. "But I can. Sophia has guided us."

Longinus stood up. This talk of divine intervention made him feel uncomfortable. His gloomy side believed a man's fate was predetermined before he born, but his optimistic side hoped that was wrong and a person could carve their own path and destiny in the world.

"I wish she was here now. We could do with some celestial help," he quipped.

"She has *always* been with you."

"Then she will be *very* shocked," Longinus replied with a rakish smile.

His misguided notion that the Gnostic holy man was more liberal than his Christian counterparts when it came to banter about the pleasures of the flesh was dashed abruptly upon the hard rock of righteousness.

Simon regarded him from under bushy, censorious brows. Longinus' smile faded, and he gave a little cough of embarrassment.

"More self-flagellation?" he enquired, innocently.

"Yes–and perhaps the succubus could assist you," Simon replied with a hint of sarcasm.

"I will see how the others are faring," Longinus said, making his escape.

Simon watched him go, then smiled and shook his head. The Revenant was a strange choice to lead their mission, but who was he to disagree? He was just the messenger. They needed warriors, not prophets. Their purpose and fates lay in the hands of much greater powers. He offered a small prayer to Sophia and asked Her to forgive Longinus' errant ways.

"Is everyone all right?" asked Longinus.

"Never better," Aeneas said, wincing. "Just some slight burns."

Longinus stared at Armilus. His bald pate was orange. He looked as though he had spent a misguided day on a sunbed.

"It looks worse than it is," said Onoskelis. "The cambion is quite resistant to Hellfire."

"And you?"

She flexed her wings, and he could see her wounds were healing.

"Good! Then we are ready to continue."

At the rear of the cave was a dark tunnel that sloped downwards. Longinus peered into it and readied his spear.

"This is the way to the Lower Depths?"

"Yes," replied Armilus.

"Can you see in the dark," Longinus asked him.

"All demons can see in the dark," Onoskelis sighed impatiently.

"Simon, Aeneas?"

"Like an owl," said Aeneas.

"I too can see quite clearly," said Simon. "It is one of the few advantages of being dead."

"Does anyone know where we can find Pazuzu?" Longinus asked.

"From what I have learned," said Armilus, rolling his eyes, "one does not find Pazuzu–he will find you. This is his domain, but other ancient monstrosities also dwell here. Some have joined Pazuzu's rebellion, but others have not and remain fiercely independent. We must be careful and avoid these creatures at all costs. They have been known to slither forth and devour unwary trespassers."

Longinus thought about the luminous abomination they had encountered at the bridge, and a shiver ran down his spine. He had no desire to meet it again.

"So we want to be found by Pazuzu, but nothing else?" said Longinus.

"That would be wise," observed Simon.

"We must proceed *quietly* and with *extreme* caution," added Armilus, with additional eye rolling.

"Thank you, Pythia," retorted Longinus.

"What is a Pythia?" the cambion asked, suspiciously.

"A frenzied Achaean hag who prophesied by sniffing her own farts," snorted Aeneas.

Armilus shook his head and wrinkled his nose in disgust. The Trojan was so uncouth.

"But will Pazuzu welcome our presence?" pondered Longinus.

"That remains to be seen," said Simon, stroking his beard. "He may treat us as potential allies or enemies. I know not. This is uncharted territory for all of us."

"There is one infinitely more dangerous than Pazuzu in this dreadful place," said Armilus. "Even archdemons speak of her in fearful whispers."

"Yes, yes. You have already told me about Lamashtu," Longinus said irritably.

"No, I speak not of the night-hag—but something much worse."

"What now?" the centurion sighed wearily.

"Demons call her Babylon the Great. She is immensely powerful, and some say she can predict the future. Very few demons have met her and lived to tell the tale. The unfortunate ones who survived became raving lunatics. To behold her is to look into the face of madness. She obeys no gods or demons. Even Satan is reputed to avoid her."

"Is she a demoness?"

"No one knows. But whatever she is, she hates men, demons and angels with equal vehemence."

"Did Satan imprison her in the Lower Depths?"

"No. I have read fragments that suggest Babylon the Great fought a great battle with an ancient goddess, but the deity defeated her and bound her here until the end of time."

"What was the name of the goddess?"

"She had many titles, but some mortals called her Ereshkigal. She was queen of the underworld before Satan and the Fallen destroyed her."

The centurion felt a stab of pain in his heart. When he was being tortured in Hell, he had dreamed that a goddess called Ereshkigal had rescued him and taken him back through time to ancient Babylon. She had been noble and beautiful. He could still remember the softness of her lips and the fragrance of her skin.

But then he frowned as a dark memory seeped up from his unconscious mind. In his dream, Asmodeus had tried frequently to pull him back through time to Hell. He knew it had been the King of Demons because he had heard his diabolical voice in his head. But the centurion had sensed another hideous presence lurking in the background. Was it possible that Asmodeus had enlisted Babylon the Great to help him? Longinus could not be certain, but his instincts warned him that this malignant being had somehow been involved.

"Longinus. Longinus!"

He started as he heard Aeneas' voice calling him. He saw the others staring at him with looks of concern upon their faces.

"Whatever is the matter?" asked the Trojan. "Are you unwell?"

"No. It was but an old memory coming back to haunt me," said Longinus.

Aeneas nodded. "You have my sympathy, my friend. Old memories have a habit of creeping up on us when we least expect it. After thousands of years of lonely wandering, I find it increasingly difficult to recall the happy times of my life but remember every single moment of despair and regret with the utmost clarity. That is why I enjoy being part of your company. It gives me less time to dwell on my past and keeps my dark thoughts at bay."

"And we are very honoured to have you accompany us," said Longinus. "It is the first time I have travelled with a king."

"Aeneas was a king?" asked Onoskelis, surprised.

"Yes," said Simon, "a very brave and great king. His kingdom was the origin of Longinus' people."

"And what is the name of your people?" she asked.

"Romans," said Longinus.

"Ro–mans," she said, with a puzzled look. "Are there no females among your people?"

"No. Just males," Longinus replied, winking at Simon and Aeneas.

Onoskelis digested this bit of information very seriously for a moment.

"So you prefer coupling with males?"

"No," Longinus responded, a faint smile hovering at the corners of his mouth.

"Your people are strange," she declared.

The men laughed, and she looked even more puzzled.

Armilus sighed at her naivety. "Of course, his people have females!"

"But he said they did not," she protested.

"He was jesting with you."

"What is this jest–ing?" she demanded.

"It is a human trait," Armilus said, scowling. "They utter incorrect, childish or stupid words to others for their own amusement. The jest is usually at the expense of its recipient."

"I see!" Onoskelis hissed, shooting daggers at Longinus.

"Do not take it so seriously," Longinus said. "It was just a little jest."

"I understand perfectly," she retorted with a terse smile. "It was a little jest from one with a little brain."

Simon and Aeneas laughed again. Even Armilus cracked the semblance of a rudimentary grin.

"I think she has grasped the concept of jesting," said Simon.

"Indeed, she has," Longinus laughed. "Right, let us be on our way. Onoskelis and I will take the lead. Aeneas, you bring up the rear."

"No," said Onoskelis. "Aeneas and I will take the lead, and you can bring up the rear."

Longinus frowned. "Why?"

"Because," she replied haughtily as she strode past him, "your people have no females!"

Aeneas clapped a hand on Longinus' shoulder and grinned. "Be not downhearted, my friend. Beautiful maidens always wish to accompany the king."

"It is a thankless task, but someone has to do it," Longinus grunted.

"That is the spirit, my boy!" Aeneas beamed before chasing after Onoskelis.

"They are both quite mad," the cambion whispered conspiratorially to Longinus.

"Then they are in good company," Longinus growled. "Are there any more surprises in the Lower Depths you forgot to tell me about? No man-eating squirrels—or cracked *nuts*?"

The cambion frowned and opened his mouth to reply, but the look in the centurion's eyes made him think better of it.

"Come, Armilus, we must catch up with them," the sorcerer murmured tactfully.

Simon did not know what had caused the tension between the centurion and the cambion, but it surprised him to discover that Longinus considered squirrels and nuts a very serious matter. "It must be a form of strange pagan religious custom," he mused, making a mental note never to mention the shadow-tailed animals or fruit in the Roman's presence.

Longinus grunted in resignation and hitched up his sword belt. He flinched as his loincloth disturbed his still tender, recovering bits.

"Oh, well. Back to watching the cambion's hairy arse again," he sighed.

CHAPTER XXVI

The companions journeyed up and down for miles through a vast labyrinth of cold, damp caverns and tunnels. The passageways varied in size: some were enormous and others so narrow they had to turn sideways to squeeze through. One tunnel ended overlooking a precipice. On further investigation, they discovered they were looking down into a vast cylindrical abyss over a mile in width where many passageways at different levels terminated. After entering a cave with distinctive boulders, stalactites and stalagmites for the third time, Longinus brought the party to a halt.

"This is useless! We are just going round in circles!" he complained.

"I agree," said Onoskelis. "Shall I fly down and see if I can discover a way to the lower levels?"

"No," Longinus replied, shaking his head. "It is too dangerous. We must stay together."

"Why? We have seen nothing," she said.

"Yes—but have you not felt that we are being watched?"

"I have," whispered Armilus, staring around with eyes like goblets. "I think we should leave."

"I too have sensed something, but I cannot discern what it is," added Simon.

"Well, I have felt nothing," scoffed Aeneas. "Your concern is but a trick of the mind. I saw such deception firsthand when my officers made the mistake of placing young, untested warriors on night guard. The high-strung pups imagined all kinds of horrors lurking in the darkness and roused the entire camp every five minutes. Neither man nor beast could get a wink of sleep. Finally, I got up and told them, 'The next time something moves, fetch me its head!' That stopped them jumping at their own shadows."

"That may be so," said Armilus, "but the shadows here have the unfortunate habit of devouring intruders."

"I tire of this pussyfooting around," growled Longinus. "If we want to find Pazuzu, we need to let him know we are here."

"What do you suggest?" asked Simon.

"Pazuzu!" Longinus roared.

"Well, that is one way of doing it," Simon murmured.

"Pazuzu, we seek an audience with you!" Longinus bellowed.

"Be silent!" Armilus hissed. "You will awaken things that should never be awoken!"

"Damn them! Pazuzu!"

"This will not end well! This will not end well!" Armilus whispered hysterically, covering his ears.

They all listened with their hearts in their mouths as the centurion's cries reverberated throughout the myriad of tunnels and caverns, followed by a deathly silence.

"Hah! I told you!" said Aeneas. "This infernal rabbit warren is as empty as a Greek's head!"

No sooner than he had uttered those words, scores of armed demons appeared from behind the boulders and stalagmites.

"Of course, I could be mistaken," the Trojan muttered, readying his spear.

Armilus screamed and scampered off down a tunnel. It never failed to amaze Longinus how swiftly the cambion could move when threatened.

A tall, horned, red demon attired in Hell armour and carrying a longsword on its shoulder sauntered towards them.

The four companions stood back to back. Longinus gritted his teeth and braced for battle. He could feel Onoskelis' thigh press against his as she crouched beside him, trident and shield poised. Simon raised his arms and prepared to unleash his power of confusion on their adversaries. Aeneas struck his shield with his spear, stamped his leading foot and adopted a strong, defiant stance.

The red demon stopped and regarded them with a smile as crooked as its teeth. It lowered the massive sword and ran a claw nail along the blade, producing a horrible screeching sound.

Everyone tensed. Muscles bulged. Eyes narrowed. Armilus screamed in the distance.

The demon bowed and said in a deep voice, "Welcome to the Lower Depths. Your request has been granted. Our master, Lord Pazuzu, commands us to escort you unto his presence."

No one answered for a moment.

Then Aeneas said, "Well–that was unexpected."

CHAPTER XXVII

Asmodeus drifted into his sanctum sanctorum deep within the bowels of his Basilica of Pain. He hovered for a moment and considered how he wished to receive his visitor. He decided a commanding and regal appearance would better serve his purpose and ascended his enormous, pulsating throne of flesh. Once comfortably ensconced, he closed his eyes and sent his powerful thoughts across the limitless, conflagrant expanse of the Abyss.

"Attend me. I would have words with you. Words to your advantage."

In less than sixty beats of a human heart, a crackling, incandescent rift appeared at the far end of the chamber. Asmodeus watched, fascinated and amused. Each archdemon's materialisation was different depending on their abilities and powers. He particularly enjoyed this one's flair for the dramatic.

As the fiery crack in space and time reached its furious crescendo, there sounded a piercing neigh and a winged, skinless horse, flames belching from its nostrils, emerged from the fissure. Sitting astride the fearsome beast was a tall, gaunt, imposing figure adorned in full plate armour. The knight's sunken red eyes burned with fervent intensity through the narrow, oblong slit of his helmet visor. In his left gauntlet, he held a highly decorative lance, from the tip of which dripped a viscous, amber pus.

The weapon was extremely poisonous and could kill lesser demons or mortals within minutes. Its effect on archdemons was less deadly, but the few unfortunate ones who had dared to cross swords with this grim rider had taken weeks to recover. Thereafter, other archdemons had studiously avoided being on the receiving end of the Lance of Eligos.

Satan had presented the horse, armour and spear to Eligos in honour of the bravery the knight had shown during the Fallen's invasion of the ancient underworlds. He was the only archdemon who had fought Pazuzu in single combat and survived. However, he had lost his groin and a good part of his abdomen; and terrible, oozing scars covered his body.

The Evil One's generosity toward Eligos had always irritated Asmodeus. He had never received such valuable gifts from his master. However, he contented himself with the fact that Satan had made him a king and Eligos but a duke. A minor distinction, to be sure, but one that held significant weight in Hell.

"Ave domine inferni!" the knight intoned in a deep voice. "You summoned me and I am here, oh, great King of Demons."

Asmodeus smiled. He enjoyed the respect that Eligos bestowed upon him. The knight was a formidable archdemon of Hell, but had always acknowledged the King of Demon's power and status. That pleased him.

"Ave domine inferni, Eligos. Pray dismount so we may speak awhile."

Eligos threw one leg over the steed's head and jumped down with a speed and agility that impressed Asmodeus. His fellow archdemon was no ponderous, clanking medieval knight. His ebony armour was light, strong and impervious to all weapons apart from the swords of the accursed archangels. He was powerful, conceited, but not too ambitious. These qualities made him the perfect candidate for Asmodeus' plan.

"I did not see you at the Gathering," said Asmodeus.

Eligos raised his visor. His face was black and shrunken; his mouth round with inward sloping pointed teeth.

"I was otherwise engaged in Purgatory. Our master tasked me with harassing the angelic scum."

"To heighten tension and goad them into fighting?"

"That is so."

"Were you successful?"

"Extremely," Eligos laughed with a peculiar wheezing sound. "During my last incursion, the accused archangels appeared. I fought them for a while and then pretended to retreat in fear. That will raise their confidence for the forthcoming battle. Thus emboldened, they shall return to Purgatory like lambs to the slaughter."

Asmodeus nodded in approval. "Very clever. Was that Satan's idea or yours?"

"Mine."

"You are a clever strategist."

"It is in my nature."

"Yet our master has not chosen you to take part in the battle."

"True," Eligos growled. "He has given that honour to others. Like you, I must wait idly in the shadows."

"Such a waste," Asmodeus sighed. "But what can we do? Our master knows best."

"That he does," Eligos hissed.

Asmodeus took his lacklustre response as a promising sign they could do business. He decided to pave the way by stroking Eligos' vanity.

"What will you do now?" he asked.

"Continue my hunt."

"For a few escaped human souls? That is hardly much of a challenge for you, the best hunter and warrior in Hell."

"A few?" Eligos chortled. "Have you not heard about the dungeons?"

"No. Tell me."

"Someone slew the inquisitors, broke the satanic seals and released the captive souls and succubi."

"All the souls?" Asmodeus exclaimed.

"Every last one of them. Hell's coffers are empty."

"But surely we can hunt them down and catch them?"

"It is too late. Baal Zebub only discovered the escape today. Most of the souls are probably in Limbo now. As you well know, the Great Tyrant's barrier only prevents demons from entering that cursed place."

"This is Pazuzu's handiwork!" growled Asmodeus.

But he was secretly pleased. Such an unmitigated disaster would lower Satan and Baal Zebub's standing among the Fallen. However, the King of Demons knew that the dearth of souls would only be temporary. There were more than ample sinners on earth to keep his cellars well stocked. It was a vintage century for evil, and the crispness, flavour, body and bouquet of the current crop was superb.

"The emperor's pet will make short work of him and his Elder scum," Eligos hissed.

"Yes, he mentioned he had released his abomination into the Lower Depths. Do you know its size now?"

"As large as a mountain with a gnawing hunger to match," Eligos laughed.

Asmodeus grimaced. He had no liking for the emperor's slithery pet. It was uncontrollable and devoured everything in its path.

"So Satan brought you back from Purgatory to hunt down the escaped succubi?"

"He did."

"They will offer you little sport."

"True. I would rather be fighting angels. Lilith's succubi whores are disappointingly easy to defeat. Even human souls have proved more troublesome."

"Really? In what way?" Asmodeus asked with a puzzled look. Shades of the dead were naught but ants to him.

"There are two souls that have evaded my grasp for millennia," Eligos snarled. "One is an ancient warrior, and the other is a sorcerer who uses some form of bastard Christian sorcery to hide his tracks. I would give anything to capture them and grind their flesh with my claws."

The King of Demons raised an eyebrow as his guest clenched his gauntlet and produced a horrible grating sound. The Hunter of Soul's taloned claws were like birds' feet, with three fingers facing forward and one pointing back. It would certainly not fare well for these errant souls when Eligos caught them, thought Asmodeus. The hunter was one of the cruellest demons in Hell. His favourite pastimes were plucking out eyes, biting off penises, and grinding testicles into pulp. Other archdemons whispered he did this because Pazuzu had ripped off his genitalia, and he now despised others with a full pouch.

But Asmodeus had his own theory. He had always suspected that Eligos, the mighty hunter, preferred males to females but concealed his predilection under the guise of torture. He imagined with some amusement that the archdemon 'lingered awhile' before biting off a cock.

Some also hinted Eligos swallowed his victim's eyes so he could relive their carnal experiences. If true, it was an impressive feat that the King of Demons wished he could replicate. It would increase his sensual pleasures immeasurably.

"Yes, sorcerers can be wearisome," Asmodeus said soothingly. "I rip out their tongues when they arrive in Hell. That puts an end to their infernal spell casting."

"Most interesting. I never thought of removing their tongues," Eligos replied thoughtfully.

"Too obsessed with other parts," Asmodeus murmured.

"Eh?" Eligos asked, glancing sharply at him.

"I said two chests and hearts," the King of Demons replied innocently.

"What?"

"The chests and hearts of the two human souls that await your talons. Hopefully, you will find them before long."

"Yes," growled Eligos, clenching his gauntlet again. "That would be extremely satisfying."

"And speaking of satisfaction, I have a small favour to ask of you."

"How can I serve you?"

"Lilith's Revenant has escaped and is somewhere in Hell. I have given the Lilitu Solomon's ring and wineskin and instructed them to find him, kill him and capture his soul."

"I have heard of this creature. What sort of demon is he?"

Asmodeus laughed. "He is no demon—merely a vampire."

"Has not Satan expressed his desire to interrogate him?"

"He has—but I would prefer he did not."

"I see," Eligos replied with a knowing smile. "So what do you require of me?"

"I wish you to destroy all of them and bring the Revenant's soul to me."

"What? You wish me to kill your little whores?" Eligos exclaimed, his eyes glistening with excitement at the thought of reliving all their carnal adventures.

"Yes. Can you do it?"

"Of course!" Eligos retorted. "The Lilitu will fall by my lance. But the task is risky and will incur Satan's wrath. I will need an excellent reason for doing it."

"Then let me provide you with the excuse you seek," Asmodeus replied suavely. "You came upon them by chance and saw them slaying the Revenant. You knew our master wanted to interrogate him and confronted them. In order to conceal their crime, they turned upon you, forcing you to defend yourself. You could not find the Revenant's soul after the fight."

Eligos regarded him silently for a moment and then said, "And what will be my reward for accomplishing this favour?"

Asmodeus grinned. Eligos was a warrior, and the King of Demons knew of something that would excite him more than playing a boy's fiddle.

"The Revenant carries a spear of great power. Mortals call it the Spear of Destiny."

"I have heard of this lance. Some say even Satan fears it," Eligos murmured, licking his lips. "What power does it possess?"

"It is a vampiric weapon that sucks the life from its victims. The more it kills, the more powerful it becomes. It can slay demons and send the souls of mortals and the undead straight to Hell. With the Spear of Destiny in one claw and the Lance of Eligos in the other, you would be invincible!"

Eligos' eyes shone with greed like rubies in moonlight.

"Very well, Asmodai, our pact is made. I will destroy Lilith's whores and bring the Revenant's soul to you."

The King of Demons scowled inwardly at his impertinent familiarity. Only Satan dared to call him by his ancient angelic name. However, he swallowed his pride and maintained an amiable countenance.

"I can rely on your complete discretion in this matter?"

"Of course. We have aided each other many times over the centuries, and I have never betrayed you."

"Nor I, you. The arrangement has worked to our mutual advantage."

"Indeed, it has. Your last gift was very satisfying," Eligos replied, leering.

Asmodeus smirked. The screaming group of pretty catamites had obviously been to the clandestine sprout nibbler's taste.

"Where did you last see the Revenant?"

"Leviathan's domain, but I can tell you where he is heading."

"Where?"

Asmodeus recounted the terms of the hunt, and the threat to Longinus' friends on earth.

"So, you believe he seeks Satan's Path in the Lower Depths?"

"I do. How else can he return to the mortal plane?"

"No matter. I know where the portal lies."

"You do!" Asmodeus exclaimed. Even he did not know its location.

"Of course. It is near Babylon the Great's cavern."

The King of Demons grimaced. He had believed that Babylon favoured him alone with her prophecies, but it now appeared that every demon he met had scuttled down into her lair. The scheming bitch's cavern must have been busier than a bespoke brothel offering free portholes to maritime mortals.

"If he enters Chaos, he will not survive, and we will lose forever the spear," Eligos said worriedly,

Asmodeus pursed his lips. Such an outcome would suit him perfectly, but he did not disclose this to Eligos.

"Then find him before he enters that vile place. But even if you cannot, worry not. I know this insect very well. He is a resourceful and resilient warrior. If anyone can find a way through Chaos, it is he."

Eligos brightened on hearing these words.

"Then he will present me with an excellent challenge. Do you have any garb worn by him?"

"I thought you might ask that," replied Asmodeus as a cloth appeared in his claw.

He threw to Eligos, who sniffed it with keen interest.

"His loincloth?"

"It is."

Asmodeus raised his eyebrows and sighed as the knight continued sniffing. He had more important things to do than watch a eunuch dream of getting an erection.

"How will you find him—the Law of Contagion, psychometry?" he asked at last.

He knew the hunter was a master of psychic tracking and could locate prey by touching inanimate objects associated with them.

Eligos issued a wheezing laugh, mounted his fiery steed, and tied the loin wrap to the pommel of his human leather saddle.

"On this occasion, I will need neither," he said, pulling on the reins and turning the beast.

"Why?"

"The stench from your harlot's cunts will lead me straight to him!"

Eligos spurred his horse savagely and with a high-pitched whinnying scream both rider and mount flew into the rift. The air crackled, hissed, and then with a dull pop, the portal vanished.

"Then good sniffing," Asmodeus replied coldly, adding Eligos' head to his growing list of imperial executions.

The road to power was littered with little shits that needed squashing and scraped from one's claws.

CHAPTER XXVIII

Pazuzu's demons escorted Longinus and his companions through the labyrinthine maze of the Lower Depths. One group led the way, and the other half brought up the rear. Longinus could not discern whether they were being treated as guests or prisoners.

"Why does it need so many to guide us?" he asked the tall demon with the broadsword.

"To ensure your safety," he answered.

"To ensure we do not escape, more like," laughed Aeneas.

The demon stopped and looked at them. "Leave, if you wish. As a sign of good faith, we have not taken your weapons from you. But you will not survive for long. There are beings down here that would take great pleasure in destroying you. They are aware of our presence, and it is only Pazuzu and the Elder demon's protection that prevents them from attacking us."

"What is your name?" asked Longinus.

"Why?" he asked, suspiciously. "Do you seek to gain power over me?"

"What?" asked Longinus, perplexed.

"Many demons are reticent about revealing their names to others," explained Onoskelis. "Human sorcerers and necromancers have used such information to bind and control us."

The centurion remembered that was true. King Solomon had used such an artifice to compel demons to build the First Temple of Jerusalem.

"My name is Longinus, and this is Simon, Aeneas, Armilus and Onoskelis."

By revealing their names first, the centurion had at a stroke negated any such threat.

The demon hesitated for a moment and then said, "Tetrax."

"You are a—renegade from Hell?"

He had nearly said 'deserter' but had chosen a more tactful term.

"I was a commander in Azazel's legions. All the demons you see here have joined Pazuzu's cause."

"Why?"

"Because he is just lord and offers us freedom from tyranny and oppression."

"And is Satan not just to his vassals?"

Tetrax gave a scornful laugh. "How long have you been in Hell?"

"Five earthly years, I think. I was Asmodeus' prisoner."

The tall demon nodded in a shared understanding of the true meaning of Longinus' understated admission, and his yellow eyes narrowed.

"Then imagine a demon a hundred fold crueler than Asmodeus: that is Azazel. Now envisage an archfiend a thousand times worse than Azazel: that is Satan. No, the Evil One is not just."

They turned a corner and Longinus and his companions gaped in astonishment as an enormous bat-like beast appeared and dropped a babbling Armilus at his feet. The cambion cowered on the ground with his claws over his eyes.

"Please! Please!" the half-demon sobbed.

"Armilus," Longinus said gently whilst keeping a wary eye on the slavering monstrosity.

"Mercy! I beg of you!"

"Armilus," the centurion sighed wearily.

"Do not consume me!"

"Armilus!" Longinus bellowed in his left ear.

The cambion lowered his claws and peered around. The look of relief on his face when he saw his companions was palpable.

"Tetrax is taking us to meet Pazuzu," the centurion said nonchalantly.

"Oh," Armilus mumbled somewhat shamefacedly.

"Are you hurt?" asked Onoskelis.

The cambion felt his body all over and said thankfully, "No!"

"Then why were you screaming?" she asked.

"Because that *thing* dragged me up and down the Abyss! I thought it was going to devour me!" the cambion replied angrily.

The flying creature tilted its head to one side and hissed. Armilus crawled behind Longinus' legs and peeked at it.

"She did not consider him tasty enough," Tetrax said, grinning. "Your little cambion led her a merry chase. He moves swiftly for a Spurned One."

"Spurned One?" Longinus asked, frowning.

"Hellspeak for a weak, deformed demon," Onoskelis said.

"Hmm," said Longinus.

It was as he had suspected. Armilus had been ostracized because he was different. Considering the plethora of ugly faces and bodies that existed in the Abyss, he thought demons should be the last to vilify and mock others. But it was in Hell as it was on earth: the weak are always the first to suffer at the hands of the strong.

"I have seen this manner of beast before," Longinus said, changing the subject. "Two were drawing Naamah's chariot."

"You have met Satan's daughter?" Tetrax asked with some surprise.

"Only in passing. I think she rather liked me."

"That is regrettable," the tall demon replied. "They say being favoured by Naamah is worse than being fed to her hounds."

Longinus remembered Naamah's cold eyes and her womb bursting open. "That I can believe."

Tetrax stroked the beast's snout, and it licked his claw with its long tongue. "She is a sharur. Asmodeus created them for his own amusement, but many escaped his power and now dwell in the Lower Depths. Not being demons, they can procreate and multiply."

"Indeed?" Longinus murmured.

The creature reminded Longinus of the shape he assumed when he was in his bat form. He wondered if that fact had influenced Asmodeus when he had created them.

The beast sniffed at him and gave a low squeaking sound.

"I think she feels some affinity to you," Tetrax said, frowning.

"Sharur was the name of the Sumerian God Ninurta's talking mace. It also means supreme hunter," said Longinus.

Tetrax looked at him in astonishment. "That is true. Your knowledge of the ancients is most impressive."

Longinus nodded graciously, but in truth he did not know how he had known it. He had just blurted it out. Perhaps, he mused, he was absorbing Naram-Sin's knowledge in the same manner the ancient vampire lord was assimilating his. Given a few years, Naram-Sin would be the very model of a modern Major-General and surpass Longinus in understanding the foibles of humankind and their society. It was an intriguing theory, and the centurion made a mental note to discuss it with Naram-Sin at some future time when slithering monstrosities were not trying to eviscerate or devour them.

"Is it friendly?" Longinus asked. He was already he was beginning to see beyond the fearsome ugliness and appreciate the true nature of the beast. He considered it kin.

"To us," the commander replied. "But I would advise you not to put your hand near its mouth."

"You mean like this?" said Longinus, holding out his hand. The sharur sniffed it with the utmost interest for a moment and then gave it a cursory lick.

Tetrax looked astounded. "It has taken me years to gain her trust!"

"I have a way with females," Longinus said nonchalantly.

He winced as Onoskelis kicked his ankle.

"What?" he said, glancing at her with apparent innocence.

She shook her head and gave him a disdainful look.

"Well, I have no intention of putting any of my body parts near that beast's dripping jaws," declared Aeneas.

"Very wise!" Armilus added, peeking out from behind the centurion's kilt.

"Perhaps we have more important matters to consider?" Simon suggested diplomatically.

The sharur uttered a series of loathsome growls and screeching noises. At first, Longinus thought they were just animalistic sounds, but he then realised the beast was communicating with Tetrax in some form of unintelligible, primitive language. He could not understand a word and thought wryly that if Sophia had indeed aided his party to converse with each other, she had forgotten to include the parlance of the sharur in her divine distance learning course.

The commander appeared to ask it a few questions in a comparable tongue, and the creature nodded its large head. Longinus could tell by Tetrax's face that something troubled him. "What is the matter?"

"Satan's pet grows larger," he replied uneasily. "That is why she brought your companion back to us by such a convoluted route. The abomination almost caught them twice."

The surrounding demons whispered to each other, and he could see the fear written upon their faces.

"Satan's pet? What is that?"

"Satan brought it back from the Realm of Chaos after the fall of Eden. He did not feed it much, and that kept it from growing. But after Pazuzu started his rebellion, the Evil One unleashed his abomination into the Lower Depths to destroy us. It consumed many of our comrades and grew in size. But there was not enough flesh here to satisfy its voracious appetite, and it found a way back into Hell and devoured demons. Evidently, Satan caught it and threw it back into the Lower Depths again. We have reports that the Evil One is sealing all known entrances to the Lower Depths so neither it nor us can escape."

"That is why the door was sealed," observed Simon.

Longinus could feel a familiar icy finger running down his spine.

"Does this creature have a name?" he asked.

"Satan called it Tiamat," said Tetrax.

Longinus grimaced. In the ancient Babylonian religion, Tiamat was the monstrous sea serpent of Chaos. Marduk, the king of the gods, destroyed her in cosmos-shaking battle, and created the heavens and the earth from her body. The centurion knew that this abomination could not be the original Tiamat; however, it suggested to him that Satan had a gruesome sense of humour, and all Abrahamic religions had common origins and myths that had been retold and reinvented from the times of the ancient Sumerians to the Christian First Council of Nicaea.

"What does it look like?"

"A glowing body with many tentacles."

"Like tendrils?"

The commander thought for a moment. "Yes. That is a better description: wet, slimy tendrils."

"I saw it twice in Hell."

"You have encountered it twice and survived?" Tetrax exclaimed. "I have seen it only once and consider myself very lucky to have escaped. Few live to tell the tale after meeting Satan's pet."

"Cannot Pazuzu and the Elder demons destroy it?"

"They can, but have not cornered it yet. The creature is not a stupid beast and displays cunning intelligence. It attacks small groups and then vanishes into the nooks and crannies of the Lower Depths. The thing can squeeze into the narrowest of fissures to hide its bulk. Then when demons pass, it strikes and devours them."

"Then perhaps we should make haste?" Longinus suggested.

"A wise decision," Tetrax replied grimly.

He emitted a series of growls and screeching noises to the sharur, and she scurried up the wall and off along the tunnel roof.

"I have asked her to scout ahead of us. She has a very keen sense of smell and will warn us if Tiamat is close. Once we reach the deepest part of the Lower Depths, we shall be safe. Pazuzu and the Elder demons reside there, and the abomination will not venture near them."

"How long will that take?" asked Aeneas.

"Not long. Once we reach the end of this tunnel, we shall come to a ledge where more sharurs await us. They will carry us down into the Pazuzu's domain."

"What! You expect us to sit on the back of one of those things?" Aeneas exclaimed.

"It is either that or walking for ten Hell days," replied Tetrax. "Flying is the safest option, believe me."

"I will not put my buttocks on one of those nightmares," Aeneas protested.

"Do not fear," Onoskelis said. "I will sit with you."

Aeneas glanced at her with an appreciative eye and pursed his lips. "Well—I suppose I could be persuaded."

"Come on, Don Juan," Longinus said.

"What is Don Juan?" asked Aeneas, frowning.

"A hero who *mounts* a sharur," Longinus replied.

"Then I am Don Juan!" Aeneas declaimed to Onoskelis. "With you by my side, I shall mount the beast without batting an eyelid!"

"Good luck with that," Longinus murmured with a wry smile, as Aeneas accompanied Simon and Armilus down the tunnel.

Onoskelis gave him a reproachful look and whispered, "Little jests from little brains."

"I thought it was rather clever. The vision of Aeneas trying to mate with a sharur rather amuses me."

"You are very childish!" Onoskelis responded with the faintest glimmer of a smile.

"It is one of my many sins."

"And what are the others?"

"Hmm. Where to start? Do you have a few centuries to spare?"

Onoskelis punched his shoulder. He winced and glanced at her in surprise. She ignored him studiously and left him wondering whether he had been on the receiving end of a painful display of succubi irritation or affection.

Longinus and Onoskelis started on hearing screams from behind them. They spun around and saw two demons in the rearguard being dragged down the tunnel by a myriad of long tendrils. The others were hacking at the predacious coils with their axes.

"Run!" Longinus roared.

They sprinted around a corner and bumped into the rest of the group.

"What is it?" asked Tetrax.

"Tiamat! Heading this way!" said Longinus.

They heard more shrieks and howls coming from behind them. Tetrax lowered his broadsword and growled. "Go! The ledge is not far. My demons will take you on the sharurs."

"What about you?" asked Longinus.

"Those are my comrades the beast devours. Flee! We shall hold the creature back until you make your escape!"

More stalking cirri drifted around the corner and headed towards them. The stems were thicker, and the repulsive suckers and barbs larger than Longinus remembered.

"Go!" roared Tetrax.

Longinus' party and the demon vanguard raced down the tunnel and came to a wide flat rock ledge where twenty monstrous sharurs and their riders were waiting. The beasts were much larger than the female they had encountered and equipped with dual saddles. Without a second thought, they jumped onto the creatures' rough leathery backs and put their arms around the waists of the demon riders. With a series of ear-splitting screeches, the sharurs leaped into the air and flapped their enormous wings.

Longinus' beast was the last one to take to flight. He looked back and saw Tetrax backing up to the ledge while fighting off scores of tendrils with his longsword.

"Wait!" Longinus cried to the rider. However, the handler paid him no heed, and the sharur flapped its massive wings and rose.

"Tetrax! Jump!" he roared.

The demon commander glanced over his shoulder. Three tendrils shot forward to grab him. He threw his longsword at them, and they snapped it into their clammy embrace.

"Now, Tetrax, now!" Longinus cried, holding out his hand. Tetrax turned on his heel, sprinted across the ledge, jumped, and grabbed Longinus wrist. The centurion gripped the saddle with his legs, and his muscles bulged as he took the strain of the commander's weight.

"Hang on!" he cried.

He grunted in pain as the demon's nails dug into his flesh. The sharur struggled to lift them and hovered above the ledge. A coil darted out and wrapped around Tetrax's waist. The sharur screeched in alarm as it smelled the monster's vile stench. Longinus glanced at the tunnel. More blood splattered tendrils were bursting through and searching for prey.

Tetrax's eyes bulged as the tendril pulled at him. Longinus felt the flesh of his wrist ripping. He tried to ready his spear, but the sharur's movement was making it difficult. The centurion knew he had only one chance and would either hit the cirrus or kill Tetrax. He roared and thrust. The spear struck the tendril an inch from the commander's chest. The sharur screeched and tried to break free. The stem quivered violently, released its grip on Tetrax, and snapped back into the tunnel.

Tetrax grabbed the wooden shaft of the spear with his free claw.

"Do not touch the spear tip!" Longinus warned.

Tetrax looked up at him uncomprehendingly.

"It cannot lift us!" Longinus roared in the handler's ear. "Tell the beast to dive straight down!"

The rider screamed words of command and thrust the reins forward. The sharur folded its wings back and dived.

As they hurled down at lighting speed, Longinus gritted his teeth and gripped the beast's flanks with his thighs. If it were not for his preternatural strength, he and Tetrax would have been thrown from its back. He looked up and saw a fleeting glimpse of a huge luminous bulk appearing high above them.

Faster and faster they fell, shooting past the other riders. Longinus could see a dark lake surrounded by rocky ground appear below them. The handler pulled viciously on the reins. The beast spread its wings and tried to slow down. But it could not. The momentum and weight were too great for it to resist. Longinus gaped as the cavern floor grew larger and appeared to rise to meet them. They were going to hit the rocks!

A winged shape appeared alongside them. Onoskelis gripped Tetrax around the waist and screamed, "Let go!"

Tetrax's mouth opened, and he released his grip. The sharur seemed to rise for a moment and then continued falling. Its large wings beat ferociously. They were slowing down at last.

Longinus watched as Onoskelis flew above them, holding Tetrax in her iron grip. Her wings were strong, but the demon commander was very heavy. They were falling too quickly. She saw the lake and hoped it was deep. She veered towards it, and they plunged into the water and sank below the surface.

The sharur managed to change its approach at the last moment and hit the ground at a steep angle. It extended its four enormous claws and skidded thirty feet before coming to an abrupt stop. The momentum threw Longinus and the handler from its back. The centurion tumbled through the air, hit a large boulder with a sickening thud, and crashed to the ground. Pain wracked his body. Blood gushed down his face, blinding him. He groaned and tried to move, but his limbs refused to obey him. The world was spinning. He heard distant shouting. It was over. He was over.

A cool hand stroked his brow, and the agony subsided.

He heard a soft female voice whisper, "Sleep, Longinus, sleep."

Darkness descended, and he knew no more.

CHAPTER XXIX

A multitudinous cacophony of shrill voices dragged Longinus back into the unwelcome realm of the waking.

"What the–?" he groaned.

He opened his eyes and saw Simon's kindly face.

"How do you feel?" asked the magus.

Longinus stretched his limbs tentatively. There was no pain and nothing felt ripped, crushed or broken.

"So far, so good," he rasped.

"You received a very nasty blow to the head, but the wound has healed remarkably quickly."

"One of the few advantages of being neither alive nor dead," said Longinus, parodying what Simon had said earlier about seeing in the dark.

"How long have I been unconscious?"

"A few hours."

Longinus grunted and looked around. He was lying on a stone slab in a small cave. His spear and shield were on the floor next to him. Two heavyset demons armed with axes and shields stood guard at the entrance and regarded him suspiciously through unblinking, garnet eyes.

"Where are we?"

"In Pazuzu's domain."

"Onoskelis?"

"She is well."

"Where are the others?"

"Outside. They are conversing with some succubi that have arrived in the Lower Depths."

The centurion grimaced. That explained the raucous sounds in the background. For a moment, he feared he was being punished in some new, terrifying form of Hell.

"Have you met with Pazuzu yet?"

"No. He will not grant us an audience until you recover."

Longinus sat up and tilted his head from side to side to loosen his neck muscles. It had been a long time since he had slept the Dark Sleep. His body had regenerated, and he felt refreshed and fighting fit again.

Tetrax strode into the chamber. The centurion thought it strange that the commander was not carrying his customary longsword until he remembered that the demon had lost it during his fight with Tiamat.

"You are awake at last!" the demon commander said, standing with his claws on his hips.

"How can I sleep with all this hubbub?" Longinus grumbled.

"There will be plenty of time to rest when you are dead again."

"Did you enjoy our flight?"

"You almost speared me!" Tetrax complained.

"I was aiming for your mouth, but hit Tiamat instead."

"Then I am fortunate your aim is so atrocious," retorted Tetrax.

"I must practice more."

"That, you must," Tetrax replied with a crooked smile.

Longinus nodded. Gratitude had been given and accepted in the manner that warriors do. There was no more to be said about the matter.

"If you are recovered, my lord Pazuzu wishes to meet you and your companions."

"I am ready. Why the guards?"

"To keep you safe."

"From what?"

"Many of Satan's spies and assassins have tried to infiltrate our forces. Pazuzu would not be pleased if one had slipped in and decapitated while you slept."

"I could do with losing some weight," Longinus said wistfully, touching his neck.

Tetrax grinned.

Longinus arose, slung his shield on his back and picked up his spear. He and Simon followed the commander from the cave.

The clamour of female voices swelled in magnitude until it reached an ear-splitting crescendo. Longinus frowned and pursed his lips. They were in a vast cavern, so enormous it could swallow a fleet of Titanics and still have ample room to spare for the doomed vessel's sister ships. Huge, irregular-shaped rocks tilted at outlandish angles, and towering mushroom stones littered the subterrane floor. In the shadowy distance, tiers of colossal stalagmites and stalactites grinned like the yawning jaws of gargantuan beasts.

In a clearing before them, Longinus' companions stood among a flock of chattering succubi. Aeneas had his arm around Armilus' shoulder and was holding court. The females surrounding them were gazing in admiration or shrieking with laughter. Onoskelis was speaking to some other succubi. Her face looked serious and drawn.

The she-demons began caterwauling and waving their tridents in the air. It was an impressive sight.

"What is happening?" asked Longinus, gazing in dazed wonderment at the jostling array of magnificent cleavages on display.

"They are hailing the cambion," said Tetrax.

"Why?"

"They call him the hero of Hell's Dungeons and say he liberated them from their oppressors."

"Oh, they do, do they?" Longinus growled.

"I believe you may have assisted him in some small way?" Simon said with a knowing smile.

"Mhmm. Just a little."

Simon laughed and shook his head. Onoskelis strode over to them with her trident on her shoulder. She looked displeased, but that did not surprise him. She always seemed incensed about something.

"You must feel better!" she said brusquely.

"Why so?"

"I could tell by your face," she replied, glaring at the succubi behind her.

He did not understand why she was so annoyed with him and dared to utter a few more words to melt her icy demeanour.

"The last thing I remember is your hand on my brow."

She regarded him stonily. "You are mistaken. I did no such thing. You were unconscious when I and Tetrax emerged from the lake."

"I must have imagined it," he sighed.

The female mind was one of the greatest mysteries of the cosmos, and it required a higher power than him to unravel its bewitching but perennially perplexing intricacies.

Aeneas and Armilus joined them.

"My good friend, Longinus!" boomed the Trojan. "I am glad to see you recovered. You had an impressive dent in your skull."

"It knocked some sense into me."

"Ah, a good jest!" laughed Aeneas. "You must indeed be better!"

"Take me away from here!" Armilus whispered imploringly. "Those harpies are driving me insane with their incessant jibber-jabber!"

"Well, if it is not the hero of the Dungeons of Hell!" exclaimed Longinus. "No wonder all beauteous buxom ones kneel at your feet and stare at you in adoration."

"I can explain," Armilus replied apologetically.

Longinus held up a hand to silence him. "Say no more. I am more than happy for you to be the centre of their full and undivided attention. Wherever you go, flocks of succubi will surround and praise you."

Armilus gurned and his shoulders slumped at the thought.

"Now I have you all gathered, shall we proceed?" Tetrax asked impatiently. He knew it was unwise to keep his lord waiting.

"After you," said Longinus.

Tetrax escorted them from the concourse. Longinus noticed the two guards accompanying them kept a close eye on the gathering of succubi. The female demons were newcomers to the Lower Depths, and their loyalty unproven.

They arrived at a towering conical rock, and the commander led them up a precipitous spiralling path to its peak. He ushered them into a large, circular gallery with scores of entrances leading off from it. They followed him through one opening and found themselves in an immense chamber lit by wall torches and ornate metal braziers.

They gasped in shock and horror. Sitting on a large rock at the far end of the chamber was a huge demon with four enormous wings; bulging crimson eyes; the semi-fleshless head of a hyena; a hairy, muscular torso; rotten genitals: large, vicious claws; and a long scorpion tail with a barb that oozed venom. To crown it all, the demon lord had a long, erect member with a serpent's head that regarded them coldly with slitted, yellowish-green eyes. To view images or statues of Pazuzu was one thing, but to see him in the flesh was quite another. Apart from Lamashtu, Longinus had beheld nothing so terrifying or hideous. Asmodeus' appearance was disgusting and frightening, but Pazuzu would win every prize in Hell's grotesque ugliness pageant.

"Perhaps this is not such a good idea!" Armilus whispered, trembling.

Longinus arched an eyebrow and lashed the cambion with a withering look.

"Really?" he murmured. "Was it not you who suggested we should join Pazuzu's forces and fight Satan?"

"I do not understand how you can be so flippant in our current predicament," the half-demon whined.

"Centuries of practice," Longinus hissed.

As they waited for Pazuzu to speak, Longinus wondered why demons bothered to use torches when they could see in the dark. Perhaps, he mused, even the denizens of the Abyss needed some good cheer in gloomy surroundings. Indeed, although fire was the natural enemy of his kind, the centurion had always enjoyed sitting by one at night, watching the elegant beauty of its flames and feeling the comforting warmth of its burning glow. Combustive scintillation repelled and yet attracted him like a suicidal moth.

"These are the trespassers we found on the main path, my lord," Tetrax said, bowing.

Longinus thought it was a strange choice of words to use after all they had gone through together, but said nothing. Despite his apparently affable manner towards Tetrax, he did not trust the demon commander or his monstrous lord and was waiting to see which way the wind blew.

Pazuzu nodded and gazed down upon them. His almost fleshless hyaenidae face gave him the appearance of having a malevolent, permanent grin. Then he spoke, and his voice rumbled like thunder throughout the cavern.

"I am Pazuzu, Lord of Fevers and Plagues, Dark Angel of the Four Winds. Why have you entered my domain? To spy for your lord and master?"

Armilus dropped to his knees, clasped his hands and adopted his most beseeching look.

"We are no spies, great lord!" he said. "We wish to join your rebellion against Satan!"

Pazuzu stared at the cambion's breastplate. "You are a messenger of Satan and one of his most trusted servants. Why do you wish to rebel against your emperor? He has rewarded you well."

"He is a cruel and tyrannical master! I spit thrice upon his name!" exclaimed Armilus, expectorating vigorously.

"Many demons have joined our rebellion, and countless have been informers sent by Satan to reveal our whereabouts. Why should I believe your intentions are any less dishonourable or devious?"

"My lord, I speak the truth!" whined the cambion.

Pazuzu regarded him disdainfully for a moment and then looked at the succubus. She trembled under his scathing gaze.

"What is your name?"

"Onoskelis, great lord," she said, bowing. "I seek sanctuary here. I am fleeing from Asmodeus."

Pazuzu cocked his head to one side and studied her. "Why does a succubus flee from the King of Demons?"

"Because I am loyal to Lilith," she stuttered.

Pazuzu turned his baleful attention to Aeneas.

"I am Aeneas, King of Latium," the Trojan said boldly, standing erect.

Pazuzu grunted and stared at Simon.

"I am Simon Magus, my lord," he said, bowing.

Pazuzu shook his head. "So, we have a cambion, a succubus, a king and a sorcerer. Well, Revenant, do you think I should trust them?"

His question startled Longinus. "You know who I am?"

Pazuzu stood up and his appearance became even more intimidating. Longinus tried his best to ignore the demon lord's rotten genitals, and the penile serpent's gaze.

"Of course, I do—demon slayer!" Pazuzu rumbled.

Longinus tensed. He could not tell whether the remark was a compliment or a threat.

"Remove the others from my presence. I wish to speak in private to Lilith's Revenant," Pazuzu said to Tetrax.

"You will do them no harm?" asked Longinus.

Pazuzu laughed. It was a horrible grating sound that chilled the soul.

"They will be safe—for the moment."

Longinus watched as Tetrax and some guards escorted his companions from the chamber. He heard Armilus continuing to assert his innocence and felt some sympathy for him. The cambion's bid for freedom was not going how he had hoped.

After they had left, Longinus looked up at Pazuzu. The centurion's face was grim, and he steeled himself for combat. He knew he could not defeat the demon lord but, as always, he would throw caution to the wind and fight with as much strength and determination as he could muster.

"How do you who I am?" he asked.

Pazuzu sat down cross-legged and rested his hairy chin upon his claw.

"Because I have a long memory. It was you who freed me from the Blood Priests of Akkad."

Longinus gasped. "I thought my journey to Babylon was just a hallucination brought on by my torture!"

Pazuzu studied him intently. "You do not remember?"

"No. I see only fleeting images as though it were but a dream."

"Let me assure you, it was no dream. The noble goddess, Ereshkigal, saved you from Asmodeus' tortures and brought you to Babylon. She revealed to you that the Blood Priests had imprisoned me, and Lamashtu was intent on breaking open the seven gates of the underworld and letting the dead could spew forth across the world."

"I cannot remember anything," Longinus sighed.

"I detect you possess the demon power of veiling your thoughts from others," replied Pazuzu. "Open your mind, and I will reveal the past to you."

Longinus rubbed his chin. He did not think it wise to allow a demon like Pazuzu access to his mind, but he was desperate to recall what had happened in Babylon. His faint recollections of that ancient city had haunted him for so long.

"Very well," he said reluctantly, opening the iron shutter that guarded his thoughts, memories, hopes and fears.

He tensed as he felt the demon lord sending ethereal tendrils into his mind. They slithered and probed like serpents until they connected with his brain. A series of vivid images flashed across his mindscape. He beheld the beautiful and lonely Ereshkigal, goddess of the netherworld; Arwia, the young, spirited high priestess; Bashaa, the dashing young captain of the king's guard; Daniel, the wise and troubled holy man; Amytis, the kind-hearted but beleaguered queen of Babylon; and finally, himself being dragged hundreds of feet into the air as Pazuzu and Lamashtu fought.

He experienced exuberant joy, followed by numbing sadness. His friends were long dead and forgotten, but their faces and voices were still as fresh in his mind as if he had seen them but yesterday. A tear came to his eye, and he mouthed a silent prayer expressing his fervent hope that Marduk, the king of the Babylonian gods, had blessed them with long and happy lives, and their souls were at peace.

He then he recalled what the noble Ereshkigal had told him about Pazuzu. The Lord of the Four Winds was not evil like Christian demons. He had been a servant of the god Anu and merely carried out his divine commands. Yes, he had brought famines and plagues to mankind when they had offended the gods—as indeed had the angels of the Judeo-Christian God—but he had also been their dark guardian. It was his image the Babylonians had used to ward off the evil of Lamashtu and protect mothers and newborns from her venomous wrath.

"Now do you remember your past?" asked Pazuzu.

"Yes," Longinus sighed.

"I was most curious to meet the champion of Babylon. Disrupting Lamashtu's insane plot was no easy feat."

"How did you know I was in Hell?"

"I heard your cries through the myriad of other screams of suffering, and your voice seemed familiar to me. I looked up through the towering levels of the Abyss and saw you being tortured by the vile and licentious Asmodeus. There was nothing I could do to help you while you were in King of Demon's Basilica of Pain. But then a spy informed me that you had escaped and travelled with the cambion. I was certain the half-demon would bring you here. The Lower Depths is the only place where one can hide from the archdemons."

"I must escape Hell and return to earth. Can you help me? The cambion told me that there may be a way in the Lower Depths."

"Earth?" Pazuzu growled. "Why do you wish to return to such a place? It has become a reeking mire of evil, corruption and death."

"Asmodeus told me that the demon, Buer, would destroy my friends. I must try to save them."

"The akhkharu maidens?" asked Pazuzu, using the Sumerian word for a vampire.

"Yes, how did you know?"

Then he remembered that Pazuzu had read his mind and cursed his own stupidity.

Pazuzu grinned at him; it was not a pleasant sight.

"We are similar and our fates are entwined."

"In what way?"

"We both were men of honour, but greater powers turned us into terrible monsters."

"You were once a man?" the centurion exclaimed.

"I was a warrior like you and fought many battles. My name was known throughout the land, and my people thought me a pious and just man. The gods knew of my exploits, and a goddess desired me. She was the most beautiful creature I had ever seen, and her very presence stole my heart and inflamed my senses. We lay together for many nights and consummated our love and earthly passions.

"I wished to remain with her for eternity, but my conscience troubled me. My wife was carrying our first child, and duty and honour dictated that I should return to her. I was foolish and thought the goddess would understand, but when I told her of my decision, her nature changed. She was no longer loving and kind, but became angry and spiteful. The goddess could not understand why I chose a mortal woman instead of her. After much passionate bickering, she let me depart. Little did I know that I would pay a heavy price for my resolution.

"One night after my son was born, she appeared in my dwelling. At first I did not recognise her; her spite and madness had transformed her into a terrifying night hag. She attacked me. I tried to defend my family, but she was too powerful. As I lay mortally wounded, she forced me to watch her tear my wife and child apart. She screamed that it was a fitting punishment for betraying her and left me to mourn and die. With my last remaining strength, I buried the bodies of my wife and son; and performed the funeral rituals that ensured their safe passage to the netherworld.

"Overcome with grief, I stumbled into the desert. As I fell to my knees one last time, I raised my hands to the heavens and pleaded to Anu, the father of the old gods, to avenge my loss. Anu heard my words and saw what had transpired. He could not bring himself to destroy his daughter, so he transformed me into a demon and gave me the power to thwart her evil. She could not destroy me, and I could not destroy her. And thus we would spend eternity locked in deadly combat."

It dawned on Longinus whom the goddess had been.

"It was Lamashtu!"

Pazuzu nodded. "That is the name men knew her by."

"Armilus said that Satan had imprisoned her in the Lower Depths."

"He spoke the truth."

"Do you know where?"

"Yes," Pazuzu sighed. "I know where she lies bound, cursing, screaming and plotting. I have visited her, but she has not changed her ways. She still blames me for what happened to her and is still evil, spiteful and completely insane."

"How could a goddess become such a monstrosity?"

"The fault was mine."

"How so?"

"When I was a mortal, Inanna, the goddess of love, sexuality, prostitution and war, also desired me."

Longinus frowned. "Inanna–later worshipped as Ishtar by the Babylonians?"

"Aye, they were one and the same. She asked me to lie with her, but I declined her invitation; I was too besotted with Lamashtu. Centuries later, I discovered it was Inanna who had laid the hand of madness upon Lamashtu."

"Why?"

"To punish me for my insolence and gain control of Lamashtu's domain. Inanna was jealous of our love and always scheming to usurp the other gods and goddesses in Heaven."

Longinus scratched his chin thoughtfully. Nothing in Heaven or Hell was ever simple. He almost felt some sympathy for Lamashtu, but the feeling vanished quickly as he remembered her vile countenance.

"She was the most hideous abomination that I ever saw," he muttered.

Pazuzu chortled. "The most hideous–until you beheld me?"

"You are–quite intimidating," Longinus replied diplomatically.

"Anu created my form so that even Lamashtu would find me horrifying. I think we can both agree that the king of the gods succeeded in his divine purpose."

"Have you ever seen yourself?"

Pazuzu's eyes narrowed, and for an instant Longinus detected a glint of anger in them. But it passed, and the demon smiled as though Longinus' boldness amused him.

"Have you seen your own appearance when you are Lilith's Revenant?" he countered.

"Yes, it was devastating. I could not believe that I had transformed into such a hideous beast. It was then that I lost all hope of escaping my fate."

Pazuzu nodded. "I understand. For centuries, I avoided seeing what I had become, but I grew curious. All demons are inquisitive by nature. One moonlit night, I stole down to the river Tigris and with great trepidation, gazed upon my reflection. I was so distraught that I never again sought to view my malign countenance. Now I am only reminded of my loathsome disfigurements when I see the looks of abject terror on the faces of my enemies before I rip them limb from limb."

"Then we have something else in common," said Longinus.

"And what is that?"

"We are both monsters without hope."

"Aye, that we are," Pazuzu murmured.

"There is something I do not understand," said Longinus.

"There are many things you do not understand, but tell me what puzzles you presently."

"You and the Elder demons fought Satan when he invaded the netherworld, but he defeated, bound and imprisoned all of you in the Lower Depths?"

"That is true. His hordes overwhelmed us," Pazuzu growled.

"Then who released you from your chains?"

"That is unknown to me."

"Do you think it was the god of the Jews and Christians?"

"I doubt it. He hates all demons. However—I have sometimes sensed another presence in the Lower Depths, but I cannot discern who or what it is. All I know is that our chains shattered when Asmodeus brought you to Hell. It would therefore appear that you have freed me twice."

Longinus rubbed his chin and tried to make sense of it. He could not and returned to a more immediate and pressing matter.

"Is there a way to earth from the Lower Depths?"

"Satan's Path?"

"Yes! Armilus said it is the way the Evil One escaped from Hell and travelled to the Garden of Eden."

"I know where the portal lies, but I would advise you against using it," Pazuzu said soberly.

"Why?"

"It is the bowels of the Lower Depths where all manner of deranged, gruesome creatures prey upon each other. Even if you avoided being devoured, the threshold leads to the realm of Chaos. You are not powerful enough to survive in that domain. Only an Elder or archdemon could endure such a perilous journey. The Lords of Chaos do not look kindly upon those who trespass upon their demesne of madness."

"Forgive me from asking, but what is the difference between an Elder and archdemon?"

"The ancient gods created the Elder demons. The original archdemons were fallen angels, but Satan has created many more. They are evil incarnate."

"Why do you think I cannot pass through the realm of Chaos? Satan did it."

"The Great Dragon is the most powerful demon in Hell, yet barely survived the ordeal."

"I must try," said Longinus.

Pazuzu pondered for a moment. "There is only one way that you may withstand such a trial."

"What?" Longinus asked, eagerly.

Pazuzu stared at him. "You already know the answer."

Longinus looked puzzled for a moment, and then his shoulders slumped.

"Allow myself to become a full demon," he sighed.

"You have the potential to become a mighty demon; I can smell the blood in your veins. Who gave you such power?"

"Lilith gave me more of her blood to heal me."

"Lilith!" Pazuzu exclaimed. "You have the pure, undiluted essence of the Mother of Demons in your body? Why do you not allow your demon nature to grow? Even Asmodeus would think twice about attacking you!"

"Because—I fear losing the last vestiges of my humanity."

"A noble sentiment, but one you can little afford to hold whilst you are a prisoner in Hell. Asmodeus seeks to recapture you and has sent many of his vassals to accomplish that task. Unless you become a full demon, you will be powerless to resist them. As Lilith's Revenant, you have many powers, but they will offer you little protection against archdemons or beings such as the Lords of Chaos."

"I understand, but I still refuse to succumb to my dark nature. In any case, I believe my full demon form will surface again when I am in mortal danger. That is what happened when I fought and destroyed Agrat Bat Mahlat."

"I learned that you defeated the Mistress of Deception in Purgatory," Pazuzu replied thoughtfully. "I do not understand how your full powers came to your aid. Usually one is a demon or is not; there is no halfway point where you transform when it is needed. But even if that is somehow true, it is clear to me that you cannot rely upon it to save you. In your darkest moment of peril, it may fail you. It is much better to transform permanently. Only then will you comprehend and hone your powers."

"What powers would I have?" asked Longinus, curious despite his misgivings.

"It varies between demons. At a stroke, you would have increased strength, swiftness and resistance against damage."

Pazuzu sprang to his feet, flew across the cavern and hit a stalactite with his claw. It shattered into a thousand pieces. Longinus crouched and shielded his face as debris rained about him. When he glanced up, Pazuzu was sitting on his rock again. The demon lord's attack had been so swift that the centurion had barely managed to follow it with his eyes.

"Impressive!" Longinus murmured.

"To see is sometimes more instructive than to hear," said Pazuzu. "What form did your demon manifestation take? Did you walk on two legs, four—or more?"

"I had two arms and two legs. I also remember having large black wings with talons."

"You were a winged demon?"

"Yes, and when I sunk my wing talons into Agrat Bat, they had a soporific effect on her. It was like my bite when I am in my Revenant form."

"How did you destroy her?"

"I bit off her head."

Pazuzu nodded. "Excellent! Your demon manifestation has inherited and enhanced some of your Revenant abilities."

"The principal thing I recall is a sense of strength, rage and fearlessness."

"This is most illuminating. You are obviously a voracious killer–like me."

"I will take that as a compliment. Could I have other powers?"

"Most Elder and archdemons can possess or control the minds of lesser demons. That is how I have come to learn so much about Hell. Satan imprisoned my body, but not my mind. Through the eyes of his vassals, I have seen much of the Evil One's empire and discovered many of its secrets."

"That would certainly be useful," conceded Longinus.

"Some can also possess the bodies of mortals; however, this is an evil practice and is used only by Satan's demons. Although I have such an ability, I have never desired to possess a human body. The very idea is unwholesome and undignified to me. We must be content, for better or worse, with the bodies the gods have given us and not stoop to stealing the lives of others."

"But it keeps exorcists in work," Longinus said with a grim smile, remembering how Pazuzu had been maligned unfairly in certain works of human fiction.

Pazuzu frowned and regarded Longinus curiously. The centurion could tell he had read his thoughts.

"Mankind," the demon lord growled, "has always enjoyed spinning tales about things beyond their comprehension. Their stories intrigued and entertained the old gods."

"Any other powers?" Longinus asked.

Pazuzu smiled at Longinus' attempt to change the subject. He knew that the centurion did not do it out of fear, but from a genuine desire not to offend him. The demon lord was unconcerned by such trifles, but he appreciated the Revenant's sense of respect.

"The ability to make yourself invisible to mortals and lesser demons, and to travel quickly from one location to another by the power of thought."

"That would be very useful in a tight spot," remarked Longinus, remembering all the times in the past he could have done with a quick escape route. He paused when he saw Pazuzu regarding him with a puzzled expression.

"You have read my thoughts again?"

Pazuzu nodded.

"You have never used it for retreating, have you?"

Pazuzu frowned. "Why should I? The chief advantage of thought travel is one can close and engage swiftly with the enemy. It offers the element of surprise."

Longinus smiled. The very concept of retreat was unknown to Pazuzu. It was a quality the centurion admired.

"How do you transport from place to place? An incantation?"

Pazuzu snorted derisively. "Incantations are for lesser demons and sorcerers! You merely *will* it to be so!"

"So it is like me using my will to transform into my Revenant form?"

"Yes. You imagine where you wish to be, and you will be transported there. It takes practice, but it is worthwhile to learn. However, that will not be difficult for you. You have one of the strongest wills that I have ever encountered. The manner in which you have been able to control your dark urges and the demon within you is quite extraordinary. Most Akhkharu would have succumbed to evil."

"I have trained for two thousand years to suppress my base instincts. How do you make yourself invisible to others? Is that also a matter of willpower?"

"Yes," said Pazuzu.

To Longinus' astonishment, the demon lord slowly disappeared. The centurion glanced around but could not see him.

"Are you still there?"

"Can you not see me?" Pazuzu chortled.

"No."

"That is because you try to see with your eyes, but these organs of the visual system are easily deceived. They are but channels through which light travels. It is the mind that transforms light into images that you can make sense of. Try to see with your mind, and all shall be revealed to you."

Longinus tried to focus his mind, but nothing happened.

"Concentrate on the rock," urged Pazuzu, "but see not just the rock, observe everything surrounding it. Imagine the tendrils of your mind exuding from you like writhing snakes in search of prey. Let these serpents see for you. See now!"

Longinus concentrated and visualised the bizarre picture that Pazuzu had suggested to him. Suddenly, his perception of the world around him changed. The rocks and walls of the cave became blurry and illuminated by an eerie blue light. The faint outline and then the full figure of the demon lord appeared gradually before him. Pazuzu was still ensconced upon the rock and had not moved.

Pazuzu nodded. "Good. Now your mind is truly open, and you will perceive many strange things that mortals and lesser demons cannot comprehend. Now see me with your eyes again!"

Longinus imagined the tendrils receding back into his mind, and the cave slowly reverted to its normal form.

"That was not too difficult," Longinus said, feeling rather pleased with himself.

"Seeing with one's mind is relatively simple, but travel by thought is quite a different matter. The greatest peril is that you transport yourself into solid rock and become imprisoned for eternity. And, of course, lava is most unpleasant."

"Is lava fatal to a demon?"

"No. But I can assure you, the experience is painful."

"Hence why the Jewish God cast the Fallen into the Lake of Fire."

Pazuzu laughed. "The Lake of Fire is not magma or lava. It is Holy fire and burns fiercer than a thousand suns!"

"So—avoid that as well?" Longinus asked, wryly.

"I would advise it."

"Or Infernus," Longinus muttered.

Pazuzu grinned, showing more pointed teeth than Longinus wished to see.

"Yes, travelling to Satan's palace would be very unwise."

"Wait, a moment! Can you transport me to earth?"

"Alas, my powers are not great enough. It is easier to enter the Abyss than to leave it. Satan holds sway over the Hell and earth."

"Over earth?"

"He is the prince of that world. I can transport you, as you call it, to Limbo or Purgatory because the Evil One has no power over these realms, but the only way to earth is through the main gate of Hell or Satan's Path."

Longinus shrugged. "It was worth a try. So, can you tell me the way to Satan's Path?"

"Yes—but I desire something in return. Quid pro quo as they say in your native tongue, centurion."

"What do you wish of me?"

"I have started a rebellion against Satan. Were you aware of that?"

"Yes, the cambion told me."

"It was my intention to disrupt Satan's plans as much as possible, but we are few, and they are legion. Now my spies have told me that Satan intends to attack Purgatory."

"How can he possibly think he can attack God and win?" Longinus said, shaking his head.

"The Christian God does not fight in battles," replied Pazuzu. "He leaves such matters to his angels."

"Are not angels more powerful than demons?"

"Possibly, but I have always considered them evenly matched. However, something has changed–something that could turn the tide of the battle."

"What?"

"For aeons, angels and demons have fought for the minds and souls of humans, and although one could defeat another in battle, they could not destroy each other."

"Like you and Lamashtu" said Longinus.

"That is so. When an angel slays a demon, the fiend's soul is sent back to Hell, where it is reborn; and when a demon slays an angel, the angel's soul is carried back to Heaven to be reborn. Neither side can eradicate the other. This is part of the Old Laws agreed by God and Satan. God will only incarcerate or destroy demons at End Times."

"So what has changed?"

"My spies have informed me that Satan has created a new weapon which can capture the souls of angels."

Longinus frowned. "But why should that bother us? We do not worship God and have no part in the war between angels and demons."

"Because if Satan succeeds, that will have grave repercussions for earth and the entire cosmos. Satan would be free to bring Hell on earth and take the souls from Purgatory and Limbo. Do you know who languishes in Limbo?"

"No? Who?"

"Your people–the Romans."

Pazuzu's words hit Longinus like a fist to the stomach. In his thousands of years of existence, he had never thought much about where the souls of his people had gone.

"Why are they held in Limbo?"

"They are Pagans, and all heathens languish in Limbo. There, they await End Times when God will judge them. On that day, He will grant the righteous salvation and a place in His New Kingdom on earth, but will cast the unrighteous into the Lake of Fire. Considering how your people treated the Christians, how many do you think He will judge as worthy?"

"Not many," Longinus said grimly.

"If the Father of Lies defeats the angelic army, he will convert the millions of souls languishing in Purgatory into demons. Then, with bolstered numbers, he will turn his attention to Limbo. Until now, it has been impossible for him to conquer that domain because the ice field protecting it can freeze demons in their tracks. But Satan is trying to create new types of fiends resistant to such glacial and boreal conditions. If he succeeds, he will invade Limbo and add millions more souls to his ranks. After that is done, he will turn his gaze to Heaven."

"But he cannot defeat God!" Longinus insisted.

Pazuzu leaned forward and spoke earnestly to him. "Let me remind you that even though Satan's forces were outnumbered two to one, he came perilously close to doing just that before he was cast out. It was the archangels who provided the final bulwark against his attack, and it was only a lucky blow struck by the Archangel Michael that saved the day. If Satan attacks with superior numbers and captures the souls of the archangels, Heaven will fall."

The sickening revelation stunned Longinus. If Satan attacked Heaven, then Lilith and his son, Gaius, would be in peril.

"Why did God not destroy Satan when He had the chance?" he said angrily.

Pazuzu shrugged his great shoulders. "The relationship between this Christian God and Satan is a mystery to me. The earliest writings of the Evil One describe him as a loyal servant of God. Some say he continues to serve God and is charged with tempting humans to separate the righteous from the unrighteous. In this way, they maintain, he still follows God's will even after his fall from grace."

"I suppose there is some merit to that argument," Longinus said grudgingly. "In the Bible, God converses with Satan in Heaven and allows him to punish a righteous man."

"You have read the Christian Bible?" asked Pazuzu.

"Yes, and the Jewish Tanakh."

"You are a most unusual Akhkharu," replied the demon lord. "Most of your kind would never touch such books."

"Reading has helped me fill the emptiness of my existence. Even my kind cannot sleep all day."

"Others maintain," continued Pazuzu, "the Evil One is completely autonomous and does everything he can to corrupt mankind and disrupt God's rule on earth. However, even so, he unwittingly still serves God by separating the righteous from the sinners."

"So God allowed Satan to exist so he could test man's faith?"

"In these two theories, yes. But there is a third explanation which is even more worrying."

"And what is that?" asked Longinus.

"It is said that Satan, or Lucifer as he was known in Heaven, was God's most perfect creation. He was also the most powerful being in Heaven, and God imparted to him the secrets of the Cosmos. Do you know which other being has this status and power in Heaven?"

"No."

Pazuzu smiled grimly. "The Son of God."

"No, the Son of God cannot be Satan!" Longinus exclaimed.

"I speak not of the Nazarene. What if Lucifer was the first Son of God? That would explain his power and why God did not destroy him. Perhaps He cannot destroy him even if he wished to do so. That would also explain why Lucifer came so close to defeating the angelic forces in Heaven. Lucifer was a divine being and may even be part of God."

"Part of God? I thought you said he was His Son?"

"You forget about the Trinity. God comprises the Father, the Son and the Holy Spirit. These three apparently separate entities are really one and make up the whole. Perhaps instead of a Trinity—there was once a Quaternity."

Longinus rubbed his forehead. He found the concept of the Trinity confusing enough without expanding it to include a fourth.

"So is Lucifer God's evil alter ego?"

"It is possible. Prior to the creation of the Nazarene, God punished mankind with plagues, famine, floods, and fire and brimstone. But after the Son appeared, God became more forgiving. His message changed from one of punishment and reward to that of redemption and hope."

Longinus frowned. Based on what Simon had told him, there was yet another explanation; namely, Lucifer was the flawed son of the Demiurge, and the Nazarene was the perfect son of Sophia. But he said none of this to Pazuzu. They could go round in circles for eternity discussing these theories and still not discover the truth. Therefore, to save time, he took a middle course.

"My friend, Simon, agrees to a certain extent to what you have said. He is a Gnostic and thinks the Nazarene softened God's attitude to humankind."

"Humankind?" asked Pazuzu.

"It is the term used by mortals to describe their species these days."

Pazuzu rubbed his hairy chin. "But the first creation was male; hence, it follows logically that the species should be termed 'mankind.' "

"Yes, but humans have become less religious. Many women of the modern world find the term 'mankind' insulting to their sex, and thus many societies have adopted the more diplomatic and less litigious term of 'humankind.' "

Pazuzu considered the argument for a moment. "It reminds me of the same idiocy that led to theological arguments about how many angels can sit on a needle's point, but I suppose there is some merit to it. I never considered my wife less important than me. Women are blessed by the gods to give life, and men are cursed to take it. But who am I to judge? I was an adulterer, a sinner who betrayed my wife's trust and loyalty."

After a long, uncomfortable pause, Longinus moved the conversation on.

"As I was saying, Simon thinks the Nazarene softened God's attitude."

Pazuzu blinked and ripped himself away from the bloodstained claws of distant, painful memories. "He may be right. After the Nazarene was sacrificed on the cross, salvation was left to man's free will. If you repented your sins, resisted the temptations of Satan, and accepted Jesus Christ as your saviour, He would save you. If you rejected Christ, you were damned. God left the choice to man—humankind."

"Then the actual battle of good versus evil is in the hearts and minds of mortals."

"It is—as it is with us. But there is greater battle fought on the spiritual level. Demons roam the earth tempting mortals to sin, and angels work to keep humans on the path of righteous. Sometimes the demons win, and other times the angels hold sway. But in the end, it is up to the individual which action he or she takes. The sisterly bond of motherhood binds all women together regardless of race, wealth or skin colour. This kinship is stronger than any army, race, or empire, but in times of war this virtue is oft forgotten and women will act selfishly and encourage their men to dash out the brains of their enemies' offspring against temple walls. These women, these mothers, these sisters of the earth will turn a blind eye to the murder of other innocents to ensure the survival of their own. Free will! It can be a blessing or a curse. God gave Lucifer free will and look what happened!"

"Many women would rather die before condoning such atrocities," said Longinus.

"And yet they still allow their men to wage wars," said Pazuzu. "What difference does it make if infants are beaten against a wall or killed from a distance by sling or arrow? They are still dead."

"I see your point," Longinus sighed. "What is it you wish me to do?"

"I intend to strike Satan's legions when they engage with the angelic army in Purgatory. We shall attack them from behind. The other Elder demons and I are powerful, but as I have already said, our numbers are too few. To have any chance of success, we must enlist the help of the souls of the Roman legions. You must travel to Limbo and convince them to join our cause."

"But why the Romans? Why not the Sumerians, Akkadians and Babylonians? These were the peoples you knew."

"The Romans are cursed because they were the greatest persecutors of the Christians and Jews."

"But the Babylonians conquered and enslaved the Jews!" protested Longinus.

"Yes, but that was God's will. He sought to punish the Jews for their idolatry. The persecution of the Christians and Jews angered Him, and that is why the Romans are damned."

"Why choose me for this task?" asked Longinus.

"Because I know you are an honourable man, and as a Roman you can plead my cause to them. There is also a prophecy."

"What prophecy?"

"What do you know of the Sibylline Books?"

"Every Roman knows of them," said Longinus. "According to the legend, an old woman arrived at the court of Lucius Tarquinius Superbus, the seventh and last king of Rome. She offered nine books of prophecies to the vain tyrant, but the king refused to pay the exorbitant price she demanded. Three of the books burst into flames and were destroyed. She then offered the six remaining books at the same high price. He again refused, and three more of the books burst into flames. She repeated her offer a final time, but this time the king relented and bought them, whereupon the old woman disappeared.

"The books were kept in the Temple of Jupiter on the Capitoline Hill in Rome for safekeeping and only consulted in emergencies or before great wars. However, they were destroyed when the temple burned down in 80 BC, and copies were made based entirely on the memories of those select few who had read them. Emperor Augustus had these copies moved to the Temple of Apollo on the Palatine Hill, and there they remained until General Flavius Stilicho burned them."

"And what of the sibyl? What know you of her?" asked Pazuzu.

"The prophetess is shrouded in mystery. Some say she was a bridge between the living and the dead."

"That is true. The Cumaean Sibyl was not a human but a creature of great power, and her origin is unknown. In the first book there was a cryptic prophecy that said 'the Sons of Mars shall fight a Great Dragon.' Do you know who the Sons of Mars are?"

"Of course," said Longinus. "They are the Romans. Rhea Silvia was a vestal virgin, but the god Mars seduced her, and she bore the twins Romulus and Remus. Hence, all Roman men consider themselves the Sons of Mars. But how do you know of this prophecy if the sibyl destroyed the book?"

"Many demons have fled from Satan's tyranny to the Lower Depths. One performed favours for the Cumaean Sibyl and was granted access to read all nine books before she took them to the king."

"Which demon?"

"The one you saved from Tiamat."

"Tetrax?"

"Yes."

"Hmm. I rather like him, much to my surprise."

"He was once a demon of whirlwinds, but Satan stripped him of his power."

"Why?"

"Because he refused to reveal all the portends contained in the Sibylline Books to the Evil One."

"Such as the prophesy about the Sons of Mars?"

"Yes."

"But why?"

"He had read prognostications in the books that had shaken his faith in Satan. Then Azazel accused him of heresy to gain control of his legions and domain. The Evil One sent Tetrax to the dungeons. They tortured him for months, but he escaped and fled here."

"So Tetrax also seeks revenge?"

"As do all in the Lower Depths. The Roman legions were the greatest armies of the ancient world, and it is upon them this important and dangerous task must fall."

"What will happen to a Roman soul slain by a demon?"

"It goes to Hell. The same holds true if one human spirit slays another."

"And if a Roman slays a demon?"

"The fiend's soul will return to Hell, be reborn, and live to fight another day."

"It seems the horntails have the advantage," the centurion muttered.

"Horntails?" asked Pazuzu, raising his eyebrow and tail.

"Apologies," Longinus said quickly. "I should have said Hell demons."

Pazuzu grinned at his discomfort. "Worry not. I prefer the term, Horntails. It amuses me."

"Thank goodness for that," the centurion replied. "What if a demon kills another demon?"

"Oblivion. Its soul returns to the dust of the cosmos; there is no rebirth."

"So that happened to Agrat Bat Mahlat when I slew her?"

"Yes."

"Hmm. I do not think the Romans will be happy to learn if they fall during this battle, they will be tortured in Hell," said Longinus.

"True," Pazuzu responded, "but if the Evil One defeats the angels, he will drag the souls of all pagan men, women and children into the Bottomless Pit. The Romans therefore have three choices: they can either wait until Satan breaches the gates of Limbo or Judgment Day comes—or they can take matters into their own hands.

"If they fight against Satan and defeat him, it will diminish his power and make him think twice about attacking Limbo. There is also a chance that the Judeo-Christian God will look favourably upon their action and take that into account at End Times. It is for the Romans to decide which course of action to take. Speaking for myself, I would rather fight than languish for aeons in a bleak place of sorrow."

"But even if they agree to help you, what will they fight with—their bare fists?"

Pazuzu waved one of his barrel-sized claws in the air. A sword appeared, and he threw it at Longinus' feet. The centurion picked it up and examined it. His eyes widened in astonishment. The weapon was a gladius: a standard issue Roman legionary's sword. It was in pristine condition, and if Longinus did not know better, he would say it had been forged recently. But that was impossible.

"Where did you get this?"

"I found it lying on the ground beyond the perimeter of the ice field protecting Limbo."

"How did it get there?"

"I presume a Roman soul escaped from Limbo."

"That means they have weapons," Longinus murmured.

"I sincerely hope so. My plan depends upon it."

"But how is that possible? I thought shades of the dead had no material possessions in the netherworld."

"I know not. That is for you to discover."

"How can you be certain I can surmount the ice field?"

"The glacial barrier prevents full demons from entering Limbo; but you and the cambion are only half-demons, and the Trojan and sorcerer are human souls. This, besides the prophecy, inspires me to believe you will succeed."

"What of Onoskelis?"

"If she is a full demon, she will not survive," Pazuzu said flatly.

"What if I cannot convince my people to help you? Will you still tell me where to find Satan's Path?"

"Of course. And to prove my trust in you, before you depart, I will give you an amulet with the power to transport you from Limbo to the portal of Chaos. Thus, even if you fail me, you can still attempt to save your friends."

"But even assuming the Romans decide to take part in the battle, how would they travel from Limbo to Purgatory?"

"I will teach your sorcerer an incantation that will open a rift between the two realms. Once your people march through it, they will arrive on the field of battle."

"It seems you have thought of everything."

"Probably not, but we have little time for priestly deliberation or claw wringing. Do you accept my quest?"

"Yes. I will do my utmost to enlist the help of the Romans, and I thank you for the trust you have placed in me."

"It is a virtue in short supply these days," Pazuzu sighed. "And speaking of trust, there is one matter you must settle before leaving for Limbo."

"What?"

"The succubus—do you trust her?"

"Yes, she saved my life."

"But you have not known her for long?"

"No, but I believe she would not betray me."

"And you desire her?"

"Perhaps, but I have little time for such trifles. What is it about her that troubles you?"

"She is not Onoskelis," Pazuzu said, studying him.

"What do you mean?"

"I have seen the demoness, Onoskelis—and that is not her."

Longinus' heart sank.

"Are you certain?" he asked, grimly.

"The Onoskelis I saw was older, had a fair complexion and the legs of a mule."

Longinus grimaced. Pazuzu's description reminded him of the succubus leader he had met in the Dungeons of Hell. She had told him her name was Satrinah, but he remembered that had caused some amusement among the other succubi. He could feel the rage building up inside him. He was angry that her deceit had made him appear foolish to Pazuzu, but more annoyed with himself for being so naïve in trusting her.

"Where is she?" he asked through gritted teeth.

"In a chamber close by. Would you like to speak to her—or should I?"

"Let me deal with her."

"Very well," replied Pazuzu, narrowing his eyes, "but if the succubus is a spy, you cannot permit her to leave. Do you understand my meaning?"

"Yes," Longinus sighed.

"Confront her and decide her fate. I shall leave the matter in your hands. When you return, I shall gift you the amulet and send you and your companions to Limbo."

Longinus nodded abruptly and marched out of the cave.

CHAPTER XXX

Longinus returned to the gallery outside Pazuzu's chamber and glared around. Armilus, Simon and Aeneas were standing nearby, but Onoskelis was nowhere to be seen. He strode across to them.

"Where is the succubus?" he demanded.

His uncharacteristic manner startled his companions, and they could tell by his face that something was amiss.

"What ails you, Longinus?" asked Aeneas.

"Pazuzu says the succubus is not Onoskelis," he hissed.

"Then who is she?" asked Simon.

"That, I intend to find out!" Longinus growled.

"I warned you not to trust her," Armilus said reproachfully. "All succubi are liars and deceitful."

"Well, you were right, and I was wrong! I hope that pleases you!" Longinus snarled.

"No—on this occasion, it does not," Armilus replied meekly.

"Where is she?"

Simon pointed to mouth of a small cave behind him. "After Pazuzu's guards released us, she wandered off in that direction."

Longinus nodded and marched towards the cave mouth.

"Do you want me to accompany you?" Aeneas called after him.

"No. I shall deal with her myself."

They watched as he disappeared into the darkness.

"This is most unfortunate," Aeneas sighed. "I liked our little succubus."

"What will he do to her?" Simon asked.

"I do not know, but this will not end well for either of them," Armilus moaned.

Simon was surprised by how distraught the cambion appeared to be.

Longinus followed a narrow passage that widened gradually and led him to a large chamber. It was empty apart from the succubus. She was lounging on a boulder and sharpening her trident with a small abrasive rock.

She looked up as Longinus entered and then continued with her work.

Longinus stood watching her for a moment.

"Who are you?"

She stopped and glanced at him. "I have told you my name."

"Pazuzu says you are not Onoskelis."

"And how would he know?" she replied casually.

Longinus moved closer to her.

"Because he once saw Onoskelis, and she was not you."

"He is mistaken."

"I think not. I knew the name was familiar to me, but I could not place it. But now I remember the description given of a demoness called Onoskelis in the Testament of Solomon: 'Her body was that of a woman with a fair complexion, but her legs were those of a mule.' She was like a Satyra—a female satyr. Do you know what the name Onoskelis means?"

She stared blankly at him and stood up.

"It can be roughly translated as 'she with the ass's legs.' Where are your ass's legs, succubus?"

"I am a demon. I can assume many shapes," she replied, eyeing the tunnel behind him.

"Then show me! Transform!"

"I need not prove myself to you!" she spat.

She attempted to walk past him, but he blocked her way. She turned and tried to walk around him, but again he stood in her path.

"I do not wish to harm you," she said sternly. "Let me pass."

Longinus looked at her with a grim expression. "And I wish you no harm, but you are not leaving until you tell who you are and why you followed us here."

"I will not warn you again! Let me pass!"

"No."

"Then on your own head be it!"

She brought up the blunt end of her trident at him. He tilted his head, and it narrowly missed his chin. In one fluid movement, she reversed the blow and brought the weapon down on his head. He stepped back quickly and parried the attack with his spear.

The succubus skipped forward and kicked him in the stomach. He grunted and scooped her leg upward with his left hand. The throw should have sent her sprawling, but she used the momentum to somersault backwards and landed nimbly on her feet.

Holding her trident at arm's length, she crouched low and whirled. Longinus leaped in the air, and the weapon missed his ankles by inches. He landed and thrust the blunt end of his spear at her chest. The succubus swept her left arm upward and outwards, deflecting his attack over her left shoulder. She arose swiftly and kicked him in the chest. It threw him onto his back. She dashed forward and thrust the blunt end of her trident at him. Longinus rolled to one side, and it hit the cave floor with a resounding crack. He stretched out his leg and spun on his back, sweeping her leading leg from under her. She crashed to the cave floor, cursing.

Longinus scrambled to his feet without taking his eyes off her. With a forward motion, she jumped up into a crouching position and regarded him warily. He had noticed that she was using the non-lethal end of her trident to attack him, and he had responded in kind by using the blunt end of his spear. He had no desire to harm her yet–at least, not until she had answered his questions.

As if reading his thoughts, she swivelled her trident and pointed the weapon head at him. His eyes became cold and hooded. Adopting a long stance, he rotated the spear so the deadly iron tip faced her. It vibrated gently and emitted a low hum as it sensed a new victim was nigh.

They circled slowly and cautiously–then she attacked him with a blistering sequence of blows that would have impaled most demons. Longinus relaxed his body and became as one with her movements. He knew when two skilled opponents fight each other they ceased to be separate beings and become conjoined in a grim, expeditious dance of death. A rhythm is established, and the first to break its frenetic cadence dies. Time seems to slow down and each fighter's senses are heightened to almost spiritual levels. Each balanced movement, every perfect action and reaction become fine brushstrokes on the crimson canvas of fate.

For the next few frantic minutes, they continued to leap, spin, duck, dive, roll and strike at each other with neither of them apparently getting the upper hand. Her athletic and acrobatic fighting style reminded him of some Chinese vampires he had fought many centuries before. They were known as Jiangshi and had been incredibly skilful with swords and spears. Their fighting style, with dramatic postures and many jumping and spinning attacks had been almost balletic. However, unfortunately for the *ballerini* of the Celestial Empire, they had crossed blades with an immortal Roman *danseur noble* and their painful deaths had followed swiftly.

Longinus did not favour complicated attacks. He had studied and experimented with many martial arts during his long existence and had absorbed many of their best techniques into his own free, eclectic style of combat; however, he had honed and simplified them, eliminating any superfluous movement or waste of energy. He believed in most cases, a straight, powerful attack to be best.

Many of the succubus' attacks were extremely skilful and well executed, but they left vulnerable parts of her body exposed for a split second–and a fraction of a second was all that an experienced fighter needed. One swift thrust to her throat, armpit or groin would destroy her. She was a natural and talented fighter, but she was not a hardened killer like him.

He focused on her eyes and used his peripheral vision to take in the rest of her body. Her eyes telegraphed each move she was about to make. He always kept his narrowed in combat to make it more difficult for another fighter to read them. She had not learned the art of disguising one's attack or making feints to deceive and confuse an opponent. She relied on speed, power, and strict adherence to technique.

But he was punishing her with his blocks. A strong block could damage an opponent almost as much as a blow. It was like striking a brick wall, and the recoil action could tear muscles or shatter bone. Their weapons locked together, and they pushed against each other. He grunted with the effort. She was incredibly strong.

He grinned savagely at her, and she glared back at him. He was about to say something witty, but before he could open his mouth, she kicked his legs from under him, and dropped him on his face. With an angry curse, he grabbed her ankle and pulled. She fell onto her back. He scrambled onto her, pinning her arms down with his knees. She struggled violently and tried to free her right hand holding her weapon, but he kept on adjusting his weight on her body, and she could not budge him.

"This game is over. Tell me who you are," he growled.

She glared at him for a moment and then burst into tears. He was so stunned that he relaxed his grip on her. That was all the leverage she needed. She grunted, arched her spine and threw him off. He landed on his back. Before he could raise his spear, she jumped on him and pinned his arms down with her knees.

They stared defiantly into each other's eyes. Her tears dripped onto his face and ran down his cheek. His anger subsided, and he could no longer find in his heart the desire to hurt her. Once again, he was in the hands of the gods and allowed them to determine his fate.

"Who are you?" he asked, softly.

"My name is Satrinah. I commanded one of Lilith's legions."

"Then why call yourself Onoskelis?"

"She was my mother and reared my sister and I. She protected and trained us. When we first met, I did not trust you, so I gave the first name that came into my head."

"I rescued her from the Dungeons of Hell," said Longinus.

"The other succubi told me."

"Where is your mother?"

"She has returned to the dust of cosmos. Eligos slew her."

"Who is Eligos?"

"He is the hunter of lost souls and heretical demons. No one withstands his fury."

"I am sorry. What of your sister? Where is she?"

She let go his arms and sat up.

"I do not know. We were trying to flee, but some of Asmodeus' incubi ambushed us, and we became separated in the confusion of battle. I think she escaped–but I am uncertain."

Satrinah sighed and moved back a little. Longinus was embarrassed to discover that his manhood was responding to her soft buttocks on his bare thighs. She felt the gathering protrusion and glanced at him in surprise.

"You wish to mate with me?" she exclaimed, frowning.

"No," he replied apologetically. "It was an unconscious reaction. I was not thinking of that at all."

She threw her trident onto the cave floor and leaned forward. Strands of her hair fell across his face. She brushed the back of her hand gently across his chin.

"I would not resist you," she whispered. "Coitus would make me forget for a while."

Her manner surprised him. She was usually so acerbic and belligerent.

"Stop, Satrinah. It is grief that makes you say such things," he said firmly.

He grunted in surprise as she grasped him in her hand. Her touch was cool and pleasing.

"Is this why you saved me? Is this what you wanted?" she asked.

She kissed him fiercely. Her lips were sweet and her long, sensuous tongue teased and explored his mouth. He tried to resist, but she conquered him. Her desperate need and passion engulfed and enslaved him.

"No!" he gasped, but he was already beyond the point of no return, the cusp of his half-hearted resistance to her luscious, feminine charms.

He had been alone for so long and yearned to be close to someone again. How pleasurable it would be to share some tender moments of intimacy with one whom he liked and desired.

"You are my first," she whispered.

He did not believe her, but was past caring. Visions of Lilith's beautiful face filled his mind as the blissful sensations of Satrinah's touch inflamed his passion.

She guided him inside her, and her eyes widened as her maidenhood broke. He filled her more than any other lover she had imagined in her dark, virginal fantasises. She moaned and her tail curled around his thigh, locking him to her. She moved sinuously on him, digging her nails into his chest and drawing blood. He groaned as the pain enhanced his pleasure and teased her rear with a fingertip to heighten her enjoyment.

Their movements became more intense and savage. He wanted to possess her, body and soul. She started shaking and he could tell she was on the cusp of her glorious crescent. He thrust deeper and her womb opened and embraced him.

"Fill me!" she cried.

Her lustful command had the desired effect on him. He arched his back and roared. She screamed and quivered as his torrent flooded into her. At the zenith of their ecstasy, their delirious eyes locked and Longinus felt himself leaving his body. He was travelling at great speed through a bright tunnel. Around him, he could see synapses sparking as they discharged electrical impulses. Then he entered vast chambers filled with vibrant, disparate sounds and images.

He saw Satrinah's twin sister; Lilith's legions amassing and taking to flight; Onoskelis trying to defend her daughters; incubi demons pursuing them; and Satrinah being captured by the Nephilim. Finally, he saw himself standing beside Armilus. This scene seemed to linger for a long time upon his face.

The visions disappeared, and he flew backward through the tunnel and returned to his own body. Satrinah jerked, trembled and collapsed on top of him. He held her and kissed her forehead. Her hair was silky and smelt good. Even her ebony horns seemed attractive to him.

Longinus closed his eyes and sighed. Her truthfulness pleased him, but accessing her memories troubled him. He had never done this before and had therefore gained a new power.

The demon inside him was growing stronger.

***

Armilus, Simon and Aeneas stood outside the cave and listened with much trepidation to their companions fighting. Suddenly—all went quiet.

"Do you think he has slain her?" Aeneas asked.

"Or she him?" Simon replied worriedly.

"I said this would not end well for either of them!" moaned Armilus.

As they waited with bated breath, strange, new sounds issued from the cave. Simon looked perplexed for a moment and then arched a disapproving eyebrow.

"Perhaps he is torturing her?" Armilus ventured.

"Hmm!" Simon said, scowling.

The noises increased in volume.

Aeneas looked at Armilus.

"Your fears were unfounded," he said, grinning.

"Why?" asked Armilus.

"It has evidently ended *very well* for both of them," Aeneas laughed.

As they walked away from the cave mouth, Armilus subjected his companions to a heated diatribe about the parlous, deceitful and seductive natures of succubi.

Aeneas stroked his beard and listened with only a half an ear to the cambion's rambling. Glancing at the alluring flock of succubi gathering at the other end of the cavern, he wondered if he should follow in Longinus' heroic footsteps.

***

Her tail uncurled from his thigh, and she pulled free of his embrace. He lay watching her as she stood up, wiped herself, and rearranged her attire. She looked cold and determined again. The flames of passion had died, and all that remained were the embers of guilt, awkwardness and regret.

"What is wrong?" he said.

"I cannot tarry here. I must go back and find my sister."

"Back? You mean to Asmodeus' domain? That is madness. He will capture you."

"You need not fear for me. I can look after myself," she replied, stealing a glance at his deflated manhood, amazed that such an inconsequential little thing had risen admirably to the occasion and brought her so much pleasure.

"What is your sister's name?"

"Ninkurra. You would favour her. She is prettier than me and has no deformities."

"That may be so, but I prefer the one that stands before me. I cannot persuade you to stay?"

"No. I have escorted you to the Lower Depths, and now I must find my sibling. I owe her that much."

"Very well. I understand. I too have someone I must save."

"Lilith?" she asked, glancing sharply at him.

"No, she is beyond my reach. My friend on earth is in danger."

"And is this 'friend' a female?" she asked.

Longinus arched an eyebrow. "Yes—but she is like a daughter to me."

"That means nothing in Hell," she laughed.

"Well, it does on earth. Fathers do not lie with daughters or mothers with sons. I consider such acts abhorrent and evil."

She studied his face for a moment and seemed almost satisfied by his answer.

"I have always wanted to see earth. I am told it is a wondrous place."

"You have never been there?"

"No."

"I thought all succubi seduced men and stole their seed?"

She smiled grimly. "They select only higher succubi for that task. I am not worthy yet. However, I have never had much interest in such things. I much prefer training for combat. Stealing the seed of mortals seems paltry in comparison."

"And you would have to couple with an incubus to transfer the seed."

"I have no desire to mate with one of those sly and repulsive creatures. I would rather pull my toenails out."

"Yes, I understand your revulsion." Longinus replied, repressing disgusting and painful memories he would rather forget. "But do not all succubi enjoy coupling with other demons? Is that not part of their nature?"

"You have much to learn about succubi. While some enjoy incessant coupling, most are not interested in such activities. They prefer combat and training for war. I am my own mistress and have my own ways."

"Indeed you are and do, and I would not wish you to be any different."

"Good!" she replied. "Then you will not prevent me from leaving?"

"I think you have made up your mind, and nothing I can say will stop you."

"Are you not concerned I may reveal your whereabouts to Asmodeus or Satan?"

"No. I trust you."

She shook her head and looked at him as though he was mad. "Trust? Demons do not trust each other. You are naive if you think they do. I caution you to trust less and suspect those around you more."

"But I am only a half-demon—and that means I only half trust you," he replied with a wry smile.

"Where are you going now?" she asked.

"Limbo. Pazuzu wishes me to find my people and ask them to fight against Satan's legions."

"The Ro-mans?" she asked, rolling it around her tongue in a strikingly Italian manner that both amused and pleased him.

"Yes."

"A thankless task," she replied.

"I was just beginning to realise that myself."

"Very well, there is no more to be said," she replied brusquely. "When I return, I shall find you—and hope you have not been too trusting in my absence. Farewell."

As she walked away, Longinus said, "I hope you find her. Be careful."

She paused for a moment but did not turn around.

"I am always careful," she said tersely, striding out of the cave.

Longinus scratched his chin and smiled. Small talk was definitely not one of Satrinah's social graces. He certainly had the knack of picking challenging females.

Then his expression became grim.

It was time to travel to Limbo.

CHAPTER XXXI

Longinus emerged from the cave and spied his companions waiting some distance away. He strode across the gallery and joined them.

"We saw the succubus fly away," said Simon.

"Without even a word of farewell," Aeneas added.

Longinus explained who she was, and why she had left.

"Then she is our ally again?" asked Aeneas.

"Yes," said Longinus.

"That gladdens me. I never believed the little one was a traitor," the Trojan replied, beaming.

"I must speak to Pazuzu," Longinus said, running his fingers through his thick, black hair.

"And I must speak to some succubi," said Aeneas, giving Longinus a knowing wink.

"Scream for Armilus if you need rescued," Longinus responded dryly.

"That will not be necessary. He is coming with me."

"What?" Armilus gasped in horror.

"No one knows more about succubi than you!" Aeneas insisted, putting his arm around the cambion's shoulders. "After all—you are the hero of Hell's Dungeons!"

Longinus grinned as Aeneas herded a protesting Armilus towards the clamourous congregation.

"What did Pazuzu say?" asked Simon.

"He wants to send us to Limbo."

"To persuade the Roman souls to fight against Satan's legions in Purgatory?"

"Yes. How did you know?"

"I foresaw this event in my visions."

"Hmm. Did you foresee anything else—the outcome of the battle, perchance?"

"No. My dreams ended with us travelling to Limbo."

"That is the problem with visions."

"What?"

"They always leave one balanced precariously at the edge of a dark chasm. You never know whether you are going to survive or fall."

"Well, assuming we do not drop into your metaphorical depths and our mission is successful, how will your people travel to Purgatory?"

"He says he will teach you an incantation that will open some sort of rift."

The magus nodded sagely. "I understand. Please inform him that I am willing, ready and able."

"Very well. I shall speak to him," the centurion said, turning to leave.

"Longinus."

"Yes?"

"I wish not to interfere in your personal affairs, but do you think it is wise to become entangled with the succubus?"

"Wisdom has eluded me for centuries, my friend. I follow the dictates of my heart and not my head sometimes. Why? Do you still not trust her?"

"I *do* trust her," Simon conceded, "but there is still something about her that troubles me."

"What?"

"I know not. It is just a feeling that I have."

Longinus shook his head. He did not have time for this; he wanted to complete his task in Limbo and reach earth as swiftly as possible.

"Well, if you can think of a more substantive reason, let me know. Anyway, she has left and may never return."

"True!" Simon sighed. "I shall accompany you and wait outside."

The centurion gave him a reassuring smile, and together they hurried to Pazuzu's lair.

Two ugly, sullen guards outside the demon lord's chamber blocked their path, but Tetrax appeared and instructed his subordinates to let Longinus pass.

"It pleases me to hear that you have joined our rebellion," the commander said.

"How could I resist your charm?" retorted Longinus.

"Our lord awaits you within," Tetrax replied, grinning.

"Call me when I am needed," said Simon.

Longinus nodded and made his way inside. The demon lord had not moved and was still perched like an eldritch gargoyle upon his rock. He eyed Longinus soberly as he entered.

"You have let the succubus depart?" he rumbled.

"She is no spy. She is Onoskelis' daughter—or one of them, I should say."

"I think you have let your loins rule your head," said Pazuzu.

"What?"

"This is my realm. I see everything that happens here."

"Oh," Longinus said, not knowing how to respond.

"I know you desire her, but that does not mean she is not an informer and will reveal our whereabouts. You should have brought her to me, and I could have probed her mind."

"There was no need. I probed her myself."

"Indeed!" Pazuzu replied, arching an eyebrow.

"I meant, with my *mind!*" Longinus clarified belatedly.

"How so?"

"It happened unexpectedly. It is the first time I have been able to do it. I saw Satrinah and her sister trying to escape from Asmodeus' incubi. She told me the truth."

"Good. This I already knew."

"You knew?" exclaimed Longinus.

"I explored her memories when you brought her before me."

"Then why did you ask me to interrogate her?"

"It was an experiment. I suspected your inner demon is released when you experience extreme passions, and you proved me right. Your motivating passions are anger and ecstasy. You attained your true demon form through rage while fighting Agrat Bat Mahlat, and you achieved the higher power of mind probing when you reached your climax with the succubus. That is why I sent you to speak to her. I knew you desired her, and she desired you. Your passion enabled your demon side to grow stronger. Rage and lust are powerful emotions. The change is upon you. You are now more demon than akhkharu. If we survive the battle ahead, I will guide as best I can. You can learn from my failings."

"Thank you, but I have just realised something that I did not consider," Longinus said rather shamefacedly.

"And what is that?"

"What if she is captured by Asmodeus, and he forces her to reveal your location?"

Pazuzu laughed. "Fear not. I have already planned for that. After you leave for Limbo, we shall prepare a trap for Hell's legions. If they dare to enter the Lower Depths and attack this place, we will crush them. That will be fewer demons Satan cannot deploy against the angels."

"Thank goodness for that," Longinus said with relief. "Can I ask you something?"

"Can I prevent you?" Pazuzu said, grinning. "Ask!"

"Why do you wish to help God?"

"I have no interest in supporting the God of the Jews and Christians. He destroyed the old gods. However, I yearn with all my being to thwart Satan's plans. When the Evil One and his demons broke open the seven gates of the netherworld, they transformed it from a place of mournful peace into one of pain and suffering. He gave the Elder demons a stark choice—join him or be imprisoned for eternity. Some Elder demons pledged allegiance to him, but most did not. We fought him, but we were too few and his Fallen is legion. He defeated and imprisoned us here in the Lower

Depths where ancient evil beings dwell."

"So you seek vengeance?"

"Yes! I wish to inflict a bloody defeat upon the Great Dragon! Is that so difficult to understand?"

"No. I wish to have my revenge upon Asmodeus. So we have something else in common."

"Indeed, we have."

"What of Tiamat? Can you destroy it?"

"Of course," Pazuzu replied, flexing his claws, "but I have a better fate in store for it. As I have told you, in the bowels of the Lower Depths exist great monstrosities with gnawing hungers. We shall drive Tiamat there, and they will devour it."

"What sort of monstrosities?"

"Dagon is one."

"The Sumerian and Philistine god?"

"It is no god, but a colossus of evil from the Realm of Chaos. It lurks in the shadows with its hideous acolytes waiting to be unleashed upon the earth."

"When will it be released?"

"That is unknown. Another being is called Babylon the Great," Pazuzu said, watching Longinus carefully.

"Armilus told me of her. I have a strange feeling that she somehow aided Asmodeus in bringing me back to Hell."

"You may be right. I too sensed her presence when I probed your mind, but it is uncommon for her to help demons. She despises the denizens of Heaven and Hell with comparable vehemence. Asmodeus must have used deceit to gain her aid, but what that trickery was, I know not."

"Still," Longinus murmured, "that information may be useful. If someone were to reveal that to Babylon, she may seek vengeance on Asmodeus."

"Or she may just devour the messenger," said Pazuzu. "Heed my advice and stay away from such beings. They are fiercer than a thousand Lamashtus. But now it is time for you to prepare for your journey to Limbo. Fetch the sorcerer, and I will teach him the incantation."

"Would you rather I opened the rift?"

"That was my original intention, but you may not return from Chaos. I must be certain that any Romans wishing to take part in the battle arrive in Purgatory in good time."

Longinus nodded. "I understand."

"Promise me one thing," said Pazuzu.

"What?"

"If you survive Chaos and save your friends, you will travel to Purgatory and fight by my side."

"Of course. I would not abandon my people in their hour of need."

Pazuzu performed his claw-waving trick and a small, oblong pendant attached to a thin leather cord appeared. He tossed it to Longinus, who caught and studied it. The arcane object was gold and covered with minute wedge-shaped Sumerian cuneiform script.

"When you wish to travel from Limbo to the portal of Chaos, touch the pendant and recite the incantation: *eme-gir-se gu-zu na-ab-sub-be-en*."

"Well, that will be easy to remember," Longinus grumbled.

"I am certain your living armour will assist you. He is quite fluent in Sumerian and has a long memory."

"You know about Naram-Sin?"

"You allowed me to enter your mind. I know everything. You have become somewhat of a Trinity yourself."

"Why?"

"You share your mind and body with two others."

"Two others?"

"The Akkadian king—and the demon that grows within you."

"Yes, it is getting rather crowded inside my thick skull," Longinus said dryly. "How do I travel from earth to Purgatory?"

"Merely touch the amulet and say, *gu-sum-ma ki-dul-dul-a-bi dal mu-na-an-e*. You will be transported to the field of battle."

"Will you remember these incantations, Naram-Sin?" Longinus asked.

"I will, centurion. This is very ancient and powerful magic Pazuzu has deigned to impart to us. I am very keen to see how it works."

"Do not be too keen," Longinus grunted.

He was not overly fond of using sorcery, but needs must.

"Has Naram-Sin committed the incantations to memory?" asked Pazuzu.

"Yes, and we thank you for helping us."

"I hope you are not too late."

"I shall do everything in my power to ensure I am there to fight alongside you."

Pazuzu seemed well pleased with his answer.

"Excellent! Now bring your three companions before me."

"What? You wish Armilus to accompany us? What good will he be?"

As far as the centurion was concerned, Armilus had fulfilled his part of their agreement, and he had no desire to put the cambion in further peril.

"Even the half-demon may be of use to you in your hour of need," Pazuzu replied enigmatically.

Longinus scratched his head and left. He was unconvinced that Armilus would be useful for anything more than moaning, whining and grumbling, but he held his peace. He had to make haste. Time was running out for

Rachel and Gabriella.

Aeneas and the cambion and had joined Simon outside the chamber. They looked expectantly at him.

"Well?" asked Aeneas.

"I thought you were off chasing succubi?"

"They were chasing him!" complained Armilus.

Aeneas winked at Longinus and seemed rather pleased with himself.

"Spare me the gory details. Pazuzu wishes to speak to us."

"Why?" asked Armilus.

"Because we four are travelling to Limbo!" Longinus answered with the faint hint of a smile.

"Limbo!" exclaimed Armilus. "I have no desire to go to that accursed place! I wish to stay here!"

"Well, you can if you wish, but Pazuzu thinks Satan's legions may attack the Lower Depths."

Armilus gaped at him.

"Come, Armilus," Simon said consolingly. "Let us see what Lord Pazuzu desires of us."

"Yes, little half-demon!" Aeneas boomed heartily. "Throw your caution to the wind and let us see what fresh adventures await us!"

Longinus smiled as the Trojan and magus led Armilus into Pazuzu's cavern. For some reason, the sorcerer and cambion had struck up a friendship. Why they had done so was a complete mystery to him. Perhaps, he mused, it was because they both knew their own kind had ostracised them. There was nothing like a little persecution and exclusion to bring people together.

Pazuzu bid Simon to come closer. The sorcerer stepped forward and knelt before the demon lord.

"I will implant an incantation into your mind," said Pazuzu. "This will allow you to open a rift through which the Roman army can pass from Limbo to Purgatory. It is in the ancient Sumerian language, and you must practice the words. If you mispronounce the spell, it will not work. Practice it only in your mind. Do not say the incantation out loud until you are ready to open the rift. Do you understand?"

"Yes, and I am ready," said Simon.

Pazuzu gazed at Simon for a few moments. The sorcerer shook and gasped.

"It is done," Pazuzu announced.

"Thank you," Simon mumbled, staggering to his feet.

Longinus dashed forward and put his arm around the magus's waist to steady him.

"I have given you more occult knowledge than any sorcerer before you. Use it wisely."

"I shall," Simon whispered.

"Very well. Are you ready to travel to Limbo?"

"I would rather stay here, great lord!" Armilus squawked.

Pazuzu regarded him sternly. "I and the Elder demons will travel to Purgatory to fight the Great Dragon. If you stay in the Lower Depths, there will be no protection for you. Therefore, may it not be safer for you to stay in the company of your companions?"

The cambion grimaced. He was caught between an unjust rock and an unsympathetic hard face. Neither miserable option was attractive to him, but, as always, he erred on the side of self-preservation.

"But then again, I may be of more use to you in Limbo, great lord!" he gushed obsequiously.

"Indeed, you may," said Pazuzu. "What think you, Revenant?"

"Armilus is an indispensable member of our party, and I would be loath to part with him," Longinus replied with a straight face.

The cambion gurned and gave the centurion a look of unparalleled filthiness.

Pazuzu stifled a smile and said, "Stand closer together."

Longinus and the others shuffled into the centre of the cavern floor.

"We will not meet again until the battle," Pazuzu said to Longinus. "May the gods keep you safe."

"And may the gods keep you safe," replied the centurion.

"May the gods keep us all safe!" moaned Armilus.

"Amen," added Simon.

"Do not move. This may be painful," the demon lord announced ominously.

"Eh?" Armilus whispered, clinging to Longinus' arm.

"Beware, Limbo. Here comes the Hero of Hell's Dungeons," the centurion muttered acerbically.

CHAPTER XXXII

Pazuzu raised his claw, and the chamber grew darker. There was a loud rumble of thunder, and a whirling vortex of darkness surrounded the companions. They held on to each other as the ground shook and the cosmos seethed and churned. Another tremendous boom resounded, and they stood blinking and disorientated on an ice field of interconnected glaziers. The sky was dark and turbulent, and the reflected light from the snow illuminated the gelid landscape like silvery moonlight. Scattered glacial islands of black rock protruded from the ice, and occasional pyramidal peaks loomed high above them. A soft, chilling breeze moaned and swirling snowflakes danced before their eyes, forming delicate and intricate carole dances of white.

Longinus spotted a rocky ridge ahead of them.

"Let us make our way up there and get our bearings."

The others nodded in agreement, and they set off. They were inappropriately attired for such harsh conditions, and Longinus hoped his companions were more resistant to cold than mortals. The party soon discovered that the fear of slipping was much worse than falling when walking on ice, and it was better to stride forward with confidence rather than taking small, tentative steps.

When they reached the crest of the ridge, they stopped and gaped in astonishment. Below them stretched a vast glacial plain where snowy blizzards blew, and icy winds howled and whistled mournfully. Towering, twisted columns of ice covered the ground and reached like Titans into the dark, tempestuous clouds.

Longinus scowled and rubbed the back of his neck. "I thought it was just an ice field!"

"And instead we discover the wind gods Boreas and Eurus exchanging fierce, wintry blows," murmured Aeneas.

"The Demiurge created this barrier to protect Limbo," said Simon. "The denizens of Hell fear such coldness. It is said that this plain can freeze a demon in its tracks."

"But I am a demon!" protested Armilus.

"A half-demon," Longinus growled. "So only one half of you will freeze."

"But which half? His head or his backside?" Aeneas asked, grinning.

"Such wit!" Armilus replied tersely. "But I suspect that all our posteriors will freeze down there."

They stood in silence for a moment and stared at the raging blizzards sweeping the plain beneath them. The snow was like a wall of white. In the distance, Longinus spied a great vertical cliff of ice towering above the plain. It was so high he could not discern its top.

"I assume the gate to Limbo must be somewhere in that cliff?" Longinus asked Simon.

"I agree," replied the magus. "We must cross the plain. Hopefully, we will find the gate without too much trouble. It is reputed to be enormous."

Armilus gaped at the wild and inhospitable landscape before them. "We will never reach that cliff! Is there no other way?"

"No, our path lies straight ahead," said Simon. "We should not tarry long. The Lilitu may return."

"I thought your sorcery had frightened them off?" the cambion asked.

"The magus shook his head. "They are Lilith's daughters and will never stop hunting us. Perhaps they will try to pick us off one by one next time."

Armilus' biggest eye widened. "But how would they know we are here?"

"How did they know where you and Longinus were last time? Someone or something guides them," Simon replied.

"Or one of Satan's spies in the Lower Depths," Aeneas added cheerfully.

"Then let us make haste!" Armilus said, making to scuttle down onto the plain.

"Hold on, Mercury!" Longinus growled.

The cambion stopped and eyed him fearfully.

"We must run as swiftly as we can!" he gasped.

"No," Longinus said patiently. "We do not know what could be lurking in that snowstorm. We have to tread carefully."

Armilus glanced ahead and behind him; and muttered an obscenity. His doom was waiting to snap its jaws in every direction.

"What do you think?" Longinus asked Aeneas.

"We cannot go back," said the Trojan. "With luck, this sea of ice will prevent the harpies from attacking us."

"Very well," said Longinus. "We will travel in a single file. I want each of you to hold on to the belt or garment of the person in front of you. If you lose your grip or fall, then cry out, and we will stop and help you. Do you all understand?"

The others voiced their agreement, and Longinus led the way down the rocky slope. Armilus was behind him, followed by Simon and Aeneas at the rear. With each step they took, they could feel the temperature drop by a degree.

Soon they were trudging through knee-deep snow and leaning forward to brace themselves against the frozen headwind that felt like a giant restraining hand upon their bodies. The bitter gusts hurt any exposed skin. They grunted and cursed as a sudden shower of large hailstones pelted down on them.

The centurion signalled to the others to kneel. They huddled together, and the warriors used their shields to protect the group from the aerial onslaught. The staccato rapping of ice on metal was deafening, and showers of crystal splinters exploded around them, stinging their arms and legs.

Longinus muttered an oath as he saw a swirling column of snow and ice drift past them. Aeneas cried in alarm as the edge of the whirlwind touched the tip of his spear, and he felt it being pulled from his grasp. With considerable effort, he wrenched it free and was horrified to observe the rotating maelstrom had polished the metal to a shine. The Trojan scrabbled back from the column to avoid it touching his legs. He could well imagine what would happen to him if sucked into the abrasive vortex.

The hailstone assault ceased abruptly, and Longinus lowered his shield.

"Up!" he cried. "We cannot stay here."

They staggered to their feet, and the weary file continued to stumble and slide across the glacial waste.

"Bring back the fires of Hell," Longinus muttered through chattering teeth as he forced his benumbed legs to keep moving.

After an hour of heavy going, the centurion stopped and looked back to determine the wellbeing of his companions. Snow and particles of ice covered them from head to foot, and they reminded him of a trio of abominable snowmen. Even Armilus' eyes had stopped watering, the tears frozen upon his cheek. Longinus knew he must appear just as grotesque to them.

He tried to utter some words of encouragement, but his face and lips were so cold, all that emerged was an incoherent mumble, sucked up and stolen by the frigid gale. He gestured forward with his spear. Lowering his head, he leaned into the wind and narrowed his eyes to keep the snow from blinding him. This was no ordinary coldness. He had once travelled in subzero temperatures on earth, but they had not affected him as severely as this. These were divine, preternatural conditions created by God to freeze the Fallen in their tracks. He knew it was imperative they kept moving and found shelter as soon as possible.

A short time later, Longinus stopped again and peered into the swirling vortex. He could see faint, indistinct humanoid shapes ahead of him. Shivering uncontrollably, he stuck his spear in the snow and blew into his hands, trying to regain some feeling in his fingers. A brief image of sausages popped into his mind. That is what his fingers felt like—huge, frozen sausages attached to his wrists. He remembered that the Romans had called this ancient food *lucania*, and it remained popular, especially during festivals, until banned in 320 AD by Emperor Constantinus I at the insistence of the Catholic Church. The clergy had considered the sausage shape too sinful and emblematic of pagan religions. In any case, his blowing met with little success: his kind was not warm-blooded and had more in common with reptiles than mammals.

He tightened his hold on his spear and concentrated. The weapon was sluggish, thrummed weakly, and produced some heat. It was not much, but enough to bring some feeling back into his hands and prove the rebellious digits belonged to him. He knelt down and motioned to the others to follow suit.

"Wha—wha—is—it?" Armilus chattered in his ear.

"Something—up—ahead! Tell—the—others—to—wait—here!"

Armilus nodded dumbly and conveyed Longinus' instruction to Simon and Aeneas. Rather than being concerned by this turn of events, they huddled together and seemed only too happy to sit and shelter from the blizzard.

Longinus grasped his spear as best he could and stumbled towards the shapes. He wanted to see what type of creatures they were before committing himself to combat. As he drew closer, the nearest figure became clearer. He saw horns and knew it was a demon. He prepared to stagger forward and thrust the spear into its guts, but stopped. The fiend did not move and just stood gaping at him. Longinus crept forward. The ice field had frozen the intruder while it was running. Its front knee was raised, and its long, bony arms outstretched. He glanced around at the other shapes. They too had been demons before the bone-chilling cold had transformed them into grotesque statues of ice. He advanced further through the blinding snow, and more glacial sculptures appeared. There were hundreds of them. Longinus suspected that this had been an expeditionary force sent by Satan to see if they could breach the ice field. Thankfully, the holy cold had done its work. They must have realised their end was nigh and attempted to retreat, but by then, it had been too late. They would remain here, frozen for eternity, as a stark warning to all demons that Limbo was beyond the reach of even their satanic master.

Longinus staggered back to his comrades and found them lying huddled together, covered in snow.

He knelt down and yelled, "S—afe! We—can—move!"

Aeneas moaned, but Armilus and Simon did not reply. Longinus shook them, but they did not respond; they were unconscious.

Longinus gritted his teeth and tried to stop shivering. He had to move them; otherwise, they would suffer the same fate as the demons. But it looked so inviting to lie down beside them and rest for a while. He wanted to sleep; he could feel his eyelids closing.

"*Awaken, centurion!*" cried Naram-Sin. "*If you sleep, you die! Stand up and keep moving towards the cliff!*"

Longinus grunted and opened his eyes. He crawled over to the Trojan.

"Aeneas! Move your arse!" he gasped.

His comrade groaned. Longinus sat back on his heels, wiped the snow from his eyes and tried to think of a way to rouse him.

"*Remember the fall of Troy. Who does he hate most?*" said Naram-Sin.

"Achaeans! Achaeans attacking! Defend Troy!" Longinus roared in Aeneas' ear.

Aeneas' eyes flashed open. He lurched to his knees and glared at Longinus.

The centurion put an arm around his shoulders and said, "We must keep going, my friend."

Aeneas nodded like a drunkard, and the centurion helped him to his feet.

"Grab Armilus by the wrist and drag him," cried Longinus.

Aeneas grunted and took hold of the cambion. Longinus held Simon's wrist, and they both started pulling for all they were worth. It was slow progress, and every inch seemed like a mile. Longinus could no longer feel his hands, and his limbs were like lead weights.

"*One step at a time,*" said Naram Sin. "*Concentrate on taking one step at a time.*"

Longinus was too cold and exhausted to answer. Summoning up his last reserves of strength, he lowered his head, leaned forward at forty-five degrees into the glacial blizzard, and kept going.

He could not remember how long he had been dragging Simon; each painful step merged into the next one with numbing regularity. He looked over his shoulder to check Aeneas was still with him. The Trojan looked as terrible as he felt. Longinus glimpsed movement ahead but kept trudging forward. He was too utterly stupefied to exert caution, and no longer cared; he just needed to keep moving.

The noise of the wind grew louder, and a large shape loomed in front of him. He wiped the mask of snow from his face and gawked. There was a giant mouth protruding from the ice. He stared stupidly as its thick, white lips puckered and discharged an immense column of snow and ice. As the gelid tempest arose, it rotated and swept across the plain. He had discovered the genesis of the holy snowstorms and whirlwinds.

"*Keep away from the mouth, centurion!*" warned Naram-Sin.

Longinus grunted. Even in his befuddled state, he understood the wisdom of the vampire lord's advice. He led Aeneas around some rocks that lay to the left of the orifice. As they drew opposite the lips, the aperture ceased blowing, and the winds died down and petered out. An eerie silence descended on the plain. Longinus signalled to Aeneas to stop, and they stood gazing at the mouth. The centurion had an uncanny feeling it was aware of their presence and listening. Although the gales had stayed, he could still hear the howling in his mind. He pinched his nostrils and blew through nose to unclog his ears. For the first time since entering the ice field, he felt a little warmer. They stood quietly for several minutes, and the mouth remained inactive. Longinus used the lull in the storm to survey the ground ahead of them. The cliff was only half a league away. If they could get past this boreal slit, they might just have a chance.

The centurion started as all too familiar ear-splitting screeches filled the air. Staggering around, he saw nine black shapes flying at them. It was the Lilitu. They had caught up with him and used the hiatus in the ice storm to attack. Longinus readied his spear and stood tottering in a weak parody of a defensive stance. He did not fear death; he welcomed it. Anything was better than this damnable cold.

The Lilitu landed and charged. Aeneas tried to raise his spear, but they swatted him aside like a fly and sent him crashing into the snow. Three were coming straight at Longinus, and the others were adopting flanking positions to attack from the sides.

He thrust his spear at Nashiram, but his attack was feeble and she knocked the weapon from his hands, grabbed him by the throat, and threw him onto the soft snow. They surrounded him, their black, leathery skins glistening in the light. The muscles of their lean bodies were as taut as bowstrings, the veins standing proud like worms burrowing under dead flesh.

"Where is your holy man, now, Revenant?" growled Nashiram.

"There he lies, sister!" cackled Oholibamah, pointing at Simon's snow covered body.

"As powerless as his God," scoffed Leah.

"He caused us so much pain with his words!" wailed Bilhah.

"Like the cuts of a thousand knives!" screamed Shelomith.

"We shall make him squirm and squeal and scream for mercy!" Sarai bayed.

"But mercy is dead," intoned Rebekah.

"This time there is no escape, Revenant!" said Nashiram. "We will take your souls back to Hell!"

"Back to Hell!" the others howled in unison.

"Slaves of Asmodeus!" Longinus gasped. "You serve the demon who usurped your mother."

"Liar!" hissed Basemath. "We and Agrat Bat deposed our mother. She was weak, like you."

Longinus gave a hollow laugh. "Fools! Is that what he told you? Asmodeus was behind everything. It was he who encouraged Agrat Bat to plot against your mother. He promised to make her Queen of the Night. You know too much. Asmodeus will destroy all of you."

"You lie!" Baileet shrieked.

"You have reaped what you have sown," said Longinus. "Once you were princesses of Hell—but now you are naught but Asmodeus' whores."

"We will rip you apart and suck the marrow from your bones!" Nashiram screamed.

Eighteen fearsome claws reached for him. Longinus screwed up his eyes and waited for death. There was a deafening roar, and a blast of freezing wind. The giant mouth had started blowing again. The Lilitu screeched in panic as the frigid ruin lashed them. Longinus opened his eyes and saw them freezing over. Some tried to run and others to fly, but there was no escape. They were too close to the great mouth, and the effect of its icy breath was instantaneous on their demon bodies. Nashiram crouched over him with her claws inches from his heart. For a moment, he saw the fear in her eyes, but they glazed over as a layer of ice covered her face. She had tried to use her last remaining strength to destroy him, her final pose capturing her seething hatred for eternity.

Longinus twisted around and stared at the mouth. Its lips puckered as it blew harder, and columns of whirling snow rose high into the air. The temperature was dropping rapidly. He had to move. Using his spear for support, he struggled to his feet and the fierce wind swept him to where Aeneas lay. The Trojan was unconscious and no amount of warnings about Greeks would awaken him this time.

Longinus dragged him to where Simon and Armilus lay and wiped the snow off their bodies. With fumbling fingers, he removed their belts and tied them together from wrist to ankle. When all was secure as he could manage, he grabbed the belt attached to Armilus' wrist, stood up, and heaved. They would not budge. Gritting his teeth, he dug his spear and heels deeper into the feathery carpet and tried once more. They slid forward an inch. He pulled again. Two inches. On the third attempt, his makeshift baggage train broke free of the snowy embrace, and he stumbled forward to maintain his momentum and keep it moving.

There was only half a league to go: two and half thousand steps. He was nearly there. Images of a dry cave with a warm fire burning flitted through his mind. Oh, what joy it would to lie down beside that welcoming conflagration!

He kept going, and no longer felt cold. He felt nothing, drained and devoid of all thoughts and sensations.

Then, through darts of ice that stung his eyes, he saw a great wall before him. To his left appeared to be a vertical crack in the ice that may afford them some shelter. Thirty more paces and he would reach it; just thirty slow and painstaking steps. The fissure was getting closer, but he was slowing.

His body was shutting down. He fell to his knees, and the belt slipped from his fingers. The glacier spun around him. He had an overwhelming urge to close his eyes and sleep. The snow seemed so enticing, so soft, like a white pillow upon which to lay his head. He fell forward, and his face sank into the freezing blanket of oblivion.

"Get up, centurion!" Naram-Sin cried.

But he could neither move nor speak.

Before he passed out, he imagined hearing a woman speak to him in dulcet tones.

"Oh, most stubborn and valorous of creatures. Death will come for you—but not yet. Not on this day."

Slithering phantoms from his past clawed at him, pulling him down into the murky charnel house of his own personal Hell.

A long, skeletal finger extinguished the solitary flickering candle of his consciousness.

And all was dark.

CHAPTER XXXIII

Longinus floated back into the algid sphere of mindfulness and groaned. The wind howled and whistled, but for some inexplicable reason, he felt warmer. He opened his eyes and tried to focus. The first thing he saw was Satrinah's worried face looking down at him, and he thought he was dreaming.

"You are awake," she said.

He raised his head and peered around. He was lying in a narrow, high roofed ice cave. Satrinah was kneeling beside him, and his companions lay sprawled on the floor opposite them.

"The others?" he gasped.

"They will survive."

He sighed with relief and stared at her.

"How are you here? You left to find your sister."

"I tried to return to Asmodeus' domain, but patrols were everywhere. Four incubi discovered my position and tried to capture me. I slew three and interrogated the fourth. Before I ended his existence, he told me that Hell is in an uproar because someone slaughtered the inquisitors and released the succubi and souls from the dungeons. Satan has commanded every demon not involved in the upcoming battle in Purgatory to find them."

"Sorry, that was my fault."

"There is no need to apologise. My sister is only one succubus, and you have saved many. Anyhow, I knew it was impossible to continue my search, so I returned to the Lower Depths and asked Pazuzu to send me here."

"Well, I am very glad that you did. I thought we were done for."

"Yes, but I have failed my sister."

He sat up and rested his back against the cave wall. He clenched and relaxed his hands. It was good to have some feeling back in his errant sausages.

"You did everything you could," he replied wearily. "They would have captured or slain you if you had tarried. That would not have helped your sister's plight."

"But I must save her!"

"And save her, you will. When this is all over, we shall find her, together."

"You would do that for me?" she asked, frowning.

He tried to give her a reassuring smile, but his cracked lips could only muster a grimace.

"Yes. I promise."

She sighed and touched his chin.

"You are far too trusting," she whispered.

He held her hand against his cheek. "Only with those I care about."

He saw the birth of a red tear in her eye. She leaned closer to him, and her red lips parted. They were beautiful and sensuous. He felt stirrings, and a surge of passion coursed through his body. She seemed so sweet and vulnerable at this moment, and that excited him. He wanted to taste her.

"What place is this?" Armilus moaned.

"Oh, joy! It has awoken!" Longinus muttered.

"And just in time. Your lips need to heal," she whispered, withdrawing her hand and wiping her eye.

"Where am I?" the cambion croaked.

"The Dungeons of Hell," Longinus said in a deep, ominous voice.

"What? No! I am innocent! They abducted me against my will!" Armilus shrieked, sitting up.

"You are very cruel," Satrinah admonished, suppressing a giggle.

At the sound of half-demon's strident protests, the others were rudely awakened.

"By the gods! I feel as though I have been kicked by an ox," Aeneas grunted, rubbing his brow.

Simon opened his eyes and sat up.

"We have reached the wall?" he asked.

"Yes. Satrinah saved us," Longinus replied.

The magus viewed the succubus with some surprise, but recovered his composure quickly.

"My thanks to you, I give," he said.

"You are most welcome," she replied, standing up and adjusting her armour.

"Your quest was successful?"

"No," she sighed.

Longinus caught his eye and shook his head, but Simon refused to be deterred so lightly.

"Why were you not frozen by the ice field?"

"I know not. I saw the Lilitu entering the icy waste when the wind stopped. I followed them, and they led me to you. The wind started again and froze them. The last thing I remember is the terrible cold and trying to drag all of you into this cave."

Simon noticed the frostbite on her body. "Most curious."

Aeneas lumbered to his feet and ambushed Satrinah with a friendly hug.

"Well, I thank you from the bottom of my heart!" he bellowed. "You have saved us from a shivery death!"

Longinus raised an eyebrow as Aeneas prolonged his gratitude a little longer than necessary. He stood up and slapped the Trojan on the shoulder.

"You are obviously feeling better," he observed, coming to the rescue.

Aeneas grinned at him. "As frisky as a mountain goat."

Satrinah gave a thin smile and disengaged herself from Aeneas' bear-like embrace.

"He is quite 'handy' to have around," she said, dryly.

Aeneas frowned and then burst into laughter.

"Ah, yes! I see your meaning. Apologies. It is has been a long time since I have held a beautiful woman in my arms."

"At least six hours," Armilus noted pithily, remembering the Trojan's antics with two succubi in the Lower Depths. "In any case, she is not a woman: she is a demoness."

Aeneas stood back and surveyed her in mock surprise at Armilus' comment. "It cannot be true! Why did I never meet demons like you when I was in Hell? That would have brightened up my lonely days and nights."

"Sorry, he has some rather ancient values concerning females," Longinus said.

Satrinah gave a little satisfied smile as she detected a hint of jealousy in his voice.

"Then I hope all Tro-jans are as handsome and strong as he," she replied.

Aeneas beamed with happiness and knelt on one knee before her.

"I am your servant and slave," he said gallantly, taking her hand and kissing it.

"I have never had a slave before. What should I do with him?" she enquired teasingly of Longinus.

"Tell him to get his big Tro—jan arse up so we can decide what to do next," Longinus muttered.

"Very well. Arise, slave. I shall call you when I have need of you," Satrinah announced.

"You wish is my command, my lady," said Aeneas, as he stood up and bowed his head.

"You have never kissed my hand and pledged obedience," she said to Longinus.

"I like to kiss other things," Longinus replied nonchalantly, adjusting his sword belt.

She laughed but enjoyed a secret thrill at his hidden message. What he had said was for her ears only, and only she could decipher its true meaning. It had taken her a little time to understand the ways of her vampire, but now she did, she was very taken with him. He appeared not to care about others, but did. She felt honoured to be coveted by Lilith's Revenant, but yet, surprisingly and annoyingly, she was also jealous. He had mated with the most alluring succubus, the mother of all succubi, and yet he had deigned to couple with her. Her! She who was nothing; she who was merely a soldier in Lilith's army. But as well as feeling humbled, she also felt anger and resentment that Lilith had known him first. She wanted him all to herself, and could not bear the inevitable comparisons he would make between her and Lilith. How could she compare to the mighty and powerful Queen of the Night? The very thought made her sad and angry: angry with him, with Lilith, but mostly with herself.

"Satan's perfervid ring!" cried Armilus. "I cannot take any more of this human emotional discourse. Send me back to the ice field!"

"You may wish to thank Satrinah for saving you," Longinus suggested.

"Yes—I *may*," Armilus said, scowling.

Longinus gave him a hard stare, and Armilus started fidgeting under his withering gaze.

"Oh, very well! Thank you—succubus," he grunted.

"You are welcome—cambion," she replied, smiling at his querulous manner.

"Come, little half-demon," said Aeneas. "We are all comrades in this adventure. I shall look after you."

Armilus accepted the Trojan's hand and was hoisted like a sack of potatoes to his feet.

"Hmm, one head, two arms, and two legs. It would seem you are still in one piece," Aeneas said, slapping him on the shoulder.

Armilus grimaced, but it pleased him that the Trojan appeared to care about his welfare. Such civilised consideration of his suffering was more than he had received from Longinus.

Simon frowned and shook his head at all this frivolity. They were still in danger and needed to make haste. It also surprised him to see this playful side of Satrinah, and he could not decide whether he liked this additional aspect of her character better than the sterner one. She was acting like a silly young girl, and he hoped she would not cause trouble between Longinus and Aeneas. The fates of these men were inextricably linked, and they would need to work together to fight the evil that faced them. They were the two heroes bearing spears that the ancient prophecy foretold. But there was a third spear-carrier, and he was the essence of evil. Simon had confronted and escaped from this fiend's grasp many times over the centuries, and he did not even want to think about his hideous face or name. One of these warriors would have to defeat this vile creature, but he did not know whether it was Longinus or Aeneas.

"So, where do we go now?" asked Longinus.

"There is a narrow shaft yonder," said Satrinah, pointing with her trident. "It cuts through the ice cliff."

Longinus strode over to the entrance and peered into the gloomy passage. He saw a reassuring speck of light in the distance..

"Well, another day, another tunnel," he said dryly. "Are we ready to proceed?"

"Lead on, my friend!" beamed Aeneas.

The centurion cast a glance back to the fissure, and the blizzard raging outside.

"Let us hope Limbo is warmer than here," he said.

"Any place is better than this hiemal nightmare!" Armilus complained, shivering. "Let us go!"

The centurion raised an eyebrow as the cambion scampered past him into the tunnel.

"Wait for me!" warned Aeneas, chasing after him.

Satrinah stroked Longinus' cheek as she walked past.

"Too trusting," she murmured regretfully.

Simon shook his head and gave the centurion a disapproving look before following her.

"Oh, joy," Longinus grunted.

He was rapidly coming to the conclusion that despite the merry, thigh-slapping tales of groups of adventurers in myth and history, most odysseys were better undertaken alone.

"One arse, one mind, one opinion!" he growled, striding into the passageway.

CHAPTER XXXIV

They emerged blinking from the tunnel of ice, and an ominous grey landscape opened up before them. It was a stark, flat valley with high mountains on either side. A layer of silvery ash covered the basin floor. An eerie, mournful wind swept across the plain and caused the choking powdery residue to swirl and create grotesque patterns and indistinct eldritch shapes. At the far end of the gorge was a towering cliff that rose and disappeared into the dismal leaden-coloured clouds. In the centre of the precipice was a massive golden portcullis.

"The gate to Limbo," Longinus whispered.

They stood in silence for a moment. The enormous size of the portal was stunning to behold.

"It is magnificent!" Aeneas said in wonder. "Only the gods could build something that size."

Satrinah was impressed despite herself. She knew the Great Tyrant was powerful, but this portal was beyond belief. The mighty gates of Hell were small compared to it.

Simon touched Longinus' arm and said, "If you convince your people to fight against the Great Dragon, this is the plain where I must open the rift to allow them to enter Purgatory."

"You cannot do it from within Limbo?"

"No. The power of the Demiurge is too strong there."

"Then we shall worry about that when the time comes. Let us make our way to the gate."

"We should proceed with caution," Simon said quietly.

"Why?"

"Have you read the *Book of Lilith*?"

"It was my favourite bedtime reading," Longinus replied.

"The scrolls hinted that a hideous winged beast guarded the entrance."

Longinus frowned. The infernal codex was older than he had surmised. Someone, or something, must have transcribed it into book form at a later date.

He could not remember the passage Simon referred to; he had been more interested in its hellish rather than divine content.

"I see nor sense nothing," he said, scouring the landscape.

"Let us hope it was just a legend," said Simon.

"Yes," Longinus retorted, glowering around.

He had no time for enigmatic prophecies or myths. Time was running out. He needed to present his request to the Romans and then save his friends on earth.

As they plodded along through the choking dust, Armilus grumbled, "Fire, ice, and now ash! Is there no end to this misery!"

Longinus noticed a red glow appear suddenly on one mountaintop. The peak differed from the others adjoining it. It was darker, almost black, and had a flat summit. The others had also seen the crimson flare and glanced worriedly at each other.

"I wonder what fresh horror lurks there?" said Aeneas.

"Let us hope we do not find out," Armilus whispered, moving closer to the Trojan.

After a few hours, the ash cleared, and the remaining two miles to the gate were easier going. Finally, they stood before the vast and imposing divine portcullis. In the middle of the gate was a circular seal, some hundreds of cubits in diameter, the bottom edge of which ended five feet from the ground. Engraved on the seal were two impressive and fearsome angels, holding a wreath. Inside the wreath was the letter X intersected by an I. Longinus knew this Christogram well. It was like the Chi-Rho or Labarum emblem used by Constantine the Great, the first Christian Roman Emperor.

"What is the meaning of this symbol?" asked Aeneas.

"It is the IX monogram," said Longinus. "It has the Greek letters I and X, iota and chi. Iota is the first letter of the Greek word for Jesus, and chi is the first letter of the Greek word for Christ. Together, they form the shorthand for the words 'Jesus Christ'. It was an early Christian symbol, but it predates Christianity. The church fathers later concluded it was far too paganistic and later replaced it with a simple cross."

"Paganistic?" asked Aeneas.

"Being a pagan. It a derogatory Christian term for anyone belonging to a religion that worships other gods," answered the centurion.

"Hmm. Do these Christians think there was not a shred of goodness or honour in the world before they deigned to appear?" Aeneas murmured.

"No. But it was not their brand of goodness, so our meager pagan offerings do not count."

"How did mankind live, love and survive for so long without these veritable paragons of morality?" Aeneas responded, dryly.

"Apparently, we were all terribly wicked and without a shred of decency," Longinus replied.

"Sanctimonious clapfart!," the Trojan exploded. "All rich, haughty priests have said the same about other religions since the world began! Those scheming backstabbers are only interested in getting more worshippers, more gold, and building larger temples to match the size of their heads!"

"Been saving that up for two millennia, have we?" Longinus asked.

"Apologies! I dislike priests!" Aeneas growled.

"Really? I would never have guessed," the centurion replied suavely.

Aeneas scowled and then realised the others were staring at him as though the hand of madness had touched him. He pursed his lips, flexed his thick neck, and adopted a more reasonable tone.

"Ahem. Anyway–what is the purpose of this 'monogram', as you call it?" he asked.

"It protects the gate from demons," Simon interjected helpfully. "No denizen of Hell can break this seal and enter Limbo."

Longinus scratched his head. "Well, we need to get in. Can you open the gate?"

"I do not know. Let me think on it," Simon replied.

"We have little time, so please hurry," said Longinus.

As Armilus and Satrinah discussed the matter with Simon, Longinus sighed in frustration and sat on a large boulder at the side of the portcullis. After a few minutes, Aeneas wandered over to join him.

"They are comparing spells and other hibber-gibber that make no sense to me," the Trojan muttered.

"I am so stupid!" Longinus said bitterly. "Did I think I was just going to walk into Limbo?"

"How were you to know, my friend? None of us knew what to expect."

"I should have known. Nothing in this miasma of confusion is ever simple."

"We shall find a way," said Aeneas.

They sat for a minute in silence and then Aeneas ventured, "If one ignores her wings, horns and tail, our succubus is a bewitching and fulsome wench."

Longinus glowered and said nothing.

Aeneas gave a tactful cough and changed the subject.

"I met one of Lilith's daughters once. She was in the guise of a woman."

"They often adopted mortal forms to deceive men," Longinus growled.

"She was not one of those who attacked us. No, she was exquisitely beautiful with long, red tresses. I encountered her as I travelled through Hell. I expected her to attack me, as all demons had, but she did not. She seemed very curious and bade me sit with her awhile."

Longinus felt a pang of jealousy in his heart. Aeneas' description suggested it was Lilith.

"What name did she give you?" he asked.

"Eldora."

Longinus breathed a sigh of relief.

"Yes, I met Eldora," he said, thinking of when she had rescued him from the army of the dead in Babylon. "She seemed the least vicious of Lilith's sorry brood."

"You say was?"

"A demoness called Agrat Bat destroyed her."

"That saddens me. She gave me much advice on how to survive in Hell and counselled me to take another route, as her sisters were not so welcoming. She was very wholesome to look upon, and I lay with her. Eldora was the only demon in the Abyss that showed me some kindness."

"Until I met you, I did not know that human souls could mate with succubi," said Longinus.

"Neither did I. But Eldora told me that while male and female souls cannot couple with each other, they can mate with succubi. It was a very pleasant surprise!"

"What surprises me is that you still have such desires. I thought shades of the dead were devoid of such yearnings."

"Well, I cannot speak for others, but I have certainly thought of such things over the last few thousand years. Perhaps it is in my nature, and even death cannot extinguish my passion. But then I was always a fool for a pretty face, the swing of hips or the knowing glance between two strangers when they first meet. Of course, when I married my first wife, Creusa, I put such youthful dalliances behind me."

"She was your wife in Troy?"

"Yes, and a sweeter and more loving woman I had never met. She bore me my beloved son, Ascanius. Our life was happy and blessed by the gods, but then that fool Paris abducted Helen and the Achaeans besieged our city."

"Was Helen as beautiful as they say?"

Aeneas gave a grim smile. "Aye, she could tempt any man that beheld her, but I never liked her. She was cold and aloof. There was also an uncanny strangeness about her. I always felt she was scheming and pleased with the death and destruction she caused."

Longinus nodded. He knew from reading the forbidden *Book of Lilith* that Helen was Lilith in mortal form, but he said nothing of this to Aeneas. Some dark secrets were better left buried in the past.

"Is the legend of the wooden horse true?"

"Oh, indeed," Aeneas replied grimly. "I begged them not to bring it into the city, but Paris, at the bidding of Helen, persuaded King Priam to ignore my warnings. I thought it was a bad omen, but they viewed it as an offering by the Achaeans to recognise that we had won the siege. Of course, I now curse my stupidity. It never occurred to me that our enemies had concealed men inside it.

"That night the people of the city celebrated the victory with wine, merriment and dancing. My wife had gone to visit her sick mother, who lived in a house near the city gates. The Achaean horde swept through Troy, raping and slaughtering. I only hope that Creusa's death was swift, and she did not suffer at the hands of those savage and uncivilised brutes."

Longinus could see by Aeneas' face that the bitter memory haunted him and moved the conversation on.

"How did you escape?"

Aeneas wiped the tears from his eyes and continued.

"It was a miracle. There was chaos and fighting everywhere, but my comrades and I found my father, Anchises, and Ascanius, my young son. My father was infirm, so I carried him on my back while my friends, Achates, Sergestus, and Acmon scouted ahead of us. We encountered other survivors and persuaded them to join us. Our party grew larger and more difficult to conceal from the eyes of the ravishers, but Aphrodite watched over us and guided our way. At one point, we ran into a party of four Achaeans, drinking and laughing. They had taken some pregnant women, cut their bellies open and stamped the unborn children into the ground. Their tiny bodies and brains lay at my feet. I put my father down, and in a red mist of madness, slaughtered them all."

"War brings out the very best or the very worse in men," Longinus said quietly.

"We made our way to the harbour and there among the myriad of enemy ships lay our own small fleet. Fortunately, most of the Achaeans were in the city, and they had only left a small contingent to guard the vessels. Under cover of darkness, we crept up on them and slit their throats. Thus as our beloved city screamed, burned, and died, we rowed silently and tearfully, into the black, inhospitable night.

"I felt like a coward! I did not want to escape; I wanted to stay and fight to the end. I could have died with my wife and accompanied her in the netherworld, but the gods commanded me to leave."

"In what manner did they impart your destiny to you?" asked Longinus.

"Before that fateful night, I had several dreams in which the goddess Aphrodite appeared to me."

"Whom we Romans called Venus. Legends tell she was your mother," said Longinus.

"My father always told me so, and I believed him. Why else would she guide my path?"

Longinus shrugged noncommittally.

"She told me that when Troy fell, as it surely would, I must flee the city and take the remnants of my people to an unknown land; a western land where a river called the Tiber flowed. There we would fight many battles, but we would be victorious. I would become king of this new people, and two of my descendants, Romulus and Remus, would found an empire that would rule the world."

"And that land was Italy, of course."

"Yes, but at that time it was not known as such. There were many kingdoms and tribes. The Latins being one of the most powerful."

"How long did it take you to reach Italy?"

"Seven years, although it seemed forever. We journeyed to Thrace, Crete, and Sicily and had many adventures. Sometimes my people lost faith and gave up hope, as did I occasionally, but I always rallied and assured them that we would find our Promised Land."

"That is the mark of a great leader," said Longinus. "It is easy to rule when things are going well, but more difficult in times of adversity."

Aeneas looked embarrassed for a moment and then said pragmatically, "I did what I had to do: no more, no less. Then we were caught in a ferocious storm and lost many of our ships and people. We were shipwrecked, tired and starving, on the coast of Africa near a mysterious city called Carthage. You know of this place?"

"Yes," said Longinus. "People remember it as one of the greatest cities of the ancient world."

Aeneas smiled. "And so it should be! Oh, Longinus, what grandeur and beauty! I thought Troy was magnificent, but my old city paled into comparison at the splendour of Carthage. I was smitten as soon as my eyes beheld her."

"Is it the city or queen of Carthage you speak of?" Longinus asked with a gentle smile.

Aeneas laughed. "Ah, so you know my story? Well, both, to be truthful. There we were, stranded on this strange land and at the mercy of its unknown ruler. We did not know whether the inhabitants would treat us kindly or make slaves of us."

"What happened?"

"A troop of charioteers appeared and surveyed us. The commander of the army, or the *tm' mhm* as they called that office bearer in the Phoenician tongue, on seeing we were a mixed band of men, women and children, said we had nothing to fear, as the Carthaginians were a civilised people. Then they rode away.

"However, we suspected treachery and built defences as best we could and waited for them to return in force. And return they did—hundreds of them! But, to our surprise, they brought supplies of food, wine and dry clothing. After we had wept many tears of gratitude and joy, the tm' mhm informed us that his queen desired to meet with the leaders of our people.

"Thereupon, my son and I, along with some other leaders, washed ourselves in the sea and donned our best armour. For although we were grateful to our hosts, we still did not fully trust them and had no intention of entering a strange city unarmed and unprotected. To give the good commander his due, he said he understood our concerns and allowed us to wear our swords and daggers. However, he warned us that no man, except members of the royal guard, could carry weapons in his beloved queen's presence. We replied that this law was acceptable to us, as such a rule had been part of the royal protocol in our homeland.

"They had brought with them spare chariots, and soon we were thundering through the mighty gates of Carthage. Such lofty buildings I had never beheld before! This city was a place of wonder to us all. Multitudes of trumpets sounded, and the streets brimmed with happy, cheering people who threw flowers beneath the hooves of our steeds. After what seemed like hours, we arrived at a large and impressive palace, decorated with lapis lazuli and gold, which gleamed and sparkled in the midday sun.

"The *tm' mhm* escorted us through long, cool corridors—lined with infantry attired in the most magnificent of armour—and ushered us into a vast, ornate throne room brimming with richly dressed and sweet-smelling officials; however, we Trojans were too eager to see what manner of queen ruled this most delightful city to mind their courtly gossiping and disparaging stares. My friends whispered naughtily in my ear that they were certain the monarch would be old and ugly."

Longinus laughed. "And was she?"

"No, Longinus, she was not! Silver trumpets sounded, and in walked the most beautiful and dignified woman that I had ever seen. I think we must have all gasped like fools in admiration. I remember stifling a laugh at my friend's astonished faces. They stood with their mouths hanging open like caught fish.

"Queen Dido ordered food and wine to be brought and asked us to tell our story. She listened very attentively and asked us to repeat and clarify many points. However, our knowledge of the Phoenician tongue, while sufficient for trading goods, was less than perfect for courtly discourse.

"I still recall, as if only yesterday, the sound of her sweet laughter when I, to the utter mortification of my comrades, mistakenly referred to her as a horse. It caused great consternation and hilt gripping among her advisors and guards, I tell you.

"After my friend, Achates, advised me of my error, I knelt before the goddess and begged her forgiveness for my impudence and ignorance. I did not fear her, but I was so taken by her beauty and sweet nature, I could not bear to contemplate she might think ill of me.

"But she smiled kindly upon me and said, 'Arise, Aeneas. You have paid me a worthy compliment. Are not royal mares the best of their breed?'"

"Her courtiers tittered in amusement and commended her wit, but Dido ignored them and had eyes only for me. Why this was so, I could not tell at the time; I felt like a blundering fool in her presence. But much later, as she lay like a beauteous nymph in my arms, she revealed to me that I was the only man to make her laugh like a carefree girl and as happy as a love struck woman. Although separated by language, rank and culture, we were both exiles and that misery of Fortune drew us ever closer together. Even a great monarch must have some cheer and companionship, Longinus. The crown of royalty bears like a crushing weight upon any ruler's head. Of that, I can assure you.

"When we had finished our discourse, she informed us she had heard of the war between the vile Achaeans and noble Trojans, and we were most welcome to stay as guests in her city. After the trials and adversities we had suffered, it was the best news we had heard in a long time."

"I have always thought Queen Dido was a remarkable woman," said Longinus.

"Indeed, she was!" Aeneas replied passionately. "She was a princess of Tyre, and her father made her and her younger brother, Pygmalion, joint heirs. But when the king died, treacherous priests and courtiers subverted his will and made Pygmalion king. He was but a boy, and they sought to control him.

"Dido married her uncle, Acerbas, who was the second most powerful man in the city. Pygmalion was a profligate and soon squandered the kingdom's wealth. He needed gold, and quickly. He knew that Acerbas was wealthy and urged on by his court officials, had his uncle murdered. Dido knew that her brother considered her a threat to his kingship, and it would not be long before his assassins put her to the sword and stole her riches to fill the royal coffers. To confuse and delay her brother's intention, she sent a messenger to him asking if she could live in the royal palace. This delighted Pygmalion, as that would make the murder of his sister much easier and less public. He granted her request and asked that she brought all her dead husband's gold with her so it could be kept *safe* under royal guard.

"When Pygmalion's guards and retainers arrived to escort her to the palace, she begged them in the name of the gods to cast her husband's bags of gold into the sea as an offering to his murdered spirit. The king's men, smitten by her beauty, tears, and the guilt of their foul deed, agreed. However, she then had them in her power. They could not return to Pygmalion and face his wrath, and so agreed to help her flee the city. Many loyal friends and senators joined them."

"If I remember correctly, she deceived them. The bags were just full of sand," Longinus said, with a wry smile.

"Yes, she was clever. She escaped Tyre with a small army of supporters and all of her husband's considerable wealth."

Longinus could tell by Aeneas' tone that he was extremely proud of Dido.

"So she and her followers landed eventually in Tunisia in north east Africa?"

Aeneas frowned. "Africa?"

"Sorry, Africa is the modern name for what the ancient Greeks and Romans called Aethiopia."

The Trojan scowled. "Hmm. The word sounds like Achaean clatfart to me, but you are correct. Dido arrived on the coast of Aethiopia."

The centurion glanced at the other members of their party and saw they were still discussing how to open the gate. Although impatient to resume his quest, Aeneas' story fascinated him.

"What happened next?"

"Dido asked the Berber king, Iarbas, for a small piece of land for her people. The king was undecided until Dido told him she would only take as much land as could be encompassed by an ox hide. The king, thinking she was a madwoman, laughingly agreed."

"But Dido cut the ox hide into fine strips until she had enough to encircle a nearby hill," Longinus replied with a laugh.

Aeneas chuckled. "It is so! The king was so impressed that a mere woman had bettered him he told her she could have a hundred times more land with his blessing. I think Iarbas was hoping there might be more between them, but that did not come to anything. She had only one concern: the welfare of her people.

"Many of the local Berbers and inhabitants from the nearby Phoenician colony of Utica joined her, and they began building a city. When digging the foundations, they found a horse's head, and that was a sign from the gods the city would grow to be powerful and win many wars."

"Why did she call it Carthage? I have always considered it such a grand and romantic name."

"I am sorry to dash your exotic dreams, but it simply means 'new town' in the Phoenician tongue. Dido was ever the practical woman."

"Really? Oh, well," Longinus laughed. "How long did you stay there?"

Aeneas looked more sober and stroked his beard. "A year. It was the happiest time of my life. Dido implored me to stay and offered to make me king, but I could not. Aphrodite came to me in another dream and commanded that I left and fulfilled my destiny."

"That must have been difficult for you. It is painful leaving someone you love," Longinus said.

Aeneas glanced at the centurion and could tell by his sad smile that the Fates had demanded the same heavy toll from him.

"It was the most difficult decision I had ever made and tore my heart apart," Aeneas continued. "I was a coward for the second time in my life. My leaving was so painful to me, I could not bear to say farewell to her. I knew if I saw her tears, I could never leave her sweet side, and the gods would seek vengeance on us. So I stole away like a contemptible thief in the night. As our ships left the harbour, I gazed one last time at the palace and saw a great fire burning on the lofty parapets. I thought she was signalling to me. It was only much later that I discovered she, in her sorrow and despair, had mounted the scorching pyre and thrown herself upon the sword I had gifted her. I have never forgiven myself for deserting her; I was not worthy of her love. This is the heavy burden of guilt I carried in life and now in death. Time does not heal all wounds: some it makes deeper."

Longinus nodded sympathetically. As he well knew, the whims of the gods were cruel sometimes and gave you the hope of happiness, only to snatch it away again.

"The gods may plot and scheme, but the Fates always wins in the end," he said.

"How true," Aeneas whispered, wiping the tears from his eyes. "Eventually, we reached the mouth of the Tiber River and were well received by Latinus, the king of the Latins. There was a prophecy among the Latins, which apparently foretold my coming, and he was determined to help us in any way he could. He proposed I marry his daughter, Lavinia, and create a union between our peoples. But Latinus' wife was a scheming shrew and opposed the marriage. She wanted her daughter to marry Turnus, the cunning leader of the Rutuli tribe. It ended in war. In the last battle, Turnus killed Latinus' son, and I had the pleasure of thrusting my sword into Turnus' belly. I married Lavinia, and we founded a new city called Lavinium."

"And thus the beginnings of the Roman Empire were born," said Longinus. "But tell me, why were you in Hell and not in Limbo with your people?"

"Because, like you, I am cursed. After I died, I arrived in the underworld and was confronted by the Erinyes."

"The Furies!" Longinus exclaimed. They were a trio of ancient crones he wished never to meet.

"Yes. They told me because of the wrong I had done to Dido, I was damned to wander Hades for eternity. That is why I am so keen to accompany you into Limbo. I have been running, hiding and fighting for millennia; and crave peace. I need to find Dido's soul and beg her forgiveness."

"But I thought you travelled with the Cumaean Sybil to the underworld when you were mortal and met Dido?" Longinus asked, remembering the legends.

"Not so. I had a dream in which I imagined I travelled to Dis, or the underworld as you call it, but I did not meet Dido. I saw only my father, who confirmed the importance of my founding a new empire in Italy. He foretold that my son, Ascanius, would build a new city called Alba Longa; and from his line would come Romulus who would build Rome; and from Romulus' descendants, a great Caesar would emerge to conquer and rule the world."

"He was right. In fact, your line was blessed with two great Caesars—Julius and his successor, Augustus," Longinus replied.

"That I am glad to hear, but I must still find Dido," Aeneas sighed.

"You will, my friend. I am certain of it," Longinus said gently. "And further to that end, let us see how the others are faring with the gate."

They grabbed their spears and returned to the divine portcullis. Simon was reciting a unintelligible incantation while making strange gestures with his hands.

"How goes it?" Longinus asked.

"We have tried every spell we know, but nothing works," Simon sighed.

"It is impossible," added Armilus. "We should return to the Lower Depths. I do not like this place. It is worse than Hell."

"You think every place is worse than Hell!" Satrinah chided.

Longinus rubbed his chin. Such demonic arguments were beyond him. He had enough trouble understanding the tortures condoned by the Christian God, never mind the stinking torments of Satan's Abyss.

"Do you think there is another way in?" he asked Simon.

"It is said there may be other gates to Limbo, but I fear ice fields and the seals of the Demiurge protect them," said the magus.

"Demiurge?" Aeneas asked, frowning.

"Do not get him started," Longinus replied blithely. "Can we climb up and over the cliff?"

"I doubt it," said Simon, giving Longinus a reproachful look. "This precipice is probably infinite. We could climb for centuries and still not reach the summits."

"Stand back and let me see if I can break it," Longinus said, staring at the seal.

"I do not think that will work," Simon enjoined him.

"No! Let him try!" Armilus insisted. "He broke the seals of Satan in the Dungeons of Hell!"

"How?" Simon exclaimed.

"With this," Longinus replied, holding up his spear.

"Your weapon has special powers?" asked the magus, surveying it with great interest.

"Mortals call it the Spear of Destiny," said Longinus. "Let us see whether our destinies lead us to Limbo."

Everyone stood well back as the centurion readied his weapon. He thrust the spear at the seal of God with all his strength and was rewarded with naught but a jarred arm and a huge shower of sparks.

"Let me try again," he said angrily.

Time after time, he struck at the seal, but it was impervious to his blows. Finally, he ceased his exertions and rubbed the back of his hand across his forehead. He had come so far, only to be stopped by a stupid gate.

Aeneas stepped forward and inspected the seal. At the bottom of the giant disc, someone had scratched the faint outline of a fish.

"I have seen this symbol many times in Hell. Someone carved it into rocks."

"So have I," said Longinus. "It is a Christian sign called the Ichthys."

"As indeed, have I," added Simon.

"But what does it mean?" asked Aeneas.

Simon pursed his lips. "Christians say that between the time of his Crucifixion and Resurrection, The Son of God descended into Hades and either freed or promised eventual salvation to all righteous souls that languished there. The faithful call this act the Harrowing of Hell."

"So you think the Nazarene made these sigils?" Longinus asked. "For what purpose?"

"To assert his authority over the demons in Hell—or to act as guiding signs for others that would follow in his footsteps."

"Who?" asked Longinus.

Simon spread his hands and shrugged. "I do not know."

"It is a most beautiful symbol," Aeneas murmured as he reached out and touched the seal.

They started as a peal of deep thunder sounded, and a vicious pillar of incarnadine fire arose from the flat-topped, black mountain and soared into the clouds.

"What the–," Longinus exclaimed.

A loud, metallic clunk followed by deep rumbling cut short his oath. The ground beneath their feet shuddered, and Armilus grabbed Satrinah for support. For once, she did not chide him and held onto him in return. They both stumbled back and gawked at the fiery summit. There was a deafening rattling sound, and the group stared in awe as the colossal portcullis opened. Longinus spread his legs to keep his balance as the ashen earth jerked and trembled. The gate rose fifty cubits and came to a grinding stop, shaking the cliff. The column of fire on the black mountain receded and disappeared with a sharp, roaring hiss.

"How did you open it?" Longinus asked Aeneas.

"I do not know! I merely touched it!" the Trojan protested.

"What do you think, Simon?"

"Either Aeneas has some hidden power that he is not aware of, or something unbarred the gate for us."

"God?" asked Longinus.

Simon narrowed his eyes. "No, this is not the work of the Demiurge. There is something else at work here. I feel we are being watched by an invisible presence."

"The sorcerer speaks the truth, centurion," whispered Naram-Sin. "I too, feel it."

"A demon?" asked Longinus.

"No. This being is neither from Heaven nor from Hell—but is ancient and extremely powerful."

Longinus gripped his spear tighter and glared around. His initial surprise and elation that the gate had opened was being replaced by an intense feeling of unease.

"Is it hostile?" he asked.

"Malignant and spiteful. I feel its terrible rage."

"Good!" Longinus growled. "If it attacks us, it will feel our anger. I am in the mood for a good fight. What say you?"

"Yes, centurion! We shall not be cowed! Let it fear us!"

"Then enough of gods and demons," Longinus snarled. "Let us see what the Fates have in store for us."

"Aye, let us hope we have some good luck for a change," replied Naram-Sin.

"It has certainly evaded us like one of Fortuna's farts in the wind," Longinus replied sourly.

After a moment of silence, they both burst into grim laughter at his crude jest.

Simon peered into the tenebrous gloom beyond the gate and wondered what lay ahead of them. He looked back at Longinus and saw him laughing to himself. The magus liked the centurion but found many of his moods and mannerisms curious. He had more than once heard the Roman speaking to an imaginary companion, and that worried him. Was the centurion becoming unhinged? What he had suffered at the hands of Asmodeus would have driven any man insane. But then he remembered that Longinus was not a man. He glanced at Aeneas and saw the big grin on his face. It seemed the two warriors were well matched in their apparent lack of concern about the dangers of their current quest. "The ways of immortal heroes are strange indeed," he thought.

Longinus turned and saw Armilus and Satrinah still clinging to each other. In the wonderment of the moment, they had forgotten to let go.

"Demon bonding?" he asked.

Satrinah frowned, glared at Armilus, and pushed him away.

"She grabbed me!" protested Armilus, somewhat shamefaced.

"In your daymares, cambion! When I seize you, you will remember it!"

Longinus shook his head and smiled. His coterie was a bedlam of conflicting views and emotions, but, in truth, he would not have it any other way. He well understood bouts of irrational madness. It was part of the human–and Revenant–condition.

Aeneas slapped him on the shoulder. "I can see those two are getting along splendidly. Shall we venture into Limbo? I am eager to explore this place."

"Just what I was thinking," he said.

"We should proceed with caution," Simon admonished.

"Why?"

"Aeneas and I are human souls, but I do not how the gate will affect you and Armilus."

"There is only one way to find out," replied the centurion. "Satrinah, what are you going to do? You are a full demon and cannot enter Limbo. Are you going to wait here for us or return to the Lower Depths?"

"I have not yet decided," she replied tersely. "But I will tarry until you have all passed safely through the gate."

"Very well. I will go first," said Longinus.

With some trepidation, the centurion strode up to the gate. He hesitated for a moment and then stepped through. He felt a burning sensation and had a brief, sharp vision in which he saw Lilith. She was flying, adorned in magnificent armour, and wielding an impressive sword. Her long tresses flowed in her wake like a regal scarlet cloak. She engaged two winged monstrosities in combat when two incubi fiends stole up from behind and struck her with their maces. Dazed and injured, she fell. A heaving sea of demons screamed and howled beneath as they waited for her to fall into their claws.

The manifestation ceased as soon as he passed through the gate, and his feet landed on the solid grey earth beyond. It had shaken him, and he rubbed his brow to clear his mind and confirm his present reality.

"Are you well?" exclaimed Aeneas. "Smoke is issuing from your body!"

Longinus looked down and saw the skin on his arm and legs was red and covered in a thin mist. He knew from experience that it was the first stage of the Final Death. The second phase was blistering, black skin and massive internal haemorrhaging. The last state was spontaneous combustion. Fortunately for him, there would be no vampire pyrotechnics display on this day.

"Yes," he replied, shakily. "I have suffered some slight burning, but it causes me no pain. Who is next?"

Aeneas looked at Simon. "Come, wise man, let us see if the gods favour us."

They both stepped up to the gate, and the Trojan took a bold step through. Simon hesitated for a moment and followed him.

Aeneas gaped in surprise as Longinus and the gate disappeared. He was in another place gazing down on a great city. He cried out in horror and despair. It was Carthage—and it was burning—like Troy! He staggered through the portal and fell onto his hands and knees.

"What is it, Aeneas?" Longinus exclaimed, kneeling beside him.

"I saw the fall of Carthage," he gasped. "It seemed so real. I could smell burning flesh and hear the screams of women and children."

Simon stumbled towards them, his face ashen. Longinus dropped his spear, stood up and dashed forward. Putting his arm around the magus' shoulders to support him, he offered his free hand to Aeneas. The Trojan took it gladly and hauled himself to his feet.

"Did you also have a vision?" Longinus asked Simon.

"No," Simon panted, avoiding the centurion's eyes. "I just need a moment to recover."

"Come," said Longinus. "Sit on this boulder."

Simon sat down and held his head in his hands. Aeneas joined him.

Longinus looked concernedly at Simon for a moment. He felt there was more to the matter than the sorcerer had admitted and decided to speak to him in private when the opportunity arose.

He turned back to Satrinah and the cambion. "Right, Armilus. It is your turn."

"I am not going in there! It could burn me to a crisp!"

"Did I burst into flames? If I can do it, then so can you."

"No, no! I cannot! It is too dangerous!"

Satrinah looked at Armilus and then at Longinus. She shook her head and look a grim determination appeared on her face.

"You think too much, cambion," she growled.

Before he could utter a reply, she unfurled her wings, grabbed him by the belt and flew straight at the gate. Armilus wailed in terror.

"No!" Longinus cried.

The succubus gritted her teeth and closed her eyes. She felt her skin burning as she passed through the divine barrier, and images from her past flashed before her eyes. She was a mewling infant. Looking up, she saw her mother's face. She grabbed her procreator's finger. Her mother laughed and told her she was strong. It was warm and safe, and she knew no harm would befall her in that soft and caring embrace. Then a red tear ran down her mother's cheek, and her face slowly disappeared. "Mother! Do not forsake me!" Satrinah cried.

To Longinus' amazement, Satrinah flew straight through the gate and deposited the cambion on the ground. Smoke wafted from their bodies but soon dissipated. As far as the centurion could see, they had suffered no harm.

"There! It is done!" she declared.

"Insane harpy!" Armilus screamed, near to tears. "You could have destroyed both of us!"

"I told you when I seized you, you would remember it," Satrinah retorted.

As they continued to bicker, Longinus turned back to Simon.

"How are you feeling?"

"Much better, thank you," the magus gasped, wiping his brow.

"I thought full demons could not enter Limbo?" asked Longinus, glancing at Satrinah.

"They cannot. There is obviously more to your succubus than meets the eye. Are you certain she is a full demon?"

"Are not all succubi full demons?"

"As far as I am aware–but she may be a half-caste of some kind."

"A cambion, like Armilus?"

"No, female cambions are quite distinctive in appearance."

"You mean they look like Armilus?"

"No, some are better looking–but not by much."

Longinus grimaced. The notion of a female that looked like Armilus was disturbing. For once, celibacy seemed an attractive proposition to him.

Forcing the hellish image from his mind, he said, "So she is only a half-demon, but we do not know what the other part is?"

"Just so, and perhaps even she does not know what she is. There has been much interbreeding in Hell. It is a place of lies and deceit."

"Well," Longinus grunted, "that suits our purpose. She is a good fighter and will be useful to us."

"I agree. I believe she is no threat to us and will be very helpful. But then, you knew that already."

"What do you mean?"

"You interrogated her thoroughly in the Lower Depths." Simon replied.

Longinus laughed at the unintended double meaning of the sorcerer's words. Simon realised his error and his brows darkened. The centurion felt distinctly uncomfortable being on the receiving end of the onslaught. He felt like a boy caught stealing an apple from a barrel by his father.

"Yes, well, I had to be make sure that she was on our side," he said awkwardly,

Simon raised his eyebrows. "Oh, yes, she is definitely on *your* side. She can hardly keep her eyes off you. I think the cambion is becoming quite jealous."

"What? No! Armilus hates her."

"Indeed? How little you know the ways of demons," murmured Simon.

Longinus stared at Armilus and then back at Simon. This was all he needed: more intrigue in the group to cause dissension and arguments. Once again, he had put his big foot in it–or something else along those metaphorical lines.

"How do you feel now?" he asked Aeneas.

"Well enough!" the Trojan growled. "Let us make haste. I dislike being near this damn gate."

"Armilus, Satrinah!" Longinus bellowed to interrupt their infernal squabbling. "We are leaving."

"Please!" Armilus rasped. "Get me away from her!"

"Did either of you have a vision when you passed through the gate?" Longinus asked.

"A vision?" Armilus replied, scornfully. "The only vision I had was of my own demise at the hands of this winged shrew!"

"What of you?" Longinus asked Satrinah.

"No," she lied. She had no interest in sharing her painful and disturbing dream with everyone and having the cambion mock her.

"Very well. Then let us proceed with hearts brimming with fellowship and joy; and discover what bountiful pleasures Limbo offers us," Longinus said wryly.

Armilus gurned, Satrinah grimaced, Simon glared, and Aeneas stood scratching his backside. Longinus sighed.

"All the world's a stage, and all the men and women are merely demonic or dead players," he muttered.

After a half mile, the gap between the cliffs opened up, and they emerged into a bleak, desolate, grey landscape with sparse clumps of petrified trees and withered vegetation. Longinus rubbed his nose and grimaced; the place stank of death and decay. Satrinah took to the air and began scouting the area. She returned after a few minutes, and her face was grim.

"What is it?" asked Longinus.

"Come," she said quietly. "You must see this for yourself."

She led them up to the crest of a hill. They gawked in horror at the vista that revealed itself beneath them. The dismal wasteland was filled with millions of crucified men, women and children. The scale of the gory spectacle was beyond belief.

"I thought Limbo was not a place of suffering?" Longinus growled.

"It is not meant to be!" Simon gasped. "I do not understand what has happened here!"

They heard the faint roars of a multitude of voices. In the far distance, Longinus saw what appeared to be hundreds of Roman legions, standing in formation around a vast, towering black edifice.

"What is that colossal building?" Aeneas gasped.

Longinus narrowed his eyes and stared at it. There was something about its shape that seemed familiar to him. Then the horrible truth dawned upon him.

"It is the Amphitheatrum Caesareum—the Colosseum of Rome."

"Was it used for religious ceremonies?"

"No. Bloody public spectacles and gladiatorial contests."

"What form of contests?" Satrinah asked, frowning.

"Prisoners and slaves forced to fight each other to the death," the magus said sombrely.

"Hmm," Aeneas replied grimly. "Then I fear the answer to the horror we see before us lies there."

"This does not bode well for us," whined Armilus.

Longinus grunted and hitched up his sword belt. For once, he agreed with the cambion.

Girding their loins, the weary band of demons and the damned stumbled down the hill to confront what new Hell awaited them in the foreboding Colosseum of the dead.

EPILOGUS

Eligos pulled back savagely on the reins and brought his hideous steed to a halt at the edge of the ice field. He scoured the frigid landscape before him and uttered a howl of frustration. The Lilitu and Revenant had passed this way not long before, but he could not follow them. No demon had ever survived the freezing temperature of this gelid wasteland, and he could not understand how Asmodeus' whores had managed it.

He flew back and forth along the periphery for hours, searching for any weakness, any gaps, he could exploit, but found none. The glacial barrier was impenetrable. He cursed God, all saints and angels. He had been so close to capturing his prey, and it angered him they had eluded him.

He dug his spurs into the steed's sides. The unholy stallion screamed in pain as the sharp points cut into its body. Its girth was a constant mass of raw, bleeding sores caused by its master's sadistic abuse. Eligos had never condescended to give it a name. To name it would be to acknowledge it was a sentient being, and he denied the beast even that small compliment. Other demons referred to it, as the Steed of Eligos and that was sufficient for him. To the archdemon, it was merely a thing, an object, to be used. It existed to serve his will and be the recipient of his frustration, rage and cruelty. And he relished inflicting unimaginable pain upon the creature.

Millennia ago, during the Fallen's invasion of the ancient underworlds, Eligos and a legion of other archdemons had cornered Pazuzu and held him at bay until Satan and the main force arrived. Although severely wounded, Eligos had fought on. He was the only survivor; the others had returned to the dust of the cosmos. Impressed by his bravery, Satan had created the steed for him and made him a duke in the new order of the Abyss. He had also had Mulciber, the architect of Hell, forge an infernal lance and armour for him.

Satan had favoured him in those distant days, and Eligos thought he would rise high in the hierarchy of Hell. But it was not to be. The Evil One had used him as he used everyone. He had a malicious talent for making every demon feel honoured for a short time and then ignoring or treating them with contempt. And afterwards, they would pine and do anything they could to regain their exalted position in Satan's eyes again. But they never could.

Satan played one archdemon against the other to encourage loyalty and competition. Demons searched endlessly for new ways of committing unspeakable evil on earth, hoping they would receive a few meagre words of praise from their imperial master. They existed only to serve and please him.

At one time, the hellish stallion had been a symbol of Eligos's star in the ascendancy, but now it was like a millstone around his neck, a constant reminder of his past glories and unfulfilled destiny. That was why he hated the steed so much and took a perverse pleasure in torturing it.

Eligos turned the beast on its haunches a half turn and made to fly back to the Lower Depths. But then he pulled on the reins and his eyes narrowed. He could not and would not admit defeat. Even if it meant his own destruction, he would not give up the hunt. No demon had every crossed the Ice Field before, but that did not mean that he could not. He was Archdemon Eligos! There had to be a way! He coveted the Revenant's spear and nothing would prevent him from obtaining it.

The Hunter of Souls turned to face the ice field, and a malevolent grin appeared on his face. He would fight ice with fire. He grabbed the stallion's mane and concentrated. The beast whinnied and snorted huge plumes of flame. Its body became hotter, turning crimson, orange, and then incandescent. Eligos' armour smouldered and glowed red hot. The archdemon howled in triumph and dug in his spurs. The steed screamed and flew straight into the frigid maelstrom. Frozen shapes in the ice flashed by underneath them. The hunter's arrogant confidence was short-lived. His mount was cooling rapidly, and he felt cold spots growing like insidious tumours on his claws, knees and elbows.

"Faster, wretch, or I will feast on your bones!" he roared.

The steed complied with its master's savage command and flew as fast as it could. The piercing cold was hurting Eligos now and felt like a thousand daggers cutting into his flesh. Ice appeared on the steed's mane, and the archdemon shivered uncontrollably.

He looked down and gaped as he beheld an enormous mouth in the glacier blasting vast swirling columns of boreal death high into the arctic vault. Then he saw the figures of the Lilitu frozen for eternity and knew that would soon be his fate. His faltering courage broke and panic set in. He had to escape! Forcing the beast into an awkward, frantic turn, he ripped its sides with his spurs and fled. He screamed in agony as the cold gnawed at his putrid flesh. He could hardly think. His brain was numb, his demonic power fading. He lowered his head and fought with all his remaining strength against the howling winds that threatened to wrench him from his saddle.

Just as the horse and rider shrieked and could bear no more, the crippling torment ceased abruptly. They shot out of the wall of white like an arrow and plummeted to the ground. The steed landed heavily and fell to its knees. A lair of frost covered it, making the beast appear hewn from ice. The momentum of the fall catapulted Eligos from the saddle, and he clattered onto his back. He groaned and shuddered as pain wracked his body. Gradually the agony subsided, and he opened his dazed scarlet eyes. Welcoming dark clouds circled above him.

It was some time before Eligos and his steed recovered from their exposure to the bone-chilling cold. The archdemon stood up, stretched his limbs and gave an involuntary shiver. The gelid conditions of the divine ice barrier had been a new and extremely unpleasant experience for him. He had grown to believe that he was almost invulnerable in his Hell armour, and it had shaken his confidence to discover that his defensive shell had a fatal weakness: it provided little protection against severe cold. This was a weakness an enemy could exploit and that irritated him. However, he consoled himself with the knowledge that no one knew of this vulnerability and there were no ice weapons in Hell. Even the accursed angels did not use swords capable of producing this form of elemental damage. Satan had once experimented with using fire axes against the spawn of Heaven, but these had proven no more effective than normal Hell weapons, and the Evil One had swiftly lost interest in the idea.

He glared at the stallion. It had recovered well and showed no ill effects from their ordeal. The steed gazed back at him, snorted, and stamped a hoof impatiently.

"Impudent cur!" Eligos roared angrily. "If you had flown swifter, I would not have suffered as much!"

He wrenched a scourge from his belt and whipped the beast mercilessly. The horse screamed as the splinters of human bone attached to the leather thongs cut deep into its raw, bleeding flesh. With a forlorn cry, the beast collapsed to its knees under the brutal onslaught. Eligos gave it one final lash and gazed contemptuously at it.

"Do not fail me again!" he hissed, his sunken eyes glistening with pleasure at its suffering.

The archdemon ripped Longinus' loincloth from the saddle, held it to his visor, and inhaled deeply. He licked his shrunken lips and felt better. The Revenant was still alive.

He would not return to the Lower Depths, but would stay here and wait. A hunter must be patient, and he had eternity on his side. When his prey left Limbo, he would strike.

Then Longinus' spear and body would be his—to savour and enjoy.

UT CONTINUED—TO BE CONTINUED…

CHAPTER 36

CHAPTER 37

CHAPTER 38

CHAPTER 39

CHAPTER 40

CHAPTER 41

CHAPTER 42

CHAPTER 43

CHAPTER 44

CHAPTER 45

CHAPTER 46

CHAPTER 47

CHAPTER 48

CHAPTER 49

CHAPTER 50

CHAPTER 51

CHAPTER 52

CHAPTER 53

CHAPTER 54

CHAPTER 55

CHAPTER 56

CHAPTER 57

CHAPTER 58

CHAPTER 59

CHAPTER 60

CHAPTER 61

CHAPTER 62

CHAPTER 63

CHAPTER 64

CHAPTER 65

CHAPTER 66

CHAPTER 67

CHAPTER 68

CHAPTER 69

CHAPTER 70

CHAPTER 71

CHAPTER 72

CHAPTER 73

CHAPTER 74

CHAPTER 75

CHAPTER 76

EPILOGUE

END

ACKNOWLEDGMENTS

I wish to give my sincerest thanks to Stephanie Lee Wesley for taking the time to edit the novel. Her help and encouragement were the epitome of Southern kindness.

Alan Kinross

Alan Kinross